CAT'S CRADLE:
WARHEAD

DOCTOR WHO – NEW ADVENTURES

Also available:

THE NEW DOCTOR WHO ADVENTURES

CAT'S CRADLE: WARHEAD

Andrew Cartmel

First published in Great Britain in 1992 by
Doctor Who Books
an imprint of Virgin Publishing Ltd
332 Ladbroke Grove
London W10 5AH

Reprinted 1993

Printed and bound in Great Britain by
Cox & Wyman Ltd, Reading, Berkshire
Typeset by Type Out, London SW16
ISBN 0 426 20367 4
Cover illustration by Peter Elson

For Ken Kessler

Prologue

The bulldozers were big blunt yellow machines, their belted tracks and superstructures spattered with mud. Brodie counted five of them. They were being carried up the sloping dirt road on a fourteen-wheeled flatbedded truck. Brodie watched from the cover of bushes at the roadside. Both the truck and the bulldozers had cartoon designs of a bee in flight and a human eye painted on their side. There were words and numbers painted beside the bee-and-eye logo.

Some of the words were in Japanese and of course Brodie couldn't read those. The other words, the English ones, he would be able to read soon. He had turned five this summer and he would learn to read in grade one, when he started school in September.

The truck made monstrous low noises as its driver struggled through low gears, fighting her way up the steep mountain track. As she approached the high-standing security camera the road levelled out and the truck began to pick up speed.

Brodie took his hands off his ears when the driver settled back into high gear and the engine noise dropped to a low rumble. Now he could hear the wind in the leaves all around him. The driver was leaning out of the cabin window and waving as she passed the camera, a small video unit mounted on a tall carbon-fibre pole. Brodie waited, crouching in the bushes. The truck was out of sight now, growling away on distant curves of the mountain road. Then there was silence, broken by the drilling of a woodpecker in a tree on the forest slopes behind him.

Brodie kept his eyes on the camera and took the smooth heavy rock out of his pocket. He'd brought it from the pile he'd collected by the big fallen tree in the woods. He had brought only the one rock because he knew he'd get only the one chance.

Brodie told himself to be brave but his heart was beating hard.

1

If he didn't move now he never would.

Brodie broke from cover and ran out into the centre of the dirt road, almost tripping on the deep ruts cut in the mud. He snapped his fist back and then forward, throwing the rock overhand at the camera on the high pole. It hit with a loud ringing noise, connecting with the support pole but missing the camera by a metre and a half. The boy stood frozen for a moment, then ran back into the woods.

Leaves on low branches whipped at his face, wiping at the tears that were streaming down his cheeks. Tears of rage.

A jeep would be coming down from the big cave now, a yellow jeep with a bee and an eye painted on the side. There would be men with guns and helmets in the jeep and they would search the woods near the road. If they found him they would take him back to his parents and his parents would keep him close to the cabin until it was time to close up for the summer and drive home. And then Brodie would never have another chance to smash the camera.

A squirrel was running through the branches above him, pausing to chatter down at him before leaping from one tree to another. The boy stood watching the small animal, a flash of red-brown among the grey branches, and then he changed direction, running along a winding side track, away from the path that would take him home.

In five minutes he was approaching the clearing with the big fallen tree in it. There would be more rocks by the tree, where he'd left them. Good-sized rocks for throwing, and he would wait until the men in the jeep went back up to the cave and then he'd —

'Possibly it's your choice of weapon.'

There was a man in the clearing.

Sitting on the stump of the long fallen tree. He looked up at the small boy standing at the fringe of the woods.

'I saw you throw that stone. It was a good throw, but a very difficult shot at that distance. You shouldn't feel bad about missing.'

Now the man looked down, at something he was doing with his hands. Brodie saw that he was carving, shaping a piece of fallen wood from the dead tree. The man put the carved piece of wood into his pocket and bent down. He reached into the long grass and selected a few small, smooth rocks from the pile under the tree. Brodie's pile.

'As I said, perhaps it's just that you didn't choose a suitable weapon for the job.'

The man stood up and Brodie got ready to run, but the man turned away from him, walking across the clearing, and Brodie found himself following. The man was putting the rocks carefully into his pocket as he walked. His eyes were a flat strange colour as he turned to look at Brodie.

'I don't like that camera,' said Brodie. He felt the need to explain under the cool gaze of those eyes.

'Clearly,' said the man.

'It used to be great here. I used to have a fort. In the woods. I built it myself last summer.'

'And then the company came,' said the Doctor.

'They're building across the valley,' said Brodie. They were walking side by side now, the man and the boy. Like old friends, back into the shadows of the woods.

'There were trees all over the mountain. Now they're gone and the squirrels are, too, mostly,' said Brodie. 'I don't even live here. But I can't stand to see somebody wrecking it.'

'I know exactly what you mean,' said the Doctor.

The Doctor?

Brodie tried to remember how long he'd been calling the man that. It was as if someone had whispered the name in his ear. No. It was as if it had been gently poked directly into his mind.

A wind was gathering behind Brodie, rushing up through the thin trees. The woods were turning cold and suddenly Brodie realized how late it was. The sun would be going down soon. Brodie shivered, his skin prickling. He remembered the stories he'd heard, about the witches and ghosts that once lived on the Catskill mountains, wandering these dense wooded hills.

The man – the Doctor – had stopped walking. He was looking at Brodie. Brodie didn't move.

'I'd better be getting home,' said the boy.

The Doctor held out his hand and showed Brodie the piece of wood he'd been carving. 'Do you know what this is?'

Brodie stared at the shape. 'A slingshot,' he said.

3

'Or catapult,' said the Doctor, walking back towards Brodie, holding out the piece of wood. 'All it needs is a strong piece of elastic or rubber.' The Doctor smiled. His eyes were calm. 'I wonder if you could help me with that?'

He handed the wooden slingshot frame to Brodie. It was nicely carved, the smooth wood fitting neatly in Brodie's hand, feeling good there. Feeling right.

Brodie looked up at the Doctor and smiled back.

The tyre was lying below a clump of splintered trees at the outside edge of a curve on the access road. It was a tight curve and a large construction vehicle had taken it too fast and crashed, months ago, when the excavation on the mountain was just beginning.

'They cleared the rest of the wreck away,' said Brodie, 'but they left this.'

A beetle was crawling across the dusty waffle-iron tread surface on the big tyre. Brodie brushed the beetle off and it flew away, its smooth glossy body dividing into wings. Brodie looked up, but the Doctor wasn't listening. He stood on the other side of the road, gazing across the valley towards the construction site, shading his eyes against the late sunlight.

The side of the mountain opposite had been shaved clean of trees and growth. A smear of raw brown earth stretched for kilometres, centred on the deep excavation hole. A single thin line of trees ran across the brow of the scalped ground, a large house above them, all glass and redwood. There were solar panels and satellite dishes on the mountainside near the excavation, and tall skeletal metal towers reflecting the pink of the evening sky. Yellow earth-moving vehicles grumbled near the tunnel mouth.

'What are those big towers?' said Brodie.

'They're for communications,' said the Doctor. 'You use them to relay to satellites.'

'Are you sure?'

'I've had rather a close look,' said the Doctor.

'That's the big cave beside them,' said Brodie. 'Do you think they're mining for gold?'

'In a manner of speaking,' said the Doctor.

4

'That's Patrick's house up there. We used to play in the woods.'

'Not any more?'

'His father won't let him.'

Smaller machinery operated among the earth-movers, running in and out of the mouth of the tunnel. Brodie shielded his eyes the way the Doctor was doing. He spotted some bulldozers and wondered if they had come up on the truck he'd watched earlier. You couldn't see the bee-and-eye emblem painted on their sides, but Brodie knew it was there. 'It just keeps getting bigger,' he said.

'I know,' said the Doctor. He walked back across the road and stood looking down at the tyre from the old wreck. 'Excellent,' he said. Brodie took a last look across the valley and turned back to the Doctor. He had freed the inner tube from the tyre and he was working on the softer rubber, cutting it with his knife, the same knife he'd used for carving the slingshot handle. The blade of the knife was made of some odd, dull metal and it cut the rubber with surprising ease. The Doctor made a last neat trim, then took the slingshot handle from Brodie. 'Find some stones,' he said, fixing the rubber to the handle. 'For practice.'

The big fourteen-wheeler was making good speed coming back down the mountain road, the trailer freed of its load. The driver slowed as she passed the observation camera and waved. As the truck accelerated and rolled past, Brodie and the Doctor moved to a tree beside the road 'Whenever you're ready,' said the Doctor. Brodie started forward, then stopped and looked back over his shoulder.

'Why aren't you trying to stop me?' said the boy.

'Sometimes it's necessary to fight back.'

'You aren't like other grown-ups, are you?'

'No.'

Brodie stepped out into the road. He didn't hurry. There was no need to hurry now. He stepped carefully over the ruts on the mud road, almost invisible in the failing light. The setting sun was a fat red disc behind the high black camera pole. Brodie took out the slingshot, settled a heavy round rock into the rubber strap and drew it tight. He held his breath as he took aim, the way the Doctor had showed him. He was squinting directly into the sun. He closed one eye and squeezed the other eye half shut, his eyelashes shattering the light into rainbow distortion curves. He released the rubber strap and the rock shot upwards into the blaze of the evening sun, rising towards the thin black pole.

The camera snapped to one side under the impact. It buzzed and twitched, trying to force itself back into the correct alignment, and that was when the entire lens housing came free, spilling open the body of the camera. Fragments of metal and glass rained musically down from the tall pole.

Brodie remained standing where he was.

They couldn't see him any more. Now he could cross the road and go into the woods on the far side. He could play there. He could play anywhere he wanted − tomorrow.

Right now it was time to go home for supper.

Brodie could hear a jeep high up the mountain, starting down from the construction site. He went back into the woods and stood for a moment, a small boy, alone and tired. Then something moved in the shadows and he saw the Doctor again. Halfway down one of the winding trails, almost out of sight in the deepening shadows of the woods. He turned and looked back at Brodie, then he spoke to him, his voice carrying strangely among the autumn trees in the quiet evening.

'You see,' said the Doctor, 'it's all a matter of assembling the correct weapon.'

PART ONE: Assembly

1

They had moved her to a new room two weeks ago. It was a private room, high up in the hospital, with a window. She knew what that meant. She tried not to dwell on the situation. Her aim these days was to keep her mind in neutral and sleep as much as possible.

It would be nice, she thought, if it could happen while she was asleep.

But it wasn't so easy getting to sleep any more.

Her body was weak, and the medication should have helped. But her mind seemed sharper and more active than ever. She sketched out a dozen articles she would never write. Thought of subjects for a hundred more.

Finally she put a stop to that. Now when she lay awake at night she managed to think of almost nothing.

She lay in bed looking up at the neutral image of the ceiling, a colourless square that filled her vision. After a while her eyes created minor hallucinations for her, meaningless patterns of motion in the non-colour of the ceiling shadow. If she kept her eyes still for a long time the images intensified. It was like watching a television after the test pattern faded, or a section of blank video with the sound turned off. The endless interference filled her field of vision and soothed her. There was a certain industrial beauty to the monochrome images. And it helped her to imagine herself as simply a machine that had failed. She stopped blaming herself and punishing herself in her mind and took comfort from this notion. The thing she was going through was just a terminal technical failure.

The thought even allowed her a little sleep, just before dawn.

That was the usual pattern of things.

Tonight was different.

Tonight she closed her eyes as soon as they took her supper tray away, the food uneaten but stirred around on the plate a bit to cheer up the nurse. And as she closed her eyes she went into a profound sleep that lasted for hours. She woke up just as suddenly, jolted out of a dream as if an electric shock had crossed her heart. She came up to consciousness with the absolute conviction that someone else was in the room with her.

She didn't stop to question whether she might still be dreaming. She groped for the lamp on the bedside cabinet. Fumbling in the dark she knocked over a get-well card and glass of water. A plastic fruit bowl went clattering off the hospital cabinet, spilling its contents. There was no fruit in the bowl, but she'd used it to hold her books and her computer. She heard them hitting the floor just as her hand closed on the light switch.

She had to close her eyes under the impact of the light.

When she forced them open they ached in the glare, tears forming. Her vision swam a little, but she could see well enough.

The man was sitting in the chair beside her bed. Sitting patiently, as if he'd been waiting for her to wake up.

'It's you,' she said.

Her heart was still racing, but that was just the aftershock of whatever dream had woken her. She could already feel her pulse slowing. She was surprised at how calm she felt.

He looked exactly the way she remembered. Pale eyes, thinning hair. Indeterminately old. But no older than the last time she'd seen him. She almost laughed when she saw that he'd taken his hat off. Holding it in his lap. It seemed so solemn. A gesture of respect at the bedside of the sick. Why have respect for this, she thought, looking down at her thin body in the hospital bed.

'Hello, Shreela,' he said.

'Hello. How did you find me?'

'Your room number is on the hospital computer.'

That wasn't what Shreela had meant, but she decided to let it pass. 'You know, in a funny way I almost expected you to turn up.'

'Really?'

'For a while I forgot about you,' said Shreela. 'I'd say that in all these years I've thought about you maybe a dozen times. But then, of course, with all this —' Plastic tubes shifted as she lifted her arm. 'With all this I've been thinking a lot of strange thoughts lately. Looking back on things. And then I started thinking about you again.' She yawned. 'We had quite a time, didn't we?'

'Yes, we did.'

'I'd almost convinced myself that it never happened. I decided you were a dream that I had. But of course here you are now.'

The plastic cushion of the chair made a faint noise as the Doctor shifted forward. He leaned a little closer to the bed. He was near enough to touch, if Shreela had wanted to touch him.

'But, of course, if I was a dream back then, I could always be a dream now.'

Now Shreela did laugh. 'That's the spirit. You never were exactly reassuring. How's Ace?'

'Keeping busy.'

The Doctor reached down past the metal frame of the bed and picked up her computer from where it had fallen on the floor. The computer was an Amstrad portable, an old model she'd used since university. Over the years she'd done most of her writing on it. If she wanted to, she could plug it into a socket beside her bed now and use it to send text files off via the hospital network.

If she wanted to. Shreela didn't see herself using the Amstrad again. She'd brought it with her out of habit.

'I don't really keep in touch with anyone from those days. Not that there are many of them left. What about Midge, eh?'

'A shame,' said the Doctor.

'I thought he had it coming, myself. I liked his little sister, though. I used to see her from time to time. What's her name? Nice kid. I wonder how she's doing.'

'She's dead,' said the Doctor.

'Christ. How?'

'Natural causes.'

'You mean her immune system went.'

The Doctor nodded. Shreela sighed and sank back on her pillows. 'There's a lot of it about. Christ,' she repeated, staring back over the years, seeing the little girl playing outside the council block. 'She must have been ten years younger than me.' She looked up at the Doctor. 'And I'm not that old myself.' He was bending over again, picking up the books that had fallen on the floor. It's funny really. That time with you I could have been killed so easily. Died any time. So I live through all that and end up like this.'

'You had the years in between,' said the Doctor.

'Just a postponement.'

11

'That's all anyone has.'

Shreela waved a hand. She couldn't manage to shrug any more. 'You know what my big mistake was?'

'No.'

'I didn't eat the food or drink the water, but I still breathed the air.'

The Doctor straightened up. He had the books she'd spilled on the floor. He put them back into the fruit bowl, one at a time, looking at each one. Several of them were Shreela's books. Her own articles, collected in paperback. Brought by a well-meaning but stupid friend. They were the last thing she wanted to read now. She waited for the Doctor to put the last book down, then she asked the question she had to ask. 'Listen . . .'

'Yes?'

'You rescued me once before. Can you rescue me now?'

The Doctor shook his head.

'No, I didn't think so.' She turned her head away, into the pillow so he wouldn't see her face. It wasn't the sting of the light this time.

The Doctor sat patiently, waiting until her voice was steady enough for her to speak again.

'So what do you want?'

'I need your help.'

Shreela laughed again. 'Oh come on. Me help you? Now?'

The Doctor handed her several sheets of paper. They felt slippery, like old-fashioned fax output. The typing on them was double spaced; large lettering. It took only five minutes for Shreela to read the article. Once she looked up at the Doctor. 'Are you sure "telekinesis" is the word you want?'

The Doctor just nodded. When she finished reading the article she set the papers on the bed beside her and lay back on the pillow.

'Pretty good. A few too many adjectives but it's my style. It would certainly fool my editors.'

'Good.'

'You want me to claim authorship of this?'

'Yes.'

'I'm a science writer,' said Shreela. 'The phenomena you're describing falls into the category of what I'd describe as pseudo-science. Superstition. Dross.'

12

'Nonetheless,' said the Doctor, 'I'd like you to put your name on it and send it to your editor.'

'Look at me,' said Shreela. The Doctor was looking at her, his disturbing eyes watching her face. Waiting. 'I've never lied in my writing and I've made damned few mistakes. I've certainly never delivered propaganda for anyone.'

'I know,' said the Doctor.

'At this point in my life I don't have a hell of a lot left.'

'No.'

'And now you want to take that away.'

'It's necessary.'

'What will you use it for?'

'Disinformation.'

'To confuse the enemy, eh? Tell me, who is the enemy this time?'

The Doctor said nothing.

'You know what I think, sometimes?' said Shreela. 'I think sometimes that perhaps you're the enemy.'

The room was quiet. Shreela had learned to judge the time of night by the changing pattern of traffic noise in the West London streets outside. There weren't many cars passing the hospital now. Perhaps ten a minute. That made it the middle of the night. Maybe two or three in the morning. 'I'll tell you what,' said Shreela. 'There's something you can do for me. You see the window there?'

'Do you want me to help you walk to it?'

'No. Just tell me what I could see. If I could walk to it.'

'It looks down on the wall of another building. There's a concrete walkway in between.'

'And if I could stand down there by the wall, what would it be like?'

'There'd be walls all around you,' said the Doctor. 'You could feel air coming from the ventilators of the building opposite. Through a metal grille in the wall. The air's warm. It smells like small animals. Hamsters, mice. Animals in the laboratory.'

'I couldn't see any green if I was standing down there? Any trees?'

'No,' said the Doctor.

'What about the fields across from the hospital?'

'The grass is all yellow on them. There were some trees there. They're gone now. That field is called the Scrubs, where the prison used to be.' The Doctor's voice was gentle, low. Shreela could feel herself drifting off a little, carried by that voice. 'Before they built the prison there it was a common. Once they held a fair on it every spring.'

'When was that?' Shreela heard her own voice at a distance. It was an effort to speak.

'A long time ago. Before that it was marshland.'

'Was it green then?'

'Very green. There were birds wading in the water. You could see them bending down to catch fish.'

Shreela could see the birds, pale under a grey sky, dipping down to disturb their reflections in the calm fen water. 'Could you see any people?'

'No.'

'It must have been nice then. Listen.' She touched the plastic tube that ran into the vein on her arm. 'They keep upping my medication. Every day now. That must mean something.'

'Yes.'

'If you've been in the hospital computer you'll know what my status is.' She swallowed. The only thing she didn't like about the drugs was the way they made her mouth dry. 'How long have I got?'

The Doctor was silent.

'Weeks? Days?'

He sat there, saying nothing. Eyes lowered so she couldn't read them.

'Hours?' she said.

He looked up at her.

The silence held for a full minute.

Finally Shreela cleared her throat. It was an unsettling sensation these days. She could feel the shifting of all sorts of unfamiliar, muscular structures. She looked down at the bedclothes. Her computer keyboard lying on the clean hospital covers, close to her pale hand.

'Well, I'd better get started, then,' she said.

14

2

The printer looked like a poised insect. It was finished in textured grey plastic with the bee-and-eye logo of the Butler Institute embossed on it. It stood on the table on slender legs, bent over its own shadow, its torso formed by the flat box shape of the paper cartridge. The cartridge was angled down so that each emerging sheet of paper slid gently out on to the surface of the table.

Mathew O'Hara picked up the first sheet as it hissed from the machine, waited for the second, then carried them with him into the kitchen. The paper was still warm.

O'Hara sat down with a fresh cup of coffee at the counter and started reading. He liked having a hard copy to read. The same information could be gleaned off a computer screen, but there was something about actually having it in his hand which helped him to concentrate. A small eccentricity. A minor vice. He supposed it was a waste of paper and therefore of trees — although of course that didn't matter any more.

O'Hara sipped his coffee and read.

The house was quiet around him. He and his wife had spent the evening with their young son Patrick. A family evening, Anne Marie called it. They'd watched television together. Then they'd given Patrick his bath and put him to bed. After that Anne Marie and O'Hara had gone to bed themselves and made love. Afterwards O'Hara lay in the dark bedroom, waiting patiently until his wife had fallen asleep. Then he'd come downstairs to work.

There was still a lot to be done.

O'Hara skimmed quickly through the day's reports from the construction crews. Cost and target completion estimates. A memo about pilfering from the canteen; a report about a fight that had broken out between the Korean and Japanese technical teams; a request for better surveillance hardware, after one of the perimeter cameras had been smashed by a boy with a slingshot. Through the windows of the kitchen O'Hara could see the dark shapes of trees and the occasional flash of light through them. He reflected that trees like this had once covered the slopes of these mountains. He had a sense of history, an important quality in a man who had a task like his.

At his wife's request, O'Hara had interfered with the clearing of the mountain and had preserved the last few trees nearest the house. As it turned out, it wasn't a bad idea. The trees acted as a barrier to the sound of construction that continued, day and night, further down the mountain slope.

O'Hara watched the intermittent lights of earth-moving machinery through the trees. He found the sight reassuring. Finally he looked back at the papers in front of him. On top were two pages of notes, one headed *Cattersan*, the other *Lindhurst*. He put these away and turned to the remaining papers. The two sheets were personnel records. On the top right-hand corner of each was a photograph. The name on the top of one sheet was *Mancuso, Tessa Anne*; on the other it was *McIlveen, James Haines*. Both the man and woman in the photographs wore police uniforms. The emblem of one of the New York City police services ran down the side of each sheet of paper.

O'Hara left the documents on the counter and wandered out of the kitchen, taking his coffee with him. In the living room he settled on to the black silk-covered couch and put his feet up. He let the matter of the decision fade from his mind. His subconscious could worry away at the problem for him.

'On,' said O'Hara to the empty room.

In a dark corner by the stone fireplace a small blue light snapped on, showing the outlines of a stack of flat black boxes. There was a faint, transient hum as the Bang and Olufsen system came to life.

'Television,' said O'Hara.

A second blue light came on at the side of a second flat box. 'News interpreter,' said O'Hara. There was a pause as the B&O analysed news broadcasts of the last twenty-four hours, choosing or discarding information according to O'Hara's recorded preferences. A small shutter opened silently and the dim light from the kitchen was caught and reflected on the precision glass of the projector's lens.

O'Hara lay back sipping his coffee and watching the hologram take shape on the dark carpet near the couch. 'Further back,' he said. Patrick had been playing with the settings. The boy always sat too close to the television.

The glowing patch skipped back t ꞏ the normal viewing position, in the centre of the carpet, halfway between the couch and the fireplace. 'A little further,' said O'Hara, and it was just as well he did.

Even so, he almost poured his coffee in his lap when the image snapped into sharp focus and the tall thin figure came racing across the carpet towards him.

O'Hara knew it was just a hologram, but he found himself drawing his legs up close to his chest in a quick involuntary move. He was cowering among the cushions as the figure strode back and forth on the carpet, as close to the couch as his chosen viewing distance would allow it to get.

Jack Blood stood leering at him in the half-light. The big misshapen pumpkin that formed his head nodded forward and twisted, as though watching O'Hara. His greasy black undertaker's suit flapped around his thin scarecrow body. The long black twigs of his fingers were wrapped around the handles of two long-bladed butcher's knives which Jack stropped together slowly. There was no sound as the blades met. That was because O'Hara's young son had sampled the image, copying it from his favourite television programme, but the Bang & Olufsen hadn't let him tamper with the sound.

'News interpretation,' said Jack, the voice coming out of his crudely carved Jack-o'-lantern mouth. 'Selection taken according to the profile set on August tenth, this year.' The voice was soft, cultured, with a slight European accent. It belonged to the attractive grey-haired woman who usually presented the news interpretation on the B&O. O'Hara sighed, straightening out on the couch and relaxing again. Now he would have to read the damned manual and find out how to return the image to its factory setting.

'International news summary,' said Jack Blood, a small worm

17

crawling out of one empty, deep-carved eye socket. The pumpkin-headed mass murderer was a modern phenomenon. Sociologists wrote books about his universal appeal. His television creators were engagingly modest about the whole thing; they'd just set out to create a good Saturday morning show.

O'Hara moved on the couch so he wouldn't have to watch the worm's progress. Jack moved his head in synchronization, tracking inexorably, offering O'Hara the best presentation of image to go along with the lifelike stereo sound. 'Increasing instability in weather patterns −'

'Skip,' said O'Hara.

'Fighting in Indonesia −'

'Skip,' said O'Hara.

'Analysis of sea water in the −'

'Skip.'

'A report on environmental −'

'Skip.'

'An article describing telekinetic −'

'Skip. No, wait a minute,' said O'Hara. 'Repeat the last item.'

'From the London *Sunday Times*, Science and Technology section, seventh of this month. Headline: "Bloody Strange!" Main text of feature as follows: "The *Sunday Times* Insight team has learned that biochemistry boffins are baffled by an article written by Shreela Govindia. A highly respected scientific journalist, dusky beauty Shreela is −" '

'Just summarize,' said O'Hara.

'The article goes on to describe how certain blood proteins may indicate the presence of "strange mental powers" in human beings.'

'Explain,' said O'Hara. 'What kind of powers?'

'No more information available. "Strange metal powers",' repeated the pumpkin-headed horror.

'Okay, hold it,' said O'Hara. He thought for a moment. 'Link with the office computer.'

'Link established,' said Jack, waving his sticky-bladed knives.

'Cross-reference with that news item. Find out the location of the scientific journalist and ask her to fly out to New York. Book a company apartment at the King Building.'

'Reference. Govindia, Shreela. Journalist. Deceased.'

18

'When and how,' said O'Hara.

'Died this morning, death recorded 11.30 a.m. local time, Hammersmith Hospital, London, England. Cause of death auto immune disease.'

'Okay,' said O'Hara. 'Memo to all departments, special attention Social and Biological Stock Acquisition. Attach copies of the article and get a hard copy for me.'

'Contents of memo?' prompted Jack Blood politely, waving his knives, dancing impatiently as near to the couch as he could get. Straining like a guard dog on a leash.

'Enclose a memo with the article requesting that everyone keeps their eyes open for any signs of unusual . . .'

'Waiting,' prompted Jack after a moment.

'Blood tests,' said O'Hara. 'All blood tests conducted by Bio-stock Acquisitions. Paste in that article you just read. And cross-reference with the database and see if there's any more technical literature you can pull out. Make a list of the blood proteins and tell Acquisition to test for them. If we find any stock reading positive, skip processing and fly them straight out here from the King Building. Put a priority on this and offer a bonus. The usual ten per cent plus seven points in the company health scheme.'

'Filed ready for action tomorrow,' said Jack. He swept his frail stick arms upward, knives clutched in black twig fingers. With a swooping motion he brought both arms swinging inwards and drove the blades through the black felt of his own jacket. He lifted his arms free and showed the knives jutting out of his wooden scarecrow torso. He took a bow and disappeared back into the B&O.

O'Hara sipped his coffee. It was cold.

There was snow falling in New York. When Mancuso looked up the sky seemed to be a low grey ceiling. All the lights of the city were being reflected back off some kind of diffuse low cloud. It wasn't a true night sky at all. It was like being inside a metal tunnel. The only thing which gave an impression of depth was the slow vertical descent of the snow, drifting down towards her face. When Mancuso was a child she would have opened her mouth to catch a flake on her tongue. She didn't do that now.

Mancuso watched the street while McIlveen secured the riotgun and locked the car. In this neighbourhood a police car was a target. The food was good here, though. McIlveen came around the car and she let him lead the way towards the diner. When his boot hit the iced sidewalk he slid, swore, and would have gone down on his ass if Mancuso hadn't caught his arm.

The waitress serving at the counter had a little silver cross pinned to the white collar of her jacket, right beside the small flag badge that signified membership of the Young Republicans. Mancuso let her pour the coffee before she said, 'There's two things I normally never talk about.'

'Hey, come on, don't start,' said McIlveen.

'I beg your pardon,' said the waitress looking at Mancuso.

'Religion and politics,' said Mancuso. 'Normally I never talk about those two subjects. But listen. Do *you* think the president will go to hell?' She smiled sweetly at the waitress. The woman put their tab down and left, heading back to the kitchen.

'Why did you have to do that?' said McIlveen. 'She's just a kid. Probably takes it all very seriously.'

'Nobody's young enough to be that stupid.'

On a rooftop across the street Lewis Christian took off his headphones. He immediately regretted it; the foam pads had been shielding his ears from the bite of the cold air. Mulwray didn't seem to be bothered by the cold. He was standing beside Christian, his camelhair coat dusted with snow. Lewis was pleased to see that somehow he'd managed to get up the fire escape without putting a black smear on it.

'Well, what do *you* think?' said Christian. 'Is Chuck going to hell?'

Mulwray just smiled. He took the rifle bag from Christian and unzipped it. The stock of the rifle was textured grey plastic with dimpled buttons under the barrel for control of the optical system. Mulwray sighted it on the warm glow of the diner window on the street opposite. The soft plastic shroud of the eyepiece formed a warm seal against his cheek. The telescopic sight brought the cops' faces sharply into view. First the woman. She was grinning. Mulwray moved the barrel of the rifle. The sight lost focus then gained it again as it tightened on the image of the male cop.

Mulwray leaned over the edge of the rooftop, making small adjustments on the rifle, swinging it back and forth.

From the man to the woman.

In the warmth of his kitchen O'Hara sat looking at the two dossiers in front of him, studying the pictures. He was coming to a decision when the telephone rang.

He took the call in the living room, routing it through the B&O. The wall opposite the big picture window lit up as the image of the callers was projected on it, flat. Northern Global hadn't yet attempted to deliver holographic images over the phone fibres.

It was a conference call, three separate images appearing in squares on the walls, like portraits without frames. Each image stabilized at a different rate, coming in over different routes, via satellites then through Northern Global's landlines.

The first caller was an Oriental woman. She was calling from an office. O'Hara could see some of the equipment on her desk at the edge of the image. She said nothing, not even looking up into the phone, continuing to work at something while waiting for the conference circuit to complete.

The second caller was young. Perhaps sixteen. He was dressed in a bathrobe, hair wet from a shower. He greeted O'Hara, combing his hair while he waited for the call to begin.

The third image remained a blank square of mint green. O'Hara couldn't tell if it was the wall behind the phone or some kind of computer-generated blind. Finally a woman stepped into frame. O'Hara didn't recognize her.

'Hello, can you hear me?'

'Who exactly are you?' said the Oriental woman on the wall above, looking up from her desk for the first time.

'I'm Mr Pegram's physician.'

'How is he?' said the teenage boy.

'I'm afraid Mr Pegram died today.'

'Again?' said the boy.

The physician seemed to take this personally. 'Mr Pegram has only died twice since I assumed supervision of his health

21

control programme —'

'We haven't got all day,' said the Oriental woman.

'Or all night,' said the boy, speaking from the other side of the world.

'All I'm asking is that you don't excite or disturb Mr Pegram too much.'

The physician's image disappeared, replaced by Pegram himself, sitting upright in his medical harness. As far as O'Hara could tell, he looked a little healthier than usual, if anything. 'What's she been telling you, that quack?' boomed Pegram. His speech was deep, mellow and virile, the synthesized voice of a young man, licensed from some popular entertainer of ten years ago and now controlled directly from what was left of Pegram's larynx.

'As much as I would love to discuss your health, Jack, there are other things which require my attention,' said the woman.

'Will you be represented at Brussels?' said the boy.

'My delegates can meet your delegates.' The woman continued working while she spoke. 'Obviously this is a very busy time and a critical time.'

'Well, let's hear it then,' said Pegram. His old eyes stared at O'Hara over his plastic oxygen mask. 'Progress report, boy.'

'We are very close to completion,' said O'Hara. 'The mountain bunker will be finished by the end of the year.'

'Is it going to be secure?' said Pegram.

'My engineers tell me that it will survive a small-scale nuclear strike or any earthquake activity that is likely to arise in this region.'

'So how long will the thing last?'

'The hardware's all self-supporting. My engineers see no reason why it should't last indefinitely.'

'Indefinitely,' said Pegram. It was hard to tell, but he might have been smiling behind the oxygen mask.

'This is all secondary,' said the Oriental woman. 'The vital aspect is the success of the software. How close are we to an assessment of that?'

'We'll be obtaining the final test subject tonight,' said O'Hara.

'Call me when you have some results.' The image went blank as the woman hung up. The boy shrugged. 'Call me also,' he said, and the second square of light faded on the wall. Only Pegram was left, staring out from the living-room wall.

In the late night quiet of the dark room O'Hara could hear noises from Pegram now. His machines breathing for him.

'This is a splendid enterprise,' said the old man. 'God will smile upon it.' Unable to move his remaining arm, he just winked at O'Hara before the computer hung up for him. O'Hara continued looking at the blank dark wall for a moment, considering the lingering traces the phonelight had left on his vision. Then he went into the kitchen. He deliberately didn't look at the two pieces of paper lying on the counter. O'Hara took a sweet pastry from the refrigerator and put it in the oven to warm up. As he did so he came to a decision. He picked up the kitchen phone, a handset, and called New York.

The bean curd satay had smelled good. McIlveen had been worried that the waitress night have taken some kind of revenge on them, sabotage in the kitchen, but the food had been fine.

That was just like McIlveen, thought Mancuso. Always worrying.

She sat at the counter, still shaking a little. The waitress was clutching Mancuso's hand in her own, gripping it fiercely. Mancuso let her. She figured it would make the waitress feel better.

There was blood on the girl's tunic, a splash of it beside the little silver cross. The waitress had done surprisingly well. She hadn't panicked. She'd been on the phone almost immediately, calling for medical assistance while Mancuso had been on the floor with McIlveen. The paramedics' feet were crunching on broken glass now. They had arrived with unbelievable speed, considering the snow and the traffic.

'Okay. Now,' said one of the paramedics. They braced themselves and lifted the stretcher off the floor. It was a life-support stretcher and McIlveen was already connected up to it. Mancuso got up to follow it out the door but one of the other cops stopped her, made her sit back down at the counter. The waitress took Mancuso's hand again and Mancuso let her.

The plates of satay were turning to cold grease on the counter. Snow and cold air blew in through the shattered window of the diner. Mancuso could see the lights of the police copter as it hovered above the building across the street, sweeping the roof with a search beam. There was nothing there. The snipers would be miles away by now.

When the traffic had eased the first paramedic glanced into the back of the ambulance. The policeman was attached to the vehicle's life support, the stretcher locked down on to the body table. The second paramedic was busy making adjustments to the drug supply.

'How is he?'

'All brain functions seem okay.'

'Thank God for that.'

The second paramedic made a last check on the vital signs readout and came forward, climbing into the passenger seat. He clipped his seatbelt on and looked across at the driver.

'That was a terrific shot,' he said.

'Well, I couldn't let us freeze on that rooftop all night,' said Mulwray.

3

Maria Chavez pulled over to let the ambulance pass her on the approach road to the King Building. There weren't any lights flashing on the vehicle, or any sirens, but it was moving at what Maria regarded as a dangerous speed as it loomed up in her rear-view mirror. She wondered what the vehicle would do when it encountered the armoured gates of the building, but as she watched the crash barriers rolled back, giving access to the parking lot. The ambulance flashed by and Maria recognized Christian and Mulwray behind the wide windscreen. She should have guessed; it was one of Biostock Acquisition's collection of colourful vehicles. They had everything from city taxis to a hearse.

Maria followed the ambulance through the open gate and parked her Toyota in the company lot. Mulwray and Christian were wheeling a stretcher trolley into the service entrance of the building and they were gone by the time she locked her car and started walking through the freezing wind to the security booth. The wind was lashing snow between the towers of the remaining skyscrapers, the crystal flakes glittering in the security floodlights. As Maria stepped over half-frozen puddles the wind changed direction and hit her from a new angle. It buffeted around the surrounding tall structures, finding a route then moving like a fast car, blowing in off the dead water of the river, chilled by its passage and funnelled by the ranks of office buildings. Gathering velocity as it swept through the gaps left by demolition and riot damage. Now it howled across the parking lot and over Maria.

The guard in his heated booth kept her waiting for five minutes while he pretended he was checking her card. In fact he was finishing off a session of MacPet on his computer screen. Maria could see the superhumanly healthy fleshtones of the imaginary woman reflecting off the lenses of his glasses. Maria didn't care. She wasn't really standing here in the cold wind.

She was dancing.

Dancing to The Clash in a hot basement, the walls crawling with sweat and condensation, floor vibrating under her. Back in California. With that vibration always making her wonder if the earthquake was arriving. The big one. The final one. The one they kept promising. Maria thought an earthquake wouldn't be such a bad way to die: most likely very quick, very exciting, and with a lot of other people to keep you company. Maria was sixteen years old again, strong and lovely, flicking the sweat out of her hair in the heat of that basement. Dancing and knowing that one day she'd have to die. Knowing it but deep in her healthy young body, on a cellular level, not really believing it.

That was a long time ago.

The guard finally pressed the release button and the wire gate slid back, allowing Maria to walk through the barrier, across another stretch of wasteground, and up on to the steps of the King Building. It was a tall structure, impressive even in this city of skyscrapers. When Maria raised her eyes to look at it the sight made her dizzy. Black glass rising forever through the cold night. But Maria didn't want to feel dizzy tonight. She didn't want to raise her eyes any more. She kept them aimed down, focused on her feet as she walked slowly up the steps to the building. Taking them one at a time, saving her strength. Not thinking about the pain.

Maria concentrated on thoughts of dancing and the smoky sunlight of the west coast. Looking back on it, those had been the good years. They had also been the years when President Norris launched the economic opportunity initiative. Local Development was one of the slogans. It meant if you didn't have a job you stayed exactly where you were until they could find one for you in your neighbourhood. No need to travel in search of work. The TV campaigns showed Okie migration of the 1930s. Skinny children eating apples in the back of skeletal Model T's. The modern-day Republican administration re-cycling dustbowl propaganda.

Those were also the years that saw the redevelopment of the

inner cities in California. Maria observed pretty quickly that redevelopment seemed to involve bigger and better barriers between her part of town and the richer suburbs, along with the private police forces expanding and acquiring newer and more devastating weaponry, some of it even approaching the quality of the stuff used by the big gangs.

Maria knew a scam when she saw one. Local development meant that the homeboys got to stay at home. Forever. You could see the rest of the world on your TV set. If you stepped outside your neighbourhood you'd get a bullet or a dog or a ground-to-ground missile that floated like a ghost and thought carefully about where its target went. A missile that could lock on to a heat image of your car and track it around five right-angle turns before it snaked up the dead-end alley where the trash cans formed a barricade and you couldn't get out again. Then it locked in and came screaming towards you and detonated in your engine block, blasting the streering column up through your spinal column.

Maria always wondered what Jerome's last thought had been. She wondered if maybe he'd been thinking of her. More likely he was cursing the approaching missile and wishing he could get at some of the hardware in his trunk. Knowing Jerome.

When Jerome died Maria decided that it was time for her to get out. Alone if necessary.

Maria's friends didn't give a damn. They were all young and living under the thunder. Life meant partying with beer and blow and listening to Black Leader. None of them read the newspapers. Neither did Maria. But she could read between the 425 phosphor lines on her TV screen. She saw the government's ads and she saw the evening news, which was much the same.

She knew what was coming. She didn't have time to dance any more. She was making plans.

Maria managed to leave California just before the economic migration laws really clamped down. Even then, if she'd tried to drive out of LA in her car she would have been intercepted and turned back. But instead Maria sold the car and caught an early-morning bus to the airport with a group of women, mostly middle-aged, who worked there on the cleaning staff. Maria was waved through the checkpoints with them, a big plastic shopping bag just like theirs in her lap. Only instead of cleaning gear Maria's bag contained the triage of a lifetime's possessions.

All the security teams at the checkpoint saw was one more coloured woman in a bus full of them, headed out to keep the blood off the airport floor. The real cleaners knew exactly what Maria was doing but they kept their mouths shut. A clan of women with varicose ankles, hands and lungs shot from the industrial-strength poisons they used for cleaning.

Maria paid for her airline seat with cash. As the jet taxied for takeoff she let herself cry a little. For Jerome and the baby growing inside. She flew out of LAX, heading east, as far as she could go. Heading into the future. As she reclined in her economy-class seat, spinning her earphone dial, trying to find some music with a little bottom to it, a little strength, she swore one thing. Whatever happened to her she would never clean floors for a living.

New York was a gamble, a chance to find work and a better way of life. Maria thought anything had to be better than home with the police helicopters slicing through the sky every night and the understreets being built and the endless drug wars where the worst gang you could imagine was always being displaced by ones that were worse still.

So she arrived in the east, landing at Kennedy, riding the subway in and stepping out of the station to be swallowed in the endless winter. With the climate going to hell all over the world they'd begun to get snow in LA on a regular basis. Maria thought she'd be ready for the cold weather. But nothing could have prepared her for that first city winter, sitting beside a searing hot radiator in a room with the windows painted shut. Icicles hanging down on the red neon sign outside the bar where she drank in the evenings. Sometimes getting drunk enough in there to dance, on her own, by the candy-coloured light of the karaoke unit. Cars outside chewed the dirty snow into rivers of slush. Maria slipped all the time when she walked home drunk, keeping her eyes on the shadows. It took her months to get the knack of walking on ice.

But it didn't take Maria long to learn that they had understreets in New York, too. You couldn't see them but they were there. Her money ran out quickly and when it did the heat in her room was cut off. Maria alone in her room, at three in the morning, New York wintertime, dancing to keep warm.

When a job finally came up, she grabbed it and held tight. She'd held on to it all these years.

The door shut behind her, cutting off the wind howl. Maria wiped her feet with care on the corrugated rubber matting then took off the plastic shoe protectors she wore; she knew what it was like having to clean up muddy footprints. On the far side of the lobby above the elevators an entire wall of black marble was devoted to the directory for the King Building. Corporate names and logos, followed by floor numbers, glowing in whatever colours were deemed to convey quiet power and wealth this year. Most of the logos were holograms but Maria knew a few of the cheaper ones were neon.

Maria walked through the warm lobby of the building and put her ID card into the elevator control console. The information on the card, along with the thin film of body oils that composed a fresh thumbprint, were sucked into the slot and passed into the building's nervous system. The computer that handled the alarm, evacuation and security procedures considered the information it had received, searched its memory, and came to a conclusion. It sent an elevator down for Maria and carried her up to the seventy-third floor. Maria didn't even need to push a button. And if she had entered the elevator and pushed any button other than 73, the elevator would have stopped between floors, doors sealed, and kept her there until the security guard could be dragged away from his bootlegged copy of MacPet to check her out.

On the seventy-third floor Maria unlocked her storage locker and trundled out the heavy trolley with its soft wheels. She checked her equipment, then went back to the elevator to continue up to 74. She would start there then methodically work her way down to 72, tidying offices, wiping screens, making sure any hard copy had been thoroughly shredded.

And, of course, cleaning the floors.

Maria pushed the trolley past the executive squash courts and the private gym and male and female saunas, the rubber wheels squealing as she manoeuvred it. The expensive leisure facilities all around her were dark and silent. Empty but with all the doors open. No need to keep anything locked. Not with security as tight as it was. She got back to the elevator and found that it was gone again. Sent up or down on some mysterious errand devised by the building's control system. While she was waiting for it to arrive she checked the trolley. The big plastic drum of industrial cleaning fluid had almost run out. She'd have to buy a new one before the weekend.

Sometimes when she was working late, like tonight, Maria's mind would just switch off, trusting muscle memory for the work at hand. In her brain other, more complex, memories were operating. Flashes of being young and the way she'd danced. Basement shaking like an earthquake. She still had nostalgic dreams of dying that way. Quickly and violently in the sunshine. Outside. Not like this. In a metal honeycomb in a cold city. In darkness with the cancer eating away, doing its own cleaning routine in a further darkness inside her. The paramedic who'd diagnosed her had also given Maria some basic counselling. He'd suggested that she try to visualize the cancer, give it an image. Like a crab or a shark. Maria said she visualized it as a drain which she poured money down. The pain was bad tonight, but manageable, thanks to the chemicals. The chemicals were expensive but there was no choice. You had to keep working, for the money. If a portion of the money went straight into pain relief, that's just the way it was.

It was a trade-off.

Life was full of trade-offs.

Like the way Jerome made her feel when he was alive, and the way he'd made her feel when she heard he was dead.

Or like poisoning her body with decades spent bent over cleaning fluids, triggering the cancer and dying before her time, in pain. But with enough money to get her son out of this city. You could still get people out to Canada if you could guarantee support finance for their first three years. Maria almost had enough money put away. And if she died the insurance policy would pay off the balance.

Maria wasn't scared of dying. She wasn't scared, but she didn't like to think about it much. Looking ahead, into the darkness. If she did think about it she visualized snow whipping around big buildings, a lot of empty space in between, and cold air. Forever. She preferred to look back and remember the dancing. Now as she bent down and loaded the floor polishers, checking their EPROMs and switching them on, she could lose herself in those memories. The simple mechanical routines of her job didn't break her revery.

What broke it was the cat.

A small grey cat, its close short fur almost silver in the glow of the lights on her cleaning trolley. At first she thought it was one of the laboratory animals that had escaped from 51. Then she remembered that the Butler Institute hadn't had any laboratory animals for years now. They didn't need them. The cat turned to look at her as it walked through the doorway into one of the stock acquisition offices.

The cat's eyes were flakes of strange flat shine, gleaming blue, then green, then yellow as the angle of its head changed, looking at her in the darkness. They looked more like the status lights of an unusual machine than the eyes of any living creature. The cat disappeared around the doorway with a flick of its tail. Maria followed.

The cat was nowhere to be seen. But even if it had been sitting at her feet Maria wouldn't have noticed it. She was looking at the man.

He was a small man, busy at the computer.

He didn't seem at all surprised to see her.

'Excuse me. Do you have clearance for this area?'

The little man looked up. 'I've got clearance,' he said, 'but only because I've hacked into your security system. I'm an intruder.' He winked at her and went back to his typing for a moment before stopping again. His head turned suddenly to the left, moving stiffy, like a bird's. He was staring intently at something on the desk surface. It was as if he'd just spotted it at the edge of his vision. He swung around on his chair to face the desk and picked up something that was lying on it among the pens and papers, a large envelope.

'What's this?'

'Company envelope.'

'I thought there would be a bee and an eye on it.'

'You can't print it on there.' The envelope was completely

black.

'You can't address it to anyone, either.'

Maria kept her eyes on the man as she casually moved away from the computer where he was sitting. 'It's for keeping documents in. It's got to be black to stop visual penetration, reading the documents inside.' She moved a good distance away. She knew most of the people on these three floors by sight. The little man didn't belong here. 'You know, satellites, that sort of thing,' she said, thinking quickly. Could he be some kind of senior executive? Some kind of software genius from the Butler Institutes in Cambridge or Eindhoven? He was weird enough. If the man had tried any kind of a story or snow job on her she would have hit the alarm already. If he made a move towards her she'd hit it. If he tried to run she'd hit it.

The small man looked at the envelope, smiling. 'I like it, he said. 'I think I'll keep it.' He put the envelope into a pocket of his jacket, then turned back to the computer screen and started working away again. His concentration complete, not pretending that Maria wasn't there or anything, but just wearing this polite little frown and occasionally glancing up at her. As if to say, Sorry I'm so busy. Just wait a minute and then I'll be happy to talk to you.

The cat was back now, circling her ankles, sniffing at them. Maria felt obscurely ashamed of those ankles; the old skin and the varicose veins. You should have seen my legs when I was dancing, she thought. 'I could punch the alarm,' she said. 'Any time I want.'

'I don't doubt it,' said the man. Now he looked up and smiled. 'I wonder if you're going to, though.' Maria couldn't stop herself liking that smile. It should have been easy. All she had to do was remember how Jerome used to smile the same way. Full of mischief and hellraising. Smiling just before he did the sort of thing he enjoyed best. The sort of thing that eventually got him killed.

'Why don't you sit down?' said the man.

'I don't think so.'

'Sit down. You're in pain.'

Maria remained standing where she was. 'What makes you think that?'

'The way you hold yourself,' said the man. 'The way you move. How long has it been bad?'

'A long time. But it won't go on too much longer.'

'No,' said the man. He knew what he was talking about. He even sounded a little sad, sorry for her.

Maria took a clean tissue from her pocket. It was a soft piece of intricately folded tissue paper with a Japanese watermark. Despite every effort to make the King Building a self-contained environment, the outside atmosphere got in. Car exhaust, ash and industrial dust leaking in through the window seals and air conditioning. This soft paper was used for wiping city grit off the screens of the computers.

Maria used it now for wiping her eyes. The little man sat, unmoving. It had been a long time since anyone had managed to get in under her radar like that. She blew her nose and wadded the screen wipe, squeezing the wet tissue hard in her fist. The shape of her fingers was moulded into the tight wet paper. She threw it across the room, crashing it dead centre into a wastepaper basket full of corporate brochures. The sound made the cat jump. Maria felt the need to throw something else as well. Preferably something with sharp edges and heavy. Dead centre in the little man's smug face. Tears were the last thing she needed now. You built a wall between yourself and your emotions, and that was the only thing that kept you going. Without it Maria knew she'd be one more weeping bag woman living in the shell of a 1989 Mazda or a shaky frail old woman in a terminal ward selling her blood to the young junkies and hookers in the adjacent beds.

The little man was watching her, aware that something was up. Sensitive to what was going on in her head. Jerome had been that way, knowing her moods like a dog that could sniff the weather, knowing when a storm was approaching. Maria kept the anger out of her voice when she spoke.

'You said you were an intruder?'

'At the very least,' said the man.

'Then I'd better tell you about the security in this place. It's pretty tight. You can do whatever you like, but I'd advise you to just sit back and relax. If you make a run for it they're happy to use what they call ultimate force. That's what the security

33

is like around here. And I'm going to call them now.'

'You don't have to do that.' The man was watching the screen again.

'I think I do.'

The little man was impatient now, speaking as if to a child. 'You do not have to call the security guards.' He'd stood up and switched off the screen. Now he was putting on a hat. 'You don't have to call them because they're already on their way.'

Christian was in the elevator. Like Mulwray, he was still armed from the night's work. They'd got the policeman secured in the medical section on 51 and by rights they should now be having a beer and taking it easy.

It was Mulwray's last week working in the biostock section. He'd been promoted, effective as of Monday. Working in Social Acquisition with that bitch Stephanie. This was the standard promotion route in the Butler Institute. You started out doing the crap work in Bio. If you survived that and they liked you, the next step was Social. Christian had found that Bio could be a pain in the ass if you worked with the wrong people. He was going to miss Mulwray. Christian had known people like him when he was in Mexico. They were always the best ones, the most fun to be with.

Christian had spent two years in Mexico during the war, with Airforce Technical Support. His job had mostly been sorting out any problems with the neural computers on the missiles. When the missiles weren't having nervous breakdowns, they were great. They had cameras fitted on the nose cones so that you could watch their flight, streaking over the villages and forests until they caught up with the columns of Mexican armour. Whenever the Mexes tried to set up a defensive position around a reservoir, the smart missiles would drop from the sky.

It was only in black and white but it was still great. Christian and the others liked to replay the missile transmissions on their VCR with a few beers in the evenings in the mess tent.

The elevator was slowing up now. Mulwray grinned at him and he grinned back. He liked the man's attitude. When the door whispered open, Mulwray was the first through. They moved down the corridor, watching for movement. There was

34

faint screenlight coming from the open doors of the offices, like light reflected off snow. And light from some other source too. As they got closer they saw it was the cleaning woman's trolley with the fluorescent bars on the side. There was a fluid container on it, open. No sign of the cleaning woman. For the first time Christian began to feel that the security alert might be something more than a hiccup in the building's control system. He could hear a sound now, coming from the door of an office just beyond the trolley. Christian was damned if he'd let Mulwray go through first this time. But Mulwray was already moving. Christian dodged ahead of him, jigging to the left as he went through the door, running low so as to present the minimum profile to hostile fire. He straightened up with his sidearm aimed in a two-handed grip looking towards the source of the noise.

'Oh, for Christ's sake.'

Mulwray was through the door now, holding his gun like Christian. Like Christian, he immediately began to lower it. 'Great,' said Mulwray. He glanced over at Christian and together they walked across the office, putting away their sidearms. The cleaning woman, Maria, was staring up at them, frozen with surprise. She was sitting in front of the big screen of one of the Apollo workstations, her hands still poised in the air above the keyboard. She was in the middle of keying something in. Looking guilty as hell. Christian wanted to see what was on the screen but Mulwray was blocking his view.

'Caught in the act,' said Mulwray.

'My God,' said Maria. 'You scared me.'

'You're going to have to be more careful than that, Maria. You were ringing bells all over the network. We got a security flash down on 51.'

Christian could see what Maria was doing on the screen now. She had the E-mail slingshot open. She was typing a letter, ready for the system to shoot right across the continent. He knew what the destination was because Maria already had the address menu set up. 'Who the hell lives in Los Angeles?'

'Old boyfriend,' said Maria. She was blushing fiercely as Christian began reading over her shoulder.

Dear Jerome, I miss you more than ever these days, in the cold out here. I especially miss you at night. I miss your arms

35

around me and the weight of you on me

'Doesn't sound like you get all that cold at night,' said Mulwray. 'Thinking about that sort of thing.'

'Woman your age should be ashamed,' said Christian.

'Do you have any idea what a phone call costs these days?' The cleaning woman was squirming in her chair, looking from Mulwray to Christian. 'I'm not doing any harm. I've done it before.' She was trying to be apologetic, you could see, but it didn't come naturally.

'Well, don't do it again, and definitely don't do it on this node.'

'I'm sorry guys.' Maria was staring down at her hands, resting on the keyboard. Christian didn't think she sounded sorry. He thought she was keeping her eyes down so they wouldn't see her natural expression. A lot of anger and defiance. She must have been trouble when she was young. He tried to avoid looking at those fingers of hers. The nails were really short, ending way back in the skin in the top of the finger. It didn't look like they'd been chewed or anything. More like they'd been melted.

'You're going to get fired when somebody finds out,' he said. 'Unauthorized use of company resources.'

'Come on, we'd better get back to the lab.' Mulwray's arm was on his shoulder. Christian turned away, a little reluctantly. He was tired all of a sudden. It was like that when you got ready for action and nothing happened. He wondered if Mulwray was free for a beer after work. They could go round to his place. Christian had some new videos, from the Philippines, which you had to see to believe.

When they'd gone the little man came out and sat beside Maria. 'I didn't know about the alarm on that terminal,' he said.

'Neither did I.' Maria was typing on the keyboard. 'There it is.' On the screen was an open folder containing a symbol which she recognized, although she'd never actually seen one before. A cartoon padlock with bulging Basil Wolverton eyes sticking out on stalks. A Norton Smartlock. 'They must have put that on here last week.' It was a security package and a very expensive one. The little man was leaning close beside her, inspecting the screen. He was nodding.

36

'Stupid of me,' he said. 'I could have avoided that.'

'No you couldn't. Anyone using this machine would have been detected.'

'Not necessarily.' The man clapped his hands and the cat came running out of the shadows and jumped. He caught the cat and held it to his chest. 'Not everyone,' he said. The cat's face was pressed close to his and as he turned to look at Maria the cat turned, too. Two pairs of strange cool eyes regarding her. 'The right person could get past it easily.'

'Stupid cow,' said Mulwray in the elevator going back down. He jerked his camelhair off his shoulders and twisted the coat into a shapeless bundle. Stuffed it tight under one arm.

'Careful you don't get creases in that.'

Mulwray let the coat flop loose. His hands were shaking a little. He smoothed out the camelhair and folded it up again, more carefully. There was a smell of sweat and aftershave in the elevator. Mulwray wasn't looking at him. Didn't want to look uncool.

Christian knew the feeling. Coming down from combat readiness without having anywhere to put all that energy. You needed an outlet. Then Christian remembered. They did have an outlet. Waiting for them down on 51. Christian was smiling as he remembered.

The man was standing at one of the floor-length windows, watching the snow. The cat was curled in his arms, like a baby. Its head was turned so it could stare out the window, too. Maria wondered if it was looking for birds. It wouldn't see any. Not in this city. 'What do I call you?' The man turned at the sound of Maria's voice. 'It doesn't have to be your real name,' she said. 'It can be like your user name on your computer.'

'The Doctor,' said the little man. He set the cat down. 'You can call me the Doctor.'

'I knew someone used to call himself the Head Doctor,' said Maria. 'That was a log-in name, too.' She thought of others, coming back to her vividly now from the years and distance. Names they used on the public access computer network back home. The libraries had installed shatterproof screens in

37

concrete booths and anyone could just go in and use them, provided you didn't mind the urine stink. Maria burned joss sticks. When the lights were smashed she brought her own, fixing big flashlights to the ceiling with gaffer tape. She taught herself to touch type and then she didn't need the flashlights any more. Working at the keyboard in the dark, eyes on the screen.

'Secretarial skills,' said Maria. She said it so quietly the man, the Doctor, could hardly have heard it. But he nodded. Sitting beside her now, watching the screen images change as she typed. Maria not looking at the keyboards, her fingers knowing where the symbols were. The big open-plan office seemed to have closed in around her. It was like sitting in a small concrete cubicle. Instead of toner and corporate carpeting she could smell piss and incense.

The public access keyboards were always being ripped off, so eventually they'd been replaced with integrated units, stainless steel set in concrete. A bit noisy, but okay to use. They even found a way of making the mice theftproof. Maria remembered afternoons spent waiting for a free terminal, sitting on a bolted-down chair reading and rereading the spraypainted graffiti on the walls, boring equivalents of the user names on the system. On the public network you got to know the regulars. Cracker Cracker, Boner, Are you Glad To Be In America and You Can't Eat A Snake (what kind of idiots had the patience to type those every time they logged on?), Eidolon, Liberty and Kool Aid. Kool Aid had been her. Named in the memory of the one time she had been busted. Jerome's idea. Putting an LSD variant into the refreshments at a police pinic. Shame it had never come off. She remembered when Jerome had outlined the plan, telling her about it in their small kitchenette, cans of beer and a pipe on the table. She felt a ticklish sensation, excitement deep in her stomach.

The same feeling she had now.

'Okay, we're there,' said Maria.

The Doctor studied the screen. Except for the small image in the centre it was blank, pale and clean. The image was a simplified diagram of the King Building. When Maria clicked on it the tiny building opened in a burst of colours. A chaotic scatter of icons appeared, all different shapes. Maria pulled down a menu, clicked on it and the jumbled screen vanished, replaced by neat rows of type. 'Have to do that or I could never find anything around here.' Maria selected and clicked, moving further in. A new mess of files appeared on the screen.

'This is the brain of the building. If you could say this place has got a brain. Operates the elevators, sniffs for fires, checks ID cards. It chews mine up about twice a year. Big expensive system but not exactly what you'd call smart. A lot of bespoke software, communications, security, maintenance, stuck together over the years.

'It controls the sprinklers?'

'The sprinklers, the cameras. All the doors and windows. Here's the interesting bit. Central or back-slash Cen, or Big Ken to his friends also has to interface with all the company networks in the building. If you've got offices here your computers have to talk to Big Ken. If there was a fire or something the Central has to know where everybody is, who's logged in at what location. Figure out optimal escape routes for everybody in the building.'

'It draws vectors,' said the Doctor, thinking aloud. 'Or it deals with it as a problem in topology.'

'It probably uses voodoo,' said Maria. 'This thing is so old it used to have a command line you typed on. Remember those?'

'But you can access any data in the building through this route.'

'Absolutely. And not only access. Big Ken has to be able to slot an evacuation message across their screens. So Central can pre-empt any process that's running on any computer in the building.'

The Doctor smiled.

'Took me years to learn my way around. I know it pretty good by now.' Maria flexed her fingers over the keyboards. 'Central also controls a lot of the cleaning hardware. Stuff I have to operate. Maintains the schedules. Reminds me when the air conditioning ducts need doing and helps me route the scrubbers. Don't want any of that legionnaire virus floating around.'

The Doctor reached over her shoulder and punched some

buttons on the keyboard. The office directory appeared on the screen, listing all the companies who leased space in the King Building. From Amoco to Zenith. Polychrome logos and badges flashed up beside some of the names. You could tell how well a company was weathering the corporate storm by the sophistication and expense of its computer graphics.

'How long have you worked in this building?' The cat was beside the Doctor now, looking at the screen. Maria had noticed that before with cats. They were interested in what you were interested in.

'Forever,' she said.

'That's a very long time. Always for the Butler Institute?'

'No. Anywhere in the building. I cleaned for other companies plenty of times.'

'But who pays you? Always the Butler Institute?'

'Yes.'

The Doctor was smiling again, but something was different this time. 'Does that suggest anything to you?' He was looking directly at her now. The light of the screen was reflected in his eyes. Like two tiny screens looking out at her, full of data she'd never be able to read.

'Tell me something. Why am I helping you?'

'Perhaps because you know what the Butler Institute is. And perhaps you can see what it will become. Can you get at their current projects directory?'

'That's highly classified stuff.'

'Can you get at it?'

'No problem.'

As she typed, Maria realized that she was making a noise. Low and rhythmic. She was singing to herself. It took her a few moments to place the song. Something by The Clash.

The system security had been improved since the last time Maria had hacked into the Butler Institute records. That had been at Christmas, to authorize a bonus for herself. Nothing too flashy, nothing that would get noticed. She'd earned it, cleaning up the wreckage after the office party. The workstation had had a sprig of mistletoe fixed over its screen and it had taken her about fifteen minutes. This took her an hour and a half, and all she found were some personnel records. Details of two cops called Mancuso and McIlveen. When the stuff flashed up on the screen, the Doctor smiled. 'Just confirming a theory,' he said. He retreated through levels of memory, closing each window down as he went. It was like retreating through a series of Chinese boxes. Sometimes he pulled down menus and ran through random processes. Maria knew what he was doing. He was removing his traces, hiding his route from the auditing software. Like brushing leaves over your footprints in a forest. When he was finished he switched the computer down, and picked up a pen and a pad of paper from the adjacent desk. 'Do you think anyone will mind if I borrow these?' he said, smiling at Maria.

They were alone in the corridor except for the vacuum units, travelling over the carpeting and in and out of the offices. The Doctor was walking, moving very quickly, but Maria wasn't having any trouble keeping up with him. She hadn't felt like this in years. 'Is that it?' she said.

'For now,' said the Doctor. 'I've got what I came for.'

'So what happens next?'

'I have to travel to certain places and meet certain people.'

'Are you coming back?'

'I'm far from finished here,' said the Doctor. He turned and looked back down the corridor. Two tiny lights shone in the darkness, moving. The cat came trotting out of the shadows and joined them. The Doctor looked at Maria. 'Thank you for your help.' He picked the cat up and turned away, moving down the corridor. Maria stood and watched him. When she opened her mouth she intended only to speak the words, but they came out as a shout.

'Take me with you.'

The Doctor stopped. He turned and looked at her. The cat wriggled out of his arms and dropped to the carpet. It walked off around the corner.

'No,' said the Doctor.

'Why not?' Maria moved down the corridor, closer to the Doctor.

'Because of 51,' said the Doctor.

'What?' Maria's voice was shaking. She could hear it herself.

41

'The fifty-first floor in this building. You know what goes on there.'

'No.'

'Yes. You've known for years, and you've let it happen.' The Doctor turned away from her and walked around the corner, after the cat.

Maria didn't try to follow him.

There was a blast of blue light, like a giant taking a photograph, a sound she couldn't describe, then a rush of air. An indoor wind, gusting past her from behind, rushing around the corner, sucking dust from the carpet. Too long since that carpet was vacuumed, she thought numbly. After a moment she made herself look around the corner. There was nothing there, of course.

It was about seven o'clock when Maria got home that morning. She found a space for her Toyota, pulled in and switched off the car. It wasn't until she tried to get out of the car that she realized something was wrong. She first noticed it in her hands as she reached for the door handle.

Shaking.

And it was as if noticing it made it worse. Now her hand shook uncontrollably. She pulled it in, tight to her body. Now her body began to shake, too. The tremors began hitting her in waves. Her legs as well. Maria looked out the window, wondering if it was an earthquake, but the storefronts and the passing cars remained steady.

Anyway, this wasn't earthquake country. This wasn't home. Was it? Outside the car were palm trees and hot blue sky shining through a moving film of fumes. Maria could feel the warmth through the glass of the window. She moved her hand to the button to open the car window. She wanted to open the window and feel the summer heat rush in on her, breathe the sweet hot tarry air.

Breathe.

Maria took a breath and found she couldn't get any air at all. Her hand was twitching feebly on the car seat. She tried to move to the window button but her hand just lay there.

But it didn't matter.

It didn't matter that her body was shaking like this. There was something familiar about the shaking. The shaking and the rhythm and the heat. Her mind was growing more remote but she could still recognize the rhythm and the heat.

Maria stopped fighting it.

She let herself go. Lost herself in the trembling of her body. She didn't feel any fear. The music kept the fear away. A steady pounding, echoing off concrete walls. She let her body follow the beat of the music. The warmth washed over her, the beer-sweat-and-basement smell.

As she went she started losing everything.

Jerome went. The sunlight on her face went. Joss stick smoke curling past a paint-stained wall. Warmth of the bong in her hand.

It didn't matter.

She was dancing.

4

They were about five blocks behind him by the time he reached the municipal library on Wendacott Avenue.

They'd been chasing Bobby Prescott for half an hour now and his batteries were running low. He used the last of the power to put on a burst of speed as he came round the corner by the mall, past Smartt Software and McCray's drugstore.

Even now Bobby Prescott felt something as he passed McCray's. He snatched a glance back. The streets were still clear. He looked around, taking in the familiar neighbourhood terrain. He found himself unconsciously trying not to look at McCray's. So he forced himself to stare at the place. He was passing near an outside corner of the mall facing Wendacott. McCray's was ahead and to the left. It was just an old drugstore with some cars out front.

Bobby Prescott shot past McCray's and the Seven Eleven, then he cut across the empty street and up on to the sidewalk, outside the library grounds. The changing texture of concrete caused his wheels to buzz. Spotlights blazed on poles in the empty tarmacked apron outside the library. Their light caused the steel bars of the library fence to strobe as he swept past. The open front gate of the library was coming up now. Bobby Prescott calculated, counting, and then he leaned outwards and grabbed at a streetlamp. He curved his leather-gloved hand around it, gripping and pulling hard.

At the speed he was travelling the manoeuvre bruised the flat of his hand and wrenched the muscles of his shoulder. But it also sent him rocketing off on a right-angle turn and straight into the library grounds without noticeably reducing his speed.

The plastic wheels of his roller skates made a gunshot sound as he crossed a narrow steel groove in the road surface. The heavy steel mechanism of the library gates had once run in this gutter, keeping the gates in alignment as they rumbled shut.

Bobby Prescott glanced back over his shoulder again. Still nothing. Just the quiet street and the open gates. Those gates had been jammed permanently open ever since the riots twenty years ago. Some grade 12 kids had taken steel bars out of the shop storeroom at their school and done the business with them, putting paid to the riot barrier by feeding the big metal bars into the cogged wheels. The wheels had churned and screamed and splintered.

Bobby Prescott had almost lost his hand that day. He hadn't let go when the gate began to chew up one of those bars.

Now he cut the power to his skates and coasted the last twenty metres, angling his skates slightly to kill the last of his momentum as he reached the bottom of the wide concrete steps of the library. The first bicycle would be coming past the mall on Wendacott, coming past Smartt's and McCray's and the Seven Eleven about now. Bobby Prescott sat down on the bottom step and rested for a moment. He looked at the sprayed and carved graffiti around him and took comfort in it.

This was as good a place as any.

Unlacing the roller skates took maybe four seconds. In the distance Bobby Prescott could hear the skimming of bicycle rubber on the street surface, approaching fast. When he had the skates off he packed them in his rucksack, leaving the top of the sack open for quick access.

The first bicycle was coming up the school entrance now, rattling as it crossed the gate gutter, the kid on the bicycle coming through the dark places between the school spotlights. Ghost white face and T-shirt swimming across the shadows, coming straight towards Bobby Prescott. The kid was very confident. Some sort of long knife was attached with clips along the main axis of the kid's bike. The kid was reaching down to unclip it. He was eager. Bobby Prescott recognized him. This kid had consistently led the pack for the past hour as they hunted him down.

But Bobby Prescott recognized the kid in another way, too. It was like looking at himself, twenty years ago.

The kid let his bicycle drop on to the ground and jumped clear of it, running for the steps where Bobby Prescott sat, knife held out to one side. Bobby Prescott strung the rucksack across his shoulder and clipped a security strap to the belt of his jeans. On the left of the belt was a battery pack like the ones kids used for their personal stereos. Bobby Prescott used it to power his skates. On the right of the belt, balancing the battery pack, he had a sealed length of heavy flexible black plastic, ribbed for easy grip and filled with lead shot. It was called a sinker. The sinker made a heavy wet sound as it connected with the bicycle kid's head. The kid dropped the knife and fell over, twitching, and Bobby Prescott picked the knife up and went over to the bike, lying there on the tarmac.

The front wheel was still spinning, a black plastic badge shaped like a bird's head rotating on the spokes. Bobby Prescott hesitated, not wanting to touch the bicycle. He was thinking about McCray's drugstore and what had happened there. He made himself touch the bicycle. He bent close, using the knife on the bike's mudguard, ruining the fine German edge on the blade. It was a shame, but Bobby Prescott needed a weapon with a decent reach.

The main pack of bicycle kids would be coming past the Seven Eleven by now. Bobby Prescott stayed calm and used the long thin knife to free the bicycle chain. He swept its oily length back and forth in the air a few times, judging the weight of it.

The rest of them were in sight now. The bicycle kids or whatever the gangs called themselves these days. Gameboys. Witchkids. Crows. Bobby Prescott had lost track.

He watched them as they came through the school gate. Two of them side by side, then three more in single file. Crows, that's what this gang called themselves. The wheel on the fallen bicycle was clicking to a halt now and the bright red eye on the crow's-head badge steadied and glinted up at Bobby Prescott.

A final straggler coasted into the library parking lot, the spotlights making the shadow of his bicycle huge and skeletal on the ground. A memory tried to force itself into Bobby Prescott's mind, the same memory that had made him flinch when he touched the bicycle. He looked up and saw the illuminated sign on McCray's drugstore glowing on the other side of the road. Bobby Prescott concentrated and forced himself to look away, back at the bicycle kids. It would be different this time.

46

He took a deep breath and prepared himself for what was coming.

The straggler made it a total of seven of the kids, if you counted the one lying bleeding by the steps. They ranged from about twelve to fifteen in age.

It took five of them to bring Bobby Prescott down.

He never really got to use the bicycle chain properly. It dropped from his hand as the youngest kid stomped his fist. The sixth one was waking now, shaking his head and moaning and throwing up as he came back to consciousness. The seventh one, the straggler, had picked up the German knife and was coming forward, getting closer, face tense and frowning with excitement. Bobby Prescott was thinking calmly and quickly, going through the options. The edge of that knife was dulled now but that wouldn't buy him any time. The kid wouldn't need the edge of it.

He was close now, looking down at Bobby Prescott. The kid was wearing a bicycle helmet that had been modified to look like a gaming helmet, with VR decals on it. That was all part of the stuff Bobby Prescott would never understand about these kids. The VR games and the bicycles and the way they hated anything that was a machine or used power. Unless of course it was one of the computers that they needed for their games.

The knife was coming close now, getting big as it neared his face. Bobby Prescott noted that the blade looked clean and for some absurd reason he was relieved. He concentrated on the brightly coloured gaming stickers as the knife's tip pressed against his throat. He didn't look at the eyes of the kid, he wasn't going to give him that satisfaction. Bobby Prescott let himself go limp. He was going to die and he knew it. He felt the fear starting in him but it was just his body, glands feeding the bloodstream. Just the animal in him. Bobby Prescott had to put that animal down. Bobby Prescott had been fighting on the streets for nearly thirty years. He'd used a knife himself. He'd killed people himself. Now there was one last fight for him to carry out. Not against the kids who held him. They were young and strong. Sweating with excitement. There was no victory there.

But Bobby Prescott was going to have a victory. He was going

47

to win a last fight. He readied himself, to confront the fear. He began to fight the fear.

He could feel himself winning already. The kid was close now. Freckles on his pale face, a ring of acne around his mouth. Little wispy moustache. The knife was beginning to enter Bobby Prescott's throat but all he felt was a warm flash of pleasure. He'd applied his willpower and he already knew that he was going to win. His breathing was beginning to ease already and his body, pressed against the hard edges of the library steps, eased too.

He relaxed, drifted away.

The fear flared one last time.

Died.

Now Bobby Prescott wasn't afraid of anything. He was grinning with satisfaction as the tip of the knife slowly cut into him, the kid holding the knife getting excited but beginning to get into it, his hand steady. He was going to really go for it any second and drive the blade right in. Bobby Prescott just grinned up at the kid as the kid began to kill him.

'That's enough,' said the small man.

Bobby Prescott had been aware of the small man for some time, standing there at the edge of his vision, but he had dismissed him as an irrelevant piece of phenomenon, background noise. The important thing had been Bobby Prescott's last fight. But now the kids holding him were loosening their grip, letting go at the man's command.

Bobby Prescott's concentration began to unlock. His mind began to come back from the death-place he'd prepared for it. The knife was moving away from him, coming back out of his throat, blood on the tip of it, the kid's hand still tight around the handle, reluctant. But moving. Bobby Prescott began to let himself think again. His memory unfroze and he could remember that the small man had come out of the glass doors and down the steps towards them. He had come out of the library, just a small man holding a big black envelope in one hand.

And now he was giving them orders, the kids, the Crows. Giving them orders and moving his hands, the envelope jabbing as he spoke. And the kids, the little animals with their bicycles and their helmets and knives, were obeying him.

The smell of the books hit Bobby Prescott even before his eyes adjusted to the darkness. 'I'm afraid the lights are dead in here,' said the smell man, walking somewhere in the shadows just in front of him.

'They're dead everywhere in the library. They have been for a long time,' said Bobby Prescott. 'Years. Ever since the big riots.' He could see now. There was enough light coming in from the tall library windows to make out the wreckage of the front desks, the shelves which had once held the latest magazines. The disembowelled overturned shape of a Xerox machine. But Bobby Prescott could have closed his eyes and still found his way through here. The smell of the books brought it all back to him.

He remembered the first time he'd ever come into this library, with the man he'd called Uncle Max. Uncle Max was there on business, looking up something to do with human anatomy, and he'd let Bobby wander off. The little boy had seen a book on a shelf, too high for him to reach, and a lady, one of the librarians, had fetched it down for him. It was the first book Bobby Prescott ever read. He couldn't remember the title, but he could still close his eyes and see the cover, and he could tell you the story.

'How's your neck?'

Bobby Prescott felt a flash of irritation. He'd forgotten about the wound. It was only a small cut, but now that the little man had reminded him about it, it began to sting like a bitch. He licked his fingers and rubbed saliva into the wound. 'It'll heal clean,' said Bobby Prescott. 'Why did they take off like that? The kids. The Crows. They just up and left when you asked them to.'

'That's because I'm paying them,' said the Doctor.

'Paying them?' Bobby Prescott looked at the blood on his fingers. He wiped it off on his leather jacket.

'To find you and pursue you. To bring you here. You see, I wanted to talk with you,' said the Doctor.

The Doctor?

Bobby Prescott felt a cold feeling beginning low down on his spine and moving up.

'They weren't supposed to hurt you,' the Doctor was saying.

Bobby Prescott recognized the symptoms of fear starting. He fought back immediately and brutally. He blocked the fear before it started. It was easy. It was nothing compared to the knife going into his throat on the steps. Feeling the fear wither away like that gave Bobby Prescott his confidence back. His mind was clear and strong. The little man was just a little man. He wasn't called the Doctor. That was just a random thought that had passed through Bobby Prescott's mind. But Bobby Prescott had firm control over his own mind. He banished the random thought.

'I'm sorry they went that far with the knife,' said the Doctor. Not the Doctor. The little man. He was shrugging. 'That's the problem with plans. They tend to take on a life of their own. People tend to get hurt.'

But Bobby Prescott wasn't listening. They were in the main hall of the library now. This was where the shelves of fiction had once stood. The smell was strongest here. The rich, spicy mustiness. The smell of books, old books, library books. Books that had gone through a thousand hands. Their pages stained and dirty.

But the stains and the dirt didn't obscure the words. All those words on all those pages. Pages you could turn on a rooftop, on a bench by a road, waiting at night under a streetlight. Words that carried you into a new world, away from the cold on a rooftop, waiting there by the satellite dishes while Uncle Max finished up downstairs in the bedrooms. And every different book was a different world. You could have a stack of them in your room, piled in the corner out of Uncle Max's way. Books with red or green covers, some with pictures on them, 'dust jackets' the ladies in the library — the *librarians* — called them, protected by library plastic until some moron tore them off to decorate a wall, or just out of malice, the idiot need to destroy.

A stack of different books, all waiting to be read, each one with its own world you could escape into. Escape from Uncle Max and the floors you had to clean for him and the funny colour of the water you had to pour away afterwards, every time.

Each book an escape route. You'd sit on your mattress in your bedroom and take a book off the pile, and open it, and the magic would begin, the escape would begin. And it always began with that smell, coming up at you from the book, that comforting musty smell.

The smell that was all around Bobby Prescott now. But deeper and stronger and different.

Stronger because there were thousands of books all around him now, lying open where they fell, the dampness making the smell stronger. It was a friendly smell. But the dampness that swelled the pages was obliterating the words. Wiping them out the way the stains of a million hands never could.

Different because Bobby Prescott still believed he could smell the charred smell, the choking smell. The book burning smell.

'You want to talk to me?' said Bobby Prescott softly, looking at the small man. They stood in one of the avenues formed when the tall bookshelves were overturned, smashing into each other with the anvil noise of the colliding metal shelf-frames. Bobby Prescott remembered the thunder as the books tumbled and spilled. Raining down bruisingly hard on his head and chest as he ran through the collapsing aisles. It was like being in a city of book buildings while it was toppling in an earthquake. Now they stood in the dark quiet aftermath, soaked with years of rain drainage from the torn roof. There were low hills of books all around them, the tilted empty skeletons of the shelves leaning against the high library windows, the colourless moonlight and the candy-coloured mall neon coming through behind them.

The small man had walked deeper into the maze of tilted shelves and piled books. He was a small figure already, moving away in the streaks of neon and moonlight in the big dim space of the library. 'Let's talk,' said Bobby Prescott, following him, moving fast, catching up.

He was about an arm's length away from the Doctor when the Doctor — the small man — turned and said, 'Destruction of the temples. Time for a new god. They always do this. The killing and the violence. It seems to be a necessary part of the process for them. Tell me —'

The little man swung around and stared up at Bobby Prescott. You couldn't see the man's eyes in the darkness, just the pale

51

shape of his face and dark shadows under the brows. 'Don't you sense any of that?' said the little man. 'Don't you feel it around you in places like this?' He moved impatiently away from where Bobby Prescott was standing, further into the dark aisles. They were in the centre of the library floor now. The centre of the building had been designed like a broad well shaft. You could look down from a circular railing to the basement level, or up at circular balconies diminishing with distance on each of the floors above. A bright oblong of moonlight came through the burst skylight at the top of the shaft, lighting up a section of wall. On the chalk white surface you could see a bold dark scrawl of spray-painted graffiti, stretching for metres above the wreckage of the library:

What's the point? We can't read anyway.

'That was sprayed up there during the riots,' said Bobby Prescott. 'When this place finally got it. Like the library at Alexandria. You heard of that?'

'Yes,' said the man.

'They burned that one, too. But look up there. Notice anything?'

The little man stood waiting, silently staring up above the dark well of the library basement. Bobby Prescott couldn't tell if he was listening or not.

'Whoever sprayed that up there got the punctuation absolutely right,' said Bobby Prescott. 'They put the apostrophes where they're supposed to go. The bastard could write. And that means they could read. They understood what all this meant.'

Bobby Prescott turned to one of the piles that peaked halfway to the ceiling and sloped down into scattered volumes, individual books, one almost touching his foot. He picked it up.

'They knew what it meant. And they still helped destroy it.' Bobby Prescott's voice was thick with emotion. He could hear himself getting louder. 'So of course I know what you mean.' He was shouting now and at last the little man was turning around, looking at him, paying attention to him. 'You mean this place is like a church,' said Bobby Prescott, letting his voice go quiet again. 'And now the church is dead because the religion is dead.' He let the book drop out of his hand. He'd checked. It was quite unsalvageable. 'It was killed by people who didn't believe in god.'

'Do you believe in gods, Bobby?'

'My god was books.' Bobby closed in on the little man. 'Books I could escape into. Books that were doorways into other worlds for me. You know about those kind of doorways?'

'Yes.'

'Like going through that wardrobe into Narnia, right? I started reading those books when I was four. I learned fast. They said I was something special. The librarians. They taught me in their own time. In their lunch hours. That was one of the first books. I went through that wardrobe. I found the lion and the witch.'

Bobby Prescott leaned in close to the Doctor, his breath warm on the Doctor's face.

'I rode on the quest for the rings of power. I went out into the desert with Kit and Tunner and Port. I've stayed in a house in England called Howard's End. It had a roof that kept the rain off my head. Even when there wasn't a real roof and the real rain was soaking me to the skin. Do you understand?'

The Doctor nodded.

'I've been down every corridor in Gormenghast. I've been on the road with Dean Moriarty. I waited for a quiet American called Pyle in the rue Catinat in Saigon. I was with Dillon and the kid when they killed Eddie Coyle after the hockey game. I went up to the castle with K. There was snow coming down on us.'

Bobby Prescott looked up at the ruined library rising around him, beyond the balconies of the dark building well. A million books, burned, torn, destroyed. The survivors dying now. Books died just like people. They died when they finally lost a critical amount of information. Pages torn out or obliterated by the dirty rainwater. When a book ceased to be legible, when it lost so much information that its ideas could no longer be transmitted, the book died. Bobby Prescott felt like a child again, sad and alone, standing in the silent heart of a mass graveyard.

He looked at the ruined books all around him. He'd rescued as many as he could, carrying bags of books home right under the noses of the librarians. They'd known. They'd switched off the alarm system when he went through. They knew the trouble was coming. Everybody did.

Bobby Prescott had been there the day the balloon went up, the day the rioting began.

One of the pitifully few. A thin line standing against the hordes. Illiterate and literacy-hating, streaming in through the gates. Shouting in their eagerness to kill. And it wasn't even people they wanted to kill. It was the books and the ideas in them. Ideas that could live almost forever if the books were cherished.

The front wave of rioters had hit them and Bobby Prescott had begun to swing his baseball bat. He had felt a wild joy matched at no other time in his young life. He had always dreamed of smashing these ignorant computer-blunted faces. Now they were being offered to him.

When he stopped swinging, it was only because the bat had been reduced to a useless stump of soggy wood.

They'd beaten the first wave of attackers as far back as the library gates. If they'd been able to shut the gates at that point things might have turned out differently. But the kids from the high school had brought steel rods with them and jammed the gate mechanism forever, just as the crash barrier began to grind shut. Bobby Prescott had almost lost a hand trying to pull one of those bars out.

Sometimes he could still feel the wound, healed but still there, deep in his hand, down among the bones. He felt it now. Bobby Prescott stood in the graveyard silence and felt that ache. It was the ache of an old defeat. There was hot air at the base of his throat. His anger made it hard to breathe. The little man had moved again. He stood looking over the circular balcony, down towards the basement well of the library. He was holding something Bobby Prescott couldn't see.

'I tried to stop them,' said Bobby Prescott. He was moving towards the little man, moving quietly. 'I tried to stop them but I didn't manage it.' The little man turned and Bobby Prescott could see what he was holding now — a pad of paper, the top sheet blank and white in the moonlight. Out of his pocket he took a pencil and he began writing on the pad. Bobby Prescott hesitated, watching him. No, he wasn't writing. The motions of his hand were too fast and sweeping. He was drawing something.

'Bobby Prescott, why were you here?' asked the little man.

'When the riots were on?' said Bobby Prescott. 'I was here because I wanted to save the books.'

'How did you intend to do that?'

'Stopping the kids.'

'Have you stopped a lot of kids?'

'They're little animals. The only time they read a word is when it's on some computer screen. That's the way I imagine them. In their safe little homes. In their warm little bedrooms with the computers their mom and dad bought for them. They've got the light from the screen on their faces and their little lips are moving, as they struggle to get through a few words and on to the next game.' Bobby Prescott sighed. 'But that's not really a realistic image. Most of them can't even read that much. They have to have pictures on their screens.'

'Why do you kill them, do you suppose, Bobby Prescott?'

'Who cares?'

'Could it just be because they're different?'

Bobby Prescott was tired of listening to the man. He began to look around for something suitably long and heavy. Or maybe he'd just use his hands. He didn't hurry as he followed the little man around the circular balcony, the man concentrating on his sketch.

'You want to know who's different?' said Bobby Prescott. 'I'm different. Out on the steps with those kids? They were fixing to kill me.'

'I know. I'm sorry about that. They got a little carried away.'

'They had the knife already going into my throat. I should have lost it right about then. You ever seen anybody die?'

The small man frowned. 'Yes.'

'I don't mean die in bed when they're sixty. I mean die in the street when they're young and think they're going to live forever. Kids always think they're going to live forever.' Bobby Prescott smiled. 'I've seen quite a few like that. And they always beg or scream or just go out of their minds. They all totally lose it in some way. But not me. Not on those steps. I felt it coming. Fear. And I stopped it. You're damned right I'm different. I'm strong. I am the iron that has been strengthened in the fire. That was my childhood, man.'

55

Now the little man looked up from his sketching. He looked into Bobby Prescott's face.

'My childhood,' said Bobby Prescott softly. 'That was the fire, all right. You wouldn't want to know about my childhood.'

'No,' agreed the little man. It was too dark to see any expression on his face.

'But that was the fire. And I was forged in the fire. It only made me stronger. I am privileged because I am strong. I am special because I am strong. You are damned right I'm different.' He was close to the little man now. Right on top of him. 'I can control my fear. It's just an enemy and I overcome it.' The little man seemed to have stopped sketching. He was still concentrating on the pad of paper, the drawing he'd just made. He wasn't looking up, but Bobby Prescott didn't mind. He'd do it to him anyway. 'I am not afraid,' said Bobby Prescott, closing in. 'If you're afraid you're an animal. And it's okay to kill animals.'

'Bobby Prescott, do I look afraid?' said the Doctor. He looked up. And then he showed Bobby Prescott his drawing.

And then the fear hit Bobby Prescott like a freight train.

'That's all.'

Bobby Prescott wasn't sure that the Doctor had heard him. He cleared his throat and said it again. 'That's all.'

The moon was gone now, only the streetlight and the mall neon coming through the library windows. They were by the front desk of the library again, near the main entrance. Bobby Prescott was sitting cross-legged on the floor, keeping some distance away from the Doctor. As far away as he could, and still make himself heard. 'Is that all you wanted to know? Can I go now, man?'

The little man was silhouetted in the window light, sitting perched on the ruined Xerox machine in the centre of the big foyer. The librarians had tried to drag it across the floor of the entrance hall and barricade the main doorway with it. They'd got about halfway.

Bobby Prescott stood up and moved around stretching his legs. He had almost stopped shaking now. Talking to the little man had allowed Bobby Prescott to calm down a bit, get himself back together a bit. He walked to ease the cramp in his legs and to feel some sense of control over himself again. He didn't walk towards the small man, though. He looked out the front window, up at the sky. He was trying to see the moon, trying to work out what the time was.

How long had they been talking? His voice was hoarse. He cleared his throat and stared through the window, looking down from the clouds. Then he saw McCray's drugstore across the street and the sight of it started him shaking again.

He had trouble walking back to the long library desk and trouble sitting down in front of it again. He looked away from the windows.

The little man was still sitting on the Xerox machine, still saying nothing, but making notes.

'Come on, let me go, man,' said Bobby Prescott, and now his voice was shaking, too. 'That's all I know. They took it away a month ago. Out of the country. I last heard that they had it on this island in Turkey. They're guarding it. They've got a lot of weaponry.'

'I see,' said the Doctor, and stopped writing. He had been making notes all the time Bobby Prescott had been talking. Occasionally he'd asked a question, but not often.

'But that's not the thing to worry about. It's what they got, what they're protecting. That's what you should be worrying about.'

'But that's exactly what I'm after, Bobby.'

'What do you mean, after?' Bobby Prescott didn't like the sound of his own voice. It was so hoarse it was getting a kind of whiny sound to it.

'I want it.'

'What would anyone want with that?' said Bobby Prescott. He couldn't help it. The whiny note in his voice was getting worse. It was a familiar kind of sound. He'd heard it from enough kids, the gameboys and the bicycle gangers. After they were cornered and while they were still trying to sound tough.

'Maybe I'd like it for my toybox,' said the Doctor. He put his pen away and carefully tore the pages off his notepad and put them in the black envelope he was carrying. He was off the Xerox machine, jumping down and striding across the floor.

The movement was so fast and unexpected that Bobby Prescott flinched, jerking back. The Doctor was right on top of him. Standing over him now. Bobby Prescott scooted back, dragging his ass back across the cold library floor. He crashed into the library checkout desks, snapping his head back on to a steel hand rail. He blinked with pain. When he opened his eyes the Doctor was bent down over him, leaning close. He was holding the black envelope. He licked it and sealed it. Then he smiled at Bobby through thin uneven teeth.

Then he moved away, deeper into the library shadows.

When the little man was out of sight Bobby Prescott climbed to his feet. The muscles in his arms and legs trembled. He had to do something. He was shaking himself to pieces. He'd lost control. For years he'd confronted his fear, faced it and defeated it and sent it away.

But now he knew it hadn't gone far.

Bobby Prescott was moving towards the front windows of the library. Every step was an effort of will. Through those windows he would be able to see the mall on the other side of the street.

He'd be able to see McCray's.

If he could just get to the window and force himself to look at it, look his fear in the face, that would be a starting point. If he looked at McCray's drugstore the memories would come back. He would have to remember how Sally and Eliot and Lyndon had died. But he would be inviting the memory. Confronting the fear on his own terms.

It would be a first act of will. Like the first small stone as you began to build a wall.

But he would build that wall. And the wall would keep the fear out. Then he would walk out of this library.

The muscles in his legs began to steady. The light from the window was on his face now. Bobby Prescott wasn't defeated yet.

He looked out the window, but he didn't see McCray's drugstore.

Instead he saw the bicycles moving back and forth outside the library.

Bicycles with kids on them. Maybe twenty or thirty kids.

58

Bobby Prescott licked his lips. There were more coming in through the library gates, in groups of twos and threes. More arriving all the time. The ones nearest the building were parking their bikes and climbing off. Moving towards the front steps. Bobby Prescott turned back in to the main hall of the library and shouted into the shadows.

'You hired them, right?' His voice echoed through the dark building. 'You hired them,' yelled Bobby Prescott. 'So you can send them away again, can't you?' He stood by the windows, legs shaking again, worse than ever, facing back into the heart of the library. He strained his ears, listening for the little man.

Silence. Silence in the deep shadows of the aisles, silence at the main desk and on the balconies and around the tumbled magazine racks.

Then a small sound.

Not coming from inside. Coming from outside.

Feet. Walking. A lot of feet.

Coming up the front steps of the library.

5

Mulwray and Christian got out of the elevator on the fifty-first floor, leaving Stephanie alone with the little boy Patrick, and the lingering smell of Mulwray's perfumed hair gel.

It wasn't an unpleasant smell. It reminded Stephanie of lavender and something else, something herbal. In any case, Stephanie imagined she was going to have to get used to it. From Monday she and Mulwray would be working together in the Social Acquisition department.

Stephanie held the little boy's hand a little tighter as they stepped out on to the roof of the King Building. The high city wind swept grit off the surface and lashed them with it. Stephanie squeezed her eyes shut and kept them shut until they were on the sheltered side of the helicopter shack. She didn't like to think about what kind of crud would be settling out of the sky on top of a building in New York these days. Get a speck of industrial waste lodged on your cornea, let it melt in your tears and you'd wake up with a poached egg rolling around in a dead socket in your head. Then wait eighteen weeks for a transplant, even on the company's priority health scheme. Considering her job, it would be easy to get an early operation and select some good stock, healthy and attractive. But a new eye would most likely be brown. Even if it was blue it could never exactly match the colour of the one she already had.

Stephanie didn't worry about the kid's eyes. He was wearing a full-head city mask. He loved it. Couldn't get into it quickly enough. It gave him a killer robot aspect, making his head bug-eyed and big on his tiny body. The mask went well with the gory, textured Jack Blood tee-shirt. The expensive Korean hardware in the mask was filtering the air so it didn't scorch his little pink lungs. The child was called Patrick and Stephanie had spent the day on what was basically a PR exercise, showing the kid around the Butler Institute office complex, a big bright smile on her face and lots of maternal gush. She made sure that Mr O'Hara, Patrick's father, was in sight when she had given the little kid a carefully timed impulsive kiss on the cheek. Set that image in the father's mind. His child and another woman. An attractive young woman, let's be frank about it.

Stephanie was in good shape and she knew it. Still in good shape despite nearly eighteen months in New York. She'd needed minor surgery only on a couple of occasions. Once for a cyst in her breast and once for lung cancer. The new lungs in Stephanie's chest had come from a young Peruvian woman who had come north. She'd intended to make a new and better life in the USA and had ended up living on one of the inner-city housing projects. When Stephanie had found her she'd been there only three weeks, so her lungs were still viable.

They'd picked up the Peruvian woman on a routine sweep of the city database. She'd been arrested for attempted murder, which under the current legislation merely meant that she'd been operating as a prostitute in an area with a high incidence of HIV7. Miraculously enough, she'd actually been clean and it was the report on her blood that had attracted the Butler Institute computers. They'd picked the Peruvian woman up within an hour of arrest and retested her. She was still clean after an hour in the cells. Another miracle. The Butler Institute made the clinical sacrifice and removed her lungs the same day and within forty-eight hours Stephanie had undergone her operation, a gift from the company.

They'd made her forfeit her Christmas bonus, though.

She could hear the helicopter now, invisible behind the solid grey overcast. A stormfront of industrial precipitate moving down from upstate. From Buffalo, blowing in off the Great Lakes. Stephanie hoped the bastard would get the helicopter down in time. She didn't want to be on the roof when those beefy clouds passed over. Patrick shifted impatiently at her side. The child's hand was lost in her grip, tiny fingers like frog bones squeezed in her strong hand.

The helicopter had broken through the haze now and they were caught in the approaching engine noise hammering off the reflective concrete underfoot. The huge weight of black machinery was settling down delicately at the centre of a painted circle. The sky above was factory sludge, dark now with approaching night as well as the storm. Stephanie sighed aloud. With the sound of the helicopter and the mask on Patrick O'Hara couldn't hear her. The day spent with the little boy had been a PR exercise all right. PR for her. But it had meant a day away from her screen and a day's work she was going to have to do this evening. The pilot popped his door open and waved from behind the plastic cockpit. Stephanie waved back as she walked towards the landing pad, ducking low under the slowing sweep of the rotor blades, forcing a smile.

Stephanie's offices were on the fifty-second floor of the King Building, one up from Biostock Acquisitions. The place was quiet now. O'Hara, the boss, had drunk his traditional democratic Friday drink with the staff then caught his own helicopter out to Albany. After he left the staff had begun to drift away to begin their own weekends. Stephanie waited around, wearing her streetcoat, joking about waiting for her date and maybe being stood up. When the last of the staff had gone she sat back down at her Apollo work station, switched it back on and booted it up again.

The company logo appeared before anything else. Not the words 'Butler Institute', but just a bold image consistin的 of a fat friendly cartoon bumble bee and, beside it, a human eye.

It always looked to Stephanie as if that bee was flying directly towards the eye, ready to sting and blind.

As the operating system woke up on the Apollo the company logo faded and a customized screen greeting flashed up for her. Then the computer presented Stephanie with a desktop featuring all her current paperwork. For ten minutes Stephanie did legitimate work. If anybody looked in on her she would just be working late. But nobody looked in.

After ten minutes she saved the document she was working on, a routine report on stock problems. Then she went into her applications folder and triggered an icon labelled 'BGSW'.

Stephanie watched it flash as the process awakened and shot away into the background of her screen.

She went back to working on another report, concentrating

on the phrasing, losing herself in it so she didn't notice the passage of time. She was doing only basic word processing but her machine had slowed down appreciably since she'd started the new process. 'BGSW' stood for 'bug sweep'. Stephanie had sent Bugsweep scurrying around the network to make sure no one was watching what she did on her computer. She worked on the report for another twenty minutes while the process waited and monitored activity. Just after midnight a small cheery icon popped up on her screen. A smiling pink cartoon elephant with a knot tied on his trunk. The cartoon elephant's tail twitched and a little word balloon appeared reading 'Don't forget Mom's birthday! Oct 27th!' The image had been pirated from a genuine piece of commercial software, a kitsch memo-pad utility she'd bought in a Mexican souvenir shop. But now it was being used as a coded message by Bugsweep to tell her that the system was clear. Stephanie saved the documents she was working on, then dumped the word processor. Only now did she begin her real work.

Bugsweep had finished and the system had snapped back to its normal response time. But not for long. Stephanie was about to unleash the Ferret.

Bugsweep was one of the goodies Stephanie had brought with her when she'd left her job at Texas Instruments. The Ferret was another. They were both software packages which had been developed for defence. Both were outgrowths of AI research − artificial intelligence − and used particular AI techniques. But the Ferret was considerably more complex than Bugsweep.

Stephanie moved her cursor to an icon showing a dripping dayglo green syringe and double-clicked on it. It was the trademark of a popular piece of virus-busting software. The syringe turned a bright red. Rather a tasteless choice, thought Stephanie. Activity on the screen was slowing down and now it seemed to freeze completely. Even the system clock came to a standstill, locking at 03:32. Stephanie hadn't noticed the passage of time. She'd missed supper and her stomach was rumbling. She'd have to eat something soon.

The small cartoon syringe flickered red and steady on the screen. If someone had looked over Stephanie's shoulder they would have seen what was apparently a virus protection package searching her hard disk.

What was really happening was the unleashing of the Ferret. The Ferret wasn't created by the AI research team at Texas Instruments. It had been bought on the grey market from the Pacific Basin, so they could take it apart and study the methods used in its searching technique. Now the screen flashed and the syringe was replaced by the Ferret front end. Originally the package had come with a terribly boring military ID screen, just some serial numbers and a diagnostic menu. The boys at Texas Instruments had replaced that with the graphics that now flashed in front of Stephanie, washing her face with coloured screenlight in the dark office.

The Ferret looked like a genuine ferret, a weasel-thin carnivore snaking around and twisting its neck, happy to be unleashed from whatever software hibernation limbo held it between excursions. Bright eyes and yellow teeth. It moved as if it was ready for the hunt, the screen animation hardly blurring. At the top left of the screen a network status panel appeared, showing the codenames of the hard disks for every terminal in the Butler Institute. The hard disks appeared as solid black rectangles, showing that they were locked and secure. Nobody could get into them through the network. Two fat boxes appeared next. These were the gateways into the Butler Institute mainframes. They were also black. Locked solid.

The Ferret thrashed on the screen.

There was a popping sound like someone opening a six-pack of soft-drink cans all at once, close to your face. Stephanie flinched. She kept the sound on her machine turned off in normal use, but Ferret could override any system defaults.

With the volley of popping noises the rectangles symbolizing the hard disks all snapped from black to white. The mainframe boxes took a moment longer. Then both unlocked with the sound of champagne bottles opening.

The whole system was wide open.

Ferret moved as if it had caught the scent of blood, tail whipping. It turned and looked at her and winked then lunged towards the top left corner of the screen. En route it split into a dozen tiny dashing cartoon ferrets. Each one darted into a box representing a hard disk or a mainframe, disappearing into it as if vanishing down a rabbit hole.

The Ferret was penetration and search software. You told it what you wanted to look for and unleashed it on a network. That's where it was now, a sly predator-process sniffing at every node in the Butler Institute, cracking open every file on every disk and nosing through it. Anything of interest that it found it would copy. It was a smart program and had a knack for choosing only the relevant material. The criteria it used were sophisticated and remarkably astute. That was where the artificial intelligence came in. The Ferret had been written using some very sophisticated techniques. The boys in her old research lab had still been scratching their heads over it when she left, a highly illegal copy of the Ferret in her briefcase. Once she knew she'd be working at the Butler Institute she'd suspected it might come in useful.

In an alcove beside the washrooms there was a small refrigerator, its top covered with dirty coffee cups, a microwave and coffee machine. Stephanie took a break from her screen and ducked in there for some coffee. It took her five minutes expertly to fix herself a cappuccino, even grating some chocolate from a bar in the refrigerator, sifting it on to the stiff white foam.

When she sat back down at her workstation there was a folder containing seven documents on the screen, with a note indicating that more were on the way. The Ferret had been busy. Stephanie cracked open the first document, unlocking its encryption using the Ferret's menu of code busters. After thirty seconds she was able to read what turned out to be a numbingly boring corporate memo. The second and third folders were stock market forecasts which she could have found in the *New York Times*. The fourth and fifth were reports about new environmental problems. Reluctantly, Stephanie binned them. She'd never find the time to fit in more reading. The sixth file was an odd piece of paperwork concerning a New York cop called McIlveen. A personnel file copied from the police database. Stephanie scanned through it quickly, chewing at a thumbnail. She set it aside to return to later.

When she opened the seventh file retrieved by the Ferret she struck gold.

It was a letter describing how the Butler Institute was in the process of buying some communications and research facilities in the Midwest. It sounded like a fairly impressive piece of corporate acquisition until you checked up on the Midwest stock and discovered it wasn't exactly a business at all. It was more like the United States Air Force. Stephanie read the document twice, heart pounding a little as the caffeine entered her bloodstream.

She slipped a floppy disk into her computer and was making a copy of the letter when all hell broke loose.

The document seemed to be taking rather a long time to copy but that didn't worry Stephanie at first. It meant only that somewhere in the network the Ferret had hit a rich seam of information and was in the process of dragging the goodies back to her. But then her screen locked completely.

For a full minute nothing happened. Now it wasn't the coffee that was pushing up Stephanie's heartbeat. She began to accept that her machine had crashed. Nothing was moving anywhere on the screen. This could be a major disaster. She could reset and reboot easily enough, but she didn't know what side effects might be involved. In normal use the Ferret would come scampering back at the end of its hunt, licking its paws, closing every file behind it, relocking the disks and restoring the mainframes to exactly their original state so there'd be no traces of the nocturnal hunt. But what would happen if Stephanie rebooted now? Would people come in on Monday morning and find muddy ferret tracks all over their files? She bit her lip and hesitated. The only sound in the office was the whirring of the air conditioning and the hum of the fan which cooled her hard disk. Then she leaned forward and pressed the start-up switch.

Nothing happened.

Stephanie hit it again. Still nothing.

It was bad enough if she couldn't cover the Ferret's tracks. But what would happen if she couldn't even switch her machine off? It would be glowing like a beacon when everyone filed back in on Monday. Might as well just hang a sign around her neck saying, *'I'm the one who did it.'*

Stephanie thought about her blonde hair swinging and the twenty years it had taken to grow it. She thought about the small fingers of the boss's child in her hand, and candy-sick breath, and about how long it had taken her to pay for just the jacket of the Otomo suit.

Then she thought about what the Butler Institute might do to her if they found her probing their secrets.

Stephanie came to a decision. Boot up and take her chances. If the Ferret was gone from the network she'd quit for the evening. Take what she had and call it a day. She'd become greedy and it was a mistake. Sweat had burst under her arms, soaking the Hamnet silk. The coffee heaved uneasily in her stomach. Stephanie found herself making bargains with a god she hadn't believed in since childhood.

Let the network be clean and I won't push my luck again. I swear. Even let the Ferret be wiped out, corrupted during the crash so I can never use it again. Just let me get out without any traces this time.

Never again.

Just let me get out.

I swear.

She was reaching to pull the power plug when the screen came back to life.

The system clock came alive again and spun through a high-speed blur of digits, recapping the time since the Apollo had gone down. The rectangles of the hard disks and the boxes of the mainframes reappeared in the top left of the screen, still coloured white, still wide open. Her active folders popped back up, one by one, reopening for her at the exact line in the exact page where she'd been reading when the system went down.

Stephanie stared and then moved the cursor on the screen.

It jerked around crazily but that was because her hand was trembling so badly. She clicked utilities on and off, ran a quick systems status check, examined the network.

There was no sign that she'd rung any bells. The system security was asleep. No one else was logged on. The network was quiet.

The Ferret's status screen had come up.

Systems failure it said.

Nine documents left to import.

Continue Or Quit?

Stephanie hesitated for a tenth of a second.

She moved the mouse and clicked on *Continue*.

New folders began to pop up on her screen as the Ferret dragged them back across the network. Stephanie thought about saving each one to floppy and then getting the hell out of the office. She thought about her promises to God.

But that wasn't the way to succeed in this life. If you didn't take the chances you didn't get the rewards. She'd stay and read each document as the Ferret decrypted them, exactly as she intended. It didn't do to let yourself get spooked. That wasn't the way to end up on the board of the Butler Institute. Maybe she should even send the Ferret out again, after she'd done a little reading, with a new set of specifications.

The miniature cartoon ferrets were coming back, scurrying out of the hard disk and mainframe icons. They grew as they ran, and merged together. Halfway in the journey back across the screen they'd coalesced into the original single big Ferret. He stopped and winked a cartoon wink at Stephanie, preening his whiskers.

He was still preening them when the green thing hit him.

It came out of the network through the hard disk icons, following the Ferret's route. It lashed down across the screen in a hot green slash of pixels, shedding a radiant series of afterimages behind it like glowing empty skins. The Ferret was just beginning to react to its presence. The Ferret sensed the arrival of security software and tried to hide. Its whiskers twitched as it began to respond. The menus and software badge vanished. The Ferret faded into a ghost image and the disguise of the syringe-shaped trademark began to appear in its place. But the green thing came crashing down on to the vanishing Ferret's shoulders and locked on with a grip of death. The syringe popped out of sight and the Ferret's colours came up bright and clear again. It tried to strike back but the green thing was sprouting long claws now.

It lunged and slashed and the Ferret went down.

'Good, isn't he?' said a voice.

Stephanie had once given herself a week of whiplash pain in her Honda by hitting the brakes when she'd had the headrest removed. It was nothing compared to what she did to her neck now, snapping her head backwards to try to look over the back of her chair. But before her eyes registered anything she'd already caught the smell.

A smell like lavender.

Lavender and something else, a scent of herbs.

Mulwray nodded towards the screen where the green scaly thing was tearing into the Ferret, lacerating it with red streaked claws. 'That's the Ferret Killer.'

Mulwray leaned forward from where he was standing behind her chair. Stephanie had to twist away so that his arm didn't touch her face. The smell of him was very strong, very close. He touched the sound-level controls on her computer. The death squeals of the Ferret rang through the office as the green thing disembowelled it. Brilliant pixel viscera sprayed across the screen, the torn body of the Ferret beginning to lose smoothness and decompose into an angular outline as its graphics controls went.

'Ever looked at this before?' Mulwray was standing hunched over the coffee maker in the kitchen alcove. 'Looked at it properly, I mean.' Now Mulwray turned towards her, carrying a cup. He gave it to Stephanie. His gun, a small automatic, a standard Biostock sidearm, remained in his other hand as he picked up his own cup and sat down beside the Krupps coffee machine. It was an antique that someone had brought from a defunct graphics art firm in Chicago.

'What about it?' said Stephanie.

'We own Krupps.'

She said nothing.

'You must know that, right? That's what you were doing on the computer.'

'I was working late.'

'What you were doing was cracking confidential files. You were reading about the corporate structure of the Butler Institute.'

'I was —'

'You were looking at things you weren't supposed to look at. You were taking information that didn't belong to you. You took it out of our computers and put it into your mind. That's the equivalent of taking money out of somebody else's bank account and putting it into yours. It's theft. And who are you stealing from? Just the company that pays for you. Feeds you. Clothes you. Heals you when you're sick.'

'This is just a misunderstanding.'

'Sure. Now tell me what you found out when you broke into the boss's computer.'

'I'm not saying anything.'

'Well, then, I'll tell you.' Mulwray smiled. He blew on his coffee to cool it. 'I'll tell you what I found out back in April.' He set his gun down now and his smile got even wider. 'Because that's when I broke into the boss's computer.' He sipped his coffee, grinning at Stephanie, and Stephanie began to feel like she could breathe again, began to feel her heartbeat slow. Lines crinkled around Mulwray's eyes when he smiled. They detracted from the perfection of his Eurasian beauty but Stephanie liked those lines. 'I found out that a big Japanese company owns the Butler Institute,' said Mulwray.

'Hoshino,' said Stephanie.

'Right. But the Butler Institute owns everything else.'

'That's not true.'

'Okay. I'm exaggerating a little. But we own every other company in this building. Every single one of them is a subsidiary, mostly acquired over the last decade. How do I know this?'

'The office rental records.'

'Right. It's a secret that BI is so big. But it makes accounting sense for them to pay all the ground rents in one lump sum from one account. They get a deal from the landlords or something.'

'And anybody who can read a tax audit can work it out. Like you did,' said Stephanie.

'Like we both did,' said Mulwray.

'It's so big it's scary.'

'Not as scary as breaking into files in the middle of the night then having somebody come up behind your chair.'

'You bastard. I never even heard you.'

'Good aren't I?' said Mulwray, amusement gleaming in his eyes.

For the first time Stephanie let herself smile. 'You scared the hell out of me, you know.'

'I know,' Mulwray chuckled and put his coffee cup down.

70

'What did you think I was going to do to you?'

'I don't know. Use me as spare parts for the organ bank, maybe. After a phone call to Mr O'Hara.'

Mulwray stopped smiling. When he stopped the little lines disappeared on his face and his eyes went flat and dead.

'That's pretty close,' he said. 'Except I think it would have more of a career impact if I delivered you in person.' He picked up his gun again, and now it was pointing at her.

They had to wait several hours for the first helicopter to the Catskills and by the end of the flight they were moving through dawn skies. She could see the yellow earth-moving machinery below her, parked in rows in the early light, like toys waiting outside the tunnel mouth in the mountain side. Stephanie had kept her coat on in the cockpit but she couldn't stop shivering. When Mulwray helped her out of the helicopter she jerked away at his touch. The grass was wet as they walked from the helicopter pad up through a screen of trees to O'Hara's house. He was waiting for them on the steps.

6

O'Hara smiled as he refilled Stephanie's glass. She picked it up with a steady hand and sipped. The bourbon was sweet and warming now. At first it had tasted bad, strong and poisonous with a flavour of rot and vomit. But that had just been her stomach complaining after the helicopter ride. The helicopter ride and all the anxiety.

'I'm sorry if you felt pressured by the way you were brought here, Stephanie.' O'Hara moved away from her to refill Mulwray's glass then returned to sit beside her on the long black silk couch. Mulwray grinned and saluted Stephanie with his glass before he drank. Stephanie didn't smile back.

'You see,' said O'Hara, 'I knew almost immediately when Mr Mulwray went into the company computers and began to — '

'Snoop,' said Mulwray.

'Let's say, began to study the corporate structure of the Butler Institute. Of course the company could have punished him. But he was a promising young employee and I like to think that I am a good man manager.' O'Hara wasn't looking directly at Stephanie as he spoke. He was staring thoughtfully out the wide dark window of his living room. The sun was rising over the treeline and in the gaps between the conifers you could see the distant yellow shapes of the excavation machinery beginning to move back and forth to the tunnel mouth as the working day began.

'I've always favoured the carrot instead of the stick,' said O'Hara. 'Reward instead of punishment. So I not only offered Mr Mulwray a promotion, I also explained about the Institute's latest and biggest project.' O'Hara turned and looked into Stephanie's eyes, smiling. 'I let him into the secret.'

Stephanie smiled right back. 'And now you're going to let me in on it, too?'

There was a small noise from the doorway of the living room

and Stephanie instantly turned towards it. She saw Mulwray move as well, coming out of his chair and reaching under his jacket, then stopping when O'Hara raised his hand. 'It's all right,' said O'Hara, getting up off the couch and walking through the doorway to the kitchen. He came back carrying a little boy, swinging him through the air and laughing. 'A spy,' said O'Hara. He sat down on the couch again, putting the boy on his lap. 'This is my son Patrick. Patrick, this is Mr Mulwray and Stephanie.'

'We've met,' said Stephanie, solemnly shaking hands with the child and smiling at him. All of them were smiling except the little boy.

'Of course you have. Stephanie looked after you at the office yesterday, Patrick.'

'I remember,' said the little boy.

'Where was I?' said O'Hara. 'The project. Well, it's a big idea and a big challenge. But we live in times that offer big challenges.' The little boy settled comfortably in his father's lap as he spoke. 'Challenges of survival. In this world health is rapidly becoming the most precious commodity. Forget gold or oil or data. Forget about water. None of these things are any good if we don't remain alive to use them.' O'Hara gestured with his hands as he spoke, lifting them up, then letting them settle back on the shoulders of his son. Patrick caught hold of one and gripped it in his own small hand. 'Stephanie, both you and Mr Mulwray are familiar with our use of surgery and transplants to maintain health. But do you know how difficult it is to find good stock? That's because the environment is increasingly compromised. We are poisoning the planet we live on. For decades we've known the dangers and for decades we have insisted on doing nothing. Now our information gatherers bring us the inevitable news. We are reaching the point of no return.'

O'Hara paused and took a sip of orange juice, offering the glass to his son afterwards. 'But the Butler Institute is taking action. We have the solution.' The boy drank the rest of the juice and then stared solemnly up into his father's face. 'It's quite a simple solution. A bright child can grasp the basic concept.' O'Hara took the empty glass from his son. 'Go on, Patrick. Explain the project to Stephanie.'

The little boy looked across at Stephanie. He was a solemn,

quiet child, taking after his mother in looks and mannerisms. Stephanie had met Mrs O'Hara a few times, at company parties. Anne Marie O'Hara had been trained as a mathematician but abandoned research to study music. She had apparently been some kind of child prodigy.

'Daddy says that we live in our thoughts,' said the little boy, speaking slowly. 'We have arms and legs and bodies. But really it's all up here.' He touched his head, small fingers in his fine pale hair. 'So it doesn't matter if our arms and legs and bodies die, just so long as we can make our thoughts stay alive. And Daddy says that our thoughts are just patterns in our heads. And that we can copy those patterns, just the way I sampled Jack Blood off the television.'

'Giving me quite a shock, too, I can tell you,' said O'Hara, chuckling. Stephanie and Mulwray both laughed immediately. Stephanie opened her mouth but Mulwray was already speaking. 'Clever kid,' he said.

'That's very good, Patrick,' said O'Hara. 'Go on.'

The little boy shifted awkwardly, embarrassed by the attention and the praise. 'Daddy says we'll copy the patterns into computers. The patterns of our thoughts. Then our thoughts will be alive on the computers. And the computers will last forever. And we'll live inside them. It won't matter what the world is like outside. What the pol-pol-'

'Pollution.'

'It won't matter what the pollution is like, or the oh-zone layer or anything. Because we'll be safe inside machines.' The boy wrinkled his forehead. 'No,' he said, slowly. 'That's not right exactly. We aren't just going to be inside the machines. We are going to be the machines.'

'What a smart little guy!' said Mulwray, again getting there a fraction of a second before Stephanie.

'But our bodies will be dead, though,' said Patrick. For the first time he looked at his father with something like uncertainty. For a second there was silence. Stephanie could see that Mulwray was trying, but he couldn't think of anything to say.

She made her move.

She slid across the couch, moving her body against O'Hara's, reaching across him and picking up the little boy before anyone could protest.

She swung Patrick up in her arms. The boy was a lot heavier than she'd imagined and she could feel him stiffening in her grasp, reacting to her uncertainty. Stephanie pushed her shoulders back, taking the weight of the little boy on her breasts, his head beside her face. As she adjusted her grip the boy relaxed and Stephanie felt a flash of triumph. 'You are a smart little guy. Very, very smart,' she said, holding him tight and carefully resting his small head on her shoulder. She turned around, carrying the little boy with confidence now, and looked at Mulwray sitting in his armchair. He wasn't saying anything. Stephanie squeezed the little boy tight. She'd read that children liked to be hugged and touched a lot.

'Brave, too,' said O'Hara. He'd got up from the couch and now leant over, ruffling the little boy's hair. Stephanie felt a flush of triumph. To touch his son O'Hara had to stand close to her, almost touching. She turned so that the boy was face to face with his father. They were like a media image of a healthy, beautiful family. 'Big and brave,' said O'Hara, tousling Patrick's hair. 'Tell Stephanie the rest of it.'

'There's more?' said Stephanie, looking at the little boy with mock wonder. The boy said nothing and the living room was silent. The distant sound of machinery could be heard through the picture window, beyond the trees, down at the excavation site.

'The next part of our project involves kids. And you'll never guess what,' said O'Hara softly. Now Mulwray's head snapped up and he looked at O'Hara. He made a sound as if he was about to say something but he remained silent.

'Patrick's volunteered for the experiment,' said O'Hara.

'Way to go, little guy!' said Stephanie. She aimed her widest, whitest, most stunning smile at the little boy but he was looking thoughtfully at his father. 'A little guy with lots of guts,' she said.

Mulwray had got out of his armchair and he was standing up now, looking at them. The boy looked at Stephanie, then over at Mulwray. The boy and the man stared across the room at each other for a moment and then Mulwray abruptly turned and walked out. Stephanie watched him go down the stairs towards the kitchen.

O'Hara opened his arms, offering to take the boy from

Stephanie. She handed Patrick to his father. 'Excuse me a second,' she said.

'Of course,' said O'Hara, taking the child and kissing him on the forehead.

Stephanie went out of the sitting room and down the pine stairs. In the kitchen Mulwray was standing at the sink, holding a glass under the big snout of the taps. Water hissed out through the filter. He drank a glass, refilled it and drank again. When he turned to Stephanie his mouth was wet and his face was an odd colour. Yellowish. Stephanie thought it was an interesting colour. 'We can call Albany from here,' said Mulwray.

'Why would we want to do that?'

'Look, the man's clearly loony tunes. So is his project, for that matter. Fine. I'm happy to go along with it. He's the boss. And I've done some fairly hairy stuff in my time. It's been my job. I'm really happy to provide Third World garbage for biostock. There are people who need that blood and those bodies. They're spare parts for real Americans. Real people. That's my job and I'm good at it.'

Mulwray set the glass back in the sink and wiped his hands. 'But all that stuff about that little boy volunteering for the experiment. You know what that means? He's talking about killing the kid.'

'Yes?' said Stephanie.

'We can't just let that happen.'

'No?' said Stephanie.

Mulwray was looking at her now. It was as if it was the first time he'd ever really looked at her. Stephanie liked the thought. Mulwray was taking a good look at her now.

Mulwray went back to the sink and picked up the towel again. He wiped his hands again, although they were already dry. He kept looking at Stephanie, rubbing his hands nervously with the towel. In the surgical fluorescent light of the kitchen she could see the lines around Mulwray's eyes, the lines he had when he smiled, although he wasn't smiling now. The lines made him look old and tired.

Stephanie liked those lines.

'Surprise,' she said.

O'Hara was still sitting on the couch with his son when she

76

went back into the living room. The B&O home entertainment system was on and the little boy was watching Saturday morning television.

'What's on, Patrick?'

The little boy answered without looking away from the screen. 'Just some kid's stuff. But *Jack Blood* is going to start in a minute.'

'That's nice,' said Stephanie, settling herself on the couch beside O'Hara.

'Mulwray is secure,' she said.

'That's good. I had my doubts about him.'

'He'll work out fine, I'll see to that.'

'You've clearly handled it very well, Stephanie. You're going to be exactly the right person for this project.'

Stephanie's face flushed at the praise. It was going red, Stephanie knew it was. She hoped O'Hara wouldn't notice in the television light. Her body felt sweaty with the relief of a job well done, and with the warmth of the praise.

'Time for *Jack Blood*,' said Patrick. He touched a button on the remote control and the software in the B&O changed channels for him. Two small lights flashed on the slim dark boxes of the home entertainment centre. One small light indicated that the television receiver was active. The other one showed that the communications system was currently transmitting. A discreet camera and microphone scanned the interior of the living room. It observed every move made by the three people watching television on the couch. It heard every word they said. This information was then routed by optical cables down to the transmission masts by the excavation further down the mountain slope. From there the sounds and images were fired up to a satellite leased by Northern Global and relayed on to the European Community data network. Coded packets of data were passed along, read and readdressed, then passed along again. Their ultimate destination was in southern England.

There the signal was picked up by a satellite dish lashed on to an ornamental spire on top of a Victorian greenhouse. The big glass structure stood in overgrown gardens that gave way to broad grounds with long grass and shrubs that had gone wild. The grounds ran up into a slope thickly wooded with old fruit trees. A broken wall ran around the perimeter of the grounds, paralleling a loop of gravel drive that wound up towards the red brick house and the long low building hidden beyond the greenhouse. It was morning in New York State but afternoon here in England. Rain was falling from a luminous grey sky and the wild garden looked lushly green. Thunder rolled in the distance beyond banked yellow clouds. A small cat broke from shelter near the greenhouse and ran towards the long building that had once housed stables. The cat didn't like getting wet and it darted through the long grass on the lawn. There was a fresh scar of turned earth running between the greenhouse and the stables and the cat ran along beside this muddy line. Buried here under the lawn was a long bundle of cabling, mixed copper wire and optical fibres, which was connected to the satellite dish at one end and the stables at the other.

The cat hurried through the open door of the long low building, into the shadows, yowling. There was the sound of rain on the wooden roof and the wind found its way through the open door in cold gusts, but it was dry in here and the cat stopped and sat down on the concrete floor. Bare light bulbs hung down from the ceiling at intervals down the whole length of the narrow building, but only the one nearest the door was glowing. The cat licked at its wet fur and got to its feet, wandering further into the building. The stable had been converted into a large garage housing half a dozen cars, two of them under paint-spattered sheets, a third one up on ramps with a plastic bowl full of sump oil under it. The cat sniffed at the oily darkness under the car, then turned and walked back towards the door of the garage. It emerged from the shadows into the yellow gleam from the single naked bulb. Directly under the bulb was a big oil-stained oak workbench. A small man was sitting on a chrome barstool at the bench, watching television. The cat rubbed against the legs of the stool and purred.

The television set was a 1940s Bakelite design with a small milky-green screen. It was connected to a bundle of gaffer-taped cables that ran out the window and into the ground. The small man was leaning forward, elbows on the bench, watching the screen with concentration. Scattered along the bench between his elbows were vacuum tubes, clipped curves of copper wire, and a large black envelope.

The monochrome image on the small screen was surprisingly sharp and clear. It showed a man, a woman and a young boy sitting on a couch, facing out at the viewer. The sound from the television was tinny but audible. 'You better not have any more of that sour mash, Stephanie,' the man was saying. 'Not on an empty stomach. I'll fix you and Patrick some breakfast in a minute. How do waffles sound, Pat?'

'Great, Dad,' said the little boy, staring out of the TV screen, not looking up.

Stephanie was finding herself wondering if television was actually good for children. It was the fixed, intense way that Patrick was staring. He sat beside her watching the television, never looking away. It was as if there was someone out there on the other side of the screen, sitting and watching, looking back at Patrick.

Stephanie shivered at the notion. She dismissed the thought. It was a beautiful morning with the sun coming up over the mountains, shining through the big picture window, breakfast smells drifting up from the kitchen. O'Hara came up the stairs with a pitcher of orange juice. He was wearing a chunky wool sweater and Stephanie wondered about asking him if he had another one. She suddenly felt cold. 'Waffles are on,' he said.

Stephanie looked up at him. 'No one's going to stop us, are they?'

'Who could stop us?' said O'Hara.

The Doctor leaned forward and switched off the small old-fashioned television. Rain was drumming on the roof of the converted stables. The cat stirred restlessly, wandering among the cars while the Doctor sat staring at the blank screen, elbows on the workbench.

Then he reached down and picked up the black envelope. He turned it over and wrote on it with what looked like a fountain pen. The pale ink had a faint luminous glow.

He wrote in big motions of the hand. Three letters.

Ace.

7

Even in the final light of the day the carpets had a jewelled brilliance. They were spread across the clean stone floor of the shop and displayed on wooden frames in the cobbled courtyard outside. Most of them were traditional Islamic designs but there were some of the newer carpets from nations to the north and east. Woven among the abstract patterns on these were helicopters, rocket launchers and lovingly rendered automatic weapons, the new icons of the Middle East.

Ace lifted a glass from the pewter tray sitting beside her on the old wooden bench. The glass was almost too hot to hold. She blew into it to cool the *ada gayi*, then set it aside. There was a chrome digital clock inset high among the thousand-year-old stones of the shop's walls. Miss David had been gone almost ten minutes. She was in the warehouse across the courtyard from the shop, conducting certain negotiations. Ace scratched idly at an insect bite on her knee. Her skin was already a deep brown after a week travelling up and down the coast. She eased off one of her cheap plastic sandals and studied the dirt on her blistered toes. She took the other sandal off and pulled a rucksack from under the bench. In the outer pocket of the pack she had an envelope full of documents and a German army-surplus life jacket with a compressed-air cylinder attached for rapid inflation. In the big inner pocket there was a plastic litre bottle of the local mineral water, half a dozen computer disks, some communication cables and a hand grenade. Down the rear of the rucksack, in a concealed pouch behind the armstraps, there was a second, slimmer envelope. A black envelope.

Ace eased the sandals in beside the water bottle then splayed her bare feet out on the cool tiled floor.

Outside, in the streets below the shop, there were the sounds of cars and teenagers laughing. Someone walked by with a ghetto blaster and Ace could hear the steady pulsing beat of a familiar song. Then the music was gone, lost under the battering thunder of a UN gunship moving through the sky over the city. The carpets that surrounded Ace gave the ancient room a curiously dead acoustic. The sound of the helicopter thudded dustily all around her for a moment then faded. Ace stirred her tea and the spoon rang with a clear note against the side of the glass. The note rang in her mind. Ace's hearing and vision had taken on a strange clarity after the sleepless nights travelling. Now she watched the big copter, standing at a window carved out of the stone wall, a box of bright flowers on the sill by her elbows. The gunship was descending in the sky over Antalya, heading out to sea to rendezvous with one of the aircraft carriers. Even at this distance Ace recognized it as an Odin, a robot-controlled drone. The Odin could strafe enemy positions while its pilot and navigator hung in sensory isolation in harnesses in a control station five hundred kilometres away. As the helicopter faded to a speck in the distance the sea breeze rose again and carried fragments of an old Western pop song up from the street to the open window.

'*My eyes are just holograms.*'

The music moved on. Ace sat on the bench in the growing twilight of the carpet shop, sipping sage tea and listening to the cadence of the street noise change. Evening was giving way to night. Through the window she could see over the stone walls of the Old Town to Karaali Park and, beyond that, the harbour. White and grey warships floated on the intense, deepening blue of the Mediterranean. Cargo copters and gunships floated down from the sky and settled on them like dragonflies.

Miss David came back into the shop folding a rug she'd taken from one of the frames outside. She set it on a table by the cash register and turned to Ace. 'They'll see you now.'

Ace cinched her rucksack shut and followed the woman, walking barefoot across the rough cobbles of the courtyard.

'Their main concern, not surprisingly, is that they will be paid.'

It was cold in the warehouse and it smelled of spice. Ace's eyes were having trouble adjusting to the dim interior after the brilliant sunlight outside. Miss David stood beside Ace, not bothering trying to conceal her contempt for the men in the room. They stood or sat on the wooden crates that filled the front section of the small building. Their clothes were counterfeits of Western designer jeans and T-shirts. There were six of them, all in their late twenties or thirties. They were mercenaries, Kurds who had been displaced by warfare since their early childhood. The four-wheel-drive vehicle they'd arrived in was parked at the back of the warehouse, just inside the mechanical wings of the folding garage doors. It was a Suzuki with what looked like a modification for mounting twin fifty-calibre machine guns over the front windscreen. The two Kurdish leaders were calling themselves Massoud and Dfewar. Ace didn't necessarily believe that these were their real names. It wasn't going to be that kind of operation.

'They would like some form of advance, or at least some sign that payment is guaranteed.' Miss David looked like she would spit. 'My advice to you is just tell them to go to hell.'

But Ace was already kneeling on the floor, opening her rucksack. One of the grey plastic cables fell on to the dirt floor and the Kurd named Dfewar instantly picked it up for her. He brushed it off and Ace gave him the other cables and the three-and-a-half-inch floppies. Dfewar was the technical expert. Ace didn't foresee any problems with him. The other leader, the man called Massoud, remained sitting on a box of carpets and chain-smoked Egyptian cigarettes, picking flakes of tobacco off his lips, occasionally looking at Ace and smiling politely.

Ace got up from the floor, brushing the dust off her knee. Some of the men averted their eyes. Not Massoud. He watched her closely as she moved and Ace suddenly found herself unpleasantly aware of the bare flesh of her arms and legs, the band of skin exposed by her knotted shirt. Gooseflesh prickled on her in the warehouse chill.

The attitude of Turks towards women was beginning to change under the reforms of President Erel, but the Kurds were a culture exiled within a culture. They held on to their traditional attitudes; it was about all they had left. Some of these men might not take kindly to accepting commands from a woman. If she was going to work with them effectively as a team she'd have to break the ice. Massoud was the weapons specialist; he'd be handling the explosives on their errand. It shouldn't be hard to establish some common ground.

Ace reached inside her rucksack again and felt for the plasticized antislip surface of the hand grenade. Designed for use with sweating hands. Ace's hand was dry as it closed over the grenade. She pulled it out. A grey egg shape with Korean script and a barcode on the flattened top. It looked like a designer soft-drink can, except for the warning label, a favourite of Ace's. *Detonate Near Enemy.* Ace tested the weight of the grenade in her hand for a moment, then casually lobbed it across to Massoud, sitting on his crate in the warehouse shadows. Ace knew he would catch the grenade, look at it with approval, then perhaps look up at her and smile. Then she would walk over and join him. They'd inspect the grenade together, perhaps have a technical discussion translated by Miss David. Mutual respect would break the ice. Then everything would be all right.

But Massoud didn't catch the grenade.

It took him by surprise and his hand jerked up awkwardly. He caught the grenade on the point of his wrist, knocking it to the floor. As the grenade rolled across the packed dirt Massoud jerked his feet away from it. For a moment there was an unmistakable look of fear on his face. Ace saw it, and, much worse, the other men in the room saw it.

The Kurds were laughing. One of them reached down and picked the grenade up, dusting it off. He passed it to his friend, who examined it. Ace registered all this at the edge of her attention. Massoud was looking at her now, with no expression whatsoever. She felt a sinking feeling in her stomach and thought of the Doctor. Sometimes he'd speak about the way events took shape, the future growing invisibly around you. And every action you took contributed to that shape, like putting your fingers to wet clay spinning on a wheel. Except the clay hardened impossibly quickly. Harder than concrete. And you were stuck with what you shaped.

Massoud was staring down at his hands, clasped tight. She could see his knuckles showing pale under tight skin. She knew she would have to deal with him. She could feel events accelerating, the wheel spinning its wet clay faster, her fingers digging in and forming ugly designs she could never change.

The air around her was hot and close. When he thought she wasn't looking, Massoud flashed a look at her in the half-light of the warehouse. Ace caught the look. She was beginning to regret leaving her handgun at the hotel.

The man who was holding the grenade was gesturing for Ace to join him. He opened a wooden crate and stood back so Ace could look inside. There in a nest of shredded fax sheets was a tray of objects, wrapped in twists of soft opaque plastic featuring Turkish printing and pictures of lemons. The man unwrapped one and grinned proudly at Ace. It was a hand grenade, identical to the sample she'd brought with her. Miss David had done her job well. Unless some of the objects actually turned out to be pieces of fruit, this crate would contain about thirty high-explosive grenades. More than enough. The man opened three more crates for Ace. The first one contained folded Afghan carpets. He'd opened it by mistake. The second contained tear gas cylinders and an anti-riot dispersal system. The third contained assorted mismatched pieces of combat body armour and the Vickers night-sight vision enhancement system, as requested.

Ace picked up the Vickers and examined it. There was an adjustable chin strap and a band inside the helmet to adapt the head size. Like the bicycle helmets she'd worn when she worked as a courier. Ace made some adjustments and checked that there was a fresh battery fitted. Then she lifted the helmet on to her head. It smelled faintly of old sweat and a scented hair oil. The warehouse vanished from view as she adjusted the dead screens of the optical unit over her eyes, a glass and rubber blindfold. Operating the power switch on the chin strap was easy, like using a remote control on a portable stereo. Ace fingered the toggle then twisted it to the On position. The black shielding over her eyes began to glow faintly, turning a milky grey, light spreading out from a point at the centre. It was like watching a monochrome desert sunrise.

The glow spread across her field of vision accompanied by a faint buzzing noise. Then images began to swim up out of the pale grey. The outlines of her surroundings, the roof beams and the warehouse crates appeared and drifted for a moment. Then the distorted shape of human figures, Miss David and the mercenaries. Their outlines were sharpening and now they came clearly into focus. As Ace looked around the optical system inside the helmet tracked her eyes, reading every minute change. It calculated the desired focus by analysing the physical behaviour of retina and iris, zooming in when she looked at distant objects. A low-intensity beam of laser light scanned the eye, supposedly without damaging the tissue. It was a fairly crude system. Ace had had one demonstrated to her but had never used the device before. She didn't find the Class One Laser Device warning sticker particularly reassuring. Also, the sighting mechanism scanned only one eye and used the data to make adjustments for both. You'd get splitting headaches if there was much variation between your right and left field of vision.

Ace studied the roof of the old wooden building, saw a tiny movement on a beam. She tracked with it and the shape instantly blossomed into a bulge on the wooden rafter and then became closer still, a huge mass of moving spiked structures crawling with insects, like squirrels among oddly smooth conical tree branches. She relaxed her eyes and the system zoomed back, individual hairs and fleas dwindling into an indistinguishable glossy pelt on the mouse. Ace watched the creature running across the dark ceiling space, its eyes glinting, small clawed feet in motion, unaware that it could be seen. She studied the wooden beam beneath the mouse, every scar and knothole visible. Ace examined a bent nail hammered into the wood and the helmet enlarged it relentless until it stood like a vast pitted metal tower standing drunkenly on a bare mountain plain. Ace grinned inside the helmet. She hadn't quite got the hang of it yet, but it would be fun learning.

She looked down from the rafters again. In the darkness at the back of the warehouse Ace could see Dfewar busy in the Suzuki. He had a battered Apple Mac clone set up on the back seat beside another computer of a different design. Ace concentrated on it and the night-sighting system zoomed in tight until the machine filled her field of vision like an art-deco office block. She could see the dirt and pits on the plastic surrounding the screen but she still couldn't find any kind of manufacturer's badge or serial number that she recognized. Ace panned down and the computer screen swept dizzyingly up and out of her field of vision. It was like falling from a window and watching the front of the building sweep past. She steadied herself and the auto focus on the eyepieces buzzed on either side of her head as they locked in. The keyboard of the computer she studied was attached to the screen unit by a thick umbilical wire, spooled like a telephone cord. It featured Cyrillic script on a black rubberized membrane. Dfewar had used Ace's cables to connect the two machines. Now he fed one of the disks into the front of the Mac clone. At some point in its life the computer had been exposed to extreme heat. The plastic shell surrounding its screen had melted and run, giving the machine a surreal look. The screen and keyboard seemed to be functioning normally. The only identifying mark on the fascia were two symbols embossed in the melted plastic. It took Ace a moment to make them out. The first symbol was a cartoon of a bumble bee in flight. The other was a human eye. A bee and an eye. Now she looked more closely, Ace decided that the other computer had previously been fitted in a vehicle of some sort. It still had bent steel brackets holding heavy bolts fitted to the back of it, obviously wrenched from a bulkhead with considerable violence. Ace imagined the computer being salvaged from a bombed-out tank on the Mongolian border and smuggled south.

Dfewar was bent over the screen of the Mac clone. Some simple cartoon graphics pulsed, showing data transmission. Ace zoomed in close enough to see the coarse staircasing on the pixels, smooth curves turned jagged by the extreme resolution. Then she zoomed out in time to see Dfewar turn and walk towards her, smiling. He'd assured himself that the disks and cables she had given him worked. Now the Kurds could download software from the half-melted machine and process it. The disks she had brought with her contained communications protocols and software links and the cables were universal adaptors for connecting different models of computer.

Dfewar was saying something to Miss David, speaking quietly.

'They're happy.'

Ace held out her hand. Dfewar returned the cables and disks. Now he'd confirmed that the merchandise was sound, Ace would retain them until it was time to make payment. Keep them somewhere safe. In this part of the world communications software had replaced gold or hashish or weapons as the universal currency.

Miss David was tapping her foot impatiently. Ace took out the black envelope containing charts and several pages of instructions on yellow legal paper. She left the drawing inside. The instructions had been written in fluent Turkish in a spidery slanted hand with an old fountain pen. The fatter envelope contained a letter of credit from a Luxembourg bank and two folded sheets of paper which had been typed using an old manual typewriter. Ace could feel the impression of the type with her fingers. Both folded sheets had been sealed with wax. She gave one to Miss David and the other to Dfewar. Miss David tucked hers away. Dfewar broke the seal on his and glanced at the instructions. He spoke to Miss David in Turkish. 'He says it's all fine,' said Miss David. 'They'll meet you on the boat in Marmaris.' She pressed a switch beside a fuse box on the wall and the large rear door of the warehouse began to creak open. A band of pale evening light appeared at the bottom of the wall and widened steadily upwards. 'They can go now,' said Miss David. 'Don't you think?'

Petrol fumes boiled in the warehouse, blue smoke clouding from the exhaust of the Suzuki as the engine revved and the Kurds climbed in. Only five of the men were seated in the vehicle as it drove out of the warehouse. Massoud remained, still sitting on the crate. He got up, moving casually and slowly, and advanced on Ace and Miss David. He came so close to Ace that his elbow slid up across her ribs when he suddenly lifted his arm. He reached above her and pulled a leather jacket down from the top of a stack of crates. He looked Ace in the eye as he zipped the jacket and murmured something. 'He's apologizing,' said Miss David. 'He doesn't mean it.'

She and Miss David left the warehouse by the side door, Massoud sauntering after them. A string of helicopters hung in the darkening sky like geese straggling home. Good target for a ground-to-air missile, thought Ace. She was aware of Massoud behind her, his eyes following her. He walked to a motor scooter leaning on a wall of the courtyard and kicked it to life. As he rolled down the cobbled yard towards the street, he glanced back at Ace. 'You can wait here a while before you leave,' said Miss David, watching Massoud. 'I can make you more tea.' The engine sound of the scooter was diminishing, the buzzing of a big insect caught between the stone walls of the old buildings.

'No. I'd better make a move. Thanks anyway.'

Ace made her way down hot twisted streets that smelled of the sea and blossoms. She walked past Ottoman houses and Roman ruins. On the broad avenues of the modern section of the city troop carriers rumbled past, freshly painted UN insignia stencilled beside the Turkish markings on their armour. Old diseased horses pulled two-wheel carriages with tourists in them. Dutch and Germans, unperturbed by the promise of war. Everywhere Ace went it seemed she could hear the buzzing of a motor scooter one street away.

At the intersection of Cumhuriyet and Ataturk Caddesi there was a narrow street lined with restaurants where she'd eaten lunch. Now Ace paused there to buy a kebab, marinated vegetables grilled and wrapped in unleavened bread. From the sealed private rooms of restaurants above her she could smell the forbidden meat grilling and touts wandered the street offering black-market meals of mutton, beef and chicken. The government directives were having little impact on a nation of seventy million carnivores. Ace waited for her kebab, standing by the hot coals of the open grill. On a table nearby she saw a Turkish daily newspaper spread open, a beer bottle anchoring it in the breeze. The cover featured an advertisement for lottery tickets beside colour photographs of an actress in a bikini and an aircraft carrier sinking in a sea of burning petroleum. They gave Ace her kebab wrapped in an earlier edition of the same paper. Vegetable oil soaked through images of soldiers in dune buggies and sitting on tanks. Smiling for the camera from behind mirrored sunglasses. Gung-ho, young and immortal. Most of them would be dead by now. The darkening stain on the newsprint obliterated their smiling faces. Ace burned her fingers, picking fragrant onion rings out of the pitta bread.

She was wolfing down the kebab when she stepped off the pavement and heard the distinctive engine note of a motor scooter in a cross street. She looked up and saw a girl on a yellow Vespa drone past. Ace realized that the muscles in her shoulders were bunched and tense, elbows held in tight to her ribs, ready to fight. She forced herself to relax. It was a lovely evening now that the motor traffic had thinned. Smiling people walked past, couples kissed, arms and legs bare under pastel shorts in the warm Mediterranean air. In a dark restaurant silver clinked and a waiter wrestled a bottle open. Ace heard the pop as the cork came free. She smiled. Then she heard the buzzing of another motor scooter and looked up in time to see Massoud swoop around a corner. He stopped then glanced up. Ace was looking directly at him. Massoud did a U-turn and went back the way he'd come. Ace stood for a moment, then hurried down a side street. Now the streets seemed to be narrowing in on her in the heat. She couldn't read the words on the shopfronts or street signs, their meaning locked away in alien lettering. An old horse tethered at a stone trough had a white film over one of its eyes. A thick cloud of flies lifted from its mane every time it stirred. Ace was still clutching the warm newspaper-wrapped bundle in her hand. It felt like a small living thing. The food she'd eaten was shifting greasily in Ace's stomach. At the first litter bin she passed she threw the rest of the kebab away, the newspaper greased to transparency, the war pictures lost to sight.

The desk clerk at the Novotel gave Ace the same look she'd received when she checked in that morning. It was not a look of approval. The clerk was a woman dressed in an immaculate man's evening suit, white shirt and black tie. On her lapel was a small crescent badge, the symbol of the new Turkish nationalism. Tourists were welcome in the new Turkey but at the Novotel they were looking for the right kind of tourist. Ace wore torn khaki culottes, a Rohan tee-shirt knotted to form a bra, and plastic sandals. She was dirty and sunburned and her hair, tied in a bun, was greasy from a week's travel in buses along the Turkish backroads. The clerk made her wait while she double-checked Ace's Visa rating on the front-desk computer. The credit card was in the name of Ms J Smith, but the validating thumb print and the recorded passport photo on the Visa database were Ace's. The clerk moved her light pen around and punched keys, trying to get the computer to ring some bells, but she couldn't find anything wrong. Finally she clucked and looked up and reluctantly handed Ace a rectangle of plastic embossed with the hotel's crest and a machine-readable barcode.

Ace slid the plastic key through the reading unit beside her door and went into her room. The air conditioning made a soft noise in the darkness. 'Lights,' said Ace, and panels of recessed halogen bulbs came on silently in the ceiling. The thick hotel carpet of the corridor had given way to even thicker carpet inside the room. She kicked her sandals off and felt the soft fibre on her sore toes. She walked to the closet opposite the bed. Her airline bag was still there, untouched. In the bathroom the fat chrome taps gleamed in the bright white curvature of an immense bathtub. Ace could see her reflection in the taps. At one touch hot water would pour into the tub. Ace turned to the sink and gathered up her toothpaste and toothbrush, sweeping them into the airline bag.

Looking at the clean smooth sheets of the bed Ace felt the weight of exhaustion settle on her. For a week she'd been travelling this alien coast, riding in old *dolmuses* thick with Turkish tobacco, ringing with Western music. She'd followed the winding backroads across mountains, her ears popping with the sudden pressure changes. For a week she had hustled, organized, made preparations. She'd met arms dealers, boat builders and black-market software hustlers. Dealing with a foreign language and the eyes of men on her all the time. Now she was in a quiet room sealed away from the world, looking down at this soft wide bed. She'd be asleep as soon as she climbed under the covers. Her head was full of dreams waiting to happen. Ace sighed and dragged the French-style bolster out from behind the pillows. She bent it in half and stuffed it deep under the quilt, halfway down the bed. Out of her rucksack she took the life jacket with the compressed air cylinder. The life jacket went into the bed snugly above the bolster and when she triggered the cylinder the quilt shuddered and slowly lifted, a shape growing under it. The inflating life jacket began to give roughly the contour of a human torso under the quilt. The bolster would pass for legs.

'Off.' The halogen bulbs went off instantly above Ace, dimming to warm orange for an instant before they died. She stood in the dark room listening to the hiss of the inflation apparatus and the sighing air conditioning. Then she locked the door and descended in the elevator, leaving the hotel through the restaurant entrance.

The automatic glass door slid open for her and she stepped out of the air conditioning into a solid wall of Mediterranean heat.

The pension where she slept that night was called the Blue House. It was a residential dwelling converted to a small hotel, centred on a system of narrow ancient alleys. Her room was high ceilinged, with tall cupboards and gleaming wooden floors. The sheets on the four-poster bed smelled of mothballs. Outside there was an old iron lamp post and a tree full of sleeping birds. From the buildings on every side Ace could hear televisions and, later in the evening, the mosques starting up. From across the dark city the recorded prayers blared, echoing and frail with distortion. Ace listened at the window that looked out on to the tree, the eerie rise and fall of the voices raising the hair on her forearms. A bird moved in the dark foliage outside. Someone shouted around the corner in an alley, followed by the frantic slap of running footsteps. Another cry.

Trouble, but someone else's. Ace listened dispassionately. She stood at the window a long time but she didn't hear any motor scooters.

The shower was a thin lukewarm drizzle, coughing rust before running clean. It was wonderful. Ace stood under it for half an hour. Her fingertips were pale and shrivelled when she came out. She wrapped her hair in a towel, pulled on a baggy tee-shirt big enough to act as a robe. 'Thirteen Years Left,' said the tee-shirt in heavy black lettering. Ace unzipped the airline bag, dumping it out on the bed. The pistol was a modified Python, a heavy American handgun with a distinctive flared sight running along the top of the barrel. This model had a MIDI control system which allowed linkage with the Vickers helmet. The gun could fire upon a target selected in the helmet system. You didn't have to pull the trigger. You just blinked your eye. It was a terrifically dangerous arrangement and a lot of people had been killed by mistake. Banned by military organizations all over the world, the system was still a best seller in the private sector.

Ace put the gun into the bed, deep under the sheets where it would be difficult for someone to see her reaching for it. The ritual reminded her of putting her teddy bear to bed, down deep where he'd be warm, when she was a child. She unknotted the towel and sat in front of the window, feet up on the cold iron radiator. When she went to bed she slept deeply, dreaming of eyes that were just holograms.

Ace woke up when she rolled over in the bed and felt the cold solid shape of the pistol pressing against her naked stomach. It left an imprint in her flesh when she got up. The echoing morning prayers drifted in through the tall windows as she dressed. She breakfasted on eggs and bread in a *pideci* near the pension, then walked in the direction of the sea, the direction of the Novotel. At the hotel she crossed the air-conditioned lobby without glancing towards the front desk. The elevator was programmed to understand English. She asked for her floor and the smooth sudden rush of acceleration dragged the blood from her brain. She rode up alone, counting the flashing lights on the indicator. In the dim quiet corridor on the seventh floor fat men and women moved between the rooms, silent on the thick carpet, pushing trolleys full of cleaning equipment and freshly laundered towels. A squat robot vacuum cleaner bearing the Novotel crest dogged their heels, scouring the floor. Ace took out the electronic key and turned the corner that led to her room. She could hear the voices as soon as she stepped around it.

The woman desk clerk from downstairs was arguing with a cleaning woman. They stood in the doorway of Ace's room, exchanging rapid, low Turkish. The cleaning woman was holding up the quilt from Ace's bed. Draped over her trolley was the life jacket, deflated and limp, air cylinder swinging at one corner. Ace didn't wait for the desk clerk to look up and see her. She turned and walked quickly back the way she'd come. When she pushed the button for the elevator her hand was steady. But as she descended in the high-speed metal cage her stomach turned over.

The quilt and the life jacket had been riddled with holes. Bullet holes.

Down by the harbour she went into a yachting shop and bought a new inflatable life jacket. Then she walked through the Old Town to the coach station to catch a bus to Marmaris. She listened for motor scooters all the way.

8

A large turtle was crawling sluggishly across the road, trying to make its way back to the water. A car thundered past, only just missing it. Ace trotted out into the road and scooped the animal up. She carried it to the water's edge, its blunt feet flailing helplessly, and set it down. The turtle crawled to the edge of the sea and studied the glittering water for a few moments. Then it looked up at Ace, tiny eyes in a shrivelled face, and turned in a slow circle and started back towards the road. Ace sighed and left it.

In Marmaris the docks had been converted to a European-style marina at one end of the bay. At the far end she'd find the boat she'd hired for the use of the Kurdish mercenaries. They'd all be on board already, along with the equipment she'd inspected in Miss David's warehouse. And Massoud would be with them.

Ace walked among the yachts. The wind whipped the lines of their sails against the masts with a sound that reminded her of flagpoles. Young Germans and New Zealanders lounged on the decks, rich kids recording themselves with camcorders, drinking and tanning in the brilliant lethal sunlight.

On the mahogany deck of one boat a tattooed teenage boy with long blond hair was sprawled out on a towel. He looked up and called out to Ace as she walked by. Despite herself Ace turned to him and immediately he reached into a plastic ice-bucket and pulled out a bottle of Polish vodka. Ice and water dripped off the bottle, glittering in the intense sea light. The boy brushed his long ragged blond hair back from his face. He smiled at her, white teeth in tanned face. His eyes were invisible behind sunglasses but then he took the glasses off and looked at her directly. His eyes were shy. He called something again, in German. He laughed at himself and shrugged, shaking the bottle. He gestured for Ace to come up on to the boat. Ace felt the nine kilos of her rucksack dragging at the sunburn on her shoulder. She could imagine the fat satisfying splash the rucksack would make when she threw it into the harbour. The German boy's boat was called *WitchKraft*. It was lolling gently on the water, a metre away from the rubber tyres nailed to the jetty. She could jump across in one smooth motion. The muscles in her legs rehearsed the action. They ached to move. Her sunburned skin itched under the abrasion of the rucksack. Ace stood on the splintering wood of the dock, flagpole noise all around her.

Two of the Kurdish mercenaries were lounging in the shade of the cabin structure, smoking and talking. Ace couldn't make out their faces. She climbed on board, lifting her rucksack carefully over the drop to the water. The boat was moored among the excursion vessels that ferried tourists among the islands, to visit the tombs and eat packed lunches. Some of the tour crews looked more piratical than her Kurds. The thought didn't make Ace smile.

Two other mercenaries were loading gear from the back of a Mercedes van, swearing and laughing. One of them, the man who'd shown her the hand grenades in the lemon crate, called a greeting to Ace. Aboard the boat now Ace could see Dfewar in the shadows of the cockpit, bent over some kind of small portable work station, typing at a keyboard. She had felt a lump of ice forming in her stomach as she walked along the jetty. Three times she almost turned back to the German boy and his Polish vodka. On the docks the rear doors of the Mercedes slammed and the men loaded the last of the equipment. They cast off and jumped on board. The men who had been smoking in the shade got to work securing the boxes and crates. Massoud was not amongst them. He was not amongst the men who had been working on the dock. He was not with Dfewar in the cockpit. The engines of the boat came alive, pushing it away from the jetty in a growing wake of foam. The marina shrank behind them. The mercenaries were all busy around her. Dfewar was working on his computer. Massoud was not on board. Ace felt shaky as relief began to set in. She leaned out over the side of the boat and let the sea breeze push into her face. When she smiled she could feel the wind pressing cold against her teeth. The German boy wasn't such a lost opportunity. Ace didn't like tattoos anyway. Eagles and tigers and hex signs on his gold skin. Nice muscles, though. The water was deep and blue, the shadow of the boat moving across it at speed. Ace's own shadow skimming the water as she raised her arm to wave at a tourist boat. It was cold in the breeze.

Ace moved away from the side of the boat, turning in time to see Massoud come out of the hatchway that led down to the galley.

The motion of the boat was lazy and gentle, despite their relatively high speed of travel. The deck rocked slightly under Ace's feet. Massoud looked at her, then away. He walked out into the sunlight on deck and unbuttoned his shirt. He was stretching his arms up, barechested in the sunshine, when something landed at his feet. Massoud reached down to pick it up. It was an inflatable life jacket. The one Ace had bought before leaving Antalya. She stood with her rucksack open, waiting, pleased with the accuracy of her throw. Massoud was lifting up the life jacket and Ace moved across the deck towards him, swaying a little with the motion of the boat. Massoud stood holding the jacket and when he looked up she saw his eyes and she knew.

It was Massoud who had gone into the Novotel, riding up in the silent elevator, gone into Ace's room and fired bullets into the bed where she was sleeping. Where she should have been sleeping. Now he stood in front of her and smiled. Ace smiled back. She had something else in her rucksack to show him. But Massoud reached out and grabbed the belt that held up Ace's jeans. He pulled hard, tanned fingers locked on the leather band, and swung Ace around. She stumbled across the deck, off balance, and collided with a tarpaulined crate, almost falling. She was still clutching her rucksack. Massoud didn't even turn to look at her. He called an order to the men at the rear of the boat. Ace was reaching into her rucksack. Except for Massoud's voice, there was silence on the boat. Ace had the pistol out. Massoud turned and saw it. Now there was complete silence.

'Jump into the water,' said Ace in Turkish. The grammar might be wrong but the meaning would be clear enough. It was one of two phrases she had memorized on the road from Antalya. Working with a Berlitz book and a flashlight in the dark bus while tourists snored on either side of her. Massoud stared at her for a moment. Ace squeezed the handgrip on the Python, holding the pistol with both hands, and thumbed the safety catch off. Massoud watched her calmly then strode back down the boat, coming towards her. Ace repeated the phrase, clearing her throat. Massoud was laughing. He was close to her, his open shirt flapping in the breeze, lazily scratching his bare chest. Then Massoud stopped.

He was looking down at his chest. There on his dark skin was a pale green lozenge of light. Massoud looked up at Ace. The light was coming from the sighting mechanism on the Python. It indicated exactly the path the bullet would follow if she pulled the trigger. It moved when Massoud moved. He scratched his chest and he watched the spot of light ripple and flow across his fingers. When he moved his hand away it hovered just over his heart. Massoud looked at Ace. The other mercenaries were all watching them. Dfewar had come out of the cockpit and was standing in the doorway. For the third time Ace repeated her phrase. Massoud didn't move. Ace lowered the Python, the spot of light sweeping down to rest on the deck between Massoud's bare feet. The bullet blew a neat hole in the plastic imitation teak veneer deck surface. Massoud didn't flinch.

Ace began to raise the pistol again. Massoud showed no sign of fear. It was Ace who was afraid. She was still lifting the pistol. The only thing left to do was to take aim and fire a round into the bare brown skin of his chest. Ace couldn't do it. If Massoud knew she couldn't do it then she had no room left to manoeuvre. Massoud wasn't moving. Ace hesitated. When she hesitated the gun barrel paused halfway in its upwards arc. The spot of light came to rest exactly on the crotch of Massoud's salt-faded jeans. Massoud looked at the spot of light and he was instantly in motion. Across the deck, over the side and into the water. It took Ace an instant to register what had happened. Then she was at the side of the boat, looking out. Massoud was swimming, doing a strong crawl away from the boat, headed back for the marina. Ace scooped her inflatable lifejacket up off the deck and threw it after him. When she turned around the rest of the Kurds were gathered in a group on the deck behind her. Their faces didn't have any expression she could read.

'Anyone else?' said Ace. It was the other phrase she had memorized, feeling a little nauseated as the flashlight beam bobbed with the motion of the bus. She still had the Python in her right hand.

Dfewar moved away from the group of men. The others watched him. He kneeled beside a crate, glanced up at Ace, frowning for a moment. Then he opened the crate, flipping up metal catches. Inside there was a densely packed white substance. Flakes of it glittered in the sunlight. Dfewar dug his hand into the ice and pulled out a can of beer. He threw it across to Ace. She almost dropped her pistol catching it. The Kurds laughed. Dfewar grinned, kneeling by the cooler, digging out cans.

Ace could see the tombs on the island hillside, caves with ornamented openings, old ruined pillars surrounding the entrances, shadowy in the heavy orange light as the sun descended. The boat rode at anchor, three kilometres from the island, riding the swell while they waited for nightfall.

The mercenaries were quiet, smoking kif, stripping their weapons and preparing for the assault. Ace found the Python's nylon shoulder holster and dug out the bubbled plastic bag containing the communications lead. She set the holstered revolver on the deck at her feet and popped the plastic bubbles, pulling out the cable. It was a flat wide wire that thinned to a tough narrow lead terminating in a DIN plug. The DIN plug jacked into the pistol grip like a lanyard. She fitted the connection at the pistol end, then got the Vickers vision system out of its box. For a moment Ace thought someone had taken the Vickers and substituted a different, cheaper unit. Then she realized that the helmet had been repainted for combat, streaked crudely with black and tan emulsion in a broken camouflage pattern. Ace tucked the flat section of the wire around the inner circumference of the helmet liner and gently worked the flat tongue connection into the output slit.

The first beer can landed too close to the boat and floated back towards her. The second one she half-filled with sea water so it was heavy enough to travel a decent distance when she threw it. The can splashed as it hit and the motion of the water carried it further away. Ace watched it twist and adjust itself in the moving sea. When the can was out of sight she put the Vickers helmet on.

The stereo eye screens offered glowing grids and menus superimposed on the image as Ace called up the scanning option. Using the switch on the chin strap she quartered the expanse of sea behind the boat, dividing it into a series of search areas. It took so long that Ace began to wonder if the can had gone under. But after three seconds the helmet had located it, still bobbing upright, weighted by the water already in it. Ace zoomed in closer until the Japanese brand name began to fill her field of vision. A smiling baseball player beamed at her above the lager logo, winding up to pitch a fastball. When she could read the tiny lettering of the ingredient list on the can, swaying in her vision with the water turbulence, she lifted the Python and let the system sight it for her.

The accurate-sighting icon flickered in front of her eyes, a ghostly smiling elf making an 'OK' sign with thumb and forefinger curled together. Ace locked on to the target. At this distance the act of pulling the trigger with her finger would disturb the aim of the weapon. The icon of the Vickers elf flickered on and off as she adjusted the aim to allow for the motion of the can, the motion of the boat and the muscle tension in her arm. She used her eyelids to cut the trigger out of the firing circuit, took the software safety catch off, then blinked her eyes to fire.

The bullet tore into the middle of the lettering describing the beer's specific gravity. Metal twisted under impact, enormous sharp edges sprouting, apparently so close to her eyes that she instinctively blinked and the pistol automatically fired again. The second bullet drove the can under a shallow wave. The can turned over, spun and sank, drifting down to the ocean floor to join ten million others.

Ace was careful to switch the system off before she blinked again. When she took the helmet off the sea breeze was cool on her scalp, sweat heavy in her hair. That was one of the dangers of using the system in the daytime. Ace remembered the photographs of Australian soldiers in Indonesia. They always wore raffish silk scarfs spun into thin cylinders and tucked around the edge of the helmet, to keep the sweat out of their eyes, and out of the vision system's circuitry. Ace wouldn't have that problem. She'd be wearing the helmet in the chill of the night. Ace unplugged the cable from the handgrip of the Python. She set the pistol down on the deck between her feet, mechanical safety engaged. The helmet was resting on top of the beer cooler where she'd left it. Ace reached down and picked it up with her left hand. The cold of the chiller box had left a slick of moisture on the smooth plastic of the helmet. It slipped as she lifted it. She lost her grip entirely and the helmet fell towards the deck. Ace grabbed with her right hand and missed.

It shouldn't have mattered. The helmet itself was virtually unbreakable. Only the glass blindfold of the vision screen was vulnerable. As the helmet fell it spun neatly in midair so the screen was towards the deck. Even then it wouldn't have mattered if the pistol hadn't been lying there. But the helmet landed on the Python, the delicate glass of the viewing system connecting with the steel frame of the pistol with a sickening intricate crash.

Ace picked up the helmet. The wide curved bar of glass that formed the optical unit hung loose from the helmet's rim. A thin band of cable was visible connecting the two.

Ace hit the On switch. The miniature screens of the eyepieces remained dark, but the laser lighting mechanism glowed faintly above them. Then the retina scanning beam flashed out, a hairline of intense hot red. The beam sliced across the interior of the helmet, taking a best-guess route directly through where the wearer's right eye should have been. The laser scorched a stinking brown burn in the plastic lining low in the back of the helmet. A tiny hole bubbled in the outer surface of the helmet. The glowing thread of the laser beam broke through the back of the Vickers and shot across the boat. Ace hit the Off switch before the beam could encounter some ammunition or a fuel tank. She swore savagely. 'Buy British,' she said, and threw the helmet to the far side of the deck, where it rolled away into an open hatch of the bilge.

The tombs on the island were still visible, but as she watched they were disappearing against the hillsides in the gloom. Using her flashlight Ace took the black envelope from her rucksack. The word *Ace* glowed on it, milky and luminous. She opened the envelope and had a final look at the map the Doctor had provided. Then she read his instructions again, a single page of his scratchy fountain-pen handwriting. On the sheet the Doctor described the general disposition of the enemy encampment, their equipment, including weaponry and a generator, and the probable numbers of personnel. Ace read the last paragraph several times then folded the sheet and put it back with the maps in a waterproof plastic case. Then she studied the drawing the Doctor had made. It showed what Ace had come to think of as *the object*, with approximate details of its size written beside the drawing. She folded the drawing and put it with the maps.

One of the Kurds had a radio playing, music quietly drifting out over the silent water. The mercenaries made no attempt to shade their lights or stay out of view, except when they were handling weapons. From the shore or a passing vessel their yacht would look like any other pleasure boat breaking its journey before taking a lazy route among the islands.

They were picking up a UN armed forces radio transmission out of Izmir, broadcasting to the American marines in the Mediterranean and Aegean. It was Bo Didley playing 'Mona'. Ace changed into a black long-sleeved shirt and a combat vest. She remembered the first time she'd heard the song, played on scratchy vinyl in a tiny hot room in a boys' college. Years ago and on the other side of the world. Her boots on the floor heavy with mud beside the boy's. His older brother had been in the Bromley Contingent. Gas fire on high and the door locked.

She checked the Python for the fourth time, unloading and reloading bullets as she listened to the ghostly harmonics of Bo Didley's guitar. This riff had first been played in a studio in Chicago in 1954, travelling out through the pickup of an electric guitar, coded as phantom patterns on magnetic tape, decoded through loudspeakers and radio towers. The song she listened to was coming at her out of the past, out of a tobacco-stained room half a century away. In a sense it was still the original signal, still coming out of that box-shaped guitar with the Gretsch neck in Chicago in 1954, still travelling. The sound waves had moved on spreading outwards but the electronic signal still propagated, along a less predictable route.

Ace watched the red dot of a burning cigarette travelling back and forth amongst the Kurds. Dfewar came forward holding the stub of it between his fingers, politely offering it to Ace. Ace bobbed her head, lifting her chin. For the first few days in the country she had still been shaking her head in response to questions. In Turkey that meant Yes. It was a common mistake which had almost led to some difficult situations for Ace when she'd been haggling with the Cypriot twins for the software.

Dfewar shrugged and showed her his wristwatch. When he pressed a stud on the side the animated analogue hands blurred for a moment and displayed a new time. Dfewar released the stud and the hands on the watch reverted to their old position. He walked back to his men, still holding the cigarette. Ace checked her own watch. They would go in and land on the island in an hour's time.

The radio played another song by Bo Didley, then another. The armed forces DJ seemed to have fallen asleep. The CD kept spinning on its transport, decoded by laser, sending its data out from a radio control room five hundred kilometres away.

I'm just twenty-two and I don't mind dying.

The moon was up when they launched the dinghy. The black rubber shape slapped the water as they lowered it over the side, settling then riding the swell. Ace was the second person aboard, sitting in the front beside Dfewar. She had a flat metal can of black dubbin she used for waterproofing her DMs. Now she thumbed the can open and applied the dark grease to her cheeks as the men behind her paddled. Dfewar studied her blackened face and nodded with approval. He borrowed the can and then passed it back to his men. When the blades of the paddles touched sand they slid over the side of the dinghy and pushed it in through the last metre of shallow water to the shore.

101

The Kurds were professionals. They dispersed in silence, the only sound the water on the beach and the faint hydraulic punching of the gasoline generator near the encampment. Dfewar touched Ace on the elbow and she moved off with him, up the hillside, away from the sound of the generator.

When the moon emerged from the film of clouds you could see the sentry quite clearly. He was moving along the skyline, holding some kind of automatic weapon with a jutting magazine. The weeds were stinging Ace's eyes. She moved her face back out of the clump of long stems. The sentry was looking away from her now. She slithered silently back down the slope. Dfewar moved with her, taking a parallel course through the dirt and dry grass. They stopped, crouching among some large shattered stones, and waited while Dfewar listened and studied his wristwatch. They could hear the sentry and, when they peered over the rim of the stones, see him following his route.

They watched for a long time, watching until the pattern was definite. He was patrolling a measured interval, walking away on the hill crest until he reached a patch of heat-stunted trees, then turning and walking back towards the ring of stones where Ace and Dfewar were waiting.

Dfewar had drawn a knife from a sheath on his webbed belt. The blade was dim, blue steel, chemically dulled so it wouldn't reflect light and betray his position. The blade was an unusual slim shape, tapering symmetrically to an acute point, like a thin flattened spike. No sawing or carving teeth on either side of the blade. There was really only one thing you could use a knife like that for. Ace moved away from it when Dfewar set the knife on the ground between them.

Dfewar rolled over on his back and lay looking up at the night sky. Particulate pollution drifting across from the mainland made the stars look faint and blunt. Dfewar didn't move or check his knife again. He was relaxing, preparing himself. He wouldn't need to move until the sentry turned and came back. He just lay there on the hillside staring upwards as though he could see the constellations. He didn't look at Ace again.

Guthrie patrolled the hillside, walking just fast enough to keep his body heat up. He remembered the photographs of Turkey they'd studied when they were planning the operation. They showed the hot blues of sky and water. Nobody mentioned how cold the nights would get.

From where he stood now Guthrie could see the encampment, the three tents, two for personnel and one, a smaller lean-to, for the generator. In the minute or so he spent watching no one moved between the tents. He could see lights on in two of them, a soft glow through thin orange canvas, and the bare bulb burning beside the generator.

At the other end of his hilltop patrol he had a good view of the best natural harbour on the island. If trouble came it would come from that direction. Perhaps a landing on a night like this. Guthrie felt a prickling of anticipation. He would watch for boats coming in. In a moment he would turn back and walk that way. But now he paused among the stand of dwarfed and twisted trees. He was supposed to maintain a steady sweep of the hilltop until three o'clock, when Sean would come and take over the watch. He should be starting back to survey the other end of the island. By now he should already be watching over the bay. But Guthrie felt suddenly lazy. There was no particular hurry. He flexed the muscles of his arms and adjusted his gun so it rested more comfortably in his grip. He leaned back against a tree. The dry old wood creaked under his weight. He moved away, following the path through the weeds, but still not swinging back towards the other side of the hilltop. Why hurry? Maybe he wouldn't bother with the other sweep at all. Leave it to Sean. He was moving in the opposite direction now, feeling the ground under him beginning a gradual downward slope. Down, towards the camp.

The path led him down among the wild herbs growing on the hillside. After the heat of the day their fragrance was intense. The smell made him feel slightly nauseated. Warren always used those herbs when he cooked for them. Warren was ridiculous. Even a girl would have been more use than the fat idiot. They'd actually discussed the idea of bringing a girl along to cook for them. It had been voted down. So they were stuck here with Warren feeding them. He had even once cooked them fish, thinking that the Mediterranean would be cleaner than his native

American waters. Presumably because you didn't find syringes on the beaches here. Yet. There had been illness in the camp for days after the fish. Guthrie had been doubled over with stomach cramps. If he hadn't been so weak he would have smashed Warren's face in with a rifle butt.

Guthrie turned away from the herb smell, starting back on the other sweep of his patrol. He marked the end of this perimeter by a cluster of huge broken stones just down the hillside. As he walked he imagined the obese figure of Warren in front of him. In the sights of his weapon. The thought led to other images of combat. Adrenalin mixed into his blood, waking him up fully. Again he thought of an assault from the sea, by night. All his senses sharpened. Now Guthrie imagined that he was about to be attacked. He felt for the safety on the gun he carried. It was a weapon developed in South Africa for riot applications. The magazine held 512 rounds which could be dispersed in less than seven seconds. It wasn't accurate but it was thorough. Guthrie rehearsed combat scenarios in his head, excitement releasing more adrenalin inside him. He imagined the enemy rushing in out of the dark. He imagined dim figures surging up the hillside.

He was ready for them.

Ace flinched as Dfewar moved. The figure of the sentry had appeared on the hill above and Dfewar was already on the last metre of the slope, running silently. In the moonlight he became an indistinct grey shape against the grey rocks of the hillside. The sentry turned just as Dfewar swept on to him.

The shapes of Dfewar and the sentry merged in the colourless light, then flattened as the two figures tumbled to the ground. Ace heard abrasive scuffing noises as heels dug frantically into dirt, digging for grip, then a single grunt. Then silence.

Nothing moved on the hilltop. Ace waited a moment, bracing herself. Then there was a burst of sound so strange it had Ace on her feet and racing up the slope.

Dfewar crouched on the ground over the sentry. The sentry's eyes were moving quickly, specks of reflected moonlight shooting across them. They fixed on Ace, wide with fear. Dfewar had one hand tight over the sentry's mouth. The other hand trembled a little, holding his knife. The blade, still clean, was pointing away from the sentry's body. The sentry had been wearing a Walkman and the headphones had come loose when Dfewar had slammed him to the ground. Now a tinny insect ringing came out of the tiny foam beads. An American thrash guitar solo, some long-haired blond playing his Viking brains out. Loud in the stillness on the hilltop. Ace grabbed the headphones and yanked the cable out of the tape player, silencing them. She stared down at the sentry's face, now looking from her to Dfewar in terror. The sentry was, at the most, fourteen years old.

Sean was nuking Indonesia. He was in the cockpit of a Loki fighter plane on a night flight, using full heat modelling and starlight vision enhancement. Black forest shot out of sight under the jet and suddenly the glowing grid of a city flared up below him. His equipment read temperature gradients rather than light and darkness, so residential areas registered as bright scarlet, office buildings as orange and bodies of water a dull rust brown. An urgent synthesized tone rang in his ears, stereo imaging making it sound as if the noise was directly behind his head. Behind and low, in that vulnerable area near the back of the neck. Sean resisted the urge to look over his shoulder. He tongued a control and instantly the image of the city below squeezed and flattened, forming a narrow band occupying the lower edge of his visual field. Directly before his eyes, front and centre, was an image from the sentry cameras situated behind the cockpit of the Loki. Sean grinned. Better than a rearview mirror. Not that he had much to grin about. Six Indonesian Hawkers were locked on behind him, coming in for the kill. Sean blinked his left eye once and his right eye twice. The fuselage of the Loki shimmered around him, orange mist coming off the metal. It was terrifyingly as if the plane had begun to smoke and burn. But the orange steam thickened and solidified, conforming to the shape of the Loki. The orange was rising steadily upwards, a second Loki jet, ethereal and glowing, lifting out of the metal of the plane. Now it was directly above him, a plane identical to his except insubstantial, a little ragged at the edges, like an afterimage on your retina. Sean checked the rear view. The Hawkers were closing fast. He blinked his right eye twice. The heat ghost of the Loki accelerated and streaked away. The real Loki dived. Sean watched as the six Indonesian fighters shot above, ignoring him, their primitive software deceived by the decoy. Sean was grinning again. He launched six Valkyrie air-to-airs. They hovered in front of his cockpit for a moment then shot away in pursuit of the Hawkers. One and a half seconds later six plumes of flame lit up the Indonesian sky in simulated night-vision colours. Sean allowed himself a single moment of grim satisfaction then returned to the business at hand. A quick status check on the Loki, and then the final missile run. He read off all the instrument outputs. The energy used to create the heat ghost had been a major drain on the system, but all flight functions were still well in the green. He cancelled the head-up analogue displays and proceeded to begin a visual inspection of the fighter's fuselage.

The first things he noticed were the white monkeys.

Dozens of quick-moving snow-white shapes, writhing on his wings, scrambling up the sidewall of the jet, pressing their obscene, debased, subhuman pink faces to the cockpit. Writhing like a giant cluster of huge maggots, they closed in on him from all sides. The cockpit was covered with their degenerate idiot faces. Drooling, squamous genetic garbage – .

'Warren!' Sean tore the gaming set off his head. He knuckled at his eyes and screamed again. 'Warren, you little suck!' The set hit the canvas floor and rolled across the tent, bouncing against Calvin's ankles. Calvin was beginning to remove his own gaming set, moving a little slowly, his fingers clumsy. Calvin had been piloting the Hawkers Warren had shot down and no doubt he was still recovering from the brilliant high-resolution colour graphics and true stereo surround sound involved in a fiery death in the air. But it wasn't Calvin he was after.

'Warren!' The fat little bastard was nowhere to be seen. Calvin had removed his headgear now and he was blinking, disoriented in the dimness of the tent after the garish colours of the virtual reality Indonesian airwar. He got up from his canvas folding chair, still a little shaky, and came over towards Sean. 'What's the matter? I –'

'It's Warren. He's ruined the game.' Sean got up and kicked his own canvas chair over. His leg muscles ached from hours accommodating themselves to an imaginary cockpit. Warren was nowhere in sight. 'What did he do?' said Calvin. 'I didn't see anything.'

'Of course you didn't see anything. You were dying.'

'But what did he do?'

'He had these things. They were on my plane. Crawling all over it.' Sean found that he was rubbing his hands hard across his arms and chest. Trying to brush off imaginary white things, crawling over his skin, maggot-wet and sticky. His stomach was heaving. He took a deep breath and forced his hands to stop. Closed his fingers into fists and jammed them into his pockets.

'What kind of things?' Calvin had put his glasses on again and he'd picked Sean's headset off the floor of the tent. He held it up to the light, inspecting it for damage.

'I don't remember. I feel sick. Yes, I do remember. They were like maggots. Or monkeys. Big white maggot monkeys. With baby faces and hands. Little pink hands. They were —' Sean stopped. Calvin was looking at him, standing close. He stepped back as Sean ran out of the tent.

The night air was cool on Sean. He was soaked with sweat. He went across to the other tent and pushed through the flap. The tent had been sealed all evening, trapping the heat of the day. It was airless and smelled like old socks. It was also empty. Just Guthrie and Warren's sleeping bags lying on the canvas floor, in a mess of chocolate-bar wrappers and soft-drink cans. Sean came back out again. He looked up at the hill then down to the sea, staring wildly around at the island darkness. 'Warren!' he yelled. 'You stupid bastard! You brought some with you, didn't you!' Was that a sound? Was it the sound of someone laughing? Sean went back into his own tent.

Calvin was staring anxiously. He had set Sean's chair upright again. 'Brought what with him?'

Sean sat down in the chair. He ran his fingers through his hair and looked up at Calvin. 'White monkeys.'

Calvin nodded. 'Cthulhu Gate software, right?'

'Yeah.'

'How could he do that? After what happened? We all

promised.'

Sean shook his head. 'I don't know. I guess he just couldn't resist bringing some with him.' He wrapped his feet around the aluminium frame of the chair. 'The moron.'

Calvin was checking the screen of their portable. 'He only joined the game about five minutes ago. He must have tapped in from somewhere nearby.' Calvin checked his watch, then went out of the tent. He was back a moment later. 'His gun is gone. It's early but I think he's gone on sentry duty.'

'He's hiding in the hills, the little creep. When he comes back I'm going to kill him.'

'Relax,' said Calvin. He had Sean's gaming set in his hand. He held it out. Sean shook his head. 'Go on,' said Calvin. 'It'll make you feel better.'

'No.' But Calvin had put the set in his lap. Sean picked it up and put it on. Calvin was already wearing his. Sean sighed as the vision screen fizzed for a moment as the system rebooted, and then he was back in the cockpit, the instrument readouts glowing against the night sky. Target shining under him. He was back in the game again. Despite himself Sean felt the old excitement building. His bladder was so full it ached but he instantly dismissed the feeling. That could wait. The body could wait.

He began a final assault run on the city, checking the status menus for his missiles. Three Niffelheims and a Ragnarok. He would get only one chance to do this properly. Even if he escaped the immediate blast of his own missiles the nuclear payloads were dirty enough to give him a lethal dose before he was out of range. This games scenario was what was known as a Bag Run. As in getting sent home in a bag. A suicide mission. Sean dismissed any feelings of fear. He allowed himself to think only about the target and victory for his nation. When the stakes were high enough you could achieve anything. Overcoming the body and its repulsive physical needs. Its shameful terrors. Fight yourself and win. Become a purified cinder burning in the jungle night, cleansed by the flames of victory. The sky tilted, islands of cloud swimming past as he turned the Loki for the assault strike. No fear, just a beautiful combat death and victory. Sean's courage flowed in him and it was good. The city was a glowing gem at the centre of his sights. His heart thundered with excitement. He locked his missiles in. He would die, but so would a million of the enemy. His life was nothing compared to the beauty of a sacrifice like that. Along with his steady strong courage Sean felt a rising note of exhilaration. The target was rushing closer now, a beautiful dayglo orange octagon.

But then the octagon pulsed, winking out for an instant. It returned, but its orange glow had diminished and it was fuzzy around the edges. The entire heat image of the city wavered, then it began to fold in on itself. The night sky suddenly snapped from mint green to a dead TV-screen grey. The head-up displays of his instruments began to swim, registering random numbers, machine-code garbage.

Sean's rage was so enormous he couldn't get the headset off. His fingers fumbled at the velcro. He heard a voice howling obscenities, muffled by a gaming mouthpiece, and the voice was his own. The virtual reality of Indonesia had faded away completely, replaced by a blank screen nowhere, nowhen. Sean knew what had happened. Someone had disrupted the gamesmaster process on their portable computer. He tore the games set off his head, knowing who he would see, knowing who would had sneaked into the tent. He would smash Warren's fat face in. Break his nose and then —

But it wasn't Warren.

It was a man. He had dark skin with some kind of black grease smeared across his cheekbones. He wore a black jacket and loose black trousers. Calvin was standing by the portable. He'd switched if off but now his hands were behind his head, fingers laced. His eyes never left the man. The man was bending over Sean's chair.

He was pointing a gun at Sean.

A real gun.

Sean felt the sudden warm rush flowing down on his leg, soaking his baggy nylon camouflage shorts as his bladder let go. The body had won after all.

9

By the time Ace and Dfewar reached the small encampment with their prisoner, Dfewar's men had already secured the place. The mercenaries had relaxed. Some were drinking cans of Fresca that came out of the American boys' small refrigerator. Others were smoking cigarettes from packets they'd brought with them in waterproof ammunition bags. There was a round of applause and a ribald cheer as Ace and Dfewar came down from the moonlit hillside. Ace was glad of the darkness so no one could see her blushing. The boy, Guthrie, was walking behind her and Ace heard him stumble on the narrow trail. Dfewar reached back and caught him before he fell. Guthrie's hands were tied behind his back, fastened with a scarf Dfewar had taken from his backpack. Ace carried the boy's automatic rifle, slung over her shoulder, unloaded and with the muzzle pointing down at the ground. She was near enough now to see the other prisoners. Two more teenage boys, handcuffed to the support pole of the tent which housed the generator.

The encampment was what you might expect from a bunch of rich kids playing wilderness games. In addition to the tents and the generator Ace could see a lot of expensive toys. A beached aluminium canoe was lying beside one of the tents, folding paddles still propped up beside it in their factory wrapping. The Kurds had a couple of expensive VR gaming headsets which evidently belonged to the kids. The mercenaries were waiting impatiently to play with the sets. The men who were currently using them were smoking kif and giggling. In the space between the tents there was a portable refrigerator, a small cooking range with natural gas cylinders, and a low opaque plastic cylinder, about a metre in diameter, standing upright on the ground. A hose ran from the cylinder to a small water pump. Ace realized it was an outdoor shower. All the comforts of home.

'What are you guys doing here?' Ace turned to Guthrie. Guthrie had opened his mouth to answer when there was a shout from the tents.

'Don't tell the skank anything!' The bigger of the other two boys had jumped to his feet, forgetting about the handcuffs. The smaller boy locked to the other cuff was forced to lurch to his feet, too. But by that time the first boy had jerked to a halt and was falling back down. They both ended up slamming to the ground again. 'That's Sean,' said Guthrie. Ace went over to where the boys were sitting, at the back of the generator tent, grimacing and rubbing their bruised buttocks.

Ace smiled down at them. 'Hello Sean. Skank, eh? I think it's time for a little interrogation.'

The drawing showed an object like a large waterbarrel with a ribbed surface. The three boys looked down at it, the sheet of paper reflecting light from the tent's naked bulb up on to their faces. Calvin was the first to look up at Ace again, then Guthrie. Sean refused to meet her eyes.

Ace folded the piece of paper and returned it to the black envelope. 'I've come to collect this for a friend. I don't know what it is and I don't particularly care. But I know you've got it and we're going to take it away from you.' Ace paused. She was trying to think of a phrase which would sound suitably threatening and which she could say with a straight face. The three boys were sitting, facing her, in the centre of the tent on folding chairs, their hands untied. The Kurdish mercenaries moved around behind them, helping themselves to food from plastic plates on a low picnic table. The boys' refrigerator stood outside, door hanging open, ravaged and dead. One of the Kurds had shot it at close range, testing a confiscated weapon. One blast had torn the small Kenwood fridge to pieces. Ace didn't like to think what would have happened if one of the boys had managed to open fire on the Kurds. Dfewar sat on the floor of the tent behind her, eating vegetarian chilli from a plastic carton. He looked like a kid with the gaming headset over his eyes. The other Kurds were smiling and laughing, all tension gone. But Ace knew that if they'd received fire from the encampment all these boys would be dead now. The Kurds were professionals. She was still trying to think of a convincing threat when she was distracted by a quiet rasping sound. She looked up and saw that the youngest boy, Calvin, had begun to cry.

'Shut up, you little suckhole.' Sean was definitely Ace's least favourite of the three. 'If you don't shut up I'll —'

'You won't do anything,' said Ace.

'We're never going to tell you where it is,' said Sean. 'Why don't you start searching the island now? It'll only take you about three weeks.'

'Why don't you act like a nice polite boy?' said Ace.

'Sit on it and rotate,' said Sean. 'None of us are saying anything.'

'It's down on the beach.'

'Guthrie!'

'Buried just below the high-water mark.'

'Guthrie, what are you doing!'

'We figured it would help to keep it cool.'

'Don't tell her, Guthrie!'

'Just shut up, Sean. I'm sick of this. I want to go home.' He looked at Ace. 'Get a flashlight and we'll show you where to dig.'

Calvin had stopped crying now. Ace handed him a handkerchief while Guthrie searched their luggage for a flashlight with batteries that weren't dead. Calvin took the handkerchief without looking at her. 'You should just leave it alone, you know. Leave it buried. We should all go home and just leave it right where it is.'

But Ace wasn't listening. There was something strange happening to the section of tent wall that was in shadow. The canvas was flattened, tight, and spots of light were appearing on it. A pattern of tiny bright circles.

Ace stared, fascinated, as the phenomenon continued, spurts of dust blasting up from the floor of the tent, tiny holes bursting in the orange fabric, the darkness of the ground visible through them. A plastic beaker had been knocked off the picnic table and was falling slowly to the floor. More holes appeared and now Ace could hear the sound, like a drill tearing at a road surface.

The Kurds were all yelling. Dfewar reached to pull Ace down

but she was already throwing herself to the floor, dragging Calvin with her. She lay on the damp canvas as the next blast of bullets ripped through the tent wall and raked the floor opposite, shredding a sleeping bag and blowing synthetic fleece up in a cloud. The Kurds had dragged the other two American boys down on to the floor. Plastic furniture exploded around them, brittle fragments showering down on Ace's back. She wished Sean would stop screaming so she could think more clearly.

The firing stopped for a moment and Ace started for the flap of the tent. Dfewar grabbed her and pulled her back just as the firing started again. He made a slamming gesture with the flat of his hand, pushing a fresh magazine into an automatic weapon. The sniper had just been reloading. A guy rope outside the tent broke, severed by a bullet, and the tent's ceiling came bellying down, losing its shape.

The Kurds were swearing, shouting to each other now. Two of them crawled to the back of the tent and started cutting at the fabric with knives. They were widening the slit so that a man could get through it when the firing stopped again. This time it didn't restart. There was a shout from the hillside.

Ace and Dfewar were the first out of the tent, running in the moonlight. Sean followed them. There was a crash of breaking vegetation as a bulky shape came rolling down the path of the hillside. 'Warren!' screamed Sean, running through the dry grass. He skidded to his knees on the ground, kneeling beside the boy who'd fallen from the path. The boy was fat, wearing a barbecue apron with a picture of a woman's bare torso printed on it. He was shaking his head and clutching his mouth. Sean tried to touch him but the fat boy batted his hand away.

One of the Kurdish mercenaries came down the path in the moonlight. He was carrying one of the American automatic rifles as well as his own. He looked at the boys on the ground, then at Ace and Dfewar. He shrugged and smiled sheepishly. Sean pointed a finger at Ace. 'You bastards,' he said. His hand was trembling. 'Warren's got a broken tooth.'

'Warren's lucky he isn't wearing his brains on his apron,' said Ace.

'You guys don't know what you're doing.' Calvin shook his head and walked along beside the sea, staring down at his feet. He scuffed his sneakers through the damp beach pebbles.

'Probably not,' said Ace. She looked back to where Dfewar and his men were digging. The barrel was almost completely uncovered now, seawater flowing into the hole as they widened it with shovels and entrenching tools. The moon was behind clouds and they worked by the chemical light of snap-sticks. Calvin brushed a strand of his long black hair away from his eyes.

'We came here so nothing like this would happen.'

'Nothing like what?'

'You people. Coming here and taking it away. The government.' He looked back at the barrel. The Kurds were wrestling it out of the ground.

'We're not the government,' said Ace.

Calvin shrugged. 'No difference,' he said.

'What are you going to do now?'

'Go back home. Back to the States. Our parents are all worried sick. I guess it never would have worked.' He looked up at the dark bulk of the island rising away from them, up from the sea. 'I came here with my parents. Family vacation when I was ten. It seemed like the other side of the world.'

'It is the other side of the world,' said Ace.

'Distance doesn't exist any more. You never heard of the information revolution? I should've known someone would find us here. When they knew what we had. We were stupid.'

'No you weren't. You did a good job.'

'Don't humour me. You think I'm going to start crying again, right?'

Ace smiled in the darkness. 'Right,' she said.

'We thought we were like the three musketeers, you know.'

'Except there were four of you.'

'There were four of the three musketeers, too. We swore we'd all work together and guard it and make sure nothing bad happened.'

'Nothing bad has happened,' said Ace.

'You really don't know what you're doing, do you? You don't know what you've got.'

'I've got a friend. He knows.'

'I hope you're right.' Calvin picked up a stone and snapped

his arm hard, throwing out into the darkness over the sea. Ace listened but she didn't hear a splash.

There were slopping noises from inside the barrel, as if it was full of liquid. Ace listened to the sound as it was unloaded and carried to the Mercedes diesel van that was waiting by the docks. It went into the back of the van with room to spare. The mercenaries crowded into the front. As far away from the drum as they could get, Ace noticed. The last of the Kurds left the keys in the cabin of the boat for the owner, then trotted to the van and slammed the door. Dfewar leaned out the window and waved to Ace and then the engine started, the van lurched, and they were gone, headlights sweeping across the marina, leaving her in a cloud of diesel that drifted away over the water.

Provided they made delivery all right they'd collect their software and cables from Miss David, who was holding them in Antalya. Then they'd be able to pump the tank computer dry of its secrets. Possibly they'd get some weapons system information.

After the noise of the van had faded the marina was silent. She looked around. Boats lifting gently on the swell. The flat-edged moon, a few nights short of full, glowed above the sea.

From the centre of Marmaris she could easily get one of the small buses that shuttled tourists back to their beach-front hotels. But Ace was still coming down from the adrenalin of the operation on the island. She needed to walk it off. She turned her back on the docks and set off, tired, empty and happy. Her feet slapped the pavement steadily, carrying her forward, a steady rhythm of sound in the soft night.

When the pavement ended she walked in the road. Past half-finished buildings, concrete shells surrounded by rubble. She was quite alone. Her head was pleasantly empty. It would take maybe half an hour to walk to her destination. Another hotel, another night in clean sheets that smelled like mothballs, then a flight back to Europe. Her ticket was already booked.

There were frogs singing in the ditches beside the road, a deeper, more liquid song than crickets. Ace crossed the quiet street, moving away from the half-finished buildings. Then she paused. There was something in the road. A small hunched shape, black under the yellow light of the street lamps. It was lying in the middle of the tarmac. The turtle, or one just like it, shell crushed by the tyres of a car. Ace looked at it for a moment then turned away and kept walking. Then she found herself turning around and coming back. She couldn't stand the thought.

Ace opened her rucksack and pulled out a flashlight. She held the beam of white light steadily on the turtle, hoping it wouldn't move, hoping it was cleanly dead. The turtle was absolutely still. Ace wondered if it had been trying to get back to the sea. She could carry it to the sea again now. It was too late, but she could send it home.

Ace bent down to pick the turtle up, and because she bent down, the steel bar hit her on the shoulder rather than the head. The blow drove her down to the road surface. Grit stinging her cheek. Smell of the tarmac and tyre rubber suddenly close against her face. There was dirt in her mouth, her lip fattened by the impact. Her shoulder was numb and the breath had been knocked out of her. Ace had been in combat. She knew the wound would begin hurting as soon as the initial shock passed. Here she was again. The slow-motion car-crash feeling as time slowed down and she tried to stay alive. Objects were spilling out of her open rucksack. A grapefruit rolled slowly past her face, looking goofy and strange. Ace felt as if she was in the middle of a very stupid cartoon. She knew another blow was coming but she didn't want to move. She forced herself into motion, twisting on the road, and the sharp curved end of the iron bar dug into the oily tarmac a few centimetres from her face. She rolled over and rolled again, then got up to face the man.

For some absurd reason she had expected him to still be dripping wet. But he'd had all afternoon to dry his clothes and get ready. He crouched in front of her holding a bent iron bar that had come out of the construction debris. He moved forward and Ace backed away. Her foot hit something. Her rucksack. She kicked it aside. It went skidding towards the ditch at the edge of the road. She tried to scan the road on either side of her. Had she heard the gun fall out of her pack? In her peripheral vision, under the amber streetlamp glare, she was aware of objects lying on the road. But she couldn't determine what they were. Ace turned her head to look for the pistol and that was when Massoud moved. He swung the iron bar in a sweeping arc. Ace evaded it easily and stepped in close to the man, punching him accurately in the stomach. The bar clattered on the road surface. Massoud was more shocked than hurt. Now Ace set about hurting him. She hit him in the windpipe with the ridge of her knuckles. He made a sound and clutched at his throat. He doubled over, not even looking at her. Ace knew she had him now. She could take her time. She moved forward to hit him again.

Ace never saw the blow. She saw the moon, a streetlight, the road coming up at her again. Massoud was moving very quickly. She hit the road and he was on top of her. For a moment they rolled across the oil-stained tarmac. Ace could smell the salt on him, the sea smell from his long swim. They were too close to hit each other effectively. They wrestled and jabbed clumsily, each reaching back to gain leverage for a blow. Ace felt her fingertips brush against the sharp edge of the turtle's shell. Sharp shell. Heavy body of the dead animal. She could feel the weight and the cutting edge of it in her mind. There was no way she could reach it with her right hand. She had to reach with her left arm. Her injured shoulder burned fiercely, muscle tearing as she began to move. Massoud was rocking back, grunting as she forced him away with the slow pressure of a knee. Her fingertips brushed the edge of the shell again. The pain in her shoulder abated, then came back in a flood. It seemed to rush into her mind.

Ace saw the string of streetlights extending away in the darkness along the deserted road. Massoud had battered her knee away from his chest and was punching at her. The streetlights looked beautiful, clean and symmetrical against the dark sky. Ace could feel herself losing her grip, drifting away. She was fainting. She pulled her arm back and the pain from her shoulder eased. She shook her head and Massoud's punch grazed her skull. She could hear him gasp at the pain in his knuckles. The sound gave her the strength to reach again.

She strained back with her damaged arm, ready for the pain this time. The turtle's shell was rough against her fingers. She clasped it, dropped it, then held it again. She lifted the shell, got a firm grip and held the thing like a killing implement. As she lifted it to hit Massoud he suddenly released her and rolled away across the road surface.

Ace sat up, breathing hard.

Massoud was standing a few metres away. Pointing something at her. A gun. Her gun. Ace dropped the turtle. She wanted to turn and run. She made herself stand her ground. She knew that the instant she turned her back on him he would fire. Massoud took a couple of steps nearer, making no sudden moves that might panic her, in no hurry now.

Ace couldn't think. Her mind had been simplified by fear. She backed away from the man with the gun. She was off the road surface, her feet making a different sound on the gravel and dirt, retreating backwards. The ground gave way under her and Ace fell. She landed on her shoulder and for a moment she thought she was going to faint with the pain. Everything faded. Darkness beat at the edge of her vision. Ace welcomed it. Escape.

But she didn't faint. The sound of the frogs came back. The damp smell of mud came back. She was in one of the drainage ditches that ran parallel with the road. Massoud was walking towards her. At the bottom of the ditch Ace's rucksack was lying in a shallow puddle, just within reach. She put her hand into it. It was empty. There was a grapefruit among some long grass and weeds, skin split, leaking juice from its soft flesh. The broken Vickers helmet was lying beside it. Massoud had almost reached the rim of the ditch. Ace picked up the night sight helmet and clutched it to her stomach. Massoud stopped walking. He stood looking down at her. Then he raised the gun.

Ace thumbed the control switch on the helmet and twisted the broken face plate. A hairline of red laser light crept along the dirt inner wall of the ditch. Ace adjusted the eyepiece, directing the beam at Massoud.

The second blow to the helmet had caused a loose circuit board to settle back into place. The control chip for limiting the intensity of the laser was still dislodged, but the sighting mechanism was functioning again. As the thread of laser light scorched Massoud's cheek the resettled chip recognized the contours of a human face. It analysed the curve of a cheek bone and error-corrected, locking in on where it expected to find the user's eye.

It found Massoud's eye, overshot slightly, swung back and directed its beam straight through his iris.

The uncontrolled laser beam needled out silently, barely visible in the dusty air of the summer night. It went in through the front of Massoud's eye and into his brain, through the frontal lobe and sweeping into the motor and sensory areas.

Massoud saw a brilliant light. It filled his vision. It was the sun over the shoulder of his sister. She was standing on a mound of drought-cracked mud in the resettlement camp, looking down at him with the sun behind her. Massoud hated her. He hated her for letting them put her in the truck that went east while they put him in the truck that went west. Darkness in the truck and the smell of fuel. Hot smell of the plastic seats. When his mother had the fever, Massoud fetched water for her. He carried it in a Coca-Cola bottle, filling it from the tap in the courtyard. His small bare feet slapped on the concrete. His mother stirred with the fever. Her lips were cracked and dry, like the mud his sister stood upon. He picked up the Coca-Cola bottle and ran down the corridor towards the courtyard. The doorway glowed brightly at the end of the corridor. The corridor was long and dark. Massoud ran along, weightless, his feet flying. But the small bright light at the end grew smaller. The corridor grew darker. Massoud ran more quickly.

Ace got out of the ditch, moving awkwardly, favouring her shoulder. Her mouth was dry. Massoud lay by the side of the road, dead. Ace found she was still clutching the helmet. She let it drop back into the ditch. She left the rucksack and everything that had spilled out of it. Now the pain in the shoulder was spreading down to her fingers. Ace couldn't move her arm. She walked back across the bare ground with the abandoned construction equipment, retracing her route towards the lights of the marina and the shopping streets.

She caught a shuttle coach from the centre of town, riding back with drunken tourists and teenage Turkish boys. Ace sat staring blankly, hugging her arms around herself. She stank of fear. When she got out of the coach at her hotel one of the boys shouted at her. Ace flinched and the boys all laughed.

10

Ace slept until the middle of the afternoon, curled into a foetal bundle, lying on her uninjured side. She slept deeply and without dreams, oblivious to the sound of the prayers and hotel construction going on outside. When she woke she went into the bathroom and stripped off the T-shirt she'd slept in. She stared at herself in the mirror. Her shoulder had a wide bruise that extended down her left arm and up the side of her neck. It looked like the map of a new continent. Her tanned skin was pale in contrast to the deep red and purple. It hurt too much to move her arm more than slightly, but nothing seemed to be broken.

Ace ran water into the sink and didn't think about Massoud. She dropped a cake of soap into the sink and watched the water turn a blind milky white, the surface trembling as the taps kept filling. She didn't think about Massoud. She soaked a sponge in the warm soapy water and wiped her body clean, using only her right hand, not thinking about him.

The *dolmus* for the airport left late that evening. Ace killed time packing and reading a battered English-language paperback she'd taken from a stack in the lobby. Most of the books in the stack were about murder. Ace was left with a choice between the complete English poems of John Donne and a slavery-and-plantation-saga. Ace took the John Donne. The book of poems fell open at 'The Anniversarie':

> When man doth die. Our body's as the womb
> And as a midwife death directs it home.

Ace went back for the plantation novel.

This last hotel of Ace's journey was called The Dove. It was located among a cluster of similar square white tourist units in Icmeler, a resort west of Marmaris. Ace bought a chilled bottle of apricot juice in the small hotel bar — three stools, a shelf and a freezer — and sat with her bags in the lobby. She had almost no luggage left now, having shed things at every stage of her journey, then leaving the rest of it last night on the road and in the ditch. Ace read her book and didn't think about Massoud. When the *dolmus* came it was full of suntanned secretaries from the north of England, drinking to kill their depression at having to fly home to the rain and word processing. Ace sat beside a young woman with tattoos and a tee-shirt that had a hologram decal of Alistair Crowley on the front of it. They passed two camels on the road and the woman photographed both of them. In the fields on either side of the road people were labouring, working their smallholdings by hand.

The flight was late. Ace had checked in and received her boarding pass three hours ago. The duty-free shop sold expensive boxes of Turkish delight, cheap computer memory and a selection of spirits. Ace was tempted to buy a bottle to obliterate the waiting. Drink half of it and simply wipe out the interval, wake up when the plane arrived. A new form of time travel. Instead she joined the other passengers stranded in the departure lounge. Their flight had been late out of Heathrow. Unexpected atmospheric conditions.

The airport was echoing and hollow, the occasional announcements ringing off the tiled surfaces, in Turkish then in English. It was three in the morning and the returning holidaymakers looked pale and exhausted under the cruel lighting. Children were crying and in one corner a young couple were having an intense argument, conducting it in whispers. Every face she saw was tired and defeated. Ace sat on one of the plastic Eames chairs as far as she could get from the smell of the brimming ashtrays. Then she lay down on the cold gritty marble floor, airline bag for a pillow. Other people were lying down around her, trying to sleep. The children had stopped crying but the young man from the arguing couple was sobbing quietly in the corner, alone. A squaddie in a grey-blue sweater and a beret tried to strike up a conversation with Ace. She picked up her bag and moved to a new position on the floor. The squaddie didn't follow. He had a downy blond moustache and a rolled-up copy of *Hustler* magazine. Ace lay staring at the airport ceiling. The floor felt good against her back. Infinitely solid.

Ace liked solid reality, when she could get it.

Uniformed guards wandered across the floor, carrying machine pistols, stepping carefully across the sleeping passengers. The departure lounge was silent now. Beyond the wide glass windows there was the black of the sky and the gleaming silver and white noses of grounded jets. Ace was thinking that the blackness was her destination. She'd be flying into it soon. Or maybe it would be blue by then. Ace saw a guard step across her. High above her. He smiled. She was certain he smiled. Ace weighed his smile against his black shoulder-slung weapon and decided the weapon won. Ace saw a pistol in her own hand. Her heart raced, a surge of fear that the guard would see it, that everyone in the room would see it. But the gun wasn't real, only a memory, and her hand was curled on the floor at her side, holding nothing. Her shoulder ached. She adjusted her position without thinking about it. Just a memory. A memory of a man who jumped off a boat. She felt cool metal against the palm of her hand but now it was just a can of beer. She saw explosions on an island and heard the buzzing of a motor scooter which sounded strange when it faded, a hissing just like air escaping from something. She saw carpets with intricate patterns and she knew that if she could make the patterns out something important would be revealed to her. Ace was angry because she couldn't see what he was getting at, the man who was showing her the carpets. Miss David had left them alone while she made sage tea in the back of the shop. The hard floor of the airport seemed to be rolling away under Ace's back, like the swell of the sea. Ace floated, dreaming sunlight on her face under the three a.m. fluorescent light of the airport.

She woke up instantly when her flight was called. All around her dazed passengers were getting up like the recently raised dead, groping for their belongings. Ace walked down the sloping umbilical tunnel to the jet, feeling numb. Tired stewardesses stood in the doorway of the plane, smiling and welcoming passengers on board while jet engines screamed beyond the thin plastic membrane. The plane smelled like hotel carpets and air conditioning. She found her seat and leaned over to the window, trying to look out at the dark airstrip. All she saw was her own breath fogging the plastic.

'I'm sorry but there's been a mistake with your ticket.'

The steward had to repeat himself twice before Ace realized he was speaking to her. People in the seats nearby were beginning to turn around and look at her. She could feel their eyes on her as she fumbled in the overhead locker for her carry-on bag, then followed the steward up towards the front of the plane.

The first-class compartment was a small bubble set into the top of the jet. You entered it by climbing a thickly carpeted spiral staircase. Inside it was dimly and discreetly lit, like an expensive bar, and half empty. Ace didn't have to check her ticket to find out where she was sitting. He was waiting for her, looking up from a book he was reading. She sat down beside him, trying to get a look at the title of the book, but he'd put it away already.

'They serve free champagne up here. You can have mine as well if you like.'

'Thanks for the ticket,' said Ace. 'I assume you were behind that scam.'

'I just asked the airline computer nicely and it upgraded your reservation.'

'Didn't expect you to meet me. I dreamed about you, though.'

'I thought I'd come to see how you are.'

'Knackered.'

'I can imagine,' said the Doctor. 'You've done very well. While I was talking to their computer I checked the cargo manifest. The item you obtained for us is secure in the hold.'

Secure? Secure from being damaged or doing damage? This was news to Ace. She'd imagined the 'item' travelling back by some separate route. A slow passage by sea, perhaps. Now she could see the ribbed grey plastic barrel in the belly of the plane, not at all far from where she was sitting. She suppressed the image.

'You were showing me carpets. In my dream.'

'Really? That reminds me. How is Miss David?'

'She can keep her *ada gayi*. I'm dying for a decent cup of tea.'

'She used to have a different name, you know. She's an old friend of mine.'

The plane was moving now, taxiing for take off. A stewardess patrolled the aisle, checking that seatbelts were fastened. She gave Ace a mechanical smile, her eyes cold. Ace saw herself from the stewardess's point of view. The sunburnt young woman with dirty feet and beat-up clothes, sitting beside the neatly dressed old gentleman, drinking his champagne.

Well, cheers. Ace poured the complimentary champagne into the plastic airline tumbler and drank the bubbles off it. They burned in her nose and throat as the huge aircraft gathered speed, engines audible now through all the first-class soundproofing. Gravity pushed Ace back in her seat, a big gentle hand. She sipped the last of the champagne as the plane came off the runway and kept going, rising into the night.

'In my dream the designs on the carpets were really complex. I was trying to make them out.'

'And could you understand them?'

'Not very often.' Ace set the plastic tumbler down on the high-friction coaster and put the empty champagne bottle into the pocket of the seatback. 'But when I did, I didn't like what I saw.'

'Sensible,' said the Doctor.

11

The slab of stone was split in two. It lay in deep weeds like an open book left on the ground by a giant. One half of the slab was angled on a rise of ground so that it caught the sunlight throughout the day. It was warm to the touch from midmorning until late evening. When you put your hand to its rough surface and pressed hard you could feel a faint vibration. Probably just the blood drumming in your own fingertips, but it was like touching the warm hide of some ancient creature, sleeping under the ground.

Justine liked to imagine a beast buried in the earth. Not buried like the dead but hibernating, sleeping, ready to wake up one day. She enjoyed sitting here on the stone and eating her rations at midday. The slab lay in the centre of a clearing in the woods, high on the slope of the hill. It was a good place to sit, with a clear line of sight through the trees down to the big house below. There were other, smaller, stones and the remains of a wall in the adjacent woods. Justine had studied them and decided that some of them, the newer ones, were merely the ruins of an old farm. The old farm was the best place to be when she wanted shelter, the smells and shadows of the trees. When she wanted to feel the sun Justine preferred the slab.

It was warm now under the torn denim of her Levis. Sitting here she would read poetry, lying back, a tuft of weeds for her pillow. Her disc player ran on solar power and she set it out in the sun beside her head, listening to the few CDs she'd brought with her. Other times she would read the magazines.

Justine was strict with herself about reading the magazines. When she read about the house in them her excitement would begin to grow and sometimes she couldn't contain it. The desire would rise in her to see the house. Not the way she could see it now, from the treeline on the hill. But up close.

Without conscious thought she would find herself walking to the edge of the woods. Once she had even come out of the trees, through the gardens, right up to the old Victorian greenhouse. She had stood there on the overgrown lawns looking up at the house. That had been unwise.

So Justine rationed the reading of the magazines and kept her excitement under control.

The sun was high now and she lay back on the stone watching coloured shapes chase each other behind her eyelids. The shapes were vivid splashes of green and blue on a field of radiant orange. They were unreal colours, romantic colours. Like the colours of tattoos. Justine watched them until it was time to eat. Today's rations consisted of charqui. She chewed each mouthful slowly, trying to work moisture into the tough strips of dried beef. There was almost no water left in her canteen. Tonight she would have to buy some from a village shop. Their rations were holding out well but water was heavy to carry and she'd brought only the minimum with them on their overland trek from London across the North Downs.

The walk had taken them three days. They could have made better time if Justine had been willing to let Sammy off the leash, a crude length of leather she'd fashioned herself and knotted loosely around his neck. Several times she'd seriously considered dispensing with the leash but ultimately decided the risk of Sammy running off was too great. Sometimes Justine wondered if she was cruel, but she always dismissed the thought from her mind. Sentimentality could get her killed.

Justine began to plan the shopping expedition. It would have to wait until nightfall. She kept a watch on the house during daylight. Each evening when the sun went down she abandoned the vigil and went back to her encampment. She read by the campfire while Sammy lay on the ground beside her, whimpering and snorting in his sleep. When the campfire burned low she would put all thoughts of the house from her mind. Even if the opportunity came, she wasn't crazy enough to try to enter the place after dark.

Now despite herself Justine found her thoughts focusing on the house, imagining exactly what she might find in it. She forced herself to concentrate on the shopping. It would have to wait until nightfall and it would have to be a long walk. It was tempting to go to the nearest village to buy water, but she didn't want the presence of a stranger to register with the locals. Word might somehow get back to the house.

Justine chewed the strips of spiced dry meat and carefully planned her walk that night. She would find an off-licence or late-night video and grocery store. She'd buy some food for Sammy in adddition to the water. She wasn't cruel. This morning when she'd left their tent she'd weighed her canteen and poured most of the contents into the old battered tin bowl that Sammy drank from. Now there was only a sip left in the canteen for her and the charqui was dry in her mouth. The muscles in her jaws ached but she didn't mind. She didn't begrudge the water left in the tin bowl. Sammy was tied to a tree by the tents and he'd need it. Lapping it up with his big pink tongue in the noon heat.

Justine swallowed the charqui. It went down a little painfully, but it did go down. Before she unwrapped the next piece she opened her leather ammunition bag and took out the magazines. When she had bought the bag in London the man had told her it was a relic of the Spanish Civil War. But that wasn't why Justine bought it. She bought it for the silver skull and crossbones and the silver lettering that said *Clean Up Or Die*. Inside the bag were the covers for the CDs, the rest of her dry rations and the magazines. She told herself she wouldn't read the magazines yet, but she found herself looking at the covers.

The magazines were thin, forty or fifty pages each. Printed on cheap paper which had begun to swell with damp after a couple of nights in the woods. The pictures in the magazines were all black and white. Some of the covers were in colour, but not the one Justine was interested in. On the cover was a grainy monochrome photograph of an old house set in wide overgrown grounds. Justine looked up from the magazine and through the trees. The photograph had been taken with a long lens, from a position very close to where she was sitting right now. Did the thought frighten her? No. It was exciting.

She leafed through the magazine, glancing at the article that went with the cover photograph. She didn't read the article. She knew it word for word.

Justine unwrapped the second strip of dried meat and put it in her mouth. Her mouth was dry meat too, she reflected as she began to chew. She'd allow herself a sip of water with this one. As she reached for the canteen she became aware of a faint background buzzing. The sound was so constant it was like silence. She couldn't say when it had started or how long it had been going on. It was a fierce buzzing and Justine instantly thought of a machine of some kind. She drew the knife from her boot.

The line of fracture between two halves of the stone slab was filled with vegetation. Weeds, grass and thin bushes had found their way up to the sunlight through the dividing crack and over time had widened it, the massed tiny strength of roots and stems shifting the thousand kilos of stone. Justine moved silently up her half of the slab, crawling over sun-warmed stone mottled with fungus. She couldn't see through the growth at the broken edge of the stone. Justine extended the knife and carefully divided the foliage, taking five minutes to create a gap she could see through. She spent another ten minutes looking through. The sound continued all the time, but as she watched it grew steadily weaker. Finally Justine stood upright and stepped over the bushes to the other side of the slab.

There by her foot was a bee. Its black and yellow stripes reminded Justine of the black and yellow capsule she carried with her, sealed in the locket she wore around her neck. The bee was lying on its back on the hot stone, kicking its legs helplessly in the strong sunlight, buzzing as it writhed. Justine studied the insect for a moment, then leaned forward with her knife held out in front of her.

Using only the very tip of the blade, with utmost care, she gently tipped the bee over. It crawled around groggily, then lay still. Justine considered for a moment then went back to get her canteen. There was even less water in it than she'd thought. It made the pale surface of the stone a deep rich grey as she poured it around the bee, careful not to pour any directly over the insect itself. She kneeled and watched while the bee moved around on the wet patch of stone. For a time it seemed the bee was growing weaker. At one point it stopped moving altogether and she held her breath. Then the buzzing started again, louder than before, and the bee jigged sideways, hovered and lifted into the air. It floated above the stone then shot away like a bullet. Justine smiled. She lifted the empty canteen to her lips and licked a final drop off the screw thread rim. Taste of metal in her mouth. She breathed the residual cool moisture from the dark tin interior. It didn't matter. It was almost three o'clock.

At three o'clock — and then again at seven — it would rain.

The rain began two minutes late, a drumming on the leaves above her. The leaves of her tree. She was halfway down the hillside now, deep in the middle of the woods. Justine had found the ruins on the morning of the second day of her vigil. Not really ruins, just the traces of foundations and two crumbling fragments of dry-stone walls. The trees were thickest here and Justine had found one particular tree that became her own. She estimated that the farmhouse had been abandoned two or three hundred years ago.

There had been a mill here, too. She knew that because of the stone. The big circular millstone which someone had left leaning against a tree one afternoon in another century. Leaning against her tree. A weathered old millstone. It was evocative of an older, saner world. Farms and the sort of farmers she associated with pastoral ad campaigns for wholemeal bread. Justine wasn't fooled. A mill was a machine. It was part of a system of exploitation. A rape that had begun centuries ago and was slowly turning into murder. But there was still a chance to resist. The way the tree was resisting. It was absorbing the stone, the bark slowly enclosing and swallowing it. One day there would be only the tree and you'd never know the stone had been there.

The leaves were heavy with the continuing rainfall, branches bowing down with the weight of it. As Justine moved through the trees some of the high leaves shed water, a secondary rainfall soaking her combat jacket until it was heavy and cold across her shoulders.

The rain had fallen at three o'clock, seeded from the clouds by small aircraft. In four hours they would fly again. Fertilizing the sky. It was a sort of machine, really, a water pump in the sky intended to replenish England's parched aquifers. It wasn't natural rain. And it wasn't working.

Justine grasped a handful of twigs and pulled the branch down to her face. She held it carefully so as not to tear the leaves off it. Rainwater streamed off the waxy leaf surfaces, spilling down to her open mouth. The leaves were soft on her lips and fragrant. The water was cold on her tongue and had a faint bitterness. It was acid rain from the industrial heart of the continent, the Ruhr and Rhine, carried back across the English Channel by the new weather systems. A reversal of the old order. Justine remembered the days when the acid rain had come from England and drifted to the woods of Scandinavia. She thought of days before that when the rain had come at random and you could drink it. Really drink it. Days before she'd been born. The rainwater she was tasting now contained tiny but measurable amounts of cadmium, dioxin, lead, and plutonium. She drank until her thirst was gone. There were some new poisons in her blood now and her life was a little shorter. That didn't matter. Justine didn't expect to live long anyway.

She wiped the moisture off her mouth and smelled her fingers. After a day in the city her fingers always stank. Here in the real world, deep in the wet green it was different. Justine liked the smell of her hands. She didn't like the way they looked though. The crude tattoo Isabelle had done for her at school with a Bic pen. Ugly and blue on the back of her hand. She had long ago acquired proper tattoos.

Her first contact with the movement, the real movement instead of the kids playing games, had come through a tattoo artist who had a damp studio above an indoor market in Hastings. There among the biker posters on the peeling wallpaper, with the smell of vegetarian food from downstairs and the pounding of music through the floorboards. He had showed Justine how he traced the tattoo designs off paper from magazines and the covers of old 33 rpm records. And he'd shown her other things.

Standing in the woods with the rain falling around her Justine thought of Alec and the way she'd felt about him at first. She'd been surprised at his pale skin. Unmarked. No tattoos on his own arms. He'd lacked the commitment. Just as she discovered that he'd lacked the commitment to the movement.

130

She remembered the way he'd looked at first, face close to hers as he put the tattoo on her shoulder with an old electric needle. Then closer still, in bed together. And the way he'd looked at the end, eyes open as he sat on the floor with his shirt off, back against the black iron radiator. After he was dead the radiator had slowly burned deep into his back, sending a smell of cooking meat drifting down to the vegetarian café. Justine sometimes had dreams about that. Sometimes she cried over Alec.

It was quiet in the woods now. The rain had stopped. It would fall again at seven o'clock. There would be another hour of light after that and when the light faded Justine would give up her watch for today. She rolled a cigarette and smoked it. She sat under the canopy of trees, waiting for someone to return to the house in the valley. Waiting for them and waiting for the automatic rain.

12

At Heathrow Ace hung back while the Doctor bartered for a taxi outside the Arrivals building. The Doctor had a knack with taxis. Within five minutes they were riding out of the airport on the back of the motorcycles, diving down a long concrete tunnel and angling low to the ground as they swept on to the curving orbital roads. Armoured cars lined the escape lanes and khaki-uniformed squaddies stood smoking and talking on the grass verges beside them.

As soon as the taxi-bikes were past the airport perimeter, they hit the traffic. A solid column of locked metal, cars extending back along the approaching roads as far as you could see. Some of the lines of traffic were moving. Most weren't. Gipsy-looking roadsiders moved up and down the stalled columns selling food, newspapers, themselves. Ragged children tagged along with some of the roadsiders. A whole subculture that had grown with the traffic problem, their numbers rising in symmetry with the falling average speed of cars in urban centres.

Ace had her arms wrapped around her taxi driver, a Sikh in a red and white leather jacket with heavy shoulder pads. In front of her she could see the Doctor sitting on the back of the other motorcycle. For some reason his hat hadn't blown off.

The bikes reduced speed as they entered the traffic pattern, slowing, dodging, threading through the motionless lines of vehicles. The fumes were thick around them now. They accelerated again, hitting a stretch where there was clearance for the bikes. Ace's driver offered her a mask, holding it over his shoulder, dangling by its strap. Ace shouted that she was all right. They'd be out of the worst of it soon, and she liked to feel the slipstream on her face. The cars on either side of them blurred as the speed of the motorcycle picked up. Ace looked at the endless stalled traffic. Passenger vehicles, giant container trucks; even some of the old-fashioned taxis. The ones that were black cars. Ace could remember when London had been full of them. Some of the drivers in the passenger cars were using phones or watching television. Some had computers on, doing work ready for when they eventually reached their offices. But most just sat passively, their engines churning exhaust and their air conditioning carrying the fumes back in to them. Ace could hear a sound, swept back to her by the wind over the driver's shoulder. The Sikh was laughing. He made a rude gesture at these sheep sitting in their cars, twisted his throttle and they roared away.

The taxis carried them down the old M2, bouncing over the ruts in the broken road surface. The air was clean and Ace was enjoying the cold sting of it on her face when the Doctor signalled, waving his arm in a slowing-down signal to Ace's driver. Ace found herself looking for a place where it would make sense to stop. They'd travelled for about ninety kilometres down the old ruined motorway heading due south. They were in the heart of Kent now, the green hills and afternoon sun a little unreal to Ace. She still felt vaguely disoriented by fragmented sleep and airline champagne. She saw the Doctor tap his driver on the shoulder and the driver hand-signalled. They slowed and pulled over to an escape lane on the left and Ace's driver followed. Up off the weed-grown band of the motorway and along a slip road. Ahead of her Ace saw the red and yellow symbol of McDonald's. The two bikes coasted into the parking lot and switched off.

The restaurant had been built as part of a complex intended to serve the motorway. It was adjacent to a service station and a modular hotel. These were all abandoned now. Ace was looking at the fuel pumps outside the service station, automatically wondering if there was any petrol left in the underground tanks and how difficult it would be to ignite. Perhaps someone had already made use of it. The sidewall of the McDonald's had the distinctive scorch patterns Ace associated with Molotov cocktails. The restaurant had been closed down even before the motorway had died, the traffic siphoning off into the new routes south. Ace remembered the headlines in the tabloids about it at the time.

An attack by Witchkids throwing petrol bombs. The tabloids were still big on the Witchkids and this had been their biggest atrocity to date. Details had been suppressed under the Official Secrets Act, but whatever had happened it was evidently enough of a disincentive to make McDonald's abandon the franchise. Now the place looked strange, its brightly coloured plastic trim holding up well against the weather but most of the glass smashed and the interior of the restaurant burned out and gutted. The wall surfaces had been covered with spray-painted hex signs.

The Doctor was paying the taxi drivers. Both of the men were Sikhs, their helmets especially adapted to accommodate their turbans, official Hackney carriage licences clamped to their handlebars. They stood beside their motorcycles, stretching their legs while the Doctor searched through a large old-fashioned wallet. Ace crossed the parking lot, feeling pins and needles in her thighs, circulation returning after the long bike ride. She looked at the bombed-out building and felt an impulse to go into the darkness and explore. There were dead leaves piled against the doors by the wind. She put her hand to the cool glass of the undamaged door. There was a decal above the handle which read *Push*.

'Watch out for glass,' called the Doctor, without looking around.

Inside there were ragged patches of sunlight on the floor, coming in through the holes in the ceiling. Dirty puddles of rainwater had collected in the seats of the plastic chairs attached to the small tables. From one corner of the roof came the crying of a small bird she couldn't identify. A brittle food carton split and shattered under Ace's foot. In the kitchen area beyond the service counter she could hear something dripping, steadily and endlessly. Bright laminated mini-posters on the table tops still offered Turkey McGuffins and Veal Nuggets. One wall was dominated by a mural of Ronald McDonald in the rainforest, helping the Indians. The dripping was louder towards the back of the restaurant. This was the area where the kitchen staff worked, unwrapping and heating instant meals. There were wide black fan-shaped burns on all the surfaces around the cooking units. The grills were thick with old congealed grease. The glass door of every microwave oven was smeared, as if something had burst during heating. Someone had cooked a final chaotic meal here, before they blew out the windows and set the place on fire. Ace stumbled over an object behind the counter. A child's high chair. She set it upright, the brightly coloured plastic toys rattling as they settled into place on their wire. In an open space on the floor there was evidence of other fires. Crude campfires built directly on the tiles. Ace was beginning to realize that the place had had visitors since the night it was destroyed. Perhaps on a regular basis. Perhaps quite recently. The wind howled around the roof and the rhythm of the dripping changed.

All the spots of sunlight on the floor vanished at once as a cloud mass drifted over the Kentish hills, cancelling the sunlight above the restaurant. Inside Ace was peering at the hex marks on the walls. These consisted of various occult symbols, each particular gang having its own set. It was the fashion to use them to mark the site of a successful attack. Ace studied them, feeling old and a little sad. When she'd been a kid she could recognize almost every spray-painted tag on every graffiti-scrawled wall in her neighbourhood.

Ace identified the sadness. She felt left out. These symbols meant nothing to her. She noticed that one was smaller than the others and more sloppily executed. Leaning close she could see that it had been daubed in something other than spray paint, dark and dull. Ace was aware of the silence now. The wind had fallen, the bird had stopped crying. The dripping had ceased. She stirred the remains of a fire with the toe of her Doc Marten shoe.

The fires on the floor actually weren't so crude. Someone had known what they were doing. This one was a well-built pyramid, wooden brands leaning in against each other, coals or small wood chips and twists of newspaper underneath to get it started. The burned wood had collapsed inward and one blackened piece protruded from the pile, a segment of branch about the length of her forearm. As Ace nudged the dead fire the piece slid out, striking the toe of her shoe. She expected it to collapse to ash. But the brand rolled out of the fire and hit the floor with a hard brittle rattle. It looked like wood but it didn't sound like it. And Ace had misjudged the length of the piece. It was more the size of the long bone in her leg. Now she looked at the remains of the fire more closely. There was something in the centre of it, half buried in ash, the burned wood covering it. About the size of a football.

The sound came abruptly from behind her, rattling off the metal edges of the cooker. A staccato spattering sound like a machine gun. Ace jerked away from the fire, getting ready to run, remembering the tent on the island, even as she realized it was just the sound of motorcycles. The taxis leaving. She turned to look across the counter, out towards the parking lot. Standing there on the other side of the counter, just a metre away from her, was the Doctor. The sound of the bikes echoed on the concrete of the car park and faded away. North, back towards London. Ace stood by the broken cash register, facing the Doctor.

'Do you want fries with that?' she said.

'What does this place remind you of, Ace?'

Ace looked around. Sunlight was coming through the holes in the roof again. The small pools of rainwater in the rows of chairs were glowing cheerfully, still and golden. A paper cup rolled in a draught, ricocheting off the legs of the tables and ending up spinning under a large hex sign by the entrance. She noticed that on the big mural at the back of the restaurant someone had added a rainforest arrow, going through Ronald's head.

'McDonald's,' said Ace.

'It reminds me of a deconsecrated church.' The Doctor walked away to stand in the centre of the restaurant. Ace slid across the counter and followed him. 'Perhaps one that has been put to a new purpose.

'That would be the altar over there.' The Doctor pointed to the scorched kitchen section, with its dead campfires. 'Those are the new decorations.' He indicated the hex signs. 'Spray paint instead of stained glass or carved stone.'

'Some of it's not spray paint,' said Ace.

'These are the benches for the congregation.' The Doctor scrambled across a plastic table top. Now he was standing in the middle of a space on the restaurant floor where several tables had been torn free and removed. 'And this would be . . .'

'The dance floor.'

The Doctor looked at Ace as if he'd just remembered she was there. 'Why not?' he said, and smiled.

'Because you don't have dance floors in churches,' said Ace.

'Depends on the religion,' said the Doctor. 'What do you know about witches, Ace?'

'Witchkids, you mean? Or real witches?'

'What's a real witch?'

The wind had risen outside and blew straight through the open space where the big front window used to be. It chilled Ace. One week in the sun and she'd forgotten about the English wind. 'I just meant proper witches instead of the kids. You know. The Goths, the Witchkids, the Crows.'

'What do you know about the Crows?'

'They did this place over. Some people got killed.' The wind was whistling through the roof again. The paper cup scuttled across the floor. Ace knew what it was but it still made her flinch. She picked it up and moved to one of the tan litter bins in an alcove. There was a sticker on the swinging lid with a picture of the planet printed in green ink. 'We Care', said the lettering on the sticker. 'Some people never pick up after themselves.' The Doctor took the paper cup from her before she could push it into the bin. 'Some people never get a chance,' he said. 'Someone was drinking from this. Perhaps they were interrupted.' He showed her the cup. Empty inside. Clean. But there was a lipstick print on the rim.

For the first time Ace let herself think about the night it had all happened and what it might have been like in this place.

Cars in the parking lot, families inside in the light and warmth. Looking out through the windows at the darkness. And then darkness coming in, smashing in through the window, claiming them. She shivered in the rising wind. 'I'm not afraid of them,' said Ace.

The Doctor smiled. 'Let's go, shall we?' They pushed through the glass doors and out into the big empty parking lot. Ace looked back over her shoulder into the gutted interior of the restaurant.

'Have a nice day,' she said.

Behind the restaurant complex there were giant waste modules with attachments designed to link with the big lifting trucks. The modules had stood here unemptied and untouched since the place had been attacked. There was a heavy smell of old rot around them. Beyond the painted squares of the staff car park there was a wire fence with a high jagged hole cut in it. Big enough for a person to walk through. Ace wondered if this was the way the Crows had come in. The Doctor held the flap of wire for her as she stepped through. She climbed with him up a shoulder of green hillside that rose up behind the complex. The first few metres was lawn that had gone wild, growing long and invaded by weeds. But further up the slope this gave way to thick bushes, nettles and brambles. Ace couldn't say at exactly what point it happened, but somewhere they crossed an invisible border and they were standing in the countryside. She looked back at the restaurant complex. From the brow of the hill the buildings were orderly geometric shapes. Nothing remotely strange about them. Perhaps they were still to be completed, waiting for the grand opening. But nothing bad could ever have happened there.

'Tell me what else you know about the Crows. You know what they've done and you know you're not afraid of them. What else?'

Ace looked at the Doctor. She liked walking with him. She liked having a chance to talk. 'At school, when I was a kid, we were all wearing Chipies and shaving brandnames into our hair. Some of the kids even had them tattooed. You know, like designer names on their faces. The Crows like their tattoos, too. But this is different, isn't it?'

'Yes,' said the Doctor. They climbed over a low barbed-wire fence and entered a field, moving diagonally across it. The grass stung Ace's bare ankles. She was working up a sweat as they walked. In the sky above them a jet fighter climbed, too far away to hear. It left twin white streaks of vapour trail behind it. Further back the neat parallel track was beginning to fragment and blur. It looked like a broken twist of DNA in the sky. They surprised some birds arguing in a thick hedgerow. The birds fell silent as they passed. Ace couldn't see them among the dense twigs and the dusty green leaves. Bright red berries gleamed. 'Are those berries poisonous?'

'They are now,' said the Doctor. He opened his umbrella. Ace joined him, walking close beside him under the shelter of the umbrella as it began to rain. Ace checked her watch. It was right on time. The evening rain, carrying industrial poisons from Germany. It made a steady gentle drumming on the fabric over them.

'I missed the Crows. I mean, I wasn't around when it got started. I was too old. When I first saw them I thought they were Goths. But they were too political. And then I thought they were hippies. But they were too violent.' Ace looked back down again towards the roadside buildings below them. A cluster of trees blocked her view. If she hadn't walked that way she would never know they were there. 'It used to be blues parties or acid raves. Or motorbikes and a fight on Saturday night.' Ace remembered the sound of bottles breaking after the pubs shut. Some of her own Saturday nights, when she was still a kid. A boy lying bleeding and crying on top of a spilled carton of Chinese food. The way everybody ran because they thought the police were coming. Ace had put a handkerchief to his face. It had been a nasty cut, but shallow. She got grease and plum sauce all over her good jeans, her Saturday night outfit. She wondered why she bothered. No blood, though. And the police never did come.

They came out of the field and through a gap in the hedge, the countryside around them looking suddenly sad in the rain. The sky was an odd yellow. On the other side of the hedge was a narrow country lane, trees close on either side, forming a canopy above them. The Doctor closed the umbrella again. 'Almost there,' he said.

'Almost where?' said Ace, but then they walked around a curve and she could see for herself.

At a wide point in the lane a small car was parked, nosed into a tangled hedge. An Austin A35, fifty years old but gleaming as if it was new. Ace didn't know which was more unlikely, finding a car there or finding one in such good nick. The Doctor was taking something out of his pocket. Keys. He turned to her and smiled.

'You drive.'

* * *

139

They drove through small villages with cherry trees edging the road. The pale pink bloom was thick in the October heat. Clouds of shed blossom drifted in front of the car like snow until the heavy rain arrived and soaked it down.

13

The rain made a constant quiet tapping on two of the three windows high on the cellar wall. At the third window it splashed softly, gathering and running in. It was running through the hole Justine had made, smashing the glass in with a brick.

Justine was aware of the noises, listening for any change in the pattern. Her feet were numb with cold. This place was unusually cold, even for a basement. Justine flexed her toes and felt them tingle. The chill was coming up from the icy stones. She walked deeper into the basement, espadrilles slopping on the floor. The power rose around her and through her, transmitted up through the soaked rope soles into the skin of her feet. Like electricity, but heavier and slower. It was prickling deep in her bones already.

Standing here, listening to the rain and the small creaking noises of the house, Justine could feel it coming into her from somewhere under the big stones of the floor. Maybe out of somewhere deep underneath the house. Up through her legs, lingering at the base of the spine to spread across her body along the Tantric lines of power, riding her backbone like domestic current running up cable into the base of her brain.

Now it was seeping into her thoughts. Just a sensation, a hint of disturbance at the edge of her mind. An awareness of another presence in her mind. As if someone else was in the basement with her. It was like seeing something out of the corner of your eye, something that wasn't there when you turned to look at it directly.

Justine knelt and touched the floor. It was formed of big, irregular slabs that had been painted and then layered with years of dust and tool-room oil. Her fingers brushed the old, cold surface. There were shapes there, blurred by paint and dirt and age but still detectable. Patterns of symbols carved in the stone.

The feeling was more intense now. She'd felt like this whenever she'd wandered near to the house. It was the nature of the place. Justine had walked in the shadows. She knew a place of power when she encountered one. Now she rose from the floor. Blood thudded in her brain, making her dizzy. Her vision swam but she could still see it in the light from the broken window.

Justine crossed the cold stone floor. Every step seemed to drive sparks up from her numb feet. The spark stung in her mind. She found herself moving off at an angle, turning away from the thing. She forced herself to face it squarely again and walk directly towards it. It was tall and its shape was indistinct. Someone had draped it with yards of old rotten cloth.

Justine reached out.

Fine embroidered sheets, torn and stained with age. Ivory coloured. Justine stroked the cloth and the tips of her fingers felt strange, suffocated by the smoothness of the material. Silk. Dust stirred and a wiry-legged black spider crawled out of a fold in the silk sheets and ran on to the back of her hand. Justine caught the spider and set it carefully on the floor. Clouds of dust swam as she gathered the sheets into a bundle. The old silk was close to her face with its smell of mildew. She held her breath. Her throat was burning and pulsing with the dust she'd inhaled. She concentrated for a moment, tightening the muscles in her neck, and suppressed the urge to cough. She folded the sheets one more time and threw them into a corner. Only then did she let herself turn and look at the thing which had been under the sheet.

One autumn Justine had hitch-hiked through the Channel Tunnel and on to Paris. She'd spent a week sitting in vigil at the cimetière Père-Lachaise, beside Jim Morrison's grave. She had fasted, living on nothing but black coffee which she drank standing up in the cafés. Standing up was cheapest. She'd fasted partly as an occult discipline, partly out of necessity. Sometimes she stole sugar cubes from the tables of cafés and ate those. Once a boy gave her a different sort of sugarcube and she ate it standing with him at the entrance of the cemetery. That night she was certain that she saw something as she sat by the sacred place, some black leather lizard-king shape moving in the shadows as she sat there weak with hunger.

But that was all.

She hadn't found what she was searching for. Justine returned to England and kept on looking, following clues and rumours. One day she knew she'd find what she was seeking.

A doorway that opened to other worlds.

Now the silk sheet was folded on the basement floor and Justine stood looking at it. A metal box like a deep wardrobe. Thick blue paint on it scarred and blistered. The absurd word *Police* written across the top of it.

Justine reached out to touch the doorway.

'How is the TARDIS now?' said Ace, breaking miles of silence.

'Waiting,' said the Doctor.

'Waiting for us?'

The Doctor didn't reply.

It took Ace a while to get used to the transmission and the brakes felt a little spongy. When the rain started she had a struggle to operate the wipers. But she soon got the hang of the car and she was even beginning to enjoy herself by the time they were nearing the house.

They passed the street sign that said ALLEN ROAD and Ace saw that someone had dabbed white paint on to the second L so that it read ALIEN ROAD. She sighed.

'Do you think somebody knows something?'

The Doctor didn't say anything.

They turned left into the gate and up the long gravel driveway. At the first big curve in the drive Ace had to slam the A35 over hard to the left as a white Transit van came storming past, travelling in the opposite direction, water spraying up from its tyres as it coasted through puddles. Ace was still swearing as they came out of the final curve of driveway and she braked outside the house.

Justine heard both the vehicles, first the van and then the car. By the time the van stopped she was turning and running across the cold basement floor, squirming out of the window, cutting herself on the broken glass. By the time the van was gone and the car had arrived she was past the tall Victorian greenhouse, running across the wet grass of the garden and into the fringe of woodland a hundred yards away from the old house. She stood under the dripping branches and watched.

Ace parked the Austin in the big garage between the Volvo estate and the Saab 96. There was just enough room to get the door open and ease herself out past the Volvo and then the Kharman Ghia. The old stables had been a large building but the cars crowded it. Ace moved through the darkness, between the Kharman Ghia and the workbench. Warm wood creaked around her in the shadows. The scent of petrol made her think of summer and lawnmowers. The Doctor was already out of the car and going into the house. Ace followed him.

There were milk bottles on the steps and a dozen newspapers. 'You forgot to cancel the *Mirror*,' said Ace, but the Doctor wasn't listening. She followed him into the living room and stopped dead.

There, standing in the centre of the Persian carpet, was the grey plastic barrel.

'How the hell did that get here?'

'That white van you saw —'

'Yeah, I worked that out,' said Ace. She went up to the barrel and stood beside the Doctor. He was smiling. That wasn't always necessarily a good sign.

The surface of the barrel was speckled with moisture. Ace wiped a portion of the surface clean. 'But how did you get it through customs so quickly?'

'Diplomatic seals are handy things,' said the Doctor. He circled the barrel, moving quickly on his neat little dancer's feet, unclipping a panel on the smooth plastic side of the barrel. It was like a small door with a compartment inside but fitted so neatly, flush with the barrel's surface, that Ace hadn't known it was there. Inside was a small packet of metal and plastic tools. The Doctor plucked the pack out. He emptied it on to a cushion of the big sofa and discarded all the tools except one, a thin bar of metal curved at one end and sharpened at the other. He used the curved end to prise up the lid of the barrel.

The thick plastic lid came free with a fat wet popping sound. Ace looked away, looking at the peeling wallpaper of the

144

living room, the mottled ceiling plaster, down at the floor. She studied the carpet. It was just like one of Miss David's. Ace rubbed the toe of her shoe against it. Part of her mind registered one of the designs on the nap, rubbed thin by a century of wear. The shape had seemed just an abstract pattern to her before. She had sat in this room on long summer afternoons, watching the dust float sleepily in the air as the sunlight crossed the floor, patiently fading the carpet. Now she could make out the rotor blades and distinctive balance fins of an Odin gunship. Ace sighed and looked into the mouth of the barrel. There was nothing to see. A taut membrane of black film sealed it shut.

The Doctor reversed the small tool and used the sharp end to rip into the membrane. A single droplet of milky liquid shot across the room and landed on the carpet.

Mist drifted out of the mouth of the barrel. There was a smell that was both organic and medicinal. An unpleasant scent of menthol and, under it, a heavy oily aroma like that of rancid butter. When the mist cleared Ace could see inside. A crust sealed the entire surface of the liquid. A thick white plug of what Ace thought at first was ice. Then she realized it was some sort of white substance, like the fat that forms on a rich broth. She felt revolted at the thought.

'What is this thing?'

'Have you ever heard of cryogenics?'

'Like when somebody gets sick with an incurable disease,' said Ace. 'They put them into deep freeze.'

'Yes?'

'And they hope one day, in the future, someone's going to thaw them out and be able to cure the disease. Like Walt Disney.'

The Doctor probed the thick white layer at the top of the cylinder, testing it with his fingers. Ace shuddered. He took a plastic spatula from the packet of tools and looked at her and smiled. 'Except with cryogenics you need a lot of technology and a lot of money. This is the poor man's version. Instead of low temperatures it involves chemicals in a gel which suspend the life processes. You take a durable container, fill it with the chemicals, put the person inside it and seal it carefully.' The Doctor studied the plastic spatula, testing its edge with his

145

thumb. 'The search for eternal life has been a recurrent motif in your cultures. It's a form of insanity and this is one of its more benign manifestations. All you need is a plastic barrel and some storage space and you've achieved immortality. Of a sort. These are very popular in California.'

'I'll bet,' said Ace.

The Doctor was using the plastic spatula to scrape back the heavy white layer. Dark liquid showed underneath. Despite herself, Ace came closer and looked down into the barrel. As she stared down into the dark fluid she saw two blue eyes staring back up at her.

14

At a distance the Victorian greenhouse looked in good repair. When you came up closer you could see the rust eating the iron-work and the missing and broken panes. Thick green tropical plants were finding their way out through the gaps, reaching for the warm autumn air. The rain had stopped but the ground was still damp, soaking through her jeans, making her feel the cold deep in her bones. It was nothing to compare with the cold she'd felt in the basement. Justine sat under a trailing length of foliage and watched the sun go down over the red-brick house. She had gone back to her encampment and put things in order, packing her bedroll and shelter, burying her campfire. She'd set Sammy free and left him behind. He'd tried to follow her and she'd had to throw stones at him until he got the message. She'd abandoned the rest of her belongings. Now she just had the clothes on her back. She was ready.

Justine waited for nightfall, watching the house.

The Doctor had brought a bulky old physician's bag down from the attic. The leather was stiff with age and the bag was difficult to open. Ace watched as he took a wooden tongue depressor from the bag and a blue glass jar. The jar had a handwritten label, the paper yellowed with age, the unreadable inscription scrawled with a fountain pen. The Doctor untied a length of string and removed the cloth seal from the jar. He scooped some gunk out with the wooden splint. The jar toppled and fell to the floor. Ace moved quickly and caught it, but the Doctor didn't even seem to notice. He was back at the barrel, looking down at the boy.

The boy's head was only just submerged in the dark fluid. When the Doctor tilted it back his face broke through the surface. The Doctor put a hand under the damp chin and adjusted the position of the boy's head. Then he pinched the boy's nose and squeezed his nostrils shut.

The boy's mouth opened like a baby bird's. The Doctor put the tongue depressor into the open mouth, feeding the boy the gunk. He stood back, beside Ace. The both waited, watching the boy. He suddenly shuddered, neck muscles and shoulders convulsing. The movement threw back his head and exposed the pale skin of his throat, tight over his Adam's apple. Ace thought she could see the flutter of a pulse in the vulnerable patch of flesh. There was something attached to the boy's neck. A cheap jewellery chain sagged around his throat, disappearing into the thick fluid. As the boy moved something shifted on the chain, floating to the surface. It looked like a leaf under dark pond water. It glittered as it broke surface. It was a metallic-looking dogtag, but so light and thin it had to be some kind of plastic. Ace recognized it as the kind of thing you won on a cheap arcade game, usually the combat simulation variety. The tag floated among the scum on the surface of the liquid. The Doctor reached in and lifted it out. He wiped the gel off the plastic, inspected the dogtag for a moment, then handed it to Ace. There was embossed lettering on the silver-coloured plastic. On one side it said *O Rh + 1794 meso/ akg dlt ugn*.

On the other it said, *Wheaton, Vincent*.

'Ace,' said the Doctor, 'Meet Vincent. And by the way, I'd put on a swimsuit if I were you.'

'Swimsuit?'

'Or go naked. You don't want to get that gel all over your clothes.'

'Why would I get gel on my clothes.'

'It will be almost inevitable when you help him upstairs.'

'Oh, good.'

'And into the bath.'

'Bath?'

'Hot, but not too hot.'

The bathtub was massive, sunken into the black tiled floor. Its wide curving inner surface was a pale ivory yellow, broken only by the daggers of green mineral deposit under the taps, heritage of fifty years of dripping water. The taps squealed and shook, pipes rattling deep in the old house as Ace turned them on.

'Don't let him move around before he eats something.'

'What?' Ace reduced the thunder of water from the taps.

'Sorry,' said the Doctor. 'I was saying that his blood sugar is extremely low. We'd better feed him before he exerts himself too much.'

Ace looked at the boy slumped unmoving in the chair. 'He isn't going anywhere.'

'And by the way, that gel is also a topical anaesthetic. Get yourself under the shower as quickly as you can. Your skin will begin to absorb it if you don't wash it off.'

Before Ace could reply the Doctor was out of the bathroom and gone.

She went back to the boy. Her arms were still shaking with the effort of getting him up the stairs and her shoulder was beginning to ache again.

The boy was sitting in a wicker chair between the sink and the shower unit, naked and pale. He had a towel under him to keep the chair safe from the gunk. The Doctor had been right. As usual. Ace's body was thoroughly oiled with the stuff after wrestling the kid up to the bathroom. She was still breathing hard.

If he'd simply been a dead weight, it wouldn't have presented much of a problem. She could have carried him, even with her bad shoulder. But part of the time he was completely slack, like his muscles were cut, then suddenly he'd move. Leaning against her and walking, staggering along like a drunk. Helping her out. He'd gone halfway up the stairs like that, a good boy, as if his body remembered staircases and how to climb them. Then, just as suddenly, the motor control had cut out and she'd had to grab him before he fell and split his skull.

He stirred now, slumped in the wicker chair. One hand spasmed, settling into an intricate movement at the wrist, fingers dancing. Like a one-handed keyboard player with an imaginary piano.

Then one eye opened, a startling blue, and orbited blindly in its socket before the lid drooped closed again. The kid's skin was bright red in bands across the soft meat of his thighs where the wicker chair made contact, as if blood was moving close to the surface. The rest of his body was still the white of fish meat and shining, greased with the barrel gunk. He smelled like Vicks VapoRub cut with chicken fat and pesticide. And after the odyssey up the stairs, so did Ace. As the Doctor suggested, she'd put on a swimsuit. If she'd been wearing her clothes they would have been a write-off. Panting in the mirror now, in the bikini with her gleaming skin, she looked like a Filipino girl wrestler between rounds or something out of an unsavoury women's prison movie.

Ace leaned on the sink, catching her breath, bracing herself for the effort of hauling him into the tub. She remembered what the Doctor had said about the gel. Already she could feel, or imagined she could feel, the stuff taking hold. The skin at the base of her neck and along her spine had begun to tingle. Her shoulder was hurting but now the pain seemed distant, overlayed with a warm rippling. She felt a little sleepy and waves of slow heat pulsed across her ribcage and the inner surfaces of her arms, where she'd picked up the most gel.

The boy in the wicker chair suddenly gulped, opened his eyes and cleared his throat as if he was about to say something.

For a moment he stared directly at Ace, blank bright eyes locked on hers. Then he nodded, spat a fat wet slug of the preserving gel on to the floor between her feet, closed his eyes and subsided again.

Ace sighed and read the name off the boy's dogtag. 'Bathtime, Vincent.'

By the time she'd settled him into the tub, sitting propped up at one end, the big bath was about ready to overflow. She wrestled with the taps for a minute and finally wrenched them back to the off position. Hidden pipes shuddered and the flow of water slowed to a dribble then a steady irritating dripping. Ace looked at the boy. His eyes were puffy and squeezed shut. He looked authentically asleep. More than that, he looked sightless, blind, born blind like some pale marine creature. She dropped a yellow plastic duck into the water of the bathtub. Not a flicker. The duck bobbed and floated against the pale milky blue skin of the kid's chest as she stripped off her swimsuit, thoroughly soaked in the struggle to get Vincent into the tub. The heavy drenched fabric puddled at her feet. She hooked it with a toe and kicked it across the room. The swimsuit hit the side of the glass shower stall with a loud slap. Ace walked across the wet bathroom tiles and stepped under the shower. When the spray hit her she soaped her elbows and began to sing.

The boy, Vincent, remained sitting in the deep steaming bath, his head nodding slightly with the residual movement of the water. The old faucet dripped, slow beads of water from its mineral-encrusted lip, gathering, hanging, falling into the hot water.

Under pale closed lids the boy's eyes were rolling.

The sound of liquid dripping.

Steady dripping.

Deep in his dreams Vincent saw the droplets gather, wait, fall. He heard the dripping sound.

Vincent dreamed and listened to the sound. It led him through his dreams.

Now the water is dripping from the sponge in his mother's hand. Vincent is ten years old and he has a fever. Nothing seems quite real. His face and forehead are hot. The water drips from the sponge as his mother wipes it gently across his skin. Noises ring around the house in a strange way. They seem to be part of his fever dreams. They echo and the echoes make him feel sick. But they aren't part of his dreams. The sounds are real. They're coming from the living room downstairs. The sounds are voices. His father's voice, loud and piercing. His mother's voice low. Vincent's father shouldn't be here. He said he was going back to university. Going to finish his degree this time. He said he'd never come home. Vincent was holding him back. Vincent's mother was holding him back. Without them he could make something of himself.

But now he's back and the voices are unbearable as Vincent walks down the stairs like a sleepwalker into the living room. His father shouting at his mother. His mother trying to be rational. Father's voice like something wild let loose in the room. Let loose in Vincent's head. His mother's voice like something small, trying to escape. Vincent walks into the living room, walking in his fever dream, just as his father hits his mother. And then his father sees him.

And grabs him, shakes him. Suddenly Vincent is dizzy with

the fever.

And that's when it happens.

That's when the Bad Thing happens.

But it must be just part of Vincent's fever dream, because when he wakes up he is back in his bed, the fever still heavy over him like a damp sour blanket. There are voices now, but they are low and quiet. He walks down the long wooden hall to the bathroom where the voices are coming from.

He sees water.

Water dripping from a sponge.

His mother is using the sponge to clean the deep cut in his father's head.

Now Vincent is standing in the doorway of the bathroom and his father is looking up at him. Water, mixed with blood, dripping from his father's chin.

His father looking up at him with fear.

Water dripping.

Water flowing.

Vincent's memories are flowing like the water. Water running into Mrs Kielowski's swimming pool as he finishes cleaning it. Vincent is fourteen years old now. Sometimes he remembers the fever time and what he did to his father. The impossible thing. Sometimes he even gets the fever feeling. But he represses it, buries it deep. Tries to forget about it. Rain is beginning to fall again, here in Mrs Kielowski's backyard. Drops of it spread ripples in the smooth surface of the swimming pool.

The tyres on Vincent's bicycle had sliced through rain puddles on the way home. His new bicycle, the red ten-speed. Its tyres hissed on the wet road surface.

The shopping mall was on Windacott Avenue, just across from the ruins of the old municipal library. Vincent always stopped there on his way home from school. It was a small development, just the Seven Eleven, a hairdresser's and eight or nine other stores.

But one of those stores was Smartt Software and another was a drugstore with a large magazine and paperback section.

Vincent got his allowance every week on Friday morning. His mom gave him cash from her wallet before she went to work. 'Make it last, okay?' she'd say. Then she'd always smile and he'd always smile back. They both knew the twenty dollars was unlikely to survive that first trip home from school, via Wendacott Avenue. His mother had given up asking Vincent to promise he wouldn't come home that way. It wasn't the money she was worried about, it was the other things. But Vincent was big enough to look after himself now and his mom was just being panicky. She just got spooked whenever she parked in that mall and looked across at the gutted hulk of the old municipal library, so close. Vincent had promised her that he'd never go in *there*, although even the library wasn't that bad these days. It hadn't been really bad since the riots two decades ago, unless you were stupid enough to go in there at night and try sleeping inside or something. They said that Bobby Prescott still went in there sometimes. At night.

Smartt Software was in a row of stores on the outside edge of the mall, opposite Seven Eleven. Vincent chained his bike up outside and automatically looked at the police posters stuck on the inside of the windows of McCray's drugstore, including the latest Bobby Prescott fax. No matter how boring the police department tried to make the Prescott faxes, they were lucky if one stayed up for more than a day before a high-school kid swiped it to put up in his bedroom. Vincent even knew Game-boys who had posters of Prescott up above their consoles. Somewhere in their minds they must know that if Prescott ever found them in an arcade or on a public access terminal, or just walking home wearing a Sega backpack, he'd go after them. But they still got a kick out of having his face up on their wall, looking down on them as they played their computer games, staring out of an official police Wanted fax.

Inside Smartt Software it was air-conditioned and smelled of plastic. Some special kind of plastic they used for shrink-wrapping the games. For Vincent, the excitement always began with that smell. It was Friday and school was over for the weekend. It was June and all the teachers were winding down. No homework. In a couple of weeks there would be two whole months of summer vacation. And now he stood in Smartt Soft-ware, listening to the Brian Eno they always played and smelling that smell. A crowd of older boys stood around the counter, sniggering at the manual for the latest release of MacPet. He casually eavesdropped and heard a couple of names he recognized. Rebecca Cox and Betty Kampinski. Girls at school who had a certain reputation. Vincent edged past them.

He hunted through the bargain bins at the front of the store. It was all cheap Korean stuff. He didn't find anything. He never did, but it was part of the ritual, delaying the pleasure. Finally, when he couldn't wait any more, he walked to the back of the store and went straight to the top twenty rack and pulled it down. They must have had a hundred copies of it. The new Cthulhu Gate strategy software. Not just a supplement or new scenario but a special AI plug-on. You just installed the strategy module in your games folder with all your other Gate software and the next time you played it woke up and started working. Vincent had the twenty dollars his mother had given him plus another ten which was the remains of last week's allowance plus money he'd saved by skipping school lunches.

The strategy module cost $24.95. The box went into the bag with his schoolbooks and then Vincent went into McCray's for a Pepsi and a bag of munchies. That took care of his remaining five dollars and change.

It was only after he'd spent his last cent that he saw it.

It was on the magazine rack rather than among the comics. Vincent later worked out that this was the reason it was still there. If it had been in its proper place someone would have found it and bought it weeks ago. But there it was, among the wrestling and weaponry magazines. A copy of *Talons* number one. *Talons* was the official Cthulhu Gate tie-in comic from Caliber. It was written and drawn by the Gilbert sisters and it was the hottest new comic of the year. Despite an initial print run of half a million it had sold out everywhere, literally within minutes. And everybody who was lucky enough to score the comic was holding on to it, waiting for the soaring collectors' prices to level out before they sold. Even Calvin Palmer, with all his parents' money, hadn't been able to pry a copy loose.

Vincent didn't have a copy. He didn't know anybody who had a copy. And here it was, red and silver cover shining between *Indonesian Mercenary* and *Heavy Metal*.

He picked it up. It was in mint condition. The price on the cover was $5.95.

In his pocket he had two quarters and a nickel.

Vincent pedalled home as fast as he could and as soon as he got home he started knocking on doors. Most of his neighbours had kids of their own and didn't want to pay anybody for yard chores. But Mrs Kielowski at number thirty-seven was a widow and childless and needed her swimming pool cleaned. Two hours of sweat and chlorine sting with autumn leaves falling around his head and Vincent had earned five dollars. He found another forty cents down the back of the couch in his mother's rec room. McCray's drugstore closed at nine. Vincent got there at seven forty-five.

The mall was empty, one last car pulling away from the Seven Eleven. Smartt Software was closed. The streets were dark, solid autumn darkness promising winter despite the hot winds. Vincent thought he was pedalling his bike as fast as he could but as he passed the ruins of the old municipal library he found himself going even faster. The parking lot lights of the building gleamed on poles, casting long shadows of the old iron railings across the road. Vincent shivered as he signalled to turn left into the mall.

When he got into McCray's drugstore the copy of *Talons* number one was gone.

He'd hidden the comic behind a stack of gun magazines where no one else would spot it. All the gun magazines were gone. He asked the guy working in the pharmacy section and he directed Vincent to a woman working on a computer in the stockroom. The woman told him that the gun magazines were out of date. They'd been returned to the distributor. The next issue would be in on Monday — as if Vincent gave a damn about *Small Arms Collector*.

He went back and searched the entire rack. Looking behind every magazine and inside, too, opening them up to check whether the comic had somehow got folded inside. It took him an hour. By the time he was finished the girl at the checkout was clearing her throat and giving him dirty looks. Vincent knew the comic was gone. Two minutes before the store shut Vincent gave up. He walked out. His route out of the store took him past the comic rack. He glanced automatically at the rack and there it was. The red and silver cover. Someone had found it among the magazines and had put it back where it belonged. Vincent just stood staring, unable to move. The girl at the check-out said something sarcastic and looked pointedly at her watch. Vincent jerked out of his paralysis. He paid, taking the money out of his wallet with trembling hands, and put the comic carefully into a plastic bag which he put inside his shirt. He pushed through the door of the drugstore and stepped outside.

'Hi, Vincent.'

Standing beside Vincent's bicycle was Calvin Palmer. If Vincent's mind hadn't been on the comic book he might have realized that there was something strange about the other boy's voice. Calvin's face was pale in the drugstore neon. But Vincent was excited and he was pleased to see Calvin.

'Hey, wait until you see what I've found.'

'Sure. Just come around here a second.' Before Vincent could reply the other boy was gone. He followed him around the corner of McCray's to the section of mall parking lot that was reserved for delivery trucks and employees' vehicles. It was a quiet enclosed square surrounded by the rear walls of stores on three sides. As Vincent walked into it he was only a hundred metres from the main road, maybe twenty metres from his bicycle.

Too far.

Calvin was standing there, waiting for him. There were four other people there, three men and a woman. Vincent didn't recognize the woman or two of the men. The third man he knew immediately. Vincent had reached inside his shirt and drawn out the comic. He was holding it, ready to show to Calvin. Now it dropped from his fingers, cover fluttering open. It lay on the ground, a meaningless flat square of colours. Oil from the asphalt bled into the corner of the cover. Vincent made no move to pick it up.

The third man smiled. 'You've recognized me, haven't you? he said. He was coming closer. 'I guess you've seen the posters,' said Bobby Prescott.

The other men and the woman moved around behind Vincent, blocking the only way out. 'In case you don't know why I'm up on those posters, it's because of the things I do with kids,' said Bobby Prescott.

No one was paying any attention to Calvin and he began to edge away towards the pile of cardboard boxes and garbage cans behind McCray's. Vincent saw Calvin's bicycle parked there. An expensive Ryohin Keikaku shaft-drive model. Calvin was moving towards it.

'I don't do those things with all kids. Just the ones like the Gameboys or the Crows. You know. The ones who play on computers all night.' Bobby Prescott pointed at Vincent. 'Like you.'

Calvin was climbing on the Keikaku now.

'And the ones who ride around on bicycles all day.'

Someone ran past Vincent from behind. The woman. She was on Calvin, pulling him off the bike and throwing him to the ground at Bobby Prescott's feet. 'Like your friend,' said Bobby Prescott. He knelt down beside Calvin. 'We promised your friend that we'd let him go if he found someone else for us. And he found you. But I don't think we will let him go.'

Calvin was crawling away from Bobby Prescott, dragging himself towards Vincent. His head was hanging down and Vincent thought he was crying. But now he looked up and Vincent saw his face and he looked too scared to cry.

'I'm sorry,' said Calvin, crawling towards him.

'It's okay,' said Vincent.

'Before we get started, I'd just like to introduce my friends,' said Bobby Prescott. 'This is Sally and Eliot and Lyndon.' But Vincent wasn't listening to him. Memories were stirring in his mind, like things moving through deep water. Things he'd been unable to face. Memories he'd buried in wasteland in his mind, then flooded with years of innocent thought like deepening water. He'd hoped to keep the memories buried forever, under old water, under heavy ground.

But now they were surfacing.

Vincent was remembering that day when he was ten and he had the fever. Memories coming up from the depths. The big wooden house on Leonard Crescent, echoing with a little boy's fever dreams. Memories surfacing fast. How he'd come downstairs, following the echoing voices. Looking into the living room and seeing his dad hit his mom. Memories and the truth, coming into the light. How his dad had looked up and seen him

157

in the doorway and bellowed with rage. How he'd grabbed Vincent. And how the Bad Thing had happened. Memories coming into the light. Vincent finally able to look at the truth after all these years.

How he'd *made* the Bad Thing happen. How his dad had grabbed him and at the moment of the touch he'd done it.

His father's one big fist had grabbed the shirt of his pyjamas, pulling the cloth up so Vincent's belly was bare and cold. The other big fist in his hair, pulling it hard. Vincent's mother crying over by the table. The mirror and the razor blade flat on the table, the way they always were when Dad got like this. And at his father's touch Vincent had struck back.

The mirror had come flying off the table, skidding through the air like a hockey puck slammed full force. Smashing into his father's head and cutting it open. Laying a big flap of skin bare and then the blood starting. His father crying out and letting go of him. The mirror falling to the floor and smashing, no longer driven by the force that had moved it.

The force from Vincent. From inside his mind.

Now Vincent stood in the shadow of the Wendacott Avenue mall, near enough to hear the traffic on the road but a world away. On three sides the blank back walls of stores sealed him in. On the fourth side, in back of him, three strange grown-ups stood. In front of him stood Bobby Prescott. Vincent's life was about to end and the shock of it brought the memories up. The truth was breaking surface.

Inside him was a power. He could cut and wound with it. It was so big it frightened him. But there was no time to be afraid now. There was no more time for the lies he'd told himself, the years of falsified memories. He could reach out with his mind and touch the world. He could fight.

On the ground Calvin moaned with fear. Bobby Prescott stood looking at them, smiling.

Vincent smiled back at him. Within himself he made an acceptance. He turned around. The other two men and the woman were closing in. The woman was holding on to Calvin's bicycle. Behind them was the open space of the mall's parking lot. Beyond that, Wendacott Avenue and freedom. Calvin was moaning louder now. 'Let's do it,' said Bobby Prescott.

158

Vincent reached deep inside his mind and felt the power there, just where he'd always known it would be. Waiting to be used. Vincent reached down and scooped the power up. He embraced it, feeling drunk with the immensity of it. It rose up like hot air rushing up from a tropical ocean. Rising and stirring into turbulence. The seed of a storm. Vincent let the stormseed spin and whirl in his mind. Spinning like a top. Then he let it loose.

The storm erupted in his mind like thunder exploding over the prairies. Behind his eyes was lightning and the scream of storm wind. Vincent let it sweep upwards from the deepest pit of his mind, moving forwards, gathering speed. He aimed it straight at the two men and the woman, a storm swelling into something bigger. It swept up behind his eyes with hurricane force.

Vincent held his breath, the power transforming, ready to take any shape at all, to perform any act, a ball of pure energy. The Bad Thing was straining at its leash, ready to happen.

But Vincent held on to it, letting the power build, his head snapping back with the effort of restraining the release, the power ready to pour out of him. Bobby Prescott's people were hesitating, as if they sensed something was wrong.

Vincent closed his eyes and aimed it straight at them. He clenched his teeth.

Now.

And he let it go.

And nothing happened.

Vincent opened his eyes.

'What are you waiting for?' said Bobby Prescott, coming up behind Vincent. Vincent heard Calvin dragging himself away from Bobby Prescott. 'Let's get started.'

Calvin made a small crying sound and reached up to touch Vincent. Maybe to apologize. Maybe just to feel some human contact before he died. The two men and the woman were starting forward. Calvin's hand groped blindly forward and touched Vincent's foot.

The touch was like lightning striking. Everybody felt it. The two men gasped. The woman dropped the bicycle. Bobby Prescott said something and stepped back. Calvin closed his eyes, not wanting to watch. He heard the metal scrape of

159

Calvin's bicycle moving across the ground. Then a strange tearing noise.

And then the Bad Thing happened.

'First of all, are you sure Bobby Prescott was there? Are you sure it was him?'

'Listen, if you're going to start doubting what I'm saying then we might as well quit now.' The drugstore girl fumbled in a pocket of her jacket and took out a pack of Camels. 'Because you really aren't going to like what comes next.'

'Okay, okay,' said the second policeman, glancing at his partner. 'Let her tell her story in her own way.'

'It was definitely Bobby Prescott. Right, kid, you saw him?' The drugstore girl looked at Vincent. Vincent nodded. He shifted on the hard metal chair. It wasn't comfortable, but it wasn't meant to be. This was the backroom of the drugstore where they took you if you were caught shoplifting. They sat you down in these chairs and sat themselves down behind the desk and proceeded to frighten you as much as they could before they phoned your parents. Vincent had been in here once before, years ago, for stealing a gaming paperback. Maybe he'd even sat in this chair.

The girl who worked at the cash register in McCray's sat beside him now, in the other folding metal seat. The cops were sitting at the desk.

'So what happened to him?' said the first cop. 'Where did Bobby Prescott go?'

'He made it to the fence in back of the mall. He was real quick.' said the girl. 'He got away. He was the only one who did.' She bent forward as she lit her cigarette and the microphone on the police tape recorder moved on the desk, automatically tracking with her.

'I'd prefer it if you didn't smoke,' said the first policeman.

The girl inhaled a deep lungful of smoke and flashed a look up at him. 'You'd what?' The second policeman looked quickly at the first one. Even to Vincent her voice sounded a little funny.

'Listen,' said the second cop, 'she's doing real good, let her smoke if she — '

But the girl wasn't letting it go. 'You'd rather I didn't smoke?'

she said. She got up from the chair and threw open the office door. The glaring fluorescent light of the drugstore beamed into the dim office. 'Look out there. Do you see that?' Immediately beyond the door was the pharmacy section of McCray's. The first team of cops had taken the body bags away but the wide splashy stains were still fresh all along the floor.

'Okay, smoke,' said the first cop, following the girl out of the office. 'Bobby Prescott gets away. And then what?' The second cop followed, bringing the tape recorder. He helped Vincent to get up and walk.

'And then the thing came after them,' said the girl.

'Okay. And I guess you're still saying this thing is −'

The second cop interrupted quickly. 'We'll get on to all that later.'

'It came after them. Walking through here.'

'Walking?'

'Sure. You've seen it. That head. Two arms. And two legs.'

'Jesus,' said the first cop, grinning and shaking his head. 'I guess when you work in pharmaceutical retail there must be certain perks, huh?'

'The kid saw it, too. Look at him. He's shaking. Hey listen, don't make him look at it again.'

'Too late,' said the cop.

Vincent stared down at the drugstore floor. The bodies were gone but the thing was still lying there, motionless, at the point where all the long dark smears converged.

'It used to be a Ryohin Keikaku bicycle. Now it looks like a sculpture by Modigliani. You know, one of these metal skeleton statues,' said the girl.

The zinc-fusion-plated diamond frame of the bicycle had been stretched, distorted and reshaped into a parody of a human being, about two metres tall. It had long tubular legs and stalks of metal that passed for arms and a stubby torso. The side-pull caliper brakes looked as though they had been melted and resculpted into delicate three-toed feet. The dull metal of the ATB-type pedals had fused into a blunt dagger jut of genitals. But the all-terrain tyres were the worst. They were split open and welded on to the ends of the arms to make huge grasping hands, the sprung spokes stretching out like long sharp fingers.

The tips of the spokes were still wet and red.

'At least, I think I mean Modigliani,' said the girl.

'It looks like one of those stick figure men you draw in that game. What's it called?' said the first cop.

'Hangman.'

'Personally it reminds me of a bad episode of *Jack Blood*,' said the second cop.

'Are you really saying that thing moved?' said the first cop.

'It didn't just move,' said the girl. 'You saw the bodies.'

'Well, it's not moving now. Was that your bike, kid?'

Vincent shook his head.

'Do you know whose it was?'

'The subject is shaking his head, indicating that he doesn't know,' said the first cop, into the tape recorder.

'Just let the poor kid go home, right?'

'Thanks for keeping me out of it,' said Calvin. He stood on the front porch of his parent's house, half in and half out of the door. For a moment it seemed as if he wasn't going to invite Vincent inside, but then he stepped back and held the door open. 'And thanks for coming around tonight.'

'It was good to hear from you,' said Vincent. 'When you didn't show up at school last week I started to get worried.'

'I wasn't feeling too well.'

'I'm not surprised after last Friday,' said Vincent.

'Maybe I shouldn't have run away and left you like that. Were the cops okay?'

'Yeah. I would have run away, too, if I could. You were just lucky. The girl in the drugstore didn't see you. Nobody saw you.'

They went into the kitchen, where Calvin stopped to pour Vincent a glass of mineral water from the fridge, then through into the living room. 'My folks are out of town for the weekend,' said Calvin. 'I thought I'd have a few friends around.' Calvin's living room had a floor plan as big as Vincent's entire house. Sitting on cushions on the floor were Sean, Warren and Guthrie. All members of the Cthulhu Cyber Club. They looked up and nodded as Calvin and Vincent walked through. But they didn't say anything as the two boys went up the staircase to the upper

162

part of the split-level living room.

'The games room is up here,' said Calvin. It was the first time Vincent had been to the house. It was an honour to be invited, something he'd been working towards for years. He wondered why he felt nothing now.

The games room had a couple of computers in it, a clamshell Mac and Sun workstation. 'The Sun's my dad's,' said Calvin. 'He runs his business on it.' In the corner was a big-screen television to interface for games. On the wood-panelled walls were posters featuring some of the most memorable monsters from the Cthulhu Gate gaming modules. Vincent sipped his mineral water. He recognized the white monkeys on one poster. They were one of the most popular software monstrosities, swarming over eager players in the virtual reality of the gaming zone. Dragging you down with damp pink paws and suffocating you. On a shelf over the fireplace there was a limited edition ceramic sculpture of three of the monkeys. Vincent estimated that it probably cost as much as his mom earned in a month. Calvin sat down at the Sun and Vincent expected him to load some exotic software on it, showing off.

But all the boy did was check departure times on an airport database. The screen listed flights to Turkey. Calvin scanned them quickly and then logged off. 'Come on,' he said, leading Vincent out of the games room, down a corridor with doors on either side. 'There's someone I want you to meet,' said Calvin. He paused at one door, looked at Vincent, and opened it. They stepped into a large bedroom which looked undecorated and sparsely furnished after the rest of the house. A guest room. Sitting on the bed was a girl. 'You know Becky?'

Vincent knew her from school. She had dirty eyes and a nice laugh and she read weird European horror novels. Her full name was Rebecca Cox. 'Excuse me a second —' said Calvin, stepping back out of the room as soon as Vincent was inside.

'Hey,' said the girl. Vincent turned to look at her and she smiled at him. Her dark eyes were wide open and luminous, deeply stoned. She had her hand on Vincent's shoulder. Just one hand on his shoulder, touching him lightly. She moved forward and put her mouth on his. As she kissed him she put one arm around him and pushed him back. Vincent felt something against the back of his legs. She pushed him further back and he fell on to the bed. It was the first time Vincent had kissed a girl. She had her tongue in his mouth now and he could taste something she'd been drinking. Something strong and aromatic. Some kind of foreign liqueur, maybe. A taste of bitter crushed herbs.

Rebecca Cox broke the kiss and smiled at him. She drew back from him, still smiling. Vincent wanted to reach up and touch her. Pull her towards him and kiss her again. But he felt a wonderful drowsy lethargy. Reaching up would be too much effort. The girl patted his shoulder and got up from the bed. He could hear her in the bathroom as he lay there on the bed, savouring the drowsy feeling. He heard water running, then the sound of Rebecca rinsing her mouth and spitting into the sink. The bed seemed to be moving a tiny bit under Vincent, undulating, riding smoothly on big soft waves. He licked his lips. They felt numb. He tried smiling and it felt funny, which made him smile even more. Now Calvin was standing, looking down at him. Calvin had come back into the room. When had Calvin come back in?

'I'm glad you invited me over,' said Vincent. When he'd first arrived he'd felt tense. His mom didn't have the kind of money that Calvin's parents had. He'd felt out of place here. But not now. Now he just felt relaxed. He could explain things to Calvin. He could talk to Calvin about anything at all.

'It wasn't me last Friday,' said Vincent. Calvin was staring down into his face. Looking serious, like he was concentrating. Like he was listening hard.

'It wasn't me who did those things. I didn't do that stuff to Bobby Prescott's friends.' Vincent frowned, trying to explain it. The frown felt funny. The muscles in his face felt tight and warm. 'Something like that happened once before, when I was a kid. My old man was hitting my mom. And he grabbed me and I did something to him. I did it with my mind. At least, that's what I always thought.'

Vincent licked his lips. He could still taste Rebecca's kiss. The bitter herbal taste. 'Last Friday at McCray's I tried to do the thing again. To fight back with my mind. I gave it everything I had. But nothing seemed to happen. I thought I'd got it wrong.

164

Maybe I didn't have the power after all. But then you touched me.' His mouth felt very dry now, and that herbal flavour was part of the dryness. 'Then the power came through. And it took your bicycle and it made that thing out of it. And the thing went after that woman.' Vincent winced. 'She was going to kill us and everything, so I guess it was okay. And then it went after those guys. The power made all that happen.' He looked up at Calvin, looking for any sign of disgust on the boy's face. But Calvin's expression hadn't changed. 'You see, I do have this power. But I'm not actually the source.'

Vincent licked his lips again. He was licking them raw. His mouth was so dry he'd have to ask for a glass of water in a minute. 'It's more like I'm a kind of amplifier, Calvin,' he said.

Rebecca Cox was coming out of the bathroom now. She walked through the bedroom and out of Vincent's line of vision. 'Like when I was a kid. Nothing happened to my dad until he touched me. And then my power came out. But it was his power, too. His emotions. Like his anger running into me. I channelled it. And I amplified it and it came back out, stronger. It cut him up with a mirror. The mirror where he chopped his blow. They were always arguing about that mirror.' The bedroom door closed as Rebecca went out. Vincent stopped talking and looked up to see if Calvin believed him. But Calvin still had the same expression on his face. Noncommittal, listening.

'And then when you touched me the same thing happened. I took your emotions and amplified them. Those feelings came out of you and into me. And they came out stronger. And they came out sort of − Oh, I didn't hear you come in.'

The boys from the living room had come up. They were standing in the doorway of the bedroom now.

'Maybe you should all hear this. Three people got killed at the mall last Friday,' said Vincent. 'Three of Bobby Prescott's people. But I didn't do it. You might say I helped. What really killed them was Calvin. His fear and anger. I just had the power to make those feelings turn into something real.' He looked at the boys standing in the doorway, reluctant to enter the bedroom, but coming in slowly. 'All that violence came out of him. I could see it. I could see Calvin's feelings and his memories. Then it went through me. Then it came out. It tore up Calvin's bicycle and built a monster out of it. Then it sent the monster after those people and killed them.'

The other boys joined Calvin and stood beside the bed looking down at Vincent. He felt the strange certainty that something was about to happen. So he spoke faster and faster, wanting to get the explanation out. 'But, you see, it wasn't my fault. Not all of it anyway. That monster came out of Calvin's mind. Because that's the way Calvin thinks. It's the way you guys think. You play those horror games. Demons and monsters on your computers. You're into gore software and Splatternetics. And maybe you believe in those demons and monsters just a little. So Calvin's fear and anger took that form.'

The boys moved around either side of the bed. Calvin and Sean to his left, Warren and Guthrie to his right. 'There's really nothing to be afraid of. There aren't really any demons or monsters, guys,' said Vincent. He said it softly. Then he shouted it as loud as he could. It didn't matter. He was only speaking the words in his mind. His numb lips and dry tongue were incapable of speech. Vincent wondered if he had managed to say anything at all. Maybe when Calvin had first come into the bedroom.

The boys were reaching down to the bed now and lifting him off it. Vincent didn't struggle, of course. Maybe Vincent had been able to make a few feeble sounds to Calvin, or maybe he'd been completely silent, chattering away without saying a word. The whole conversation had been remarkably realistic, but sometimes hallucinations were like that. Hearing his own voice in his mind was no big deal. Vincent felt a little sorry that he hadn't been able to explain things to Calvin, but it didn't really matter.

The boys were carrying him out of the bedroom and down the hall now, two on either side of him, carrying him on their shoulders. Vincent couldn't move at all. The drug had paralysed everything except perhaps his respiratory system. Perhaps that as well — now that he thought about it, he could feel his breathing slowing down. He wondered if he was about to die. The ceiling of the corridor was close to his face as they carried him. He saw cobwebs in the corners of the ceiling and he was pleased. His mom would have liked that. Rich people had cobwebs in their houses, too.

Vincent wondered what the drug was. Its effect was frighteningly pleasant. He felt relaxed and euphoric, even now. The boys were carrying him down the stairs to the living room. Rebecca Cox was sitting there on one of the big cushions. She glanced up as the boys carried Vincent past her, but her only expression was one of drowsiness. Vincent wasn't surprised. She must have ingested some of the drug, too. She'd probably held the capsule in her mouth and bitten into it just before she kissed him, passing the drug across in her mouth. He wondered if Rebecca had been holding lifelike conversations in her own head. The boys were carrying him through the side door of the house, out into the car port.

As they lowered his body Vincent saw that there was a big sheet of plastic spread across the floor of the car port. Standing at the centre of it was a tall grey barrel.

It was the last thing he saw before the drug began to encroach on his field of vision. He lay there on the plastic sheet with the darkness coming in from all sides. But he could still hear the boys talking as they worked on him.

'Somebody cut off his underwear.'

'Let Guthrie do that. He's a homo.'

'Shut up, Warren.'

Sleepily, distantly, Vincent felt his bowels let go.

Distant voices ran musically in the darkness.

'Gross.'

'Shut up, Warren. Careful with that gel.'

A sensation of being lifted. Being placed naked into the barrel. The gel inside the barrel closing over his body, over his mouth and nose. Over his eyes. It wasn't at all an unpleasant sensation. Then he heard the lid being sealed over the rim of the barrel. It echoed through the liquid that covered his ears. The rim of the barrel had a curving inner lip that collected moisture and the last thing he heard was the sound of liquid dripping from that lip. Droplets hitting the surface of the gel and transmitting heartbeat sounds through the thick mixture to his ears.

A restful sound.

The sound of liquid dripping.

Steady dripping.

Now he was hearing that sound again. Irregular splashes of

liquid on liquid.

Deep in his sleep in the barrel Vincent heard the droplets gather, wait, fall. Whatever drug they had given him suspended his vital processes in an interesting way. He found that he was still dimly conscious, floating in the gel. It was the sort of fleeting consciousness you have between dreams in deep sleep. And the dreams came, too.

Some of the dreams were unpleasant.

Other dreams were comforting and cheerful. Like this one.

Vincent was dreaming he heard a dripping sound and that when he opened his eyes he wasn't in the barrel any more. He was in a bathtub full of warm water. In a big old bathroom with a glass shower stall against the far wall. Someone was in the shower, just a pale shape through the misted glass. The person in the shower was singing. A girl.

It was very nice dreaming that he was out of the barrel. Dreaming that he was sitting here in the warm water, listening to the girl sing. But he was terribly sleepy. Time to roll over and find deep, restful sleep. Leave all the dreams behind forever.

Vincent let himself lay back in the warm bathtub, easing his legs further down. He dreamed that his face went under the water.

He dreamed pretty bubbles rising up in front of his face. And he dreamed the warm water invading his lungs.

When Ace had finished washing the goo off herself she took the handshower and aimed it at the floor of the stall. She used the spray to wash it clean. All around her feet there was a thick clinging layer of the coagulating gel. Ace drove it down the drain with needles of water. Her toes were completely numb, as if they'd frozen standing in the gel that floated in the warm runoff. She hung the shower head back on its fixture and slid the glass door open.

The first thing she then was the front door closing downstairs, a boneshaking vibration transmitted through the sturdy joists of the house.

The second thing she heard was the boy in the bathtub drowning.

15

Vincent was having a new dream. The old dream kept trying to come back, the warm bathtub and the choking water, but it was growing more distant. Floating away into vagueness. Now Vincent had a dream that he was back home in his bedroom. It was Saturday afternoon and his mother had just gone up the road to have a few beers with Mrs Kielowski. She'd be gone for at least three hours. As soon as she was out the front door, Vincent went upstairs and locked himself in his bedroom. Now he was lying on his bed, wearing his gaming unit over his head and eyes, booting up some new software with his tongue.

It was a new version of MacPet that was circulating among the grade 9 kids. The computer game displayed colour graphics on the inside screen of Vincent's gaming helmet, filling his field of vision. The opening sequence showed him a stream of beautiful faces of women, movie-star faces, all smiling, all radiant with health. They flashed across his vision, the images changing with almost subliminal rapidity.

Then the screen changed to a background of gleaming red crushed velvet and a menu appeared.

Select hair colour.

Vincent chose *Blonde*.

Select eye colour, said the menu.

Vincent chose *Blue*.

Select behaviour.

Three long menus followed this, with submenus attached. Vincent scanned them and chose *Submissive/zany*.

Select surroundings.

Vincent paused and considered. The options on offer included *Bed*, *Bathtub*, *Tropical Lagoon*, *Elevator*, *Backseat of Car* and *Abandoned Warehouse*.

Vincent selected *Elevator* and set the program running.

Immediately he knew that something was wrong. There was a loud splashing sound, in lifelike stereo, and the image before his eyes distorted, giving an illusion of movement, as if his face was being dragged up through water. And then he broke surface. The computer graphics were amazingly convincing. Vincent stared around himself, the screen image tracking with him in virtually perfect 3-D. The bathroom was presented in beautiful detail, right down to the cracks on the tiles and the tiny froth of bubbles riding the agitated swell of the bathwater.

But, damn it, he hadn't selected *Bathtub*. And here he was, slopping around in hot water with the girl.

And the girl was all wrong. She was lovely and she was naked, all right. But she was dark-haired rather than blonde and she didn't have the standard busty MacPet physique. Water shone on her smooth brown shoulders and her sleek muscular stomach. A dark brown disc of nipple flashed across his vision as the girl leaned over him. She was crouching in the bathtub, dragging him up out of the water. He studied the movements of a smooth brown forearm slick with hot water. The computer graphics really were lifelike. But there was definitely something wrong. Her skin wasn't perfect. Vincent could see a broad purple bruise on one shoulder, a flash of dark hair under her arm as she reached for him.

Clearly this was some kind of cheap pirate software. Maybe a Korean copy of the real MacPet game. And yet, he found it oddly exciting. Vincent decided to relax and enjoy the game anyway. He reached out to touch one small brown computer graphic breast.

He was shocked at the sensation of touching warm taut skin.

And he was amazed at how hard the girl hit him.

The Doctor hurried up the stairs and along the frayed ragged carpeting in the hallway. He stopped and looked in through the open door of the bathroom. The entire expanse of the tiled floor was awash. Ace was kneeling in the half-empty tub, bent over the pale boy. The Doctor cleared his throat and Ace turned to look at him.

'Oh, yes, I forgot,' said the Doctor. 'Be careful he doesn't drown.'

'No shit,' said Ace.

'Is everything all right?'

'Well, he's definitely recovering.' She climbed out of the tub and began towelling her hair. They looked down at the boy, lying back in the old enamelled bathtub, head safely above the water level now. His eyes were shut and thin strings of water were running out of his nose and mouth.

'He's gone back to sleep.'

'Yes,' said the Doctor. 'He'll have intermittent flashes of wakefulness followed by periods of sleep until he recovers fully from the effects of the gel.'

'Which is when?' said Ace. She reached down into the bath-water between the boy's feet and pulled the plug. The tub began to drain with moist gurgling sounds.

'A day or so,' said the Doctor. 'Plenty of time before we leave.'

'Leave?' said Ace.

'Good idea, emptying the bathwater. We'll just let him lie there until he dries off.' The Doctor turned and left the bathroom.

'Leave for where?' said Ace. She pulled on a robe and knotted it around her waist, striding out of the bathroom after the Doctor.

Vincent lay in the drained bathtub, eyes rolling under closed pale eyelids, snoring faintly.

In the living room all the windows had turned to mirrors. It was dark outside now, full night. Ace felt the jetlag and the night on the airport floor catching up with her. Her shoulder was aching in earnest. Her feet were wet on the Persian carpet and she was beginning to feel how cold the house was, a chill settling on her after the shower and the exertion of saving the boy.

'You said we're going to leave soon. Where are we going?'

'New York,' said the Doctor.

'Fair enough. Who is the tumescent adolescent upstairs?'

The Doctor perched on the arm of an old sprung armchair. He reached down under the fat dusty cushions, as if he was looking for something. 'I'll tell you all about him.'

'Good.'

'I'll tell you about him very, very soon.'

'Very, very good.'

'But first I'd best tell you about someone else.' The Doctor tugged something out from under a cushion in the armchair. He passed it to Ace. It was a thin magazine, printed on cheap paper. The title was *Seeing*.

'What is this?'

'Turn to page twenty-seven,' said the Doctor. 'Do you see the photos?'

On page 27 was an article entitled 'A Doorway to Other Worlds?' Three large photographs were set above the text. Ace didn't need to do more than glance at them. 'It's this house. Someone's been up on the hillside.' She looked at the photographs and estimated the position of the photographer. 'Up in our orchard with a long lens.'

'That's right, it was me,' said the Doctor. 'I wrote the article as well.'

' "A Doorway to Other Worlds?" ' said Ace.

'That publication is what you might call a fanzine. It is sold to a certain, small, specific audience.'

'The Crows,' said Ace. 'The Witchkids, that lot.'

'Young people who are adopting new belief systems. A blend of ecological activism with older ways of thinking.'

'What you're talking about is black magic,' said Ace.

'Sorcery, to be more accurate,' said the Doctor. 'In any case, that article was written to appeal to a special kind of individual. It was calculated to attract their attention to this house and to provide them with just enough information to find it.'

'Find it?'

'We have a battle to fight, Ace. The boy in the bathtub is part of it. But so is this other person. They are vital to my plan. I put information into that magazine that would act as a lure to someone with a certain profile of beliefs and obsessions. Exactly the kind of person who would be most useful to us. Think of it as a kind of job advertisement.'

'I don't suppose you want to tell me a little more about the applicant.'

'Well,' said the Doctor. 'They are likely to be violently

opposed to the destruction of this planet. They will be full of anger and aggression, coupled with a belief in supernatural forces. Of course, as a result of this, the person is likely to be somewhat unstable.'

'Oh boy,' said Ace. She sat down in the armchair beside the Doctor. 'Unstable and potentially dangerous,' she said.

'Potentially very dangerous.'

'Well, thanks for telling me. I don't suppose I've got a day or two to catch up on my sleep?'

'I'm afraid not.'

'Okay. When is he turning up?'

'It may be a she instead of a he,' said the Doctor. 'And she's already here.'

'Here in the sense of here in the general neighbourhood?'

'Here in the sense of upstairs in the bathroom.'

Justine wasn't sure if the boy in the bathtub was alive or dead. She leaned over the bathtub and reached out to check for a pulse in his throat. As she did so the boy's hand drifted up blindly and collided with her own. Justine didn't flinch. She watched pale fingers open and slowly close around hers. She felt the chill in those fingers.

And then she felt something else.

Vincent's eyes wouldn't focus properly. He closed them again. The enamelled iron bathtub was cold and hard against his body, but in a strange way it was comfortable. He felt drowsy. He was holding someone's hand and that was comforting. He tried to open his eyes again. His eyelids stuck together, some gummy substance gluing them shut. Then they popped open. Transparent clots of crud swam in his eyes for a moment before his vision steadied. He could see the girl. She was wearing clothes now. No, it wasn't the same girl. This girl had darker eyes and paler hair. Dirty and tangled. She was looking down at him, holding his hand. Her grip tighter and tighter.

Somewhere deep in Vincent's mind the seed of a storm began to stir.

He tried to let go, to relax his hand, but his muscles didn't obey. It was as if he'd forgotten how to operate them. Then he felt a tremor. A stirring of feeling around his knuckles and his fingers, a sensation of unknotting. And he could move his hand again. He pulled hard, tugging with all the strength of his arm, but she wasn't going to let go. The girl felt the jerky movement and just tightened her grip. She was far stronger than he was. Vincent pulled again, then gave up. His head lolled. The girl was no longer in his visual field. Now all he could see was the bathtub enamel, a blank ivory landscape curving away to infinity at the edges of his vision. He closed his eyes.

It was going to happen again and there was nothing he could do about it.

His body jerked. He forced himself to fight back. It was like trying to lift something heavy underwater. He twisted his head, pulling his cheek away from the pleasant cool smoothness of the tub. He forced his eyes open and stared dreamily up at his hand and the girl's, still locked together. He stared at intertwined fingers, his clean and pale, hers dirty and tanned. The girl's fingernails were bitten to the quick. His were long and translucent and softened from the long months in the barrel. He could see them bending back easily where they touched her. He could see the pale blue skin under those nails.

The sensation of holding hands and the colour blue.

Memories stirred in Vincent's mind. They were stronger than the fear. And they weren't his memories.

Feeling a hand in his and seeing the colour blue. And then he seeing something else.

Blue.

Blue shoes.

Tiny blue shoes on tiny feet.

She's very proud of her shoes. She is wearing her favourite shoes. She is looking down, watching her own feet as she walks. Her mother had told her not to do this because she might trip over. So she looks up again, a well-mannered little girl. Looks around herself. The world is huge. Grown-ups walk past, benign giants on incomprehensible missions. Ignoring little kids the way they do. Sometimes you wonder if they even know you are there.

In the bathtub Vincent Wheaton twisted and shook. It was like the time Calvin touched him, but much more intense. Much worse. He felt himself sinking into the girl's memories. *She*

174

is seven. Experiencing the feel of childhood again. *Her name is Justine*. Childhood's simplified desires and the furnace-hot intensity of vision.

Her name was Justine.

A hand was clasping Justine's. Her friend Cheryl. Cheryl was only six but that was all right. She was very grown-up for six and there was no shame in being seen with her. Justine and Cheryl were coming home from school, walking out of the tube station.

Justine loved this moment. The station was made of old concrete, paint peeling off the dirty walls. It was grey and dead and cold and shadowy. But as you stepped out of the station everything changed. There was a burst of green. Trees grew thickly along the streets that led to the station. There were big houses and outside the houses there were trees. The houses belonged to rich people, her father said. When the trees were in leaf there was nothing but green as far as you could see. Justine loved walking under the towering green trees. She could feel the thick weight of leaves above her head. A ceiling of green to protect her.

They had taught her about trees in school, how they drew food and water up into their long bodies, into their graceful branches and leaves. And the way they sucked up bad things and dirt in the air and breathed out clean air.

Justine was walking under the trees. School was over and she was free and she was walking with Cheryl. She loved this moment.

It didn't last long, however.

Halfway down the street from the station you began to hear the traffic. No matter how slowly you walked the trees only lasted five minutes. Today it was less because it was Cheryl's brother's birthday and Cheryl was in a hurry to get home. Five minutes of green, then you arrived at the big road. The road they had to cross every day. Five minutes among the trees, then perhaps fifteen minutes waiting for a break in the traffic.

Today Justine didn't wait. She saw a gap and ran straight across. She was laughing with triumph when she reached the other side. The traffic was an enemy and today she had beaten it. She was standing on the far side of the road, almost home,

175

laughing, but she was standing alone. Where was Cheryl? Justine stopped laughing. She didn't remember letting go of Cheryl's hand. The road was dangerous. Her mother and father told her that twice a day, but they didn't really need to. Justine could feel that it was dangerous. Something to be feared and hated. Now cars sped past her roaring, sweeping their stink over her. A little girl standing at the roadside. Standing alone.

Where was Cheryl? Justine spun around, searching for her friend. Then she stopped.

On the far side of the road Cheryl was standing, laughing at Justine's confusion. She waved at Justine, then leaned out, looked at the approaching cars. There was another brief break in the traffic coming up. Justine looked, too. There was a moment's silence on the road. Fumes danced in the heat, twisting images in the distance. The small bright colours of cars, far off and approaching. The rising sound of powerful engines began to fill the silence.

Justine squinted into the gritty oil-heavy air. The cars were a long way off but they were approaching very fast. Cheryl was looking at them, too. She hesitated, then stepped out into the traffic lane, hesitated again and then stepped back on to the roadside. Justine decided to call to her, to tell her to wait. She took a deep breath of the roadside air and began to cough, the fumes burning her throat and eyes. But Cheryl was back in the road again now, running towards her.

There was a long scream.

But it was all right.

It wasn't Cheryl. It was a car making the noise. It was the *breaks* of the car. Justine's mother had told her the word. Justine never forgot it because she imagined something breaking, something precious which you could never repair again.

Now there was that screaming sound but it was all right. It wasn't Cheryl. It was the *breaks*. The *breaks* stopped a car. They would stop the cars before anything happened to Cheryl. Things were happening quite quickly now. Where was Cheryl? Justine squinted out through the thick fumes, looking out into the road. The long mechanical scream of the car was ending. There was a noise like something hot hissing on a stove. It was the noise of tyre rubber on the road surface. Then a heavy wet sound.

Justine kept looking for Cheryl. Cars were stopping. Other cars kept moving, driving up on the pavement so they could get past the blockage. After all, this was supposed to be the high-speed route out of London. Justine was looking back and forth, twising her neck, blinking her eyes in the blurred stinging air. Then she saw Cheryl. Cheryl was on the same side of the road as her. The safe side. The home side. Very close to Justine. In fact, Justine had seen her several times as she swept her eyes around. But it had taken a little time for Justine to accept that this was Cheryl, lying here just in front of her. To accept that Cheryl could have been hammered into this blunt, bloody shape.

When the ambulances eventually arrived they couldn't do anything about Cheryl. But they gave Justine an injection that stopped her screaming.

In the early hours of the following morning Justine's parents found that her bed was empty. After a frantic search they realized she wasn't anywhere in the house. She was in the garage. They found her standing there, swaying with the sedative, eyes a little feverish. She was staring at the family car and talking about brakes and braking. Or at least, that's what Justine's parents thought.

Breaks will stop the cars.

A ten-pound sledgehammer was best. When it hit the windscreen of a car the whole big slab of reinforced glass crunched up in the middle and released at the edges.

Justine is standing on a bridge above a motorway and thinking about sledgehammers. Justine is seventeen now and desires are no longer so simple. The intensity of vision has been blunted, so drugs are essential to recapture it.

In an empty bathtub in an old house Vincent Wheaton was twisting on cold porcelain. A girl was holding his hand.

And the girl was smiling.

The ten-pound sledgehammer is a weighty fist of metal on a strong wood handle. Your muscles feel good as you swing it up. Justine was swinging it up. Justine swung it at three in the morning until her arms were tired. Running down the car-choked streets of West Kensington. And it feels even better as you bring it down. But there were other methods.

Petrol bombs, for instance.

The kind you make with three tablespoons of sand, a milk bottle and a piece of cloth. The kind Justine had lined up beside her elbow on the concrete ledge of the motorway bridge. Three days after her seventeenth birthday. Watching the endless stream of traffic pouring out of London below her. The Friday night rush. Justine is lighting a match.

Now Vincent writhes in the dry bathtub. Justine holds on to his hand, knuckles white and popping with strain. In Vincent's mind is a firestorm of anger and the image of cars, neverending lines of cars.

But the cars are beginning to burn.

And then the Bad Thing happens.

'Jesus Christ, what was that?' said Ace.

The explosion blew the front window of the sitting room in on the Doctor and Ace. The Doctor was standing in front of Ace and facing her, nearest to the window. His body created an impact shadow, sheltering her from the fine spray of broken glass. She was fighting her way up out of the armchair, the glass spilling from her hair, running towards the front door. The Doctor was already there.

It was pitch dark outside but Ace didn't have any trouble seeing. Flames were rising into the air from a scorched tangle of wreckage on the gravel driveway. From the size and shape of it, Ace recognized the remains of the Saab. There was a hole in the wooden wall of the garage where the car had been slammed through. Ace didn't have any problem working out what had happened because now another hole was punched through the west wall, the Kharman Ghia emerging in a spray of bricks and torn planking. The small sports car went spinning across the garden, tearing lawn, slamming the earth with a wet pounding sound and clawing up clods of mud and grass. It was as if a giant foot had kicked it and sent it splintering through the garage wall. The car tore through a hedge and kept rolling away from the house, towards the orchard on the hillside. It became an indistinct shape, lost in the darkness, but not for long.

The petrol tank ruptured and ignited, first in a twisting halo of pale blue, then in hot orange flame. The car collided with a tree, bounced back and lay still on the lawn, burning.

There was a creaking sound behind Ace. She turned away from the open door and looked up at the staircase. The firelight from the burning Saab shone through the window on the landing. Standing there was a girl in jeans and a leather jacket. The Doctor came back in through the front door and stood beside Ace, looking up at the girl on the stairs. She stood watching them, ready to run at any moment. The Doctor looked at the girl, then out the door at the burning cars, then back at the girl again.

'Excellent,' he said, smiling at Ace.

16

The bedroom had evidently once been used for some other purpose. There were special fittings on the windowsills for mounting a telescope, the kind you had in seaside houses to watch the shipping.

But this house was fifty miles from the sea in every direction.

Fat old-fashioned lead wiring entered the room through corroded lengths of pipe which had been set into the walls, high up, in three corners of the room. At night the wind came through the pipes with all kinds of odd atonal noises. The lead wiring ran along the moulding near the ceiling of the room, lines of wire connecting with the crude pipe ducting in the three corners. In the fourth corner of the ceiling the wires met and ran down the wall in parallel. They ended halfway down the wall, curling raggedly. There was a large stained space on the wall just below where a large piece of machinery had once been attached.

You could get on to the red tiled roof of the house from the windows and Ace had often climbed out there with a blanket to sunbathe. Once she had tried following the wires. They had led her across the roof to a large lump of cement that had been trowelled crudely on to the tiles at the base of one of the chimneys. The wires ran into the lump and disappeared. The cement looked like it had been slapped down in a hurry and there was something simultaneously familiar and disturbing about the shape of the lump. It certainly looked too large to be cement all the way through. It was hard to tell, standing there on the roof with the birds singing and the sound of the wind, but Ace had thought she could hear a faint electrical humming sound. The low buzz of something like a transformer.

Ace had crouched by the chimney, the sum warm on the skin of her back, and studied the cement shape for about five minutes before she came to a decision. She'd wiped sunbathing sweat from her eyes and reached out to touch the cement.

Luckily she'd been able to pull her hand back quickly, before it had been too badly burned.

She looked at the burn now, on the edge of her hand between her wrist and the knuckle of her little finger. A slightly swollen red line of scar tissue. She'd climbed back through the window and gone down to the kitchen. There had been plenty of ice in the refrigerator and she'd spent the next hour with her hand in a bowl of ice cubes, telling herself that on a summer's day like that, with sun bright and constant, a piece of cement could naturally acquire a very high temperature.

'He's breathing too fast,' said Justine.

Ace looked up from her hand, over to where Justine was standing by the bed. The girl was looking at Ace, frowning with concern. The emotion made her look younger and Ace revised her estimate of the girl's age downwards again. At first she'd guessed early twenties. Now she thought maybe sixteen or seventeen. 'Don't panic,' said Ace. She went over and stood beside the girl, looking down at the bed. 'At least he's breathing.'

The boy, Vincent, was lying under a dusty floral quilt in a bed that Ace sometimes used. He was propped up on two fat pillows. His eyes were shut but he didn't look as if he was asleep. He looked like a runner who had just finished a difficult race, lying with his eyes shut, trying to get his breath back. Ace went over and sat in a wicker chair beside a window that was open to the cool night air. Justine stayed by the bed, watching over the boy.

There was an old card table covered with boxes beside Ace's chair. She put her feet up on it now, trying to look casual. She wished Justine would sit down or something, get away from the thing in the bed.

The boy, rather.

Ace remembered the sound the Kharman Ghia had made when the gas tank went. She had spent the last three months restoring the car and had just fitted it with a new automatic Porsche transmission. All that was left of it now was a slug of melted metal cooling under the pear trees.

Justine was standing bent over the bed listening to the kid's breathing. Ace found herself listening as well, and staring blankly at her wristwatch, unable to register what time it said. 'Just relax, would you? The Doctor said he'll be fine. Everything will be fine.'

The other girl didn't reply and Ace made herself look away. She turned to the card table and studied the boxes piled on it. Ace had looked through them once before. She'd found jigsaw puzzles from the 1930s, oddly shaped chunky pieces with garish colours on them. Fragments of movie stars' faces and paintings of country estate gardens. In the other boxes she'd found kids' games. Cluedo, Monopoly, Snakes and Ladders. All from the 1930s and '40s. In one box under a yellowing playing board and a dice shaker she'd also found a miniature pair of Zeiss binoculars. Now she opened a box at random. Inside was half a playing board for some forgotten prewar game and, underneath it, an octagonal-barrelled service revolver with a lanyard attached and five bullets. Beside the gun was a heavy chrome syringe, dried blood crusted in its glass barrel. Ace set the box aside and turned away from the table.

In the daytime this room was spacious and full of light. It had windows on two sides and caught the sun through most of the day. The walls were covered with floral wallpaper of yellow roses. At least, the roses had faded to yellow years ago. There were large patches of damp spreading down the walls from the ceiling, engulfing the pale flower patterns. Ace liked this room in the summer.

She went over and joined Justine at the bed again. The boy's colour was a little more normal now. You could see adolescent patterns of acne around his mouth and on his forehead.

'Hard to believe that he has so much power.'

Ace and Justine both spun around, startled by the Doctor's voice. He came into the room and walked over to the card table. He looked into the box Ace had opened. He picked up the syringe. 'I've been looking for that,' he said, putting it into his pocket as he walked over to the bed.

'What is it, anyway,' said Ace, 'this power?'

'It seems to be an odd hybrid form of psi talent. Telepathy combined with some kind of telekinesis.' The Doctor reached down and put a hand on the boy's forehead. The boy stirred in his sleep and muttered something. 'Vincent has the power to make things happen with his mind.'

'I noticed,' said Ace.

'But he is only a kind of conduit. He channels power from elsewhere. It is the emotions and memories of others which provide the raw energy.' The girl, Justine, was listening carefully to the Doctor. He looked at her and smiled. 'You might say Vincent's power is a kind of midwife's power.' He walked to the door, checking his watch. 'Give him another three hours' sleep, then wake him up. We'll all have supper together.'

'Breakfast,' said Ace, looking out at the night sky. She looked back at the Doctor but he was already gone. The boy rolled over in his sleep, one bare arm flopping over the side of the bed. The muscles in his arms were slack and flabby. He was snoring wetly into the pillows.

'He's an ugly little creep, isn't he?'

'Look within,' said Justine.

'Look what?'

'Deeper than the skin. That's what love is, after all.'

'I don't think we're talking about love here.'

'It's the same thing. It isn't the outer surface that matters. It's the entity within.'

'Entity?'

'The demon that dwells inside this boy.'

'He's not a demon. He's a kid. An American. His name is Vincent, for Christ's sake. His friends probably call him Vinnie.'

'He's a creature of power. A demon.'

Ace sighed. If it hadn't been so late and she hadn't been so tired, she might have let it pass. It was dangerous to tamper with someone's beliefs. People cherished their delusions. But it was late, and Ace was bone tired, and she didn't feel like letting it pass. 'Crap,' she said. 'Crap and superstition. You heard what the Doctor said.'

'He said that for your benefit. Didn't you see the way he looked at me when he said it? Didn't you see him smile at me? He was talking about midwives. Midwives were the wise women. They used the sacred herbs and poisons. They wielded power. He was talking about witchcraft.'

'Maybe. But he was just conning you.'

'He was conning someone.'

'He's using the things you believe in. Demons, witches, all that black magic crap. He knows it's crap but he's using it to manipulate you.'

The girl looked thoughtful. 'Demons. Witches. Black magic crap,' she said. There was a wistful note in her voice, a hint of sadness. 'Well, it certainly is one way of describing reality.'

Ace began to feel a little guilty. It was cruel to attack someone's beliefs. Sometimes they were all a person had.

'Just words to cover the truth,' said Justine. 'You're saying he chose those words because he knows they're a necessary illusion for me.'

'That's right,' said Ace.

'That's the way a sorcerer behaves,' said Justine.

Ace sighed. 'Sorcerer, sure. I thought we were beginning to make some progress here. There aren't any sorcerers, there aren't demons. There is no black magic. I'm sorry if that hurts. I'm sorry if it scares you. But why don't you try wrapping your tiny brain around the concept?'

'He is a sorcerer. He makes realities to accommodate belief systems. He knows you couldn't stand the truth. That's why he had to invent that story about Vincent's powers. All those words like telepathy and telekinesis. Do they explain anything? Those powers are clearly a black blessing. They're conferred by the Lords of Hell for use on this plane of reality.' Justine sat on the bed and took the sleeping boy's hand in hers.

'Plane of reality, right,' said Ace. 'You know, I just feel sorry for you.'

'Don't try and make me angry.' Justine brushed a strand of hair away from the boy's face.

'It seems pretty easy to do. I suppose you believe in elves and unicorns, too.'

'Of course not.'

'Why not? You believe in everything else. You go dancing in the moonlight naked, don't you? Where do you go? Down in Deptford every midsummer? Up on the Isle of Dogs?'

'Have you been there?'

184

'No. And I haven't been to the masses in Blackheath, either. I just read about it in the *Mirror*. I think they're just a bunch of kids with nothing better to believe in. And you're just like the rest of them except maybe you haven't quite gone the full leather-and-death metal trip. You sit around listening to Kate Bush in the forests and oathing to the earth mother. I feel sorry for you.'

'You're right. It is quite easy to make me angry.' Justine looked up and Ace could see for the first time just how upset the girl was. Once again she began to regret what she was doing.

'You didn't have to do this to me, did you?' said Justine.

'Look, all right, I'm sorry.'

'A person's belief system is their world. And it can be a delicate thing.'

'I know.'

'It can be devastating to have your view of reality challenged.'

'I know. All right. I'm sorry.'

'And now you've made me angry. So that's what I'm going to do to you.' She looked up at Ace and Ace found it hard to meet that unwavering dark stare. 'The Doctor. Your friend. He has powers.' said Justine.

'Listen, I think maybe it would be better if we just stopped talking,' said Ace.

'He has power and you know it. How did he account for that power? What did he tell you he was?'

'Let's talk about it in the morning.' Ace went to the window. 'It must be bloody nearly morning now.'

'You have your necessary illusions as well. But in your case they involve science. You don't believe in magic but you believe in machines. So when he explained himself to you, he used your terms of reference. That's the way a sorcerer behaves.'

Ace yawned. 'Why don't you just try to get some sleep?' she said. 'It's been a long night.'

'Let me tell you something about yourself,' said Justine, speaking quietly from the bed behind Ace. 'When you were a kid your favourite reading was science fiction. Maybe books, maybe comics. Space ships, time travel, that sort of thing.'

Standing by the window Ace felt a cold chill along her spine and in the pit of her stomach.

185

'You work from a paradigm of technology. So when he encountered you he offered a description of reality which worked with your terms of reference. Let me guess . . . He said he was some kind of eccentric scientist? A mad inventor?'

Ace said nothing. She didn't shake her head. She didn't dare move at all. Maybe if she didn't move, Justine would stop speaking.

But Justine didn't stop.

'Did he say he was an android? A wise and powerful robot? An alien?'

Now she stopped, sitting there on the bed and staring at Ace's face. Then she laughed with genuine pleasure.

'He's from another planet! That's what you believe.'

'Shut up,' said Ace.

'You don't believe in magic but you believe he's from another planet and you're his girl companion.'

'Shut up.' Ace was turning away from the window.

'And that thing in the cellar. The door. The gateway to other worlds. How does he account for that? A space ship? A time machine?'

'Shut up,' shouted Ace, but it came out as a howl. She lunged across the bedroom and lashed out at Justine. The girl made no attempt to fight back. She just held up her arms to protect her face. When Ace stopped hitting her, she lowered her arms. Her face was flushed but her eyes were calm. Ace stood panting in front of her.

Justine began to undress. She tugged off her shirt and shucked off her jeans. Her eyes were cold and ugly. 'You insulted me and you thought you could walk away unscathed. As punishment I have begun to peel away your view of reality. It was easy.' Justine was naked now except for a tarnished silver locket that swayed at her throat. She turned away from Ace and climbed on to the bed where the boy was sleeping. 'Now get out of here,' said Justine, 'before I tear your world apart completely.'

As Ace fled the room she saw the boy's arm drift sleepily around Justine. Running down the corridor she heard the sound of bedsprings beginning. The sound seemed to pursue her down the stairs.

17

'No appetite, Ace?'

Ace stared at the plate in front of her and shook her head. In the centre of the kitchen table was a large platter with fried eggs, bacon, sausages and fried slices of potato heaped on it. The Doctor stepped away from the stove, holding a heavy black frying pan. He scraped brown crescents of mushrooms out of the pan on to the platter.

'No thanks,' said Ace.

'I'll have some more, sir,' said Vincent. The boy was wearing a frayed velvet smoking jacket which Ace usually wore. His hair was tousled and his eyes were bleary. He wiped a piece of bread across his plate, mopping up a yellow smear of egg yolk.

'He's worked up quite an appetite,' said Justine. She tried to catch Ace's eyes, but Ace refused to look at her. Justine shook her head as the Doctor offered her the frying pan. 'I'm all right,' she said.

'He hasn't eaten anything for a long time,' said the Doctor, watching Vincent. 'And he's going to need his strength for what lies ahead.' Justine nodded, listening carefully to what the Doctor said. She took a last drag on her handrolled cigarette and ground the butt out on her plate.

Ace said nothing. She sat looking out the kitchen window, a small slit high on the tiled wall. The sky outside was a deep dawn blue and birds had begun to sing in the dark garden.

When Vincent had finished the Doctor cleared the table and placed a tin box on it. The box was old-fashioned, brightly painted with a hinged lid. Then he ceremoniously placed a stemmed glass in front of Justine, Ace and Vincent and poured a small amount of red wine into each one. He sat down at the table, opposite Justine, and opened the tin box. Inside were small

187

Italian biscuits wrapped in coloured tissue paper. The four of them ate the bittersweet biscuits, dipping them in the wine and then, at the Doctor's instruction, each of them took one of the discarded wrappers and carefully smoothed it out.

They rolled the squares of tissue paper into cylinders and set them upright on the table. Then the Doctor took out a box of matches and each of them set the biscuit papers alight.

The wrappers were different colours but they all burned the same intense eerie blue-green shade. As they burned, the papers became delicate charred black cylinders which rose weightlessly off the table, ghost husks that drifted up towards the ceiling.

The Doctor looked across the table at Ace.

'Make a wish,' he said.

PART TWO: Detonation

18

Men and women mixed spices and stirred pots of curried goat over open fires. Artisans carved up abandoned tyres to make thonged footwear and hats for foul weather. Hawkers sold bracelets and necklaces, circles of silver jangling on their arms while musicians played strange low-voiced instruments under skeletal trees.

'I've never been to New York before,' said Vincent. 'How about you?'

'Never been out of England,' said Justine. 'Well, across the Channel a few times, to Paris and Amsterdam. But never out of Europe before.'

Vincent took her hand as they turned away from the spattering grease and laughter and scents of the market place. 'That used to be something called The Inn on the Green,' said Vincent, 'before the riots took care of it.'

They walked side by side, occasionally bumping against each other, still a little clumsy with each other, moving deeper into Central Park. Vincent looked at Justine whenever he thought she wouldn't notice. They had been able to take off their breathing masks once they were a few hundred metres inside the park and he couldn't get enough of looking at her.

Justine was wearing her hair in dreadlocks with bright beads fastened in it. Under her eyes she'd pencilled circles of kohl. The beads rattled close to his ear when he hugged her.

When Vincent thought she might see him looking at her face, when he thought he might embarrass her or annoy her, he'd just look at her hands. Small vulnerable-looking hands with bitten nails and dirty fingers. He wanted to kiss her fingers. He wondered how much longer they could spend in the park.

'Won't the others be getting worried about us?' he said. 'The Doctor and what's-her-name. Heart? Queen?'

'Ace.'

'Yeah. They said for us to meet them somewhere on Fifth Avenue, didn't they?'

'Number One, Fifth Avenue,' said Justine. 'Don't worry. We've got plenty of time. I just had to see some trees.'

'I guess it's okay,' said Vincent. But Justine wasn't looking at him. She was watching a pack of boys coming towards them along the footpath. They were jogging in a group, all with shaven heads and sleeveless tee-shirts. Vincent didn't recognize their image. New-style skinheads, maybe. Oi Boys, they called themselves. The Eastern European synthesis. Or maybe it was some new kind of youth gang Vincent hadn't heard of yet. Justine had let go of his hand and was watching the boys.

'Maybe we should go back to the market,' said Vincent.

'I don't think we have time.' Justine didn't take her eyes away from the approaching group. The jogging boys seemed to be heading directly towards them.

'We could run,' said Vincent.

'I'm not running. I'm your bodyguard. The Doctor said to look after you.'

Vincent felt a queasy warm excitement in his stomach. 'Look after me? We can look after each other,' he said. 'Take my hand.'

Justine clasped his hand again, her fingers cold against his. Immediately he began to pick up images. Recent memories coloured with her emotions. They were fresh and raw, flashes of New York she witnessed since their arrival.

The innocent gap-toothed smile of a child prostitute. The same smile on her mother's face, the family resemblance striking, as the mother haggled with a group of soldiers over her daughter's price. The little girl had coloured squares of foil braided into her long blonde hair to make her look pretty. Inside the foil squares were condoms. Her mother was looking after her.

Skyscrapers against a sky the colour of weak tea. Air so thick with hot rolling dirt that you swallowed it instead of breathing it. If you didn't wear a mask on the streets the air choked you, but the masks were expensive. Old men and women tottered past with pieces of bedsheet taped on their faces. There were three neat black patches on those white masks, a small black dot by each nostril and a large one over the mouth.

Cars. Cars everywhere. The taxi drivers were all armed and they advertised their weaponry, stencilled paintings of automatic rifles on the doors of the cabs, to reassure customers and discourage robbery. The Sikhs were the most heavily armed. The cabs also advertised in-car entertainment including well-stocked bars and television, to keep the customers amused while they sat for hours in gridlocked traffic.

Cardboard shelters built in doorways where the homeless slept standing upright.

Dirt that settled, stinging, into your eyes and gathered on your hands and on the bridge of your nose where the breathing mask stopped.

Dogs lying panting under parked cars, trying to get enough air to breathe. Thin cats with fat tumours on their faces prowling on the stoops and in the alleys.

Vincent saw it all through Justine's eyes. He felt his heart beating with her anger. The beating stirred the power inside him. Pressure grew behind his eyes, mounting so fast it took him by surprise. It was getting quicker every time.

The emotion and memories surged out of Justine, fast and unstoppable. They ignited the power inside him. He looked at the pack of boys running towards them.

Vincent let it happen.

It was over as quickly as a flash photograph.

Suddenly the boys were all sitting on the footpath, flat on their asses, coughing and choking. Some crawled into the thin yellow grass to vomit. They showed no interest in Justine and Vincent as she led him along the footpath, walking through their midst. Some of the boys moaned, rocking back and forth uncontrollably, hugging themselves or hugging their friends. Others just sat, staring blankly, their lips moving, like shell shock cases in a psychiatric ward. As Justine reached the far side of the group she began to smile, then she turned to Vincent and laughed. They broke into a run, both of them laughing.

They ran through a tunnel under a low bridge and out again, then off the footpath into a patch of bare trees. As they paused to catch their breath, Vincent reached for Justine. His fingers were in her thick braided hair, drawing her face towards his, when he felt her go rigid. She was staring over his shoulder, looking back at the footpath. Four women in white overalls were walking among the stubs of the melted park benches, examining the piles of newspapers and damp cardboard where the winos slept.

'It's just the Butler Institute,' whispered Vincent. 'They sweep the park every couple of hours.' The women in white were pausing, bending over, lifting up a big sheet of corrugated cardboard. Underneath it was a man, an unconscious drunk or junkie. The women unfurled a stretcher and rolled the man on to it. 'They pick up anything that's warm and breathing,' said Vincent. 'Use them for biostock. Spare parts for the organ banks.' Justine put her fingers on his lips. She kissed him and they clutched at each other, trying to keep their balance, clumsy in their thick jackets as they got their arms around each other. They stood there under a dead black tree with the smell of wet newspapers and methanol all around them. It was a golden afternoon in late autumn and dead leaves covered the park. Somewhere in the bushes nearby an OD was moaning.

'You know,' said Vincent, 'we never really kissed before. You didn't kiss me the other night.'

'We were too busy doing other things.'

Vincent sighed and held her as close as he could. 'You know, the last time a girl kissed me something bad happened. I guess my luck's —'

He looked down at the sharp pain in his arm.

Justine was holding a heavy old chrome syringe. She had slid the needle into his wrist, into a thin blue vein.

Vincent looked up into her eyes. They were as beautiful and as unreadable as a cat's. He looked down again and now there was a flowering of blood in the syringe. As she finished draining it, he looked up again, feeling his muscles moving slowly, sad and slow, looking for her eyes. But her eyes were gone and the world was rushing out from under him.

Justine watched the boy's eyes as they flickered shut. She dragged him to one of the few remaining intact benches, checked his breathing, and left him lying there.

She waited, watching from the trees, until the next sweep by

194

the Butler Institute bio-acquisition unit team found him and collected his unconscious body. Then she left the park, slipping away into the darkening city.

'Everything is going according to plan,' said the Doctor. He closed the door behind him and strolled casually over to join Ace. The door had a sign on it which read 'Employees Only'. He had been inside about ten minutes, according to Ace's watch.

'Fine,' said Ace. 'But what is the plan?' She was looking at a display advertising children's vitamins. It featured an image of a pumpkin-headed humanoid in a greasy old-fashioned black jacket. He was holding two hideously sticky carving knives. His fingers looked like twigs.

'Why don't you tell me?' said the Doctor. 'Tell me how much you've worked out and I'll fill in the blanks.' He turned and walked down one of the long aisles. They seemed to extend for miles and this was just the vitamin section. Ace followed.

'Okay,' she said. 'You need a weapon. Those two kids are the weapon. I don't know what the target is but I can guess.' They were in the homoeopathy section of the drugstore now. A smiling boy in an apron was offering samples of an all-natural toothpaste. 'That girl's got a thing about cars, pollution, the environment. She's a bit psychotic.'

'Perhaps. But she also happens to be right,' said the Doctor. 'This planet is reaching the point of no return. Ordinary people don't have the ability to alter the course of events. Only the big corporations and the very rich have the power to do that.'

'Yeah, but eventually they'll have to do something,' said Ace. 'They have to breathe the same air we do.'

'Not necessarily,' said the Doctor.

'But I'm right otherwise,' said Ace. 'Right?'

'Yes.'

'So tell me why we're standing in the middle of New York city in a chemist's.'

'Drugstore,' said the Doctor. 'Try to speak the language and adopt local ways.'

A man brushed past Ace, not apologizing or even glancing at her. He wore the uniform of a private security guard. 'Are we supposed to meet somebody here?' said Ace. 'Besides

Vincent and Justine, I mean.'

'Yes,' said the Doctor. 'And Vincent isn't coming back. Justine is arranging for him to go directly to the Butler Institute.'

'The Butler Institute. They're the target?'

'Yes. Or, to be more specific, one of their research projects. We have to put a stop to it.'

'Just tell me what I have to do,' said Ace.

'Well, please don't be startled if you hear some alarms go off. Or gunfire.'

'Do you mean there's going to be a robbery in here?'

'It's already started,' said the Doctor.

'And that's part of the plan, too?'

They were nearing the end of the homoeopathy section now, the Doctor strolling as if he had no particular destination in mind. 'Not exactly. But the security guards will send a signal which summons the police.' A girl in a leather jacket was standing, her back to them, staring up at a display that showed idealized endless vistas of rainforest. 'And thanks to modifications I've made to their computer,' said the Doctor, 'we can be sure that a certain specific police officer will get the call. And she will come here.'

'And she's part of the plan.'

'No, she isn't part of the plan. But her partner is.'

'And he'll be with her.'

'No. He's dead, as a matter of fact.'

The girl in the leather jacket turned away from the rainforest display and fell into step with them. 'Am I on time?' said Justine.

'Yes,' said the Doctor. 'I was just saying to Ace that everything is going according to plan.' Two security guards came past them, running along the aisle. 'Did you manage Vincent all right?'

Justine was toying with a silver locket that she wore around her neck. 'I did what you wished,' she said, pressing the edge of the locket. 'But now I must do this.' The locket opened with a click, spilling a large yellow and black capsule into the palm of her hand. There were tears in her dark eyes.

'No!' roared the Doctor.

Justine put her hand to her mouth and swallowed the capsule. 'Forgive me, my lord,' she said. Then she reached out and grabbed one of the racks beside the aisle. Her body convulsed and bottles of homoeopathic mouthwash began to tumble off the shelves. She let go of the rack and reached out towards Ace. Her face was white and the kohl under her eyes stood out in stark black arcs. She took a clumsy lurching step forward and Ace involuntarily backed away. Justine's body folded at the waist and she slumped towards the floor.

'Is she dead,' said Ace, searching for a pulse.

'Yes,' said the Doctor.

'Is that part of the plan?'

'No.'

Then there was the sound of alarms going off.

And the gunshots.

19

'What do you think of it?' The new weapon system consisted of two thick black tubes, connected side by side, with 'Manhattan Police Service' and the Butler Institute logo picked out in thin elegant red. The bee and eye symbol was slightly larger than the lettering.

Mancuso held the gun in her lap, feeling the weight of it across the top of her legs. She studied the magazine-release catch which looked a little intricate and prone to jamming.

'So, what do you think of it?' repeated Breen, glancing across at her.

'Keep your eyes on the road,' said Mancuso. 'And slow down.' They were passing the restaurant where McIlveen had been shot. Breen was looking at her as if he expected some kind of reaction. 'On the road,' repeated Mancuso, and finally he looked away. The police car swayed a little as it accelerated past the burnt-out brownstone buildings, picking up speed. Their red light cut regular slices in the night, sweeping across blank walls and burst windows. Sweeping through pitch darkness where the road widened into wasteland. There hadn't been a street light working in this neighbourhood for ten years. 'Put the siren on,' said Mancuso.

The brownstones gave way to wasteland, a burned-out bus shelter, and then they were back among buildings again. Mancuso relaxed a little. Now their siren made a steady high scream that bounced back at them off the solid old stone faces.

Instead of easing up on the gas pedal, Breen was relentlessly creeping it down a little further.

The new weapons systems were an annual joke. Mancuso had spent three hours that evening waiting outside Research and Development. Waiting to be issued with the latest joke. Every month R&D blew a portion of their annual budget on technology licensed from the Butler Institute. Hastily organized designs were sent to industrial conglomerates in the Pacific Basin where each component was manufactured by the lowest bidder. Then the equipment was issued to the various police services and the Butler Institute got its technology field-tested for free.

'What's that over there?' said Breen. There was an orange glow from a building lot, ahead and to the right. Breen eased up on the accelerator and the patrol car coasted to a crawl. Mancuso studied the building lot through the bulletproof plastic of the passenger window. It was a space of waste ground created by the destruction of a medium-sized office building. Orange light washed out on to the dark pavement through a wide gap in the corrugated tin sheets of the fence. Through the gap Mancuso could make out the tall shapes of vitrification rods jutting out of the earth. Their shadows swayed on the packed dirt. The source of the orange light was a car on its side, a taxi, burning.

Mancuso's fingers were already moving across the rubber keyboard of the dash computer. There was something else there in the darkness, standing beside one of the vitrification rods. It gleamed like metal, dark blue or black. It was hard to tell in the shadows. It had a light on top of it, like the revolving lights on old police cars. Mancuso looked back at the taxi. The windows were cracked but not broken. The interior of the car was a misted, glowing box. There was a dark shape in there. Maybe it was the driver.

As Breen swung back out into the street Mancuso finished typing, logging the location and the general nature of the incident. Just another routine robbery and murder of a cabbie. She flagged the call as urgent. A car would be sent. Help would arrive. Eventually. Now Breen had his foot down hard. Side streets swept by. Mancuso didn't say anything. In the rear view mirror the orange glow was shrinking. They turned a corner and then it was gone. 'Did you see that? On the top of it?' Mancuso had seen it. Black spray paint on the yellow cab roof. The shape that looked like a crooked star. 'Hex sign,' said Mancuso.

'It's going to be a long Hallowe'en,' said Breen.

At the edge of her vision Mancuso registered a change on

the dashboard screen. Above the street map a string of flashing numbers changed colour, amber to dark red. They were now more than half an hour late responding to their own urgent situation. Mancuso realized that her right hand was still clutching the contoured plastic grip of the gun. She forced herself to relax, feeling the grooves that the handgrip had made, moulded deep in the flesh of her palm.

Sometimes the faults in the new guns were subtle and nasty. Sometimes it was difficult to get anyone to test them. Nine years ago, when she was still a trainee, Mancuso had refused a direct order concerning a new gun. Her training sergeant, who hated Mancuso, had tried to force her to use the latest model. Mancuso was a rookie but she knew her rights. When she wouldn't budge the sergeant had been forced to demonstrate the weapon herself. She was now collecting a fifty per cent disability pension.

'So what do you think of the new gun?' said Breen.

Mancuso felt her body jerk minutely at the sound of his voice. She realized that she'd been half asleep. Eyes open, hypnotized by the passing street. Eighteen hours yesterday. Twenty hours on shift the night before. She shook the images of McIlveen out of her head and forced herself to concentrate. She looked at the map on the screen, checking their location against the location of the alarm call. Two glowing dots merging.

The site of the call was a giant drugstore on Fifth Avenue, deep in the centre of the combat zone. Before the riots it had been a fashionable restaurant in a chic neighbourhood. Now the area was marginal slum: games arcades, discount stores, student housing for the Butler Institute. 'Cut the siren,' said Mancuso. She could feel the adrenaline rising, the lift of dealing with a situation. On the street, at night, your back to the patrol car. Sussing the situation and dealing with it and coming out on top.

Breen eased the car to a stop a block away from the site of the call. Mancuso grinned and popped the car door open, swinging it out from its thick rubber seals.

The night was cool and the air was so clear you could breathe without a mask. Mancuso crossed the street, watching for movement. The drugstore was at Number One Fifth Avenue. The government had requisitioned the place during the state of emergency and retained the property rights ever since. Mancuso did a quick sweep along the storefront. These places usually had private security guards, paid to keep a high profile. Where the hell were they?

As she glanced in the front door she found out. A young man in a black uniform lay against the chrome turnstile inside the glass doors. Head slack, bloodstains on his tunic. Mancuso went back across the street.

Breen was busy with the car computer, logging their location and filing a routine request for backup. 'This is way the hell out of our patrol area. Why did we get this call?'

'Ask the central computer,' said Mancuso. 'Take care.' She thumbed the rocker switch on her gun from 'wait' to 'ready'. Breen leaned across the front seat to release his own gun from the weapons rack.

Mancuso kept glancing up to watch the interior of the drugstore as she waited in the entranceway, crouching over the security guard. By the time Breen arrived she had checked for a pulse and used a BT stick on the man. She was just going through the motions; she could see that he was well and truly gone. The triamine level indicated by the BT stick showed that he'd been fatally wounded at least an hour ago. Even the organ banks wouldn't be interested in him now. Breen waited while she closed the guard's eyes. He looked about nineteen. Mancuso moved into the drugstore, Breen following.

The drugstore seemed to occupy about three acres of glaring floorspace. It was split into two levels, ground floor and mezzanine, illuminated by old-fashioned high-consumption fluorescent lights hanging from the yellowed ceiling. You could still see something of the old restaurant elegance behind the shelves and displays. The place had been designed to look like a twentieth-century luxury cruise ship. There were fake portholes visible on the walls behind the government sun-cancer posters.

Mancuso and Breen moved between the shelves of products, crouching low, moving quietly. The only noise was the sound of the fluorescents buzzing and the asthmatic gulping of air filters somewhere. They passed a deserted credit point. No sign of the staff and any late-night customers seemed to have fled.

201

Mancuso scanned on either side of her.

The shelves stretching ahead were stacked with brightly coloured containers for dozens of competing brands of popular medicines. Vitamins, ginseng, herbs. Further back in the store, on the mezzanine, was the secure section. That's where they had the bottle shop and kept the tobacco and different brands of diamorphine and bitter alkaloid. It was the most likely target for a robbery.

Mancuso turned a corner into the skincare department and instantly swept her gun up to shoulder level, clicking the safety off. On the scuffed tile floor she registered another security guard, a woman. With figures standing above her.

As Mancuso's finger tightened she felt resistance on the trigger. The gun's scan was reading no danger. The guard was lying motionless on the stained marble floor with three other women standing over her. Beautiful women in culottes and vests. Milky-skinned, grinning. They flickered a bit as they smiled down at the woman on the floor. A display for blocker cream. Cheap Korean holograms. Mancuso stepped past the imaginary women and over the real one on the floor. She didn't bother with a BT stick this time. The top of the guard's head was gone. She checked that Breen was following and moved deeper into the drugstore.

Mancuso was ready for the next set of holograms. Which was just as well because they were a Hallowe'en display. A pumpkin-head creature with a long knife and two multicoloured grinning hags. They were imaginary mass murderers with a huge popular following. She recognized them from Saturday morning kids' cartoons. Beyond the holograms was a wall full of squat orange canisters. Glow-in-the-dark paint in jack o'lantern spraybombs. Beyond that was the girl.

The girl was moving casually enough, backing away down the aisle. But she was the first real, living person they'd seen since entering the store. That was automatically suspicious. And something about her caught Mancuso's eye. She was dressed conservatively, the way Mancuso herself had dressed, twenty years ago, when she'd run with a gang. Black bomber jacket, black leggings, DMs. The girl was young, maybe teens, maybe early twenties. Hair tied back. The jacket open. Not obviously carrying any weapons. But something wasn't right. Breen thought so, too. He came silently out of an aisle at the girl's side and put his handgun to her head. Polite hand on her shoulder and he was escorting her back down the aisle. Towards the main entrance. As she turned to follow him, Mancuso saw the back of the girl's jacket. A big red letter 'A'. Then a sound came from a few metres away and Mancuso was sprinting, not even thinking about it, gun held braced to her body and ready for use.

Under a Hallowe'en banner was a shelf of seasonal herbs and preparations. Cinchona bark, butcher's broom, tannis. Below the shelf a small man was crouching over something. Another body. The body was a girl, a white kid with dreadlocks and beads in her hair. There were no obvious external wounds but Mancuso could see the kid was dead. The little guy bending over her didn't appear to be the assailant. He seemed to be examining the kid the way a paramedic would. He stirred from his inspection as Mancuso closed in on him.

When the little guy began to look up from the dead girl Mancuso was looking directly at him, looking at his face. A faulty fluorescent tube overhead buzzed, flickering and strobing their shadows a bit. The muscles of the little guy's face were set. He looked angry. As he turned around he should have ended up looking directly into Mancuso's eyes. It was pure instinct that made Mancuso glance away. A spasm of the nerves, like jerking your fingers from a hot pan. She told herself that she was staying alert, checking out the situation around her. But she was suddenly aware that she was sweating under her uniform. Her heartbeat was racing a little.

She forced herself to look back at the little guy, look at him directly. She moved towards him, keeping him in the sweep of her weapon. On top of the situation. Doing the job. Mancuso could bust the little guy. Shoot him if it came to that. No problem. She just didn't want to look him in the eye when he was angry.

'Nice, eh?' The girl was looking at Jack Blood, Heather and Hetty as they walked past. The long curved knife suddenly switched from one of Jack's twig-fingered hands to the other. The girl flinched. Breen didn't blame her. He still got the creeps if he was standing beside an ordinary store dummy. The hologram's gouged-out pumpkin eyes rotated to follow them, a glint of ruby in the darkness of the vegetable head.

'That's Jack Blood,' said Breen. 'That's who my kid wants to be when he grows up.' The hags grinned, mouths opening to show realistic threads of saliva.

'Bloody hell. Kids,' said the girl. She had an accent that Breen couldn't quite identify. She hadn't offered any resistance but Breen hadn't holstered his handgun yet. Breen and the girl walked past a display of cardboard cats, witch hats and ghosts. Dayglo orange vests with 'Trick or Treat' screen-printed on them, so your kids wouldn't get run over by a car when they were out collecting poisoned candy. Breen would be happy to get back into the saner parts of the drugstore. Hallowe'en was the worst, in all sorts of ways.

'There's something I'd like you to see.' The little guy looked as if he was about to move towards Mancuso, get close and have a friendly conversation.

'Take it nice and easy,' she said. She was holding her gun steadily on the little guy but keeping her attention all around them. The little guy hadn't killed the girl with dreadlocks, Mancuso was pretty sure of that. And she still hadn't found any sign of the robbery in progress that had triggered the alarm call. She looked across the tops of the aisles, up towards the secure section of the store.

'That's an interesting weapon,' said the little guy.

'It will blow your interesting ass into the next street,' said Mancuso, studying the mezzanine level. 'Now back away please.'

The little guy moved back from the body of the girl and Mancuso moved forward. 'The upper cylinder is obviously the muzzle and a cooling unit,' said the little guy. 'Now what about the other cylinder? Control system? Have you wondered about that?'

Mancuso bent to the corpse, checking for weapons in the girl's jacket. 'Control and scanning,' she said, keeping the little guy covered. She heard movement, a shuffling sound from deeper in the store.

'There's something I really think you should see,' said the little guy.

'Just shut up,' said Mancuso, concentrating on the sound. It was coming from above. Something big, being dragged. The sound stopped and Mancuso's full attention returned to the little guy. 'Turn around and spread your arms. I'm going to do a body search. While I do it you read your rights off this card. Do you read Spanish, Portuguese, English, Gujarati or Patois?' Mancuso took a card out of her jacket pocket.

'Yes,' said the little guy, turning and spreading his arms. Mancuso flicked her wrist, sending the card skimming across the shiny stone floor. It was sliding towards the little guy's feet when the explosion came.

Mancuso spun. The noise was coming from above again, from the secure section. A vast shattering and crashing. Too extended to be an explosion. Like a ton of glass breaking. Even as Mancuso was turning she saw movement out of the corner of her eye.

The little guy was making a break. She couldn't believe how quickly he moved. As Mancuso cursed and started to run he was already three aisles away, turning a corner. Moving through the kids' section he grabbed something off one of the shelves. Mancuso checked the shelf as she ran past in pursuit. He'd taken one of the pumpkin canisters. A spraybomb of paint. Mancuso hated that stuff. Her apartment building was covered by a layer of paintbomb graffiti about a centimetre thick. And it all glowed in the dark.

The little guy slammed through a swinging door marked 'Employees Only' and Mancuso followed. Through a broad room partitioned into office cubicles, chipboard dividers and workstations, then a narrow room with tables and food machines, street clothes and street masks hanging on wall hooks. There was the sound of a crash bar being hit and another door opening. Mancuso got to it just as the door was closing on its pneumatic lever. It led down concrete stairs into darkness. Mancuso hesitated then stepped through.

The steps descended to the loading bay behind the store. Mancuso felt for the pressure pads beside the door that should have controlled the lights. She jabbed at the rubberized indentations. Nothing happened. As she moved down the steps small fragments of broken glass ground under her boots. Someone had smashed the lights. Mancuso stood motionless, holding her gun out in front of her. She realized that she hadn't been briefed on how to work the infrared on it. Down below her was the loading bay, a wide concrete space opening into darkness. Mancuso began to descend.

The loading bay was a big rectangular area with a sloping ramp that led out to street level. No light came in from the street because the ramp curved sharply as it descended. The street entrance was out of sight from the loading bay itself. But as Mancuso's eyes adjusted she realized that there was light coming from somewhere. A small patch of milky green glowing in the darkness. Moving in on it she realized it was a splash of graffiti. Fresh. From that spraycan the little guy had grabbed. The landing bay was silent. From the other end of the curving cement tunnel she could hear faint traffic sound. Like sea noises in a shell.

The glowing graffiti grew in the darkness as she moved towards it, assuming shape and scale. It was sprayed on the side of a massive bulky object in the centre of the loading bay floor. Mancuso walked towards the glowing mark, eyes fixed on it, wading through the darkness. Her boot hit something on the floor and she stopped and reached down. Her fingers curled around spokes, brushed across curved rubber, sharp edges of a finned metal block, the smooth bulk of plastic and padding. Mancuso stepped around the motorcycle and kept moving.

The graffiti was sharp and clear now, glowing in spooky Hallowe'en green. Not a word or a tag, just a single symbol. Not a hex sign. A long curved loop ending in a dot: '?'

Mancuso studied the glowing question mark on the crest of the big shape in the darkness. The shape was big enough to be a garbage module waiting for collection. Far too big to be a car. The wrong shape for a van or truck. She approached, moving cautiously, and reached up to touch the paint and see if it was still wet. As she reached, before her fingers even made contact, she realized what the thing was.

In the faint glow of the luminous paint she could make out the surface of the surrounding metal. It had a familiar pattern of grooves and hollows in it. Mancuso began to grin in the darkness. She rubbed her hand across the high curved surface until she found the familiar dimple. Her fingers locked around the recessed grab bar and she pulled herself up, her foot lifting in the darkness and finding the rubber step where she knew it would be.

Careful not to make any noise on the metal surface, Mancuso released the grab bar and knelt on the curved top surface of the big metal box. Her fingers traced the fine grooving on the surface that outlined a big square, about half a metre on each side. She touched the lock mechanism lightly, resisting the urge to press down on it. She remembered quite vividly how much noise the hatch would make if it wasn't oiled. And they never were oiled. Besides, if they had any brains it would be locked securely from the inside.

Mancuso set her gun down, gently, remembering how alert she used to be for noises on the roof. She moved forward both hands free. She looked down at the hatch, the spray-painted question mark glowing on it, dead centre. Maybe she should try to open it after all. It might be unlocked. There might not be anybody inside.

And then the ghost-green question mark began to slide, rising up into the air. Mancuso's heart slammed and she leaned back, reaching for her gun. The question mark rose and tilted as the metal surface rose and tilted beneath it. Mancuso's arm strained. She didn't dare move her body. She never should have moved so far from her weapon. Her finger tips brushed the cylindrical barrel of the gun.

The glowing question mark was rising silently as the hatch opened. The bastards must have drowned the release catch in oil. A dull glow spread out from under the hatch as the inner shield was swung back. The head and shoulders of a big man became visible, emerging from under the hatch, dim cabin light behind him. Mancuso grabbed for her gun and knocked the barrel to one side. It slid along the metal roof, sliding away, out of her reach, rasping as it followed the curved metal surface, sliding and falling towards the concrete floor three metres below.

While the gun was still in midair Mancuso stood up, stepped forward and put her combat boot on to the chest of the man who was coming out of the hatch. She put all her weight on her foot and pushed, driving him back through the hatch. As he fell she put her other foot on his head and followed him down.

The interior of the hovercraft was cramped and shadowy, lit only by the pale fluorescence of the screens at the weapons station and the pilot station. Mancuso landed more or less on top of the man. He was wearing a ribbed biker's jacket and an open-necked shirt. Now that the surprise was over he was reacting, fighting back, and he was strong. Mancuso could smell peppermint on his breath and the leather of his jacket.

There was a knife sheath sewn on to the sleeve of his jacket, a carved bone handle protruding from it. Mancuso let the man reach for it, right arm going for left sleeve, and while his hand was exposed she broke his wrist. It didn't even slow the man down. He was on some kind of powerful dexedrine analogue, blocking out pain and speeding up his reaction time. His pupils were open wide and his eyes as flat and glassy as a doll's eyes. As his broken wrist dragged down he simply reached across, left to right, and pulled the other knife out of the other sleeve.

Ambidextrous was the word that registered in Mancuso's head as she backed away, slithering across the floor, the knife lashing out at her.

They were both on their feet now, crouching in the confines of the hovercraft cabin. Neither of them moved. He held the knife so that the blade was flat, parallel to the floor, angled to slide easily between her ribs. Mancuso watched his eyes, waiting for a sign that would prefigure action, though she was so wired she might have been better off watching his feet.

The cabin was hot. It always was, despite the clumsy mass of air-conditioning equipment that jutted down from the ceiling. Mancuso began to move, neither towards the man nor away from him. To one side. Circling in the small cabin space. The man circled with her. Now she was at the front of the cabin, by the control panel and the pilot's seat, and he was at the rear by the air conditioning. Mancuso reached down and put her hand on the pilot's seat, as if for support. She slid her fingers down and hit the adjustment lever and pulled hard. The detachable seat back came away in her hands and she threw it straight at the man.

Moving with fantastic drugged speed and grace, the man darted to one side, the seatback missing him completely. But he jumped straight into the air conditioning, head slamming hard against the ceiling-mounted unit. Mancuso knew how he felt. She'd spent her first three weeks on a hovercraft banging her head on the damned thing. The man's eyes had closed for an instant with the impact of the blow and before he could open them again Mancuso was on him, kicking solidly into his midriff so he bent double, knife leaving his fingers, rattling on the floor. Then she was pushing him back, her forearm against his neck, her free hand pulling back the velcro cover of her wristband. He knew what was coming, but it was too late.

She held the medicated pad to the bare skin of his neck. He groped at her elbow with his good hand, trying to break her grip, but Mancuso held tight. The massive dose of tranquillizer on her wristband was being absorbed directly through his skin. She'd got him right over the carotid artery and the sedative took hold almost immediately.

He kept struggling but it was like wrestling with a child. His body loosened under her as his muscles relaxed and he settled into a profound sleep. Mancuso held on a little longer, to compensate for the stimulants that were already in his bloodstream, then let him sink to the floor.

Mancuso retrieved the seatback from the rear of the cabin and slotted it back into the pilot's chair. She sat down at the controls and sighed. It was a G-8, the same model she'd trained on and flown in combat. She'd still be piloting a G-8 now if the police service hadn't dumped the whole programme as part of their financial streamlining. The G-8s had been sold off at auction to help with departmental cash flow. They'd been snapped up by armed robber teams and terrorists who knew a good thing when they saw one. Ten years later the vehicles were still providing excellent service. Like this one. Mancuso began to punch buttons, checking status.

The screen reported the rear doors of the craft as open. They gave access to the cargo bay. Whoever was robbing the store would need them open for loading up their merchandise. Mancuso moved a cursor on the screen and the doors closed. Scrolling down a menu she sealed the hatch on the roof. Her gun was still out there somewhere, on the loading bay floor, but that was okay now. Mancuso looked around the cabin. The NYPD logo on the bulkhead had been painted over with hex signs and graffiti.

Some new equipment had been fitted, thick bundles of wiring secured overhead with masking tape. The man in the leather jacket was snoring peacefully under the air conditioning. Mancuso stretched her shoulders, relaxing. It was nice to be home.

She switched the screen from status check to environment simulation. The cameras on the exterior armour tracked with infrared lights, sending a description of the loading bay back to the screen. The screen simulated the image, iconizing, high-lighting, filling in details in an accurate cartoon replica of the world outside. The image was monochrome and precise. She scanned the floor and saw her gun lying by the rubber skirt of the craft. She saw the motorcycle she'd walked into and three others. A Kawasaki, two BMWs and a Honda. They were on the floor of the loading bay near the steps, ready for a quick getaway. No sign of the little guy or anyone else. No movement at all.

Mancuso scanned the tunnel exit. The screen displayed a string of figures and a wireframe diagram, showing where the curve of the tunnel would lead, as if she could see through walls. Mancuso looked at the tunnel mouth and then back at the motorcycles, presented on the screen in dull precise shades of cream and grey. She punched some buttons on the keypad. What the hell. The screen instantly blossomed into brilliant, garish colours. The same images as before but now hot pink, turquoise and lime green. Mancuso suppressed the urge to giggle.

The hovercraft lifted from the concrete floor in a spray of fine grit, shuddering slightly as it gained speed. Moving through the darkness to the mouth of the tunnel.

By the time she hit the sloping ramp of the exit tunnel Mancuso had the hovercraft halfway to full speed. She banked gently, smoothly nudging the control stick as she took the G-8 around the tight curve. The screen gave a continuous estimate of the hovercraft's position, animated hovercraft icon moving through animated tunnel. The icon made it very clear that the

G-8 was too large to turn sideways in the tunnel.

As soon as she was fully around the curve Mancuso twisted the control stick, turning the craft sideways in the tunnel.

The hovercraft hit the tunnel walls with a grinding of metal that stopped as its twisting motion brought the rubber skirts against the concrete. The G-8 gave a final shudder, trying to turn in the impossibly narrow space, then locked solid. The engine note spun into a high-pitched squeal as the hovercraft hung there motionless, blocking the tunnel from wall to wall.

Mancuso switched the engines off before they could shake themselves to pieces. The roof of the craft was tilted at a steep angle and it was difficult climbing out of the hatch. Mancuso sealed the hatch cover behind her and hung for a moment from a grab bar. She dropped to the floor and jogged back up the ramp. Before she rounded the curve back into the loading bay she looked back over her shoulder and saw the luminous question mark glowing dead centre in the tunnel.

In the loading bay she paused to retrieve her gun before going back up the steps into the store.

Breen was crouching beneath shelves featuring a hundred different brands of shampoo, watching the secure area of the store. Mancuso knelt beside him. The secure area was thirty metres ahead and above them, on the mezzanine, with escalators running up to it on three sides.

Mancuso could see movement among the shelves. At least three people. There had been four motorcycles in the loading bay. Plus however many had crewed the hovercraft. The mezzanine overlooked quite a wide spread of the drugstore floor space.

It would be hard to get any closer without being visible to someone looking out over the railings. Actually getting up there unseen was going to be even harder. Breen put his head close to hers.

'I've got it all figured,' he said.

Mancuso rode up on the escalator lying down. Flat on her back on the grooved metal stairs, her gun held above her. She watched the egg-crate fluorescent lights slide by on the slanted ceiling.

On either side of her safety brushes edged the moving stairs. She saw small trapped bits of debris. Candy wrappers, coins, a child's lost glove. She hit the mezzanine floor shoulders first, gathering her knees to her chest and rolling clear of the escalator to land in a combat stance. Hiding behind a pyramid display of Polish vodka she realized that she was wet. The floor all around was wet. There were fragments of broken glass everywhere; the necks and sharp semicircle bases of bottles. Mancuso remembered the crashing sound she'd heard, when she'd looked up and the little guy had made his move. She hunched lower behind the vodka display as a man came by.

He was carrying a packing carton on one shoulder. There was a silhouette of a bottle drawn on the side of the carton and 'handle with care' warnings in several languages. The man moved to the back of the mezzanine and disappeared among the shelves. Mancuso could hear voices back there, and a humming noise that was growing louder. The voices of three men and one woman, maybe two. There was a metallic thud and the humming stopped. The sound of metal doors sliding open. Freight elevator. More voices and the sound of packing cartons dragging as they were loaded into the elevator.

Mancuso checked the analogue sweep hand on her watch. Ninety seconds. She carefully refastened the velcro covers on her wristbands. McIlveen had once forgotten and left his wristbands open after sedating a suspect. He'd been changing his clothes in the station locker room, wearing just his boxer shorts. He'd leaned forward to clip his toenails or something and the wristband had come in contact with his knee. The guys coming on the next shift had found him like that, sitting there in his boxer shorts, deeply unconscious.

Sixty seconds. McIlveen's leg had been numb for a week.

Fifty. Mancuso had never let him forget it. She moved the rocker switch on her gun to its third position. The light went from amber to red. The digital readout above the magazine read full.

Thirty. Twenty. Ten.

Mancuso was up and moving. Past shelves of Jim Beam and Cutty Sark. Past the smoking section. Bright packets of tobacco, diamorphine and alkaloid. On the other side of a pillar were

212

rows and rows of mineral water in glass bottles. A man was running between the rows, from the far side of the mezzanine, running parallel with her. Breen. Exactly on time. He wasn't McIlveen, but he wasn't bad.

There were twin freight elevators at the back of the mezzanine, behind the checkout terminals. Dead ahead. One elevator had its doors open and boxes of bottles stacked inside. One man stood inside, organizing the stacking. A man and a woman passed cartons in to him. A second woman stood by the terminals at the checkout, supervising things. She had some kind of blunt small-barrelled submachine gun slung on a strap from her shoulder. She was wearing an antique military tunic with epaulettes and big brass buttons. The submachine gun looked like a Weber, or a clone of one. The man inside the elevator had a similar weapon, set on top of a stack of cases beside him. The others either had concealed handguns or nothing.

It was the man inside the elevator who saw them first.

He didn't even bother shouting a warning. He just turned, scooped up his Weber and began firing. The two carrying the packing cases screamed and ducked out of his way, throwing themselves on to the floor. The woman supervising fumbled for her gun, trying to drag it up across her body, and the strap snagged on a button on her tunic.

The man in the elevator was firing single rounds now, deliberate and carefully aimed. Breen popped up from behind a display for Tanqeray showing a hologram of a boar's head and fired once, holding his pistol in a two-handed grip. It was about twenty metres to the man in the elevator. The man went down, wounded in the shoulder, his Weber switching to automatic fire as he fell, blasting wildly all around in the confined space of the elevator, shredding packing cases and blowing apart bottles.

The woman on the floor in front of the elevator shouted something and jumped in among the cartons, trying to wrestle the gun away from him. The woman by the checkout had freed the strap from her buttons and was raising the Weber when Mancuso fired a long burst that tore the checkout terminal in half and shredded the plastic countertop beside her elbow. The woman dived clear of the exploding plastic.

Inside the elevator the other woman had grabbed the other Weber from the wounded man and was fumbling to change magazines. Outside the elevator the man with the boxes was lying flat on the floor, clamping his hands over his head. The woman from the checkout leapt over him and into the elevator. She knocked the other woman aside just as she was reloading the Weber. The wounded man was lurching forward, clutching his shoulder, blood flowing down his tee-shirt. He let go of his shoulder and hit the freight elevator button with his good hand. The doors began to close and the man outside on the floor scrambled forward, throwing himself in among the others, elbowing aside the kneeling woman just as she loaded the Weber and was trying to take aim. The metal doors were sliding closed. Breen and Mancuso were both up and running. The woman with the Weber finally got it sighted and pulled the trigger. Mancuso fired from the hip as she ran. Ricochets screamed off the steel doors. The woman in the elevator fired wildly through the narrowing gap as they closed. A fluorescent tube imploded with a blue flashbulb pop above Mancuso. Delicate small fragments of glass snowed down on to her shoulders. Behind Breen a shelf rocked with the impact of a blast. Then the doors were shut and the elevator was heading down.

Mancuso's ears were ringing in the sudden silence. Colourful liqueurs flowed smoothly out of pierced plastic bottles on a shelf by Breen, running down the shelves on to the aisle floor, mixing in a bright tangle. She thumbed the switch on her gun back to mid position. The light on the barrel went from red to amber. The soles of her shoes were sticky with the spilled liqueurs. The indicator above the sealed doors indicated the main floor, then flashed as the elevator descended towards the loading bay.

'We take the other one,' said Breen. 'Take the other elevator down.' Mancuso nodded but she wasn't listening to him. She was counting in her head. Three in the elevator plus the one Breen had hit. Four. One for each motorcycle. One in the hovercraft as pilot. And then one for the weapons station.

Her gun suddenly moved in her hands as if someone had grabbed it. The barrel was twisting to the right with a harsh ratchetting sound, her fingers still gripping tight to the handle and trigger guard, fighting the movement. Breen was still saying something, in midsentence, his eyes just beginning to drift to the right, registering movement.

The status light on Mancuso's gun had gone from amber back to red. Directly beyond the gun barrel was the intersection of two rows of aisles. Coming out of them between a Johnny Walker display and a rack of red wine was a woman. Tie-dyed shirt and a flak vest. She was holding something in her right hand. Holding it as if offering it. A pistol. Mancuso recognized the weapon, her mind automatically trying to classify it even as the woman swung it to aim at her. Pointing directly at Mancuso and now there was the sound of gunfire. But it was Mancuso's own gun. She wasn't pressing the trigger but the gun was firing, a short burst. It caught the woman high and centre, in the chest, as if the tie-dyed circle on her shirt was a target. The impact of the bullets threw her back. Her arms were spread wide. Her handgun went off, aimed now at the air above her. A bullet rang as it hit a ceiling-mounted spigot for the fire sprinklers. Breen was reacting, moving, gun raised, turning to face the woman. But it was all over. The woman was lying on the floor between the aisles, out of it, a body.

Breen stared at the woman on the floor. Disturbed dust and paint fragments floated down from the ceiling in a fine cloud. Mancuso was looking at the gun in her own hands. At the top of the hand grip, where it joined the tubular barrel, there was a metal disc. The barrel of the gun was twisted off centre along the disc. Mancuso moved the handgrip and it shifted smoothly with the same ratchetting sound as before, locking solidly back into position. The barrel was aligned with the handgrip again. The rocker switch had gone back to mid position again. She hadn't touched the switch. The status light was amber.

'Nice reflexes,' said Breen.

'Yes,' said Mancuso looking at the gun. 'I wish they were mine.'

She pulled open the doors of the second freight elevator and stepped inside.

Mancuso and Breen got down in time to hear the motorcycles being kick-started. The empty loading bay was visible in the light that shone through the opening doors of the freight elevator. Breen was out before they were fully open, moving into the other elevator, Mancuso covering his back. The cartons of bottles were still stacked on the patterned metal floor of the elevator, abandoned. There was blood on several of the cardboard cartons. 'How the hell did they expect to carry that stuff on bikes?'

The motorcycle noise faded a bit as the bikes sped around the curve in the exit tunnel. 'They used to have a hovercraft,' said Mancuso.

Breen stepped out of the elevator and looked at her. 'What happened to it?' From the far end of the tunnel there was the sound of several voices screaming in unison and the squeal of rubber on concrete as brakes were applied at high speed. The engine noise of the four motorcycles died almost simultaneously, transforming into the sound of shattering glass and rending metal.

'It's up there in the tunnel,' said Mancuso, 'creating an obstruction.'

They collected the girl in the black jacket on the way out of the drugstore. She was where Breen had left her, handcuffed to the metal upright of a turnstile by the main entrance. 'Don't mind me,' she said as they approached. 'I like being tied up while other people fire guns.'

Breen unlocked her cuffs and they went out through the glass doors into the hot October night. The girl began to cough as soon as they hit the street air. Her eyes were streaming by the time she reached the squad car. Breen locked her in the back, handing her a mask to wear until the car air conditioning took hold. By the time she got it on the girl was coughing so hard that Mancuso's chest was aching in sympathy.

She must be from out of town.

20

The helicopter was late.

Stephanie didn't mind. It gave her more time to observe Mulwray's increasingly interesting behaviour.

The two of them were still working together, although Mulwray had twice asked to be transferred. Both times O'Hara had routed the requests back to Stephanie and Stephanie had torn them up. She was enjoying herself. Things had reached the point now where Mulwray wouldn't even look her in the eye.

The longer the flight was delayed the more nervous Mulwray became. Eventually he went to sit in the control shack with the pilots. Stephanie remained outside on the rooftop, watching big clouds moving over the city. She was wearing a breathing mask today to protect her face against the hot sooty winds blowing in from the west.

Finally the Biostock technicians brought the teenage boy up. Two of them came out on to the roof, wearing the standard white overalls with the Butler Institute logos on the back. They wheeled the stretcher across the roof surface towards the painted circle where the helicopter sat. The boy's head was lolling, a small plastic tube taped to his cheek so it remained fixed in his nose. His arms were lashed down on top of the blanket in case he regained consciousness.

Stephanie read the boy's name off the ID tags that were hanging outside the blanket. *Vincent Wheaton.* The technicians on the fifty-first floor had found the tags around his neck when he was being processed.

Vincent was the reason the flight had been delayed. He had been picked up on a routine sweep of the junkies in Central Park and would normally have gone straight into Biostock. He looked cleaner and healthier than the average derelict or street dweller, but the park sweeps were unpredictable and by rights the boy

217

should have been spare parts by now.

But there was a new memo from O'Hara which altered the Biostock protocol. It was apparently based on an article in a British newspaper and it specified a new range of blood tests to be carried out on all incoming stock. Vincent's blood had rung bells on all the tests, so the clinical sacrifice was postponed, the boy was flagged as something special and his unconscious body was scheduled on the next flight out to the Catskills.

Mulwray came out of the flight shack now and watched as the technicians put Vincent in the back of the helicopter. They strapped him down on a portable life-support unit with heavy sedatives being fed into his bloodstream in a glucose solution.

'If they're pressed for space I can fly out later,' said Mulwray. 'I've got a lot of deskwork to catch up on.'

Stephanie said nothing.

'So long as it's okay with you,' said Mulwray.

Stephanie smiled.

When they reached the construction site after the flight, Stephanie made Mulwray wait while she pulled on some rubber boots in the site office. There had been some drainage problems at the site, with runoff from the mountainside above flooding the tunnel. As soon as Stephanie had the boots on she set off for the tunnel mouth, not giving Mulwray time to change. She was fascinated to see what he would do. He came trotting after her, still wearing his expensive, gleaming street shoes. By the time they were inside the tunnel they had been reduced to muddy ruin.

Men and women in white coats were trudging back from lunch in the company canteen on the surface, picking their way among puddles in the rutted mud of the tunnel floor. The excavation work was complete now but the ground was still crisscrossed with the tyre tracks of the heavy machinery. Japanese and Korean technicians in hard hats were inspecting the wall and studying blueprints, studiously avoiding each other as they planned the installations of the mainframes and the multiple generators. Lengths of plastic piping were stacked along the tunnel walls and fat power cables were hung in loops along the ceiling.

The suite of prefab huts which Stephanie used as her offices

218

were located 150 metres down the sloping length of the tunnel. But even this deep it was impossible to see how much further the tunnel went. It faded away in the thick mists of evaporating runoff that glared under the harsh beams of the temporary lighting system. Stephanie unlocked the offices and flicked on the lights, leaving Mulwray outside trying to scrape the mud off his shoes and the cuffs of his suit pants. She went directly to the telephone on the nearest desk and dialled the number for O'Hara's house.

She knew it must be a difficult day for him and she wanted to lend her support.

The signal from Stephanie's phone travelled a kilometre via land lines, routed through the communications centre, up to O'Hara's redwood house on the slope above the excavation site. Inside the big house the B&O home-entertainment computer detected the incoming call and came to life.

The video sample created by O'Hara's son was still in the memory of the machine and it was the default image for all communications. So instead of a simple telephone bell ringing, the B&O created a holographic image of Jack Blood and sent him stalking through the house, looking for the inhabitants, eager to inform them of the phone call.

The pumpkin-headed killer strutted across the wide empty living room, the image of a jagged carving knife waving in one holographic hand and the image of an old-fashioned telephone, presented on a silver butler's tray, in the other.

Jack wandered the length of the silent living room, his image fading a little and the colours turning watery in the mountain sunlight as he crossed in front of the floor-to-ceiling picture window. He then quartered the room, exploring it carefully, empty pumpkin eye sockets scanning from side to side as he searched for someone to take the call.

Once it was clear that the living room was empty the hologram promptly vanished, only to appear in the kitchen. Projectors mounted high on the walls of the room picked up the signal from the home-entertainment unit and projected Jack in full colour and apparent solidity, striding the tile floor between gleaming refrigerator and cooking unit. The kitchen was bare and peaceful, only a slight buzzing from the refrigerator disturbing the silence. Jack paused, standing in the quiet sunlight, then turned and strode through the wall, the projector in the master bedroom picking him up and flashing his image into the shadows as he appeared again. The blinds were down in the master bedroom and the silence was heavy. Jack stood there only for a moment before moving on to Patrick's bedroom at the back of the house.

He prowled up and down the little boy's room, stalking among the colouring books and crayons and computer scattered on the floor. He peered into both layers of the bunk bed but all he found was a tangle of sheets and blankets. Jack stood in the doorway of the empty closet. Finally he walked over to stand with his back to the window, the unanswered telephone still sitting on the silver tray in his rotted twig hand. His misshapen head was tilted to one side, giving an illusion of regret, as if Jack was sad that he couldn't complete his mission.

Now Stephanie abandoned her phone call and hung up the receiver a kilometre away. The disconnect code pulsed along the wire and the B&O cancelled Jack.

Just before the hologram vanished, the tall pumpkin head did a final turn, as if giving the child's bedroom a final survey. The computer graphics faded when he was halfway through the turn. The image froze and lingered for a moment, apparently staring out the window at the mountain slope below the house.

It was almost as if he could see through the glass, as if he was looking at the man and his wife sitting out there on the lawn.

Outside the house O'Hara stood up and began to pace down towards the treeline. His wife remained sitting in one of the expensive white plastic all-weather chairs. O'Hara came back across the lawn to the chairs and set his glass down beside his wife's. Ants had already discovered the other drink and were crawling around it, up the slick sides and into the glass.

O'Hara sighed. 'I'm sorry you had to find out the way you did. But you must have suspected. All the research has been heading in this direction.' He turned and looked down towards the excavation site beyond the thinning trees. 'And now we're almost ready to get started.'

O'Hara's wife said nothing and he hurried on, filling the

silence. 'All right. I know how you feel. I know your side of the argument. In fact I can probably put your own case better than you can.' He crouched on the lawn and searched for a moment, then he plucked something out from among the strands of grass. One of the small wild flowers that had seeded itself, blown there on the mountain winds. He held it carefully between thumb and forefinger, inspecting it in the sunlight.

'You might look at this flower,' said O'Hara, 'and you might see something of beauty. Perhaps you'd be moved by it. I know I'm moved by it. But when we look at this flower we see different things. I see the end processes of millions of years of evolution in action. Life replicating itself, changing, taking new shapes.

And the thing I'm doing, that project down the slope, that's the end product of the same processes. That is evolution, too. It's no different than the colours and form of this flower.

'You see, we stand at the threshold of a new age. Industrialization has had a massive impact on our planet. Our machines have brought us many boons but you might argue that they are also destroying the natural world. You might say that degradation of the ecosphere is reaching crisis proportions. That if we don't take action now there will be no turning back.' O'Hara looked at the flower again, then let it drop from his fingers, falling back to the grass. 'And you'd be right.

'But there's something you don't understand. The machines that are polluting our world are built by human beings. Human beings who have evolved on this planet. Our species has stopped evolving physically, but not mentally. Our minds keep on developing. And our machines are the creations of our minds. They are the next stage of our evolution.' Now O'Hara's voice took on a note of excitement. He paced back and forth in front of the white lawn chairs.

'We don't need the natural world any more. It doesn't matter if the flowers and trees and animals all die. It doesn't matter if we fill the sky and sea with poison. Because none of those things can harm a world populated with machines. And our minds now have the skills to lift themselves out of our bodies and place themselves into those machines.'

O'Hara pointed to the line of trees and the construction site

221

beyond. 'Down there we're building the first outpost of a new world. A deep bunker with generators that will last forever. Maintenance machines that can repair the generators and repair themselves as well. And we will fill that bunker with computers and we'll fill those computers with people. Minds that can live forever in the memories of those computers. And that's just the beginning.' O'Hara sat down near his wife's feet, sitting cross-legged on the damp grass among the small wild flowers. 'Soon we'll be building sites like this all over the world. And they are the blossoming of evolution just as surely as these flowers are.

'What hurts,' said O'Hara, 'is that you look at me as if I'm some kind of monster. I'm not saying this will be just the salvation of a super-rich few. They will be the first beneficiaries, certainly. But eventually we intend to offer this salvation to everyone. The project is in its infancy, but we already have the first prototypes out in the field, where the technology will be shaped by market forces. It will evolve and it will evolve quickly. The first human beings have already been saved from a poisoned world. We had two pilot tests, and they showed that the method worked. Then we took the mind of an ordinary policeman and transformed it. And now our son has volunteered to be part of this project.' There were tears in O'Hara's eyes. 'Right this minute he's down at the site, beginning his evolutionary journey. And you should be proud of him. You should be proud of me. I've offered him a new world.'

O'Hara reached down and picked his wife's glass off the lawn. A dozen small ants were floating in it, all dead. 'If you had been just a little more patient, a little more willing to listen, I could have offered it to you as well.'

He got up holding the glass. He closed his wife's eyes and he touched her cold hand. Then he went into the house.

The playroom was full of toys.

It was brightly lit, with a floor made of clean blond wood. You would never have guessed it was inside the smallest of the prefab huts, at the rear of the group that made up Stephanie's suite of offices. The windows were sealed with blackout material so that you couldn't see the mud walls and raw construction of the tunnel outside.

Now a five-year-old boy entered the room. Patrick O'Hara came in slowly, looking around. He ignored the toys.

Instead he looked at the large vents in the floor.

Then he came directly over to the mirror and looked at it.

He stared into the big square of reflective glass above the sink. It was as if he expected it to be a window into another room, rather than just a mirror.

Smart kid, thought Stephanie, sitting in the darkness of the adjacent room. She moved her chair a little to the left. Now Patrick was staring right at her through the two-way glass. He wasn't looking away, even though he must be able to hear the gas by now. Stephanie had expected him to go over to the floor vents and look at them. But instead the small boy just stood there, watching the mirror above the sink. Staring into the next room at Stephanie, his little face looking somehow sad and knowing.

Stephanie thought it was a fascinating expression. She wished she'd thought to record it. Record the whole procedure, in fact. But on second thoughts the gas was coming into the playroom pretty quickly, filling it with thick white mist, and pretty soon a camera would be unable to pick up any image.

There was already a thin mist between Patrick's face and hers, the boy's face softening in the white vapour, losing details of its expression, becoming a blank slate. Now you could imagine any expression on it.

Stephanie imagined the face smiling at her, with that heart-catching smile kids sometimes have. Then any suggestion of a face was blurred away, lost like a pattern you had imagined in a cloud, staring up into the sky on a hot summer's day.

Mulwray was sitting in a chair just behind Stephanie's. She'd made sure that he had a clear view of what was happening in the playroom. Stephanie would have liked to stay in the observation suite a little longer, even though there wasn't much to see, but this whole visit was something of a luxury. O'Hara was promoting her to the position of project organizer and soon she'd be on site permanently, moving into his house. There would be plenty of room now.

But before she transferred from New York Stephanie had to

clear her desk. That meant flying back in an hour and paying a final visit to the office and doing one last sweep of the police cells. She would take Mulwray with her. Stephanie liked having him around.

When the lights came on Stephanie stood up and went to the door, wasting no time. Mulwray blundered to his feet and came stumbling hastily after her, as if he was afraid to be left alone in the small room.

They emerged into the bright flat lighting of the tunnel and she had a good look at Mulwray's face. He was looking very old indeed.

As they left, the surgical teams were entering the playroom their faces concealed behind breathing apparatus.

21

Ace didn't know what the time was. She'd been wearing a wristwatch when she was brought into the big cell, a circle of armed guards standing just inside the cell door, then retreating quickly as she was shoved inside. The door had chunked shut behind her on a remote control lock and then the other prisoners had begun to move forward, a slow tide.

The watch had been torn off her during the first fight. It didn't matter; Ace didn't need it. She could estimate the passage of time with a fair degree of accuracy. She guessed she'd been in the cell for about two and a half hours. She'd had to fight three men and two women. The women had been the worst. Then some fresh prisoners had arrived, two teenage boys. And because of them, and because she'd won the fights, Ace had been left alone.

Now she squatted in a corner of the cell, balanced so that the ball of each foot was on the concrete floor while she sat back on her heels. It was comfortable when you got the knack, although you had to rise up every so often, like doing deep knee bends, if you didn't want your muscles to lock. There was a bench running the full length of one wall of the cell, but it was fully occupied and ruthlessly defended. You didn't necessarily have to fight to get a place, but the other things you had to do were worse.

After the teenagers arrived Ace had a chance to sit back and look and listen, learning everything she could about this new environment. But then she'd heard the man talking about how his first month in the cell had been the worst, and someone else agreeing and saying it hardly ever took more than a year before you got your first court hearing. And then she'd seen the woman nursing a newborn child in one corner, a pale, quiet baby. And that was when Ace stopped looking and listening.

As she rocked back and forth on her heels Ace kept her arms hugged tight around herself, her bruised shoulder aching savagely now.

'You're the one, right?'

Ace looked up. She recognized the man from the crowds that had gathered during the fights. He had watched with interest and kept a safe distance. He was better dressed than the other prisoners and seemed to be able to move through any part of the cell with impunity.

'I'm from the committee,' said the man. 'Actually, to tell you the truth, I am the committee.' He smiled at Ace. 'You're a good fighter, I'm sorry to lose you.' He signalled and two big men moved in quickly and dragged Ace to her feet. She pulled free but the men had already released her and moved back. 'I was going to give you a week and then, if you held out, I was going to nominate you for the committee,' said the well-dressed man. 'But that's the way it goes. Come on.'

Ace didn't move.

'We haven't got all day,' said the man. 'Even the committee can't hold them back forever.'

What Ace recognized as a group of the most dangerous prisoners were creating a human corridor, their backs to her, facing outwards towards the other prisoners in the cell.

Ace walked along the coridor, the man from the committee beside her. 'Listen, next time you're arrested, see if you can get them to put you back in this cell.'

'I'm not coming back.'

The man was looking past Ace at the cell door. 'Maybe not,' he said.

Waiting beyond the barred door were a man and woman. The woman looked just a few years older than Ace, the man's age was harder to guess. He had beautiful Eurasian features but he was stooped and old looking; beaten looking. Ace found herself thinking that he wouldn't last long in the cells.

The woman leaned forward and passed something through the bars. It looked like a telephone. The man from the committee accepted the telephone and took an American Express card out of his shirt pocket. Ace saw that the portable phone had a small screen on the handset. The man ran his credit card down a groove in the side of the phone and the screen lit up, showing numbers and a dollar sign. 'That's equitable,' said the man. There was the chunking sound Ace had heard once before and the cell door shivered.

The man stood aside politely to let Ace by. Ace stared at the open door and the man and woman who stood waiting on the other side. The man from the committee winked at Ace. 'I haven't figured out a way of charging them for incoming prisoners yet, but I'm working on it.' He smiled as Ace walked past him and out of the cell.

The man and woman were immediately beside Ace, a little closer than she would have liked. Ace's heart was racing.

The cell door was locking behind her. She was out. Ace couldn't quite believe it. She felt like running, before someone could change their mind. Now that she had time to think, the pain was coming back. Her shoulder pulsed with pain and sweat crawled down her sides. She felt a little feverish.

The woman was smiling at her. She had perfect teeth. She caught Ace's hand and shook it. 'My name is Stephanie, this is Mr Mulwray.'

'Are you sure?' Petersen was saying. 'The subconscious mind can respond with amazing speed.'

'You're talking about reflexes,' said Mancuso. 'I know what my own reflexes feel like.'

'It was a moment of extreme stress —'

Mancuso set aside her cup of powdery, machine-tasting coffee. 'Listen, I didn't do anything. I was standing there in the drugstore. The situation appeared to be under control. I was trying to do a count in my head, working out if we'd dropped all of them. Then the gun swivelled. It moved on some kind of universal joint just over the handle. It moved by itself.'

Petersen sighed and took a Phillips screwdriver out of a coffee mug full of pens on his desk. On the coffee mug there was a big letter *I*, then a drawing of a heart, then big letters *NY*. The heart had bullets holes in it. 'They never tell us exactly what to expect with the new weapons systems.' He opened a concealed panel on the underside of the gun and began to work at a recessed screw.

'I thought you guys designed them,' said Mancuso, pacing the laboratory area. The R&D lab was a big open space occupied by work stations, desks and long benches. It was silent except for recurrent deep rumbling and a regular high-pitched beeping sound.

'Mostly we do,' said Petersen, 'but sometimes we get government or company specifications. Features they want us to test.'

'Features they want *us* to test,' said Mancuso, returning to stand at the desk beside Petersen. 'When was the last time one of you guys fired a gun?'

'When was the last time you dismantled one? These thing have been known to blow up when you take them apart. Greetings from the Pacific Basin.' Petersen's fingers had found the seam that divided the lower cylinder of the gun and he was prying it apart.

'Where's that noise coming from? The beeping.' Mancuso crushed her coffee cup and dumped it in a bin of junk fax and printout.

'Why don't you settle down? Read a book or something.' Petersen indicated his desk screen. 'That noise is the coder on the door lock. The side entrance, down in the alley. Ignore it. It's just some wino punching numbers, trying to get lucky.' On the small screen digits flashed on, in time with the beeping sound. Petersen watched the sequence of numbers for a moment, then returned to the gun on his desk. 'Come and see this.'

The black metal cylinder was lined with a white plastic honeycomb matrix that supported the gun's control system. There were surprisingly few components. A complex optical unit with a shatterproof quartz lens that peeked out of the front end of the tube, just under the muzzle. A bus cable that ran the length of the cylinder. A little silver sticker that said 'Made in Korea'. Some drops of spilled solder. A rack of chips and a large, non-standard chip with a luminous line framing it. Petersen pointed with the screwdriver. 'That's special. It's powered all the time. It has its own long-life battery on the underside.' Petersen's fingers moved to the bus cable, gently working it free. A flat tongue of clear plastic emerged with a network of copper lines embossed on it.

Petersen had connected an earthing line to his wrist so that

228

static wouldn't fry the circuitry.

'So what's it for?' said Mancuso, leaning closer.

'The other chips are just on-board memory and the operating system. That big one's the intelligence. They don't call it a smart gun for nothing.'

Mancuso pointed at the display above the magazine sleeve on the gun. The magazine itself lay on Petersen's desk, grey and copper bullets visible in the glow of the desk lamp. ' "M-T". What the hell does "M-T" mean?'

'It means no ammunition. The gun is empty. It also means the bastards were too cheap to give you anything more than a three-character display. You can also use that readout to do a general systems check when you dismantle the weapon. It'll probably also show the time and date and store phone numbers for you.' Mancuso picked the magazine up and thumbed bullets out of it on to the desk, the spring easing a new round up each time. She remembered bright colours flowing out of plastic bottles, gathering at her feet.

'I was holding it, talking to Breen. This witchy girl came out of nowhere, from behind some shelves. She had us. We were finished. She had her gun right on me. Then this thing moved, aimed and fired itself.'

'That's pretty smart.' Petersen was carefully working the intelligence chip out of its socket. The thin glowing light around its edges remained on as it left the mother board.

'Maybe you can examine that, tell me something about it.'

Petersen set the chip on his desk and adjusted the lamp over it. 'Maybe,' he said.

'I wouldn't mind some answers before I go off duty. I might be able to get some sleep if I know what I'm carrying on the street tomorrow.'

But Petersen didn't reply. He was no longer looking at the chip. His eyes were on the desk screen, watching the numbers from the door coder flashing. He stared at the numbers for a moment, then began pulling magazines out of the piles of paper that buried his in-tray.

'What is it?'

Petersen ignored her. He had a magazine open and was looking at the screen again. The magazine was printed on cheap yellow paper with occasional high-quality ivory-toned pages for colour illustrations. It was a scientific journal of some kind.

'Jesus,' said Petersen. He was running his finger along a row of figures printed in the journal, looking up at the screen and back down at the magazine.

'What's going on?' said Mancuso. 'What is that?'

'It's an article in the math section. Not really my field. It's about the ozone holes and modelling their behaviour. The big problem is predicting the movement in the atmosphere.'

'I know. I had a cousin in Oregon.'

'Well, they've got these equations.' Petersen was looking at the screen again. 'Basically, all you have to understand is that it's an unsolvable problem,' he said, reaching for the release button for the door lock, 'and that someone standing down there in the alley is solving it.'

The steel bars securing the street door made a dull thudding noise as they drew back into the wall.

He was smaller than Mancuso remembered. In the drugstore she'd thought of him as the little guy, but somehow in her memory he'd grown. Now she was startled to see how small he was. She looked into his disquieting eyes, then down at his small, delicate hands. They were empty. Mancuso held her own hands out of sight behind Petersen's desk.

'There's no need for that,' said the man, looking at her. Mancuso lifted her hands and brought her Colt sidearm into view. She didn't point it at the man, but she didn't point it away from him either. Petersen ignored both of them, concentrating on his desk screen. He was ransacking the buffer, retrieving as much as he could of the sequence of numbers the man had keyed in on the door coder. 'It's chaotic but patterned,' said the man.

Petersen glanced up and smiled, then bent back to his work. He was happy. He was going to get a paper out of this.

'Did you find the hovercraft?' said the man. 'I thought you ought to know about it.'

'That was a really stupid move,' said Mancuso.

'Not only was it illegally parked, but I also suspected it of being involved in the commission of a felony,' said the man.

'I can't remember if I gave you your rights,' said Mancuso.

'I've still got the card, right here.' The man's hand moved and Mancuso's handgun automatically swayed up, aiming dead centre at the man's chest.

But he just smiled as he reached in a pocket and took out the card. 'There's a misspelling in the Gujarati,' he said.

Stephanie was very tall and very blonde. Mulwray was slim and muscular, with oriental eyes. His skin was golden and he had thick black hair, cropped short. Very pretty, but very tired. When he looked at Ace he wouldn't quite meet her gaze.

'What's the matter? Your posture's all wrong,' Stephanie was saying. 'You look like you're hurt. What happened in there?'

'I had to fight.' Ace's voice was hoarse. She cleared her throat. 'The first couple of times I was okay but then one of them got me down and held me while another one kicked −'

'Oh my God.' The woman was looking at her with concern in her eyes and touching her. A light, professional touch, a physician's touch. 'Jesus, those animals.'

Stephanie and Mulwray steered Ace a short distance down the hallway from the cell and seated her on the first bench, sitting close on either side of her. Stephanie bent over her, fussing. A woman walked past, pushing a trolley. She slowed down to take in the three of them sitting on the bench. 'Careful girl,' she said, 'they just want your body.'

'Shut up,' snapped Stephanie.

Breen was beginning to wish he'd flipped a coin with Mancuso. A visit to R&D about a weapons malfunction wasn't much fun, but registering a prisoner involved dealing with Cooper on the data console. It had taken three hours just for Breen to finish doing the documentation on the English girl. Now he had to get over to the lab and pick up Mancuso. Then maybe they could see if there was anything useful they could do in what was left of the shift. He was hurrying past the data section, on his way to the car, when he ran into them.

Sitting on a bench near the cells. Three of them. Two clowns from the Butler Institute and the English girl. Breen dismissed the man as no threat. He looked like one of the walking wounded. The BI woman was different; hard. She just looked right through Breen, as if he wasn't important enough to register. The English girl smiled, recognizing him.

'Hello,' she said. 'All right?'

'No, not really,' said Breen, unclipping his holster and resting his hand on his pistol.

'Good evening, officer,' said the female BI, acknowledging Breen now that she had no choice.

'Good evening,' said Breen. He looked at the woman. 'What are you doing with my prisoner?'

'This young lady has been released into our care.'

'That's interesting. To the best of my knowledge this young lady hasn't even been charged yet,' said Breen.

Through the glass he could see Cooper easing his fat bulk out from behind the data console and coming towards them, sensing trouble.

'Come on now, time to go,' said the female BI, taking the girl by the arm and moving away from Breen.

The girl pulled free. 'No thanks,' she said. 'This young lady has plans of her own.'

Cooper was hurrying towards them.

'This is ridiculous. We have custody of the girl and we're going,' said the woman.

'I understand you people have very good health-care schemes. They say you can replace just about anything these days,' Breen said.

Cooper was beside them now. 'Hold on, Breen.'

'I am holding on,' said Breen. 'They're not taking her. It's bad enough letting these ghouls into the parks but now they're taking prisoners out of the cells. She hasn't even been charged yet.'

'There are no charges,' said the woman. 'She's no longer under arrest.'

Breen looked at Cooper. He nodded, his double chin wobbling. 'She's off the charge list,' said Cooper. 'She's free.'

'That's great,' said Breen. 'How long has this scam been going on?'

The woman smiled and signalled to the man. They grabbed the English girl, each taking an arm. The English girl tried to pull away but they hung on tight, clutching the black cloth of her jacket. Breen reached in and helped her pull free. The Butler Institute couple looked at him.

'If she's free, then she's free to go without you,' said Breen. The female BI moved forward, as if she was going to go for Breen. He just smiled at her, hoping she was stupid enough. But the man touched the woman's arm and she stared at Breen for a moment then relaxed. She reached into the jacket of her silk suit and took out a small blue card that resembled a credit card. Printed on it was the bee-and-eye logo of the Butler Institute. 'If you need a place to stay while you're in town, just put this in any public phone. It will dial our number for you.' She slipped the card into the English girl's pocket and left, the man following her.

Breen and the English girl stood looking at Cooper. Cooper shifted uncomfortably and shrugged. 'They must have read her medical records as soon as we logged her. The Butler Institute is in very tight with the service and . . .'

Breen just kept looking at him until he stopped talking.

'I don't know how much they're paying you,' said Breen. 'I hope it's worth it.' The English girl stifled a yawn, standing beside him. When Breen turned to leave she followed him.

'Well, what am I supposed to do with you?'

'Where are you off to now?' said the girl.

'I'm supposed to find my partner,' said Breen.

'So am I.'

'I don't believe it,' said Mancuso.

The Doctor said nothing.

Mancuso turned and looked at Petersen. 'He could be lying, couldn't he? He could have rigged this up.'

Petersen didn't reply, either. He was examining the dismantled control sections of Mancuso's gun, spread out on his desk. A thin coiling cable connected the gun to the scientist's computer. Petersen looked at the display above the gun's ammunition clip, then back at his computer. Mancuso came and stood behind him, looking over his shoulder at the gun's small ammunition counter display.

'I refuse to believe it,' she said.

'You've been talking to the Doctor, I can tell.'

Mancuso's head jerked up, startled by the voice. The English girl from the drugstore on Fifth Avenue had come into the lab. She was standing just inside the doorway.

'Hello, Ace,' said the Doctor.

'Who let you in?' said Mancuso.

'Bloke called Breen. Claims to be your partner.' The girl came over and sat beside the Doctor. 'He said to tell you he's going home to bed. He'll see you tomorrow.'

Mancuso automatically checked her watch.

'Your shift isn't over yet, is it?' said the Doctor. 'McIlveen would never have done that.'

'Who is McIlveen?' said Ace, covering a yawn with the back of her hand.

'He used to be Mancuso's partner,' said the Doctor, going to the computer on Petersen's desk. 'Until he was shot from a rooftop.'

'I'm sorry,' said Ace. She watched while the Doctor typed at the computer keyboard. 'Is he dead?'

'In a manner of speaking,' said the Doctor. On the screen of the computer the words he was typing appeared, letter by letter.

Who are you?

The Doctor pressed the Return key on the keyboard and the message was transmitted, travelling through the thin communications cable that connected the computer to the gun. The words were converted to ASCII codes which flashed into the gun's control system, entering the large chip with the luminous line around it. There was a brief pause and then symbols flashed up on the gun's ammunition counter. The tiny LCD screen was only three symbols wide, being designed to indicate how many bullets were left in the clip.

But now instead of numbers it began to display letters of the alphabet.

MCI

LVE

EN

'Does that mean what I think it means?' said Ace.

'McIlveen, James Haines,' said the Doctor.

The lab was silent. After a moment the letters on the

ammunition counter faded away. Mancuso watched the tiny screen go blank, then she looked over at Petersen. He just shrugged.

Mancuso moved to the chair where the Doctor was sitting. 'Here, out of the way.'

The Doctor got out of the chair and Mancuso sat in front of the computer, typing on the screen.

Why should I believe you?

After a moment a response began to appear on the gun's display.

ISA

VED

YOU

RAS

S

Mancuso began to smile. She remembered the woman in the tie-dyes and flack vest and the way the gun had moved on its own, aiming and firing for her. 'I guess you did save it.'

Now a new message was coming up on the gun display.

HEL

PME

'Okay, don't worry, Jimmy,' said Mancuso. 'I'll do whatever it takes.' She began typing at the computer. 'What do you want?'

GET

EVE

N

'Okay.' Mancuso turned to the Doctor. 'Let's assume for a moment that I buy this. In that case the people who did this to Jimmy are the same ones who shot him. Right?'

'Right.'

'And you know where to find them?'

'In a place called the King Building,' said the Doctor.

Mancuso picked up the outer casing of the gun, careful not to disturb the large control clip. She examined the bee-and-eye logo engraved on the metal. 'You're talking about the Butler Institute.'

'The BI has been doing some very interesting work,' said Petersen. 'Neural networks. Artificial intelligence.'

'Yeah,' said Mancuso quietly. 'But I didn't know they were

big on black magic.'

The Doctor took the gun casing away from Mancuso and set it gently back on the desk. 'Our minds are processes that run in our brains. A mind is an electrical and chemical pattern. And patterns can be transferred and copied.'

'The Butler Institute,' said Ace. 'I think I'm beginning to get this. Breen said that they use people for organ transplants. Keeping rich people alive with poor people's bodies.'

'They've been doing that for years.' Mancuso got up from the computer. She walked across the lab, moving restlessly. She looked angry. 'Where have you been?'

'So if someone is found dead at the scene of a crime, like the drugstore on Fifth Avenue —'

'The body goes to the Butler Institute,' said Mancuso.

'And that's where they took Justine.' Ace was looking at the Doctor accusingly. She was thinking about a black and yellow capsule and an old silver locket. She was thinking about a girl with beads in her hair, falling to the floor, spilling plastic mouth-wash bottles. 'I saw your face when she did it. You really did look angry. You said it wasn't part of the plan.'

'It wasn't,' said the Doctor. 'She took that pill far too soon.'

Mancuso was back on the computer now, concentrating. She quit out of the communications software and called up a database of the city's streetplans. In thirty seconds the blueprints of the King Building were up on the screen. 'We have to get somebody inside there.'

'You haven't been listening,' said Ace. 'I think we already have.'

22

Justine was walking through west London streets under a cold blue sky. The houses around here were big old brick structures. Some of them had corner turrets with conical roofs and the black shingles made them look like witch hats. Justine had never noticed that before and it worried her. She felt like she might be losing her grip. She found herself beginning to sweat under the leather jacket, a familiar symptom. The condition was called stoned paranoia. It was particularly likely to hit you when you were on your way to score, as Justine was now.

But Justine knew a sure cure for stoned paranoia. She kept walking, feet clattering on the pavement, aware of her own breathing, watching the streets telescope endlessly on this unreal day. As soon as she saw a policeman, she crossed the road and went straight up to him and asked for directions, asking him the way to Portobello Market, just like a tourist.

She didn't even bother listening to what the policeman said. She just stared attentively up into his face, her sense of control returning. The policeman was white. He wore the traditional London cop headgear and a heavy coat against the cold. He was young and tall and handsome. But his face was so pale and he had such dark rings under his eyes that he looked like he was a fever victim. There was something wrong with his skin as well: a mottling and a dampness. Justine stared at his face in fascination; you don't expect policemen to have skin conditions. He smiled at her and his teeth were marvellously even and white.

And sharp.

'Whatever happened to the traditional greasy roll of banknotes?' said Mrs Woodcott, scooping the one-quid and five-quid coins off the table. 'It's just not the same doing a deal any more. You young junkies these days. You just don't know what you're

237

missing.' She counted the money as she put it into her purse.

'I'm not a junkie,' said Justine. 'I'm a soldier for a cause.'

'Of course you are, dear,' said Mrs Woodcott. And as she said the words they seemed to echo in Justine's head. A rush of *déjà vu* began to hit her.

She had heard exactly those words before, in exactly this place. In a pub called The Moonchild on the corner of Powys Square. In a small backroom of the saloon bar with nicotine-coloured walls and ceiling and heavy old wooden tables. A glass of Polish vodka was in front of Justine, ice melting and thinning the alcohol. The old woman called Mrs Woodcott was sipping a port and lemon. Any moment now Mrs Woodcott would say —

'What are you looking at, dear?'

'The policemen.' There were three policemen over by the crowded bar. One of them met her glance as she looked across at them. None of the men wore uniforms but Justine could spot a policeman in plain clothes, even in the Saturday crush at the bar. The undercover men all had something subtly wrong with their faces. An unhealthy colour, pale and splotchy. It made Justine think of mushrooms you found in the autumn, on the damp underside of a log. You rolled the log over, looking for treasure, and all you found was the wood rotting away to dark coffee granules to feed the clinging fungus.

Or maybe it was the just the lighting in The Moonchild. A line of multicoloured Christmas lights was strung up over the bar. Above the Christmas lights was a crossed pair of sabres from some antique war. They were old but they looked remarkably clean and sharp. Justine had to tear her eyes away from them, from the light gleaming on their blades.

Now two of the policemen were staring at them, not bothering to conceal their interest. Mrs Woodcott stared back at them, unperturbed.

'London's finest.'

'Has this place become a CID boozer or something?'

'Not as far as I know,' said Mrs Woodcott. She made no move to hide the pill she'd placed on the table. It was a fat shiny black and yellow capsule. Justine quickly put it away in the place she prepared.

'That's a nice locket,' said Mrs Woodcott.

Justine wasn't listening. She was looking at the policemen again. They were all smiling. Their teeth appeared to be unnaturally sharp.

'I know what you use those pills for, you know,' said Mrs Woodcott. 'You young people. All you goths and punks and crows. You use them for nice things like morgue parties.'

Justine nodded, unable to reply. She was sweating heavily again. The door of the pub had opened, bringing in a flood of cold air that found its way to the saloon bar. Justine shivered as it hit her. Following the cold air through the pub door was the uniformed policeman. The one she'd asked about directions. His face looked worse than before.

Mrs Woodcott had a large fabric Harrods bag. She put her purse back inside it and as she did so Justine got a look at the other contents. Old jam jars full of the black and yellow capsules. Mrs Woodcott saw her looking and took out one of the jars, setting it on the table in plain sight. The policemen were all staring, including the PC who'd just walked in. Justine tried not to let it bother her. She was still shivering although the pub was warm again. Mrs Woodcott picked up the jar and shook it. The pills rattled loudly. 'Beautiful aren't they?' Did you know that the yellow and black colour combination is used in nature to signify a virulent poison?'

'Poisons are drugs and drugs are poisons,' said Justine. 'It's just a matter of terminology.'

'Commendably suicidal attitude,' said Mrs Woodcott. 'Now, let me tell you about this capsule. I like to think of it as what our American friends call a "double header". The first and most significant component is a synthetic variant on tetrodotoxin. Tetrodotoxin is a naturally occurring and highly potent neurotoxin. It is found in the puffer fish and the Japanese *fugu*. The method of operation of the substance is to block nerve signals by interfering with the sodium process through cells. Symptoms of tetrodotoxin poisoning included pulmonary oedema, hypotension, cyanosis, hypothermia, respiratory distress, paralysis and death. Sound good so far?'

Justine nodded. The policemen were talking together in a small huddle. Their faces were strange and getting stranger. Mrs Woodcott kept on talking, oblivious.

'It is a folk poison capable of pharmacologically inducing an apparent state of death. In Haiti its sacramental use is central to the zombie phenomenon. You've heard of zombies. At any rate, you've seen the videos, I'll warrant.'

The policemen were all turning to look at Justine. They were all smiling. They opened their mouths quite wide when they smiled.

'The second component is a popular amphetamine derivative in a thick gelatine coating that takes several hours to dissolve in stomach acid. At the deepest part of the trance the amphetamine kicks in and begins to brings you back up to consciousness. Imagine the surprise of the poor bloody morgue attendant when you come out of your trance on a trolley. Imagine *your* surprise if they've already locked you in a refrigerated cabinet with a limited air supply.'

'What's the amphetamine analogue called?'

'Billy whiz,' said Mrs Woodcott. She sipped her port and lemon. 'At least that's what I like to call it.' She turned the yellow and black capsule over in her hand. 'It really is a lovely little drug. I'd say the dosage in one of these would be about perfect for someone with your body weight.'

'How come you know so much about this drug?'

'How come? Because I built it, dear.'

Over by the bar the policemen were beginning to undress. With each piece of clothing they took off their gestures grew more extravagant and stylized, like the movements of a dancer. Their fangs appeared as they smiled and leered, blowing kisses to the people sitting in the booths near them.

'And is it possible,' said Justine, 'that there might be hallucinations as I come back up to consciousness?'

'Certainly. Vivid dream hallucinations.'

A punky girl sitting beside the policemen got up hastily and tried to leave. One of the policemen grabbed her hand.

'And could they be partly pure fantasy and partly take the form of a flashback?'

'Do you mean like a summer-of-love-style acid flashback? How sweetly nostalgic. Flashbacks were partly propaganda of course. Take a tab of acid at the student union fresher's hop and ten years later you crash head on into a semi while you're

driving your family to church. But they do sometimes occur.'
Mrs Woodcott drained her port and lemon and smiled. 'The
human mind is a strange and dangerous place, as I'm sure you've
discovered, dear.'

The policeman who'd grabbed the punk now spun her around
as if they were going to dance in a Fred Astaire musical. But
instead of dancing he swooped forward, his mouth latching on
to her throat. Justine noted that the big fangs were basically just
for show. Getting the blood out of the girl's neck involved some
kind of fungoid extrusion where the policeman's tongue ought
to be. A damp grey pipe locked to the punk's throat, pulsing
as it drank. Some excess blood splashed on to the surface of
the bar. The fat publican sighed and wiped it up with a rag.

'For instance,' said Justine, 'I might seem to be reliving an
episode from my recent past, with some weird shit thrown in?'

'Absolutely.'

The other policemen were doing a striptease, but not a very
pleasant one, unless you were attracted to human skin with
unusual textures and colours. The kind of texture and colours
you might find in a mushroom that had been left too long in
the fridge in a sealed plastic bag. The kind of mushroom that
was beginning to melt. Justine reflected that she had never liked
mushrooms. 'Like the time I went to Notting Hill and went into
a pub and scored a drug?'

'The hallucination could adopt any sort of delusional archi-
tecture. So yes, why not?'

One of the policemen was mincing across the pub, towards
the saloon bar, towards the corner where Justine and Mrs
Woodcott sat. 'And could I be explaining something to myself
in my head? Like a dream where you're telling yourself you're
alseep?'

The policeman's tongue, such as it was, was flickering wetly
in and out of his mouth.

'Yes, dear. You might even have a person in it who seemed
absolutely real. And that person might just be a construct, made
from memories of someone you met.'

'Telling me it's all a dream.'

'Well, they might not actually come out and *say* it, dear.'

* * *

The last of the trees had been cut down and dragged away.

Now you could see the tunnel mouth of the project site quite clearly from the picture window, even when you were sitting down.

Stephanie was admiring the view, sitting on the couch beside O'Hara. She had her feet up on a cushion on the coffee table beside the printer. While O'Hara was waiting for his call she was printing out a questionnaire that had been prepared by the Butler Institute's psychology consultants. Stephanie caught the last sheet as it slid out of the printer. She got up and sauntered out of the room.

O'Hara remained sitting on the couch, waiting to take the call that was coming in on the hour. Jack Blood appeared on the carpet in front of him. He was holding a rotting newspaper and a huge fan of yellow pages, and was wearing a 1930s newsboy's cap. 'Priority news,' said Jack. The words came out of his carved mouth in the voice of the B&O television newswoman. The computer in the B&O had picked up something it deemed O'Hara should know about.

'Pause,' said O'Hara. Jack Blood froze, the newspaper extended in one twig-bundle hand, hanging in midair. The woman's voice faded. 'Resume when this phone call is over.'

Three images stabilized on the wall. The first to snap into focus was Mr Pegram's physician. She advised O'Hara against exciting Mr Pegram, then disappeared to be replaced by Pegram himself. O'Hara had never seen the old man looking so ill. The next image to arrive was that of the Oriental woman. Next was the teenage boy. He was wearing his ceremonial robes today.

The woman was the first to speak. 'Our shareholders are applying a great deal of pressure. People are becoming frightened.'

'My subjects are frightened as well,' said the boy.

'We've done our best to keep a lid on the situation,' said Mr Pegram, the rich virile voice coming out of his withered face. 'But too many people know. Word's getting out to the public. They know about the point of no return.'

On the floor under the living room, at the front of the house, Stephanie knocked and went into what used to be Patrick's bedroom. There were still toys on the floor, dragged into piles to make room for the stretcher from the helicopter. It was a bulky paramedical unit with on-board life support equipment and some monitoring hardware. Mulwray was sitting in a child-sized chair, supposedly on guard duty. He got up when Stephanie came into the room and shambled out, heading for the kitchen. He was carrying a handgun and, considering his increasingly erratic behaviour, Stephanie might normally have been a little worried. But she had ordered the weapon especially for Mulwray from an armaments subsidiary, with a request that the firing pin was removed.

When Stephanie was alone she presented Vincent with the questionnaire, removing one set of handcuffs and giving the boy a pen to write with. She kept the other set of cuffs locked, one end attached to his wrist, the other to the frame of the bunk bed. Stephanie looked at the small decals that covered the heavy metal bunk bed. O'Hara had told her that his son loved this bed. Just one of those dumb things kids become fond of.

As Stephanie turned to leave the room she had a strong impulse. She wanted to touch Vincent. Turn and go back into the room and touch the teenage boy handcuffed to the bed.

It was an odd desire. It wasn't as though there was anything special about Vincent. He certainly wasn't good looking. But there was something about him. You wanted to grab his hand. Touch his face. Make contact.

Vincent was watching her now. Lying there on the undersized bunk bed. His eyes were afraid but there was some other emotion, too.

Stephanie turned and hurried out of the bedroom.

Upstairs in the living room the hologram of Jack Blood stood waiting patiently for O'Hara to finish his conference call.

'Frankly, I don't care what route we follow,' the Oriental woman was saying. 'So long as profits continue and there is agreement. But I have to know soon.'

'Don't be mistaken,' said the boy. 'Unless there is continuing progress I will cease to back your project.'

'Have some faith,' bellowed Mr Pegram.

'I agree with the prince,' said the Oriental woman. 'My company withdraws its support if there are any setbacks.'

'There will be continuing progress. There won't be any

243

setbacks,' said O'Hara.

'That's more like it,' said Mr Pegram.

As Stephanie came into the room the Oriental woman disappeared from the wall, closing her call. The boy went next, leaving just Mr Pegram's image. The old man, his face huge on the wall, stared at O'Hara.

'You must succeed, my friend,' said Mr Pegram as his image began to fade. 'We must triumph over the flesh.' One of his pinkish eyes was spasming wetly, buried deeply in its nest of wrinkles. He might have been trying to wink.

O'Hara turned to say something to Stephanie. But before he could speak, the hologram of Jack Blood unfroze, the B&O coming off pause.

'The exciting life of one hovercraft continues its eventful course in New York City,' said Jack, speaking in his newsreader's voice. 'In a bizarre accident a G-8 hovercraft has crashed into a security installation outside the King Building, killing one guard and injuring three others. Once a police vehicle, the hovercraft was sold into private ownership and has only just been confiscated for use in a robbery. However, it now appears to have been stolen from the police pound and abandoned in spectacularly destructive style.'

'So, which drug is doing this to me?' said Justine.

The floor of the pub consisted of bare planks scattered with sawdust, and the sawdust was doing a surprisingly good job of soaking up the blood. However, there were thick puddles here and there, and it was in the puddles that the policemen were dancing. Most of the policemen were completely naked now except for their socks and big clumsy boots.

The one coming towards Justine's table was also still wearing his striped CID tie.

Justine leaned closer to Mrs Woodcott, who had put on her spectacles and was now watching the policemen with some interest.

'Is it the neurotoxin or the billy?' said Justine.

The pale damp skin of the policemen had a pronounced mottling now, a diseased fungus appearance. They moved and danced more or less as a single unit and now they began to caress each other lasciviously.

'Right, that's it,' the fat man behind the bar sighed and stopped drying beer mugs. 'Gents, gents, you're well out of order.' He was reaching to ring the brass bell over the bar when two of the policemen dragged him to the floor and began to dismember him.

'In answer to your question, most likely neither,' said Mrs Woodcott.

'Neither?'

The CID man with the tie reached the table just as Justine ran for the bar. She jumped up on the beer- and blood-soaked surface and pulled one of the ornamental sabres down. The blade snagged on the string of Christmas tree lights but it had an edge on it like a razor blade. It sliced through the wire as Justine pulled it free. It went through the CID man's neck almost as easily.

'No dear,' said Mrs Woodcott. 'These hallucinations are almost certainly being caused by a little something extra I slipped in. A mind-bendingly powerful psychedelic, for instance.'

'You mischievous old bitch,' said Justine, swinging the sword again.

Mrs Woodcott's white-haired old head went spinning across the pub floor and struck the brass foot rail in front of the bar. It sounded like a bowling ball hitting the brass.

'Ouch,' said Mrs Woodcott's head. 'I didn't do it purely because I was a mischievous old bitch, however.'

The other policemen had begun to pay a little more attention to Justine since she had decapitated their colleague. They were closing in on her. Justine kicked Mrs Woodcott's head through the half-opened door to the men's toilets, and followed it through. She slammed the door behind her and bolted it.

'You see,' Mrs Woodcott's head was saying, 'these hallucinatory dreams are triggered to occur after the amphetamine takes effect. They happen as you begin to wake up. They help you orientate yourself and prepare yourself for consciousness.'

'They've been a great help, thanks,' said Justine. She nudged Mrs Woodcott's head with the toe of her shoe and sent it splashing into the brimming urinal.

The head surfaced, spluttering and blinking. 'You should

listen to me, dear. I am, if you like, the voice of your conscience. You are probably close to waking up and there are things you must remember.'

'I know. I'm beginning to remember some of them. Like Vincent. He's the reason I'm here.' Justine had to shout to make herself heard. The policemen were outside the lavatory door, trying to batter it down. 'I like all sorts of stupid things about Vincent. The way he talks and the way his mouth looks when he's smiling. And I like the fact that he's got powers. It's like he has a demon inside him.'

'That's nice, dear,' said Mrs Woodcott, bobbing in the reeking urinal puddle.

'I want to get rid of that crap haircut of his and teach him things. Teach him not to say any of those stupid American things. Get him to dress nicely. Go to the pub with him. Show him off to people. And, you know, maybe use that demon in him a bit.'

'Ah, young love,' slobbered Mrs Woodcott's head. Bubbles were trickling up from her mouth as she began to go under.

Justine dragged her out of the urinal and slammed her into the nearest sink. 'I guess I really do like him a lot.' She ran the taps, cleaning off Mrs Woodcott and her own hands. 'That's why I took that capsule in the drugstore. It was supposed to make me look like I was dead.'

'Oh it did, believe me, it did.'

'Then I was supposed to be picked up by a medical team. It's a bit like a morgue party. They take me somewhere and I wake up inside, when they least expect it. Except I'm going inside a place called the King Building. That's where they took Vincent. It's all part of the Doctor's plan.'

'But the point is, they didn't keep Vincent there,' said Mrs Woodcott from the sink. 'And don't talk to me about the Doctor's plan. You didn't even wait until you were properly briefed.'

The battering noises were getting louder. It sounded as if the door would come off its hinges any second.

'I'm supposed to wake up inside the King Building and let the others in.' Justine took Mrs Woodcott's head out of the sink. She set it upright on top of a cigarette-burned towel holder. Mrs

246

Woodcott's eyes were on the same level as Justine's now.

'But you couldn't wait for the proper time could you? You stupid girl.' Mrs Woodcott's voice was changing. It was more like a young woman's. And there was something subtly different about her eyes. Justine noticed that the pounding at the door was subsiding. It wasn't as if the policemen were giving up. They were still attacking with ferocity but the sound itself was growing distant. It was as if someone was turning the sound down on a video.

'Am I coming out of the drug now?'

'I certainly hope so,' said Mrs Woodcott in her young woman's voice. There was something familiar about that voice. And the eyes. Justine could identify the eyes now. They weren't Mrs Woodcott's.

They were Ace's.

In fact it was Ace's face she was looking at. Ace standing in front of her, instead of Mrs Woodcott's head propped up on a towel container. Justine looked around herself. She wasn't in the men's room of a pub any more. She was in a big open-plan office with floor-to-ceiling windows. Beyond the windows was the night skyline of New York, glass skyscrapers with random small squares of light where people were working late. This office was deserted. From what Justine could see it was full of desks and computers, each desk divided into its own little area by lightweight partitions. But the partitions around this one had all been knocked over, as if there had been a struggle. Some of the partitions had computer-printed charts on them. Others had large coloured photographs of spreadeagled young women. A man was lying beside the computer, sprawled across the desk, his face discoloured and bruised. Justine looked at the man, then at Ace. She realized that Ace was breathing hard, as if she'd just worked out or run a footrace.

'Geezer's name is Christian. He was down on the fifty-first floor when their equipment blew the whistle on you. Unfortunately that drug still leaves detectable brain activity.'

'What happened?' said Justine.

'They detected it. So Christian brought you up here. If the biostock isn't dead he gets first dibs, apparently.' Ace looked at the unconscious man. 'I hit him a bit harder than I meant to.'

'Thank you,' said Justine.

'You've been a right pain in the arse to everyone,' said Ace. She took something from the pocket of her jacket. It was a small blue card like a credit card. Ace threw it on to the desk beside Christian's face. 'I had to do your bit. It was me who had to let the others into this place.'

'Have you got Vincent with you?'

'No, it's the Doctor and a couple of cops.'

'I've just had a dream about very strange policemen,' said Justine.

'You ain't seen nothing yet,' said Ace. She sat down at the desk, shoving the unconscious man over so she could get at the keyboard of the computer. Justine saw that there had been some kind of modification to the computer. A communications cable connected it to a single large chip that sat in a small box on the desk. The chip had a luminous line glowing all around it. Ace was typing on the screen. Glowing words appeared on the computer screen.

Where's the Doctor?

A moment later a response pushed up on the screen in a strange format, only three characters wide:

ONR
OOF
WIT
HHE
LIC
OPT
ER

How do we get up there? Ace typed.

ELE
VAT
ORC
OMI
NGU
P

The corridor outside the office was dim except for access lights and silent except for a whisper of air conditioning. Ace and Justine stood on the thick carpet waiting for an elevator. The flashing lights on the control panels showed that all six elevators were heading for their floor.

'Which one is ours?' said Justine.

'We've got a friend who can play this place like an arcade game,' said Ace. She showed Justine the box with the chip inside it. The thin line around the chip glowed in the half-light. 'All of them are ours.'

But the first elevator to arrive had two Butler Institute security guards sitting in it, blank-eyed and dead. Ace and Justine stepped back quickly and the elevator stayed open for a minute, light shining out into the corridor. Then its doors whispered shut. Behind them, on the other side of the corridor, another elevator was opening. Ace and Justine turned to see a figure in combat armour, holding a gun. The figure's face was a blank curve of mirror: the faceplate of a Vickers weapons helmet. It hinged up as one gloved hand pulled it back. Mancuso's eyes frowned from inside.

'Are you coming or what?'

From the roof of the King Building the Saturday-night traffic looked like toys. Justine began to feel a sense of vertigo, so she pulled herself back from the guard rail and retreated from the edge of the roof. She stared up at the sky. It was the middle of the night but the glow of the city illuminated grey rolling masses of cloud. The air was almost clear enough to breathe. Justine turned and walked back towards the centre of the rooftop. Ace was waiting for her by the helicopter, wind blowing in her hair. 'Ready to go,' she said.

Inside the helicopter the Doctor and Mancuso were already strapped into their seats. 'Can you fly this?' said Justine, choosing the seat immediately behind the Doctor.

'No,' said the Doctor.

'Neither can I,' said Mancuso. 'But I know someone who can.' She made some final adjustments on the communications link she had attached to the autopilot. The other end was connected to the large chip in its box, resting on the seat between Mancuso and the Doctor. Ace settled into the seat behind Mancuso, fastening her seat belt as the engines began to pulse and the helicopter rose into the night.

23

'Christ, it's massive. It's even bigger than the Channel Tunnel.' Ace wiped at the window where her breath was fogging. The heating in the canteen building seemed to have been left on high for the weekend and the window misted again as soon as she wiped a portion clear. Through the filmy glass she could just about see the excavation in the early morning light.

'Wider at the mouth, but not as long, of course,' said the Doctor. 'It's essentially just a large bunker built to protect the machinery inside. You could say it's just one vast computer room built into the mountain.' The Doctor was sitting at one of the big tables that filled the prefabricated hut. Justine was back at the door of the building, trying for the third time to make it stay shut. Ace wished she'd just give up. The constant rattling noise was beginning to get to her. She still felt a little airsick after the flight in the helicopter. And besides, the lock was broken beyond repair; Ace knew that because she had been the one who kicked the door in.

The helicopter had landed in the first light of dawn, settling expertly on to the landing circle in a cleared section of forest, the rotors sweeping frost off the grass and battering it to dew. There had been ground mist rising among the surrounding mountain trees. They walked through a thin fringe of forest before they reached the wide cleared zone of the project site. The helicopter pad was situated halfway between O'Hara's house and the big excavation on the mountainside.

Mancuso had gone uphill to the house while the Doctor led the others down to the excavation.

'Why do we have to wait in here?' said Justine.

'We don't,' said the Doctor. 'But I wanted you to have a good look at the construction site. Our target.'

'It's like a ghost town. Where is everyone?'

250

'Read the bulletin board,' said Ace. 'On Sunday all employees have the day off. They go into Albany for shopping or worship at the church of their choice.'

'There's still a skeleton maintenance staff in the tunnel, so keep the lights off in here.' The Doctor's chair scraped back as he got up and joined Ace, looking out the window. The day was getting steadily brighter as the sun came up over the mountains. The square kilometre of ground outside the excavation was clearly visible now, an ocean of mud with bare patches of concrete rising out of it. Vehicles with bee-and-eye logos were parked on the concrete. 'And the security guards of course.' Spotlights gleamed in the tunnel mouth and on the bare rock brow of the mountain above. Further up the slope was O'Hara's large redwood house. The Doctor was peering through the glass, looking up towards the house. Ace noticed that for some reason his breath wasn't fogging on the window.

'How long do you think it will take up there?' said Justine.

'They're coming down now,' said the Doctor. 'Mancuso has got him.'

A hundred metres from the canteen prefab there were stacks of timber, each about the dimensions of a small house. The timber in the stacks consisted of logs cut to the size of telephone poles. The trees had apparently been chopped down recently; their cut white ends were still sticky and aromatic with resin. Ace stood hidden behind one stack, breathing in the resin smell. As she exhaled her warm breath came out like cigarette smoke on the cold morning air. The Doctor and Justine waited with her, watching the figures come down the slope from the house. Ace felt a deep fatigue waiting somewhere in the background of her mind, a promise of exhaustion as soon as the pressure was off. A wave of sleepiness rolled over her, making the morning and the mountainside unreal. She pressed her thumb against the sticky splintered stump until the flesh under the nail went white. The pain woke her up a little. She needed to be ready. They were entering the final phase. She made herself watch the woman and the boy coming down from the house.

In the lead was the figure in police armour, wearing a Vickers helmet. She was walking beside the teenage boy, watching that he didn't stumble.

'Vincent,' said Justine, staring up at the boy.

'Wait,' said the Doctor, 'Make sure.' But Justine was already beyond the stack of logs, out in the open, running for the path. Ace looked at the Doctor and he shrugged. They followed Justine out into the open. The two figures on the slope were near enough to see now, picking their way down the muddy footpath carved into the mountain rock. The teenage boy was definitely Vincent. The woman's face was concealed behind the mirrored visor of the police helmet. But now she reached up with a gloved hand and thumbed the visor back.

A wisp of blonde hair curled out from the helmet.

Justine was running up the footpath, holding on to the metal handrail that zigzagged up the slope. Now she stopped. The woman in the combat armour was holding a gun, pointing it first at Vincent, then at Justine.

The boy looked thin and tired. He began to speak but the wind carried his words away. He cleared his throat and started again. 'They know everything. They know we're here to destroy the project. And they know how we were planning to do it. Stephanie says that if you come any closer she'll shoot Justine. She knows what will happen if Justine touches me and she won't let that happen. She'll shoot me as well if she has to.'

Vincent hesitated then added, 'Your friend the policewoman is back at the house. I think she's dead.' The mountain wind howled past them in the following silence.

Stephanie glanced back up towards the house to confirm that Mulwray and O'Hara had come out. They were coming down the slope, careful not to slip on the fresh mud. Both of them had handguns. Ace thought she recognized the one O'Hara was holding. It was Mancuso's police sidearm.

The Doctor and Ace stood unmoving behind Justine, at the bottom of the footpath. 'What do we do?' said Ace.

'Don't do anything now,' said the Doctor. 'If we get a chance we have to try to bring Justine and Vincent into contact.'

'But you heard what she said —'

'Quiet,' said the Doctor.

The two men from the house had joined Stephanie and Vincent now. They were all coming down the footpath together. Justine came backing down the steps, moving slowly until she was standing with the Doctor and Ace again. Stephanie followed, removing her police helmet now and letting her long blonde hair loose. She stayed between Justine and Vincent, watching both of them.

'It's all right, Stephanie,' said O'Hara. 'I'll look after them. You go and get some security personnel. There'll be some staff on duty in the tunnel.'

'I can use the phone in the canteen,' said Stephanie. She set Mancuso's helmet on the ground as she gathered her hair and folded the braid, securing it with an elastic band to keep it out of her eyes.

'No. Go into the tunnel and make personal contact. Choose people you can trust. Don't tell anyone else.' O'Hara looked at the small group. The teenage boy sat on the bottom step of the footpath, looking alone and miserable. The Doctor standing beside one of the tall stacks of logs, Ace and Justine beside him. 'We may have to take radical action.'

'Right.' Stephanie finished fastening her hair and set off for the tunnel mouth, jogging across the flat expanse of mud and concrete. The mountain wind stirred debris from around the site and sent fragments cartwheeling after her — styrofoam packing from a computer box, an empty soft-drink can, some autumn leaves. Mulwray watched her go. His eyes were red-rimmed in a slack grey face.

'I understand the general concept,' said O'Hara, looking at the Doctor. He seemed excited, eager to talk. 'I understand that you've constructed a two-component weapon to use against us. This girl and this boy. They're like a bomb made up of an explosive and a detonator.'

'That's one way of describing it,' said the Doctor.

'But the boy has a unique power. What is it that makes the girl so special?'

'Ask her.'

'All right,' said O'Hara, beginning to move eagerly towards Justine, then thinking better of it. He remained standing beside Mulwray. 'What is it you have?'

'It's a bit hard to explain,' said Justine. 'Let Vincent come over here and I'll show you.'

'I don't think so,' said O'Hara.

Justine said something else but Ace wasn't listening. She was looking at the police helmet on the ground. It was similar to the one she had used in Turkey. Ace was measuring distances, wondering if she could get to it before they could fire at her. There was no way she could expose the laser sighting system in that kind of a hurry. But the helmet was heavy enough to use as a weapon in itself. If she could get it and throw—

'Go!'

Someone was shouting.

Ace was so deep in concentration that she missed the beginning of the action.

O'Hara was already falling headlong into the mud, his gun flying from his hand. Mulwray's arm was still swinging with the force of the blow that had knocked the other man to the ground. Mulwray's face was still contorting as he shouted. Vincent was gaping at him, seated on the steps. O'Hara was pulling himself out of the mud now. Mulwray grabbed the teenage boy and flung him towards Justine. 'Go!' he yelled again. O'Hara was groping for his gun in the mud. Now the boy was running towards Justine, and she was running to meet him.

O'Hara had found his gun. As she ran Justine saw him pick it up, clutch at the muddy handgrip, and drop it again. Vincent was perhaps twenty paces away from her now. Mulwray was striding over to where O'Hara was thrashing in the mud. Fifteen paces. Mulwray stood over the other man. O'Hara was fumbling on the ground for his gun. Ten paces. Mulwray aimed his own handgun at O'Hara's back. Five paces.

Vincent heard an incoherent shout of rage and he glanced back over his shoulder as he ran. He saw that Mulwray was pointing his gun, pulling the trigger again and again, but the gun wasn't firing.

It didn't matter.

He had Justine back. She ran straight into him, colliding so hard they almost fell.

Contact.

They wrapped their arms around each other. Vincent had her back. The weight of her was real in his arms. He could smell her, the leather of her jacket and the scent of her hair and face.

254

And he could feel the detonating passion surging out of her, the huge muscles of her emotion flexing and moving in his own skull.

The power had been building in Vincent ever since he'd been brought to this place, building in the long hours he stayed handcuffed to a child's bed in a child's room.

Now he twisted around, moving with Justine like two clumsy dancers in the mud. He whirled to face the tunnel mouth, whirled to throw the huge bolt of energy straight into the excavation site, to scour it off the mountainside forever.

Vincent squeezed his eyes shut and shouted with sheer exhilaration, bracing himself for the rush of images from Justine, bracing himself for the thunder of destruction.

But he could feel her emotions already, and immediately he knew that something was wrong. There was no blossoming rage, no gasoline stink of aggression. The hatred was there, and so was the need to smash and burn. But they were faint echoes lost in the background.

The emotions that surged into him, dominating everything else, were keen sadness, fear, and now, rising above the others, a simple powerful joy.

The memories that rushed out of Justine were a single unstoppable image, repeated over and over. A little girl was standing by a roadside. There were people all around her, passing her every second, but she was alone because the people were sealed inside cars. The traffic poured past the little girl and the little girl stood there all alone. The little girl had had a friend. The friend had held her hand just a moment ago. But now the friend was gone. There had been a screaming of *breaks* and her friend had disappeared. She could still feel the pressure of that hand in hers. The girl didn't really understand where her friend had gone. She never would understand. She understood only that no one was holding her hand now. That she had been left alone.

She had been left alone for a very long time.

But she wasn't alone now.

A hand holding hers again. Vincent could feel it in his mind. His hand in hers.

He felt Justine's loneliness like a twenty-year headache that was suddenly gone. A rigid muscle unclenching.

Images of relaxation. Calmness and peace rushing out of Justine now. Rushing into Vincent.

Giving the power inside him no purchase, nothing to grip. Like a storm roaring over smooth stone. Nothing to pick up and throw. Nothing to smash with.

No way of destroying the project site.

Mulwray was standing in the mud at the bottom of the footpath, standing over O'Hara as he scrabbled for his gun. Mulwray was firing his own gun again and again. But nothing was happening. The firing pin had been disabled and nothing was happening. Mulwray had seen the boy and girl run towards each other, meet and embrace. In the following second he had expected the project site to be wiped out by a force like the wrath of God.

But it seemed the firing pin had been wrecked on that, too.

Now O'Hara had picked up his gun from the mud and he was rolling over, aiming at Mulwray and firing. Mulwray actually saw the bullet racing up towards his face, a dark blur like a fat bee moving with impossible speed. Straight up towards his eye.

He never heard the sound of the shot. He never felt the bullet go in. As his brain came apart the last thing he thought of was a small boy in a room full of toys, the boy's face disappearing into a mist.

O'Hara climbed off the ground, wiping mud from his face with one hand. The other hand held the gun. He stepped over Mulwray's body. He aimed the gun at Justine and Vincent, and then at the Doctor and Ace.

'It looks as if your weapon is broken,' he said.

'Vincent,' said the Doctor, speaking in an unhurried, conversational tone. 'Let go of Justine. Let go of her now. And run.'

'Stay exactly where you are,' said O'Hara. But Vincent wasn't listening. He was looking over Justine's shoulder at the Doctor, listening to what the Doctor said. He turned away and began to run. He was weak from months in the barrel and drugs and captivity. He stumbled clumsily through the mud. O'Hara ran after him.

O'Hara was well fed and well rested. Muscled with years of

exercise. He caught Vincent easily.

He grabbed the boy.

Locked a hand on to Vincent's shoulder.

Contact.

'Oh my God,' said Ace.

Stephanie was in her suite of offices deep in the tunnel. Sitting across the desk from her was the chief electrician from the Korean technical team. He was a chubby, smiling man wearing a white paper hat and white overalls. From his personnel records Stephanie knew that he had once worked with the South Korean security services, on interrogation assignments. He would be the ideal choice for help with the current problem. There would no doubt be some more burials in the quiet woods up above O'Hara's house, but first they would need to ask certain questions of the man called the Doctor and the two girls.

Stephanie had just begun to explain the situation when she heard the noise outside.

It was hard to believe it wasn't some living thing howling up at the mouth of the tunnel. But the sound was too gigantic, and mixed in with it was the echoing tumbling sound of big objects being thrown around. The Korean was staring out the window, perplexed, but Stephanie recognized the sound from her Midwestern childhood. It was the sound of a prairie storm, but bigger. Considerably bigger.

The Korean electrician was opening the door of the hut. Stephanie wanted to tell him to stop, but it was too late. She wondered what could have gone wrong. She glanced out the window and just had time to hope that O'Hara was all right. The Korean had begun to open the door, but he only pushed it outwards a fraction before the door was caught by the wind and torn off its hinges. He had been holding on to the handle as the door went and his arm went with it, torn off at the shoulder. Stephanie was retreating to the rear of the office and she managed to get through the inner door as the Korean was sucked out into the wind, screaming and bleeding.

Stephanie heard gunshot sounds from the office as she shut the door. She knew instantly what the sounds were. The windows in the office blowing out. The windows had been made of some kind of plastic which would simply bend and bulge and were normally impossible to break. But Stephanie had seen ice crystals forming on them as they froze down to some unimaginable sub-zero brittleness.

The corridor where Stephanie stood was as cold as a meat freezer already. There was a window at the far end, on the side of the hut facing away from the tunnel mouth. A small portion of the window was still clear of ice and Stephanie was able to look out. She saw lights exploding all down the tunnel's length and great curved panels of computer circuitry peeling off the tunnel walls. All the metal structures lining the excavation were shattering under the sledge-hammer winds and the impact of temperatures that should never have occurred on Earth. A small group of Japanese mainframe consultants were sheltering in the jagged remains of some crane machinery, trying to fix themselves to the metal frames with belts. She saw them being plucked off one by one by the wind before the window blanked out completely, ice crystals growing across it.

The corridor was freezing now. Every breath was a cold stab deep in Stephanie's lungs. She pulled a bunch of keys out of her pocket and the metal of the keys welded to her flesh with the cold. She fought her way to the door in the centre of the corridor. This was an inner room with no windows. She might have a chance inside. Stephanie unlocked the door and entered.

Stephanie could hardly see now. The emergency generator under the prefab was still operating, providing light, but there was something wrong with her eyes. Crystals of frost had formed on her lashes. It was getting difficult to breathe. Her body was reluctant to take in the killing chill of the air. Stephanie turned to close the door as the mirror in the far end of the room exploded. As the mirror went it exposed an opening and through that opening was another room, with three windows in it. A fast wind found its way in those windows and knifed towards Stephanie. It picked up toys from the pale wooden floor of the room and lashed at Stephanie with them. Through the ice on her lashes she could see the far wall of the hut being torn open. She blinked, trying to clear her vision, but when she shut her eyes she found that she couldn't open them again.

* * *

Cold.

A cold like permafrost, extending forever in layers below. Into dark earth frozen hard as steel.

As soon as O'Hara touched him, Vincent began to feel the cold and to see the images.

He saw O'Hara as a child, a serious little boy sitting in a dusty backyard. His parents had just explained to him that one day he would have to die, like everyone else. In his rage O'Hara had beaten his hands raw against the fence in the backyard. Now he sat staring at his bloody knuckles, staring in disgust at the fragility of the skin. Hating his own flesh, the warmth and weakness of it.

Cold.

O'Hara sitting in a university library, working late. Refusing to go to sleep. Refusing to eat. Refusing to let the flesh win.

Cold.

O'Hara making love to his wife. Using his body like a machine. It was just a machine he lived in. He tended it and exercised it, but it meant nothing to him. It was just the flesh. It wasn't O'Hara. O'Hara was the mind that watched his wife's face, calculating when to move and where to move his body, timing each motion and controlling each muscle. He was the mind that watched her face strain sadly with pleasure and he was the mind that made his mouth kiss her afterwards.

Cold.

O'Hara in the delivery room of the hospital. Holding his newborn son and feeling disgust at the tough, living piece of muscle that writhed in his hands and cried.

Cold.

So cold that Vincent felt as if he had become frozen himself. Frozen at the centre of the great storm. The storm came from behind his eyes and went into the mouth of the tunnel, blowing across the deep ice of O'Hara's emotions, picking up the cold and carrying it along.

In the end, the cold was so intense Vincent wanted to let go. But he couldn't. A lifetime of emotions were tearing out of O'Hara, emptying him. O'Hara was fighting but it was doing no good. The storm in Vincent was sucking everything out. And Vincent felt it all travelling through him. It was like touching a bare wire, feeling a thousand volts running into you and being unable to let go.

But hands were pulling him loose.

He heard Justine saying, 'Is he all right?' And the Doctor saying, 'Get him up to the house.'

And Ace saying, 'Jesus, what a mess.'

They found Mancuso lying in the kitchen of O'Hara's house, shot three times but still breathing. The Doctor hooked her up to the life-support stretcher they found in Patrick's bedroom. When the software reported that the wounds were too numerous and too complex, the Doctor tore out the motherboard from the medical computer and replaced it with a large computer chip, one with a luminous line glowing around it.

Ace sat in the child's bedroom, watching Mancuso breathe and occasionally getting a readout from the life support screens. She nodded off to sleep and woke to find herself on a bunkbed covered with decals of cartoon characters, a pair of handcuffs locked on to the frame above her pillows.

When she accessed the medical computer, asking for Mancuso's status, the reply was immediate:

TOO

MEA

NTO

DIE

Ace wandered through the wrecked kitchen and into the living room. The Doctor was sitting, watching some kind of television programme involving three screens, each showing a person's face. One face was of an Oriental woman. She was saying, 'This is exactly what I was afraid of. I never had full belief in this project, or in his ability to manage it. Now we are in an extremely difficult position.'

On another screen was a teenage boy wearing ceremonial robes. 'Well, obviously we have no choice. There will have to be a policy U-turn. But don't be too disheartened. A clean-up on a global scale will require many years, and a great deal of money applied to technology. Your people can start selling that technology.'

On the third screen was the pink wrinkled face of an enormously old man. The old man was saying nothing. He was just weeping.

The Doctor was evidently enjoying the programme very much. He turned and smiled at Ace as she came into the room. 'Off,' he said, and the television switched itself off, cancelling each of the images in turn.

'Would you like to go for a walk in the woods?' said the Doctor. 'It's a beautiful day.'

Instead of going immediately to the woods they found themselves drawn by the noises from the cavern mouth. The ground outside the excavation was covered with an ellipse of brilliant white that extended from the tunnel like a tongue. What remained of O'Hara was lying at the outer edge of the frost, the black husk of his body presented in sharp contrast against the white ground.

The noises were loud this close to the tunnel. The sound of earth and steel collapsing as the tunnel slowly buried itself. While Ace and the Doctor watched a final landslide thundered up the axis of the tunnel and sealed the excavation with tons of dirt and rock. The fall punched the last air pocket out and a muddy cloud blew up to the surface, settling like a fine spray of ink on the frosted ground, destroying the pure white of the landscape.

The rush of air plucked at Ace's hair and the Doctor's hat. It lifted O'Hara's weightless corpse and sent it spinning up through the air. Ace remembered the taste of red wine and small sugared biscuits. Blue flame on tissue paper.

'Make a wish,' she said.

They walked in the woods until they met Justine and Vincent, coming back up from the old logging road. A boy was tagging along behind them and he smiled and yelled when he saw the Doctor.

'I'm sorry,' said Justine. 'We told him not to come up here but he followed us.'

'That's all right,' said the Doctor. 'Brodie and I are old friends.'

'My parents are back at the cabin,' said Brodie, approaching the Doctor. 'We're going to be here every weekend until

Thanksgiving.'

'Well, you can go anywhere you want in the woods now. No one will bother you.' The Doctor sat on a wide stump beside Ace, leaving enough room for the small boy to join them. But Brodie was eyeing Ace with shyness and now he fell silent and remained where he was standing. The only sound was the stir of bare autumn branches and the occasional chattering of a squirrel.

'We'd better check on the cop.' Justine took Vincent's hand and they turned and started back up the path. They walked slowly through the deep fallen leaves, kicking red and yellow shapes aside with each step. As they moved away Brodie edged forward and hesitantly sat on the stump between the Doctor and Ace. He reached into the big pocket in the front of his jacket and drew something out. Two pieces of wood and a length of black rubber.

'It's the slingshot you made for me,' said Brodie.

'So it is,' said the Doctor.

'It's broken now.' The boy looked up at the Doctor hopefully.

But the Doctor wasn't looking at the little boy, or at the broken weapon in his hand. He was staring after Vincent and Justine as they walked away through the slanting sunlight, disappearing among the trees.

'It's probably broken for good,' said Brodie.

'Yes, but it's served its purpose,' said the Doctor. 'So that's all right.'

TIME'S CRUCIBLE

Marc Platt

You're on your own, Ace.

The TARDIS is invaded by an alien presence and is then destroyed. The Doctor, seemingly crushed by the fate of his ship, disappears.

Ace, lost and alone, finds herself in a bizarre, deserted city ruled by the tyrannical, leechlike monster known as the Process.

Lost voyagers drawn forward from Ancient Gallifrey perform obsessive rituals in the ruins.

The strands of time are tangled in a cat's cradle of dimensions.

Only the Doctor can challenge the rule of the Process and restore the stolen Future. But the Doctor was destroyed long ago.

Before Time began.

This is the first novel in the CAT'S CRADLE series of Doctor Who New Adventures. Written by Marc Platt, author of *Ghost Light* and *Battlefield*, it is a strange, haunting story that shows an Ace changed beyond all recognition and reveals something of the history and development of Gallifrey and of time travel.

ISBN 0 426 20365 8   Paperback

WITCH MARK

Andrew Hunt

Shattered by the events that have taken them from the twisted dimensions of the TARDIS to the gang-ridden streets of a hideous future, Ace and the Doctor go to a sleepy Welsh village for some peace.

A police officer charged with investigation of the paranormal is called to investigate an accident involving a holiday coach in which all the passengers are killed. None can be identified, yet each carries a distinctive mark on the side of the neck.

All over Wales, there are reports of mythical creatures appearing on farms and in the hills. Stuff and nonsense, of course — Ace has been all over the galaxy by now and knows that creatures like these don't exist. Daleks and haemovores, maybe, but unicorns and centaurs? *Please*.

And yet, something is definitely wrong in Llanfer Ceirog.

This is Andrew Hunt's first novel, a marvellous science fiction story disguised under the cloak of fantasy.

ISBN 0 426 20368 2   Paperback

TIMEWYRM: GENESYS

John Peel

The Doctor and Ace are drawn to Ancient Mesopotamia in search of an evil sentience that has tumbled from the stars — the dreaded Timewyrm of ancient Gallifreyan legend.

ISBN 0 426 20355 0

TIMEWYRM: EXODUS

Terrance Dicks

Pursuit of the Timewyrm brings the Doctor and Ace to the Festival of Britain. But the London they find is strangely subdued, and patrolling the streets are the uniformed thugs of the Britischer Freikorps.

ISBN 0 426 20357 7

TIMEWYRM: APOCALYPSE

Nigel Robinson

Kirith seems an ideal planet — a world of peace and plenty, ruled by the kindly hand of the Great Matriarch. But it's here that the end of the universe — of everything — will be precipitated. Only the Doctor can stop the tragedy.

ISBN 0 426 20359 3

TIMEWYRM: REVELATION

Paul Cornell

Ace has died of oxygen starvation on the moon, having thought the place to be Norfolk. 'I do believe that's unique,' says the afterlife's receptionist.

ISBN 0 426 20360 7